Passions & Reflections

A Collection of 20th-Century Women's Fiction

PASSIONS & REFLECTIONS

A Collection of 20th-Century Women's Fiction

EDITED BY JUDY COOKE

With an introduction by
DEBORAH MOGGACH

VOLUME II

First published in Great Britain 1991
by Lime Tree
an imprint of the Octopus Publishing Group
Michelin House, 81 Fulham Road, London SW3 6RB

Introduction © Deborah Moggach 1991
Novel extract introductions, biographical notes and
selection © Judy Cooke 1991
The authors have asserted their moral rights

A CIP catalogue record for these books is available
from the British Library

ISBN 0-413-45291-3

Typeset by Falcon Typographic Art Ltd.,
Edinburgh & London
Printed in Great Britain
by Clays Ltd., St Ives Group

Cover Illustration:
Volume I Henri Matisse:
Interieur à Nice, Jeune Femme Lisante, c. 1919
© Succession H. Matisse/DACS 1991
Philadelphia Museum of Art:
Given by Mr and Mrs R. Sturgis Ingersoll

Volume II Henri Matisse:
Femme Assise, le Dos Tourné Vers la Fenêtre Ouverte,
1921-3, oil on canvas, 73 x 92.1 cm
© Succession H. Matisse/DACS 1991
The Montreal Museum of Fine Arts; purchase, Tempest
Fund; 1949. 1915
Photo Marilyn Aitken, MMFA

Contents

Acknowledgements	vii
Katherine Mansfield *Prelude*	1
Alice Munro *Miles City, Montana*	59
Iris Murdoch *The Bell*	89
Edna O'Brien *Girl With Green Eyes*	143
Kathy Page *The Ancient Siddanese*	179
Sylvia Plath *The Bell Jar*	203
Jean Rhys *Wide Sargasso Sea*	237
Françoise Sagan *Bonjour Tristesse*	265
Ntozake Shange *Sassafrass, Cypress & Indigo*	289
Elizabeth Smart *By Grand Central Station I Sat Down and Wept*	313
Amy Tan *The Joy Luck Club*	321
Alice Walker *Everyday Use*	343
Fay Weldon *The Hearts and Lives of Men*	357
Edith Wharton *Pomegranate Seed*	429
Jeanette Winterson *Sexing the Cherry*	471
Virginia Woolf *To The Lighthouse*	487
Biographical Notes	559

Acknowledgements

The original publication details of the texts in this anthology are given below. Copyright material is reproduced by kind permission of the publishers and authors. Every effort has been made to trace copyright owners correctly and credit them accordingly. Apologies are made for any errors or omissions.

Katherine Mansfield, *Prelude*. From the collection *Katherine Mansfield Short Stories*, selected and introduced by Claire Tomalin, published in Everyman Paperback 1983. *Prelude* was first published by the Hogarth Press in 1918 © Katherine Mansfield.
Alice Munro, *Miles City, Montana*. From the collection *The Progress of Love*, first published 1987 in Great Britain by Chatto & Windus Ltd; copyright © Alice Munro 1985, 1986. Originally published in *The New Yorker*.
Iris Murdoch, *The Bell*. First published 1958 in Great Britain by Chatto & Windus Ltd; copyright © Iris Murdoch 1958.
Edna O'Brien, *Girl With Green Eyes*. First published as *The Lonely Girl* 1962 in Great Britain by Jonathan Cape Ltd; published as *Girl With Green Eyes* 1964 by Penguin Books; copyright © Edna O'Brien 1962.
Kathy Page, *The Ancient Siddanese*. From the collection *As In Music*, first published 1990 in Great Britain by Methuen London; copyright © Kathy Page 1990.
Sylvia Plath, *The Bell Jar*. First published 1963 in Great Britain by William Heinemann Ltd; copyright © Victoria Lucas 1963.
Jean Rhys, *Wide Sargasso Sea*. First published 1966 in Great Britain by Andre Deutsch Ltd; copyright © Jean Rhys 1966.

Françoise Sagan, *Bonjour Tristesse*. First published 1955 in Great Britain by John Murray (Publishers) Ltd. Translated by Irene Ash.

Ntozake Shange, *Sassafras, Cypress & Indigo*. First published 1983 in Great Britain by Methuen London; copyright © Ntozake Shange 1982.

Elizabeth Smart, *By Grand Central Station I Sat Down and Wept*. First published 1945 in Great Britain by Editions Poetry London (Nicholson & Watson); copyright © Elizabeth Smart 1966.

Amy Tan, *The Joy Luck Club*. First published 1989 in Great Britain by William Heinemann Ltd; copyright © Any Tan 1989. Reprinted by permission of William Heinemann Ltd.

Alice Walker, *Everyday Use*. From the collection *In Love and Trouble*, first published 1984 in Great Britain by the Women's Press; copyright © Alice Walker 1984.

Fay Weldon, *The Hearts and Lives of Men*. First published 1987 in Great Britain by William Heinemann Ltd; copyright © Fay Weldon 1987. Reprinted by permission of William Heinemann Ltd.

Edith Wharton, *Pomegranate Seed*. From *The World Over*, first published 1936 by D. Appleton-Century Co. Inc. and Hearst Magazines Inc. Copyright © 1936 D. Appleton-Century Inc. and Hearst Magazines Inc.

Jeanette Winterson, *Sexing the Cherry*. First published 1989 in Great Britain by Bloomsbury Publishing Ltd; copyright © Jeanette Winterson 1989.

Virginia Woolf, *To The Lighthouse*. First published May 1927 in Great Britain by Hogarth Press; copyright © the Estate of Virginia Woolf 1927.

Katherine Mansfield
Prelude

I

There was not an inch of room for Lottie and Kezia in the buggy. When Pat swung them on top of the luggage they wobbled; the grandmother's lap was full and Linda Burnell could not possibly have held a lump of a child on hers for any distance. Isabel, very superior, was perched beside the new handy-man on the driver's seat. Holdalls, bags and boxes were piled upon the floor. 'These are absolute necessities that I will not let out of my sight for one instant,' said Linda Burnell, her voice trembling with fatigue and excitement.

Lottie and Kezia stood on the patch of lawn just inside the gate all ready for the fray in their coats with brass anchor buttons and little round caps with battleship ribbons. Hand in hand, they stared with round solemn eyes, first at the absolute necessities and then at their mother.

'We shall simply have to leave them. That is all. We shall simply have to cast them off,' said Linda Burnell. A strange little laugh flew from her lips; she leaned back against the buttoned leather cushions and shut her eyes, her lips trembling with laughter. Happily at that moment Mrs Samuel Josephs, who had been watching the scene from behind her drawing-room blind, waddled down the garden path.

'Why nod leave the chudren with be for the afterdoon,

Brs Burnell? They could go on the dray with the storeban when he comes in the eveding. Those thigs on the path have to go, dod't they?'

'Yes, everything outside the house is supposed to go,' said Linda Burnell, and she waved a white hand at the tables and chairs standing on their heads on the front lawn. How absurd they looked! Either they ought to be the other way up, or Lottie and Kezia ought to stand on their heads, too. And she longed to say: 'Stand on your heads, children, and wait for the storeman.' It seemed to her that would be so exquisitely funny that she could not attend to Mrs Samuel Josephs.

The fat creaking body leaned across the gate, and the big jelly of a face smiled. 'Dod't you worry, Brs Burnell. Loddie and Kezia can have tea with my chudren in the dursery, and I'll see theb on the dray afterwards.'

The grandmother considered. 'Yes, it really is quite the best plan. We are very obliged to you, Mrs Samuel Josephs. Children, say "thank you" to Mrs Samuel Josephs.'

Two subdued chirrups: 'Thank you, Mrs Samuel Josephs.'

'And be good little girls, and – come closer –' they advanced, 'don't forget to tell Mrs Samuel Josephs when you want to . . .'

'No, granma.'

'Dod't worry, Brs Burnell.'

At the last moment Kezia let go Lottie's hand and darted towards the buggy.

'I want to kiss my granma goodbye again.'

But she was too late. The buggy rolled off up the road, Isabel bursting with pride, her nose turned up at all the world, Linda Burnell prostrated, and the grandmother rummaging among the very curious oddments she had had put in her black silk reticule at the last moment,

Prelude

for something to give her daughter. The buggy twinkled away in the sunlight and fine golden dust up the hill and over. Kezia bit her lip, but Lottie, carefully finding her handkerchief first, set up a wail.

'Mother! Granma!'

Mrs Samuel Josephs, like a huge warm black silk tea-cosy, enveloped her.

'It's all right, by dear. Be a brave child. You come and blay in the dursery!'

She put her arm round weeping Lottie and led her away. Kezia followed, making a face at Mrs Samuel Josephs' placket, which was undone as usual, with two long pink corset laces hanging out of it. . . .

Lottie's weeping died down as she mounted the stairs, but the sight of her at the nursery door with swollen eyes and a blob of a nose gave great satisfaction to the S.J.'s who sat on two benches before a long table covered with American cloth and set out with immense plates of bread and dripping and two brown jugs that faintly steamed.

'Hullo! You've been crying!'

'Ooh! Your eyes have gone right in.'

'Doesn't her nose look funny.'

'You're all red-and-patchy.'

Lottie was quite a success. She felt it and swelled, smiling timidly.

'Go and sid by Zaidee, ducky,' said Mrs Samuel Josephs, 'and Kezia, you sid ad the end by Boses.'

Moses grinned and gave her a nip as she sat down; but she pretended not to notice. She did hate boys.

'Which will you have?' asked Stanley, leaning across the table very politely, and smiling at her. 'Which will you have to begin with – strawberries and cream or bread and dripping?'

'Strawberries and cream, please,' said she.

'Ah-h-h-h.' How they all laughed and beat the table with their teaspoons. Wasn't that a take-in! Wasn't it now! Didn't he fox her! Good old Stan!

'Ma! She thought it was real.'

Even Mrs Samuel Josephs, pouring out the milk and water, could not help smiling. 'You bustn't tease theb on their last day,' she wheezed.

But Kezia bit a big piece out of her bread and dripping, and then stood the piece up on her plate. With the bite out it made a dear little sort of gate. Pooh! She didn't care! A tear rolled down her cheek, but she wasn't crying. She couldn't have cried in front of those awful Samuel Josephs. She sat with her head bent, and as the tear dripped slowly down, she caught it with a neat little whisk of her tongue and ate it before any of them had seen.

II

After tea Kezia wandered back to their own house. Slowly she walked up the back steps, and through the scullery into the kitchen. Nothing was left in it but a lump of gritty yellow soap in one corner of the kitchen window-sill and a piece of flannel stained with blue bag in another. The fireplace was choked up with rubbish. She poked among it but found nothing except a hair-tidy with a heart painted on it that had belonged to the servant girl. Even that she left lying, and she trailed through the narrow passage into the drawing-room. The Venetian blind was pulled down but not drawn close. Long pencil rays of sunlight shone through and the wavy shadow of a bush outside danced on the gold lines. Now it was still, now it began to flutter again, and now it

Prelude

came almost as far as her feet. Zoom! Zoom! a bluebottle knocked against the ceiling; the carpet-tacks had little bits of red fluff sticking to them.

The dining-room window had a square of coloured glass at each corner. One was blue and one was yellow. Kezia bent down to have one more look at a blue lawn with blue arum lilies growing at the gate, and then at a yellow lawn with yellow lilies and a yellow fence. As she looked a little Chinese Lottie came out on to the lawn and began to dust the tables and chairs with a corner of her pinafore. Was that really Lottie? Kezia was not quite sure until she had looked through the ordinary window.

Upstairs in her father's and mother's room she found a pill box black and shiny outside and red in, holding a blob of cotton wool.

'I could keep a bird's egg in that,' she decided.

In the servant girl's room there was a stay-button stuck in a crack of the floor, and in another crack some beads and a long needle. She knew there was nothing in her grandmother's room; she had watched her pack. She went over to the window and leaned against it, pressing her hands to the pane.

Kezia liked to stand so before the window. She liked the feeling of the cold shining glass against her hot palms, and she liked to watch the funny white tops that came on her fingers when she pressed them hard against the pane. As she stood there, the day flickered out and dark came. With the dark crept the wind snuffling and howling. The windows of the empty house shook, a creaking came from the walls and floors, a piece of loose iron on the roof banged forlornly. Kezia was suddenly quite, quite still, with wide open eyes and knees pressed together. She was frightened. She wanted to call Lottie and to go on calling all the while she ran downstairs and out of the house. But IT was just behind her, waiting at the door, at the head of the stairs, at the bottom of the stairs, hiding in the passage, ready to dart out at the back door. But Lottie was at the back door, too.

'Kezia!' she called cheerfully. 'The storeman's here. Everything is on the dray and three horses, Kezia. Mrs Samuel Josephs has given us a big shawl to wear round us, and she says to button up your coat. She won't come out because of asthma.'

Lottie was very important.

'Now then, you kids,' called the storeman. He hooked his big thumbs under their arms and up they swung. Lottie arranged the shawl 'most beautifully' and the storeman tucked up their feet in a piece of old blanket.

'Lift up. Easy does it.'

They might have been a couple of young ponies. The storeman felt over the cords holding his load, unhooked the brakechain from the wheel, and whistling, he swung up beside them.

'Keep close to me,' said Lottie, 'because otherwise you pull the shawl away from my side, Kezia.'

But Kezia edged up to the storeman. He towered beside her big as a giant and he smelled of nuts and new wooden boxes.

III

It was the first time that Lottie and Kezia had ever been out so late. Everything looked different – the painted wooden houses far smaller than they did by day, the gardens far bigger and wilder. Bright stars speckled the sky and the moon hung over the harbour dabbling the

Prelude

waves with gold. They could see the lighthouse shining on Quarantine Island, and the green lights on the old coal hulks.

'There comes the Picton boat,' said the storeman, pointing to a little steamer all hung with bright beads.

But when they reached the top of the hill and began to go down the other side the harbour disappeared, and although they were still in the town they were quite lost. Other carts rattled past. Everybody knew the storeman.

'Night, Fred.'

'Night O,' he shouted.

Kezia liked very much to hear him. Whenever a cart appeared in the distance she looked up and waited for his voice. He was an old friend; and she and her grandmother had often been to his place to buy grapes. The storeman lived alone in a cottage that had a glasshouse against one wall built by himself. All the glasshouse was spanned and arched over with one beautiful vine. He took her brown basket from her, lined it with three large leaves, and then he felt in his belt for a little horn knife, reached up and snapped off a big blue cluster and laid it on the leaves so tenderly that Kezia held her breath to watch. He was a very big man. He wore brown velvet trousers, and he had a long brown beard. But he never wore a collar, not even on Sunday. The back of his neck was burnt bright red.

'Where are we now?' Every few minutes one of the children asked him the question.

'Why, this is Hawk Street, or Charlotte Crescent.'

'Of course it is,' Lottie pricked up her ears at the last name; she always felt that Charlotte Crescent belonged specially to her. Very few people had streets with the same name as theirs.

'Look, Kezia, there is Charlotte Crescent. Doesn't it

look different?' Now everything familiar was left behind. Now the big dray rattled into unknown country, along new roads with high clay banks on either side, up steep hills, down into busy valleys, through wide shallow rivers. Further and further. Lottie's head wagged; she drooped, she slipped half into Kezia's lap and lay there. But Kezia could not open her eyes wide enough. The wind blew and she shivered; but her cheeks and ears burned.

'Do stars ever blow about?' she asked.

'Not to notice,' said the storeman.

'We've got a nuncle and a naunt living near our new house,' said Kezia. 'They have got two children, Pip, the eldest is called, and the youngest's name is Rags. He's got a ram. He has to feed it with a nenamuel teapot and a glove top over the spout. He's going to show us. What is the difference between a ram and a sheep?'

'Well, a ram has horns and runs for you.'

Kezia considered. 'I don't want to see it frightfully,' she said. 'I hate rushing animals like dogs and parrots. I often dream that animals rush at me – even camels – and while they are rushing, their heads swell e-enormous.'

The storeman said nothing. Kezia peered up at him, screwing up her eyes. Then she put her finger out and stroked his sleeve; it felt hairy. 'Are we near?' she asked.

'Not far off, now,' answered the storeman. 'Getting tired?'

'Well, I'm not an atom bit sleepy,' said Kezia. 'But my eyes keep curling up in such a funny sort of way.' She gave a long sigh, and to stop her eyes from curling she shut them. . . . When she opened them again they were clanking through a drive that cut through the garden like whiplash, looping suddenly an island of

Prelude

green, and behind the island, but out of sight until you came upon it, was the house. It was long and low built, with a pillared veranda and balcony all the way round. The soft white bulk of it lay stretched upon the green garden like a sleeping beast. And now one and now another of the windows leaped into light. Someone was walking through the empty rooms carrying a lamp. From the window downstairs the light of a fire flickered. A strange beautiful excitement seemed to stream from the house in quivering ripples.

'Where are we?' said Lottie, sitting up. Her reefer cap was all on one side and on her cheek there was the print of an anchor button she had pressed against while sleeping. Tenderly the storeman lifted her, set her cap straight, and pulled down her crumpled clothes. She stood blinking on the lowest veranda step watching Kezia, who seemed to come flying through the air to her feet.

'Ooh!' cried Kezia, flinging up her arms. The grandmother came out of the dark hall carrying a little lamp. She was smiling.

'You found your way in the dark?' said she.

'Perfectly well.'

But Lottie staggered on the lowest veranda step like a bird fallen out of the nest. If she stood still for a moment she fell asleep; if she leaned against anything her eyes closed. She could not walk another step.

'Kezia,' said the grandmother, 'can I trust you to carry the lamp?'

'Yes, my granma.'

The old woman bent down and gave the bright breathing thing into her hands and then she caught up drunken Lottie. 'This way.'

Through a square hall filled with bales and hundreds

of parrots (but the parrots were only on the wallpaper) down a narrow passage where the parrots persisted in flying past Kezia with her lamp.

'Be very quiet,' warned the grandmother, putting down Lottie and opening the dining-room door. 'Poor little mother has got such a headache.'

Linda Burnell, in a long cane chair, with her feet on a hassock and a plaid over her knees, lay before a crackling fire. Burnell and Beryl sat at the table in the middle of the room eating a dish of fried chops and drinking tea out of a brown china teapot. Over the back of her mother's chair leaned Isabel. She had a comb in her fingers and in a gentle absorbed fashion she was combing the curls from her mother's forehead. Outside the pool of lamp and firelight the room stretched dark and bare to the hollow windows.

'Are those the children?' But Linda did not really care; she did not even open her eyes to see.

'Put down the lamp, Kezia,' said Aunt Beryl, 'or we shall have the house on fire before we are out of packing cases. More tea, Stanley?'

'Well, you might just give me five-eighths of a cup,' said Burnell, leaning across the table. 'Have another chop, Beryl. Tip-top meat, isn't it? Not too lean and not too fat.' He turned to his wife. 'You're sure you won't change your mind, Linda darling?'

'The very thought of it is enough.' She raised one eyebrow in the way she had. The grandmother brought the children bread and milk and they sat up to table, flushed and sleepy behind the wavy steam.

'I had meat for my supper,' said Isabel, still combing gently.

'I had a whole chop for my supper, the bone and all and Worcester sauce. Didn't I, Father?'

Prelude

'Oh, don't boast, Isabel,' said Aunt Beryl.

Isabel looked astounded. 'I wasn't boasting, was I, Mummy? I never thought of boasting. I thought they would like to know. I meant to tell them.'

'Very well. That's enough,' said Burnell. He pushed back his plate, took a toothpick out of his pocket and began picking his strong white teeth.

'You might see that Fred has a bite of something in the kitchen before he goes, will you, Mother?'

'Yes, Stanley.' The old woman turned to go.

'Oh, hold on half a jiffy. I suppose nobody knows where my slippers were put? I suppose I shall not be able to get at them for a month or two – what?'

'Yes,' came from Linda. 'In the top of the canvas holdall marked "urgent necessities".'

'Well, you might get them for me, will you, Mother?'

'Yes, Stanley.'

Burnell got up, stretched himself, and going over to the fire he turned his back to it and lifted up his coat tails.

'By Jove, this is a pretty pickle. Eh, Beryl?'

Beryl, sipping tea, her elbows on the table, smiled over the cup at him. She wore an unfamiliar pink pinafore; the sleeves of her blouse were rolled up to her shoulders showing her lovely freckled arms, and she had let her hair fall down her back in a long pigtail.

'How long do you think it will take to get straight – couple of weeks – eh?' he chaffed.

'Good heavens, no,' said Beryl airily. 'The worst is over already. The servant girl and I have simply slaved all day, and ever since Mother came she has worked like a horse, too. We have never sat down for a moment. We have had a day.'

Stanley scented a rebuke.

'Well, I suppose you did not expect me to rush away from the office and nail carpets – did you?'

'Certainly not,' laughed Beryl. She put down her cup and ran out of the dining-room.

'What the hell does she expect us to do?' asked Stanley. 'Sit down and fan herself with a palm-leaf fan while I have a gang of professionals to do the job? By Jove, if she can't do a hand's turn occasionally without shouting about it in return for . . .'

And he gloomed as the chops began to fight the tea in his sensitive stomach. But Linda put up a hand and dragged him down to the side of her long chair.

'This is a wretched time for you, old boy,' she said. Her cheeks were very white, but she smiled and curled her fingers into the big red hand she held. Burnell became quiet. Suddenly he began to whistle 'Pure as a lily, joyous and free' – a good sign.

'Think you're going to like it?' he asked.

'I don't want to tell you, but I think I ought to, Mother,' said Isabel. 'Kezia is drinking tea out of Aunt Beryl's cup.'

IV

They were taken off to bed by the grandmother. She went first with a candle; the stairs rang to their climbing feet. Isabel and Lottie lay in a room to themselves, Kezia curled in her grandmother's soft bed.

'Aren't there going to be any sheets, my granma?'

'No, not tonight.'

'It's tickly,' said Kezia, 'but it's like Indians.' She dragged her grandmother down to her and kissed her under the chin.

Prelude

'Come to bed soon and be my Indian brave.'

'What a silly you are,' said the old woman, tucking her in as she loved to be tucked.

'Aren't you going to leave me a candle?'

'No. Sh-h. Go to sleep.'

'Well, can I have the door left open?'

She rolled herself up into a round but she did not go to sleep. From all over the house came the sound of steps. The house itself creaked and popped. Loud whispering voices came from downstairs. Once she heard Aunt Beryl's rush of high laughter, and once she heard a loud trumpeting from Burnell blowing his nose. Outside the window hundreds of black cats with yellow eyes sat in the sky watching her – but she was not frightened. Lottie was saying to Isabel: 'I'm not going to say my prayers in bed tonight.'

'No, you can't, Lottie.' Isabel was very firm. 'God only excuses you saying your prayers in bed if you've got a temperature.' So Lottie yielded:

> 'Gentle Jesus meek anmile,
> Look pon a little chile.
> Pity me, simple Lizzie,
> Suffer me to come to thee.'

And then they lay down back to back, their little behinds just touching, and fell asleep.

Standing in a pool of moonlight Beryl Fairfield undressed herself. She was tired, but she pretended to be more tired than she really was – letting her clothes fall, pushing back with a languid gesture her warm, heavy hair.

'Oh, how tired I am – very tired.'

She shut her eyes a moment, but her lips smiled. Her breath rose and fell in her breast like two fanning wings.

The window was wide open; it was warm, and somewhere out there in the garden a young man, dark and slender, with mocking eyes, tiptoed among the bushes, and gathered the flowers into a big bouquet, and slipped under her window and held it up to her. She saw herself bending forward. He thrust his head among the bright waxy flowers, sly and laughing. 'No, no,' said Beryl. She turned from the window and dropped her nightgown over her head.

'How frightfully unreasonable Stanley is sometimes,' she thought, buttoning. And then as she lay down, there came the old thought, the cruel thought – ah, if only she had money of her own.

A young man, immensely rich, has just arrived from England. He meets her quite by chance. . . . The new governor is unmarried. . . . There is a ball at Government house. . . . Who is that exquisite creature in eau-de-nil satin? Beryl Fairfield. . . .

'The thing that pleases me,' said Stanley, leaning against the side of the bed and giving himself a good scratch on his shoulders and back before turning in, 'is that I've got the place dirt cheap, Linda. I was talking about it to little Wally Bell today and he said he simply could not understand why they had accepted my figure. You see land about here is bound to become more and more valuable . . . in about ten years' time . . . of course we shall have to go very slow and cut down expenses as fine as possible. Not asleep – are you?'

'No, dear, I've heard every word,' said Linda.

He sprang into bed, leaned over her and blew out the candle.

'Good night, Mr Business Man,' said she, and she took hold of his head by the ears and gave him a quick

Prelude

kiss. Her faint far-away voice seemed to come from a deep well.

'Good night, darling.' He slipped his arm under her neck and drew her to him.

'Yes, clasp me,' said the faint voice from the deep well.

Pat the handy-man sprawled in his little room behind the kitchen. His sponge-bag, coat and trousers hung from the door-peg like a hanged man. From the edge of the blanket his twisted toes protruded, and on the floor beside him there was an empty cane bird-cage. He looked like a comic picture.

'Honk, honk,' came from the servant girl. She had adenoids.

Last to go to bed was the grandmother.

'What. Not asleep yet?'

'No, I'm waiting for you,' said Kezia. The old woman sighed and lay down beside her. Kezia thrust her head under her grandmother's arm and gave a little squeak. But the old woman only pressed her faintly, and sighed again, took out her teeth, and put them in a glass of water beside her on the floor.

In the garden some tiny owls, perched on the branches of a lace-bark tree, called: 'More pork; more pork.' And far away in the bush there sounded a harsh rapid chatter: 'Ha-ha-ha . . . Ha-ha-ha.'

V

Dawn came sharp and chill with red clouds on a faint green sky and drops of water on every leaf and blade. A breeze blew over the garden, dropping dew and dropping petals, shivered over the drenched paddocks, and was lost in the sombre bush. In the sky some tiny stars floated for a moment and then they were gone – they were dissolved like bubbles. And plain to be heard in the early quiet was the sound of the creek in the paddock running over the brown stones, running in and out of the sandy hollows, hiding under clumps of dark berry bushes, spilling into a swamp of yellow water flowers and cresses.

And then at the first beam of sun the birds began. Big cheeky birds, starlings and mynahs, whistled on the lawns, the little birds, the goldfinches and linnets and fan-tails, flicked from bough to bough. A lovely kingfisher perched on the paddock fence preening his rich beauty, and a *tui* sang his three notes and laughed and sang them again.

'How loud the birds are,' said Linda in her dream. She was walking with her father through a green paddock sprinkled with daisies. Suddenly he bent down and parted the grasses and showed her a tiny ball of fluff just at her feet. 'Oh, Papa, the darling.' She made a cup of her hands and caught the tiny bird and stroked its head with her finger. It was quite tame. But a funny thing happened. As she stroked it began to swell, it ruffled and pouched, it grew bigger and bigger and its round eyes seemed to smile knowingly at her. Now her arms were hardly wide enough to hold it and she dropped it into her apron. It had become a baby with a big naked head and a gaping bird-mouth, opening and shutting. Her father broke into a loud clattering laugh and she woke to see Burnell standing by the windows rattling the Venetian blind up to the very top.

'Hullo,' he said. 'Didn't wake you, did I? Nothing much wrong with the weather this morning.'

Prelude

He was enormously pleased. Weather like this set a final seal on his bargain. He felt, somehow, that he had bought the lovely day, too – got it chucked in dirt cheap with the house and ground. He dashed off to his bath and Linda turned over and raised herself on one elbow to see the room by daylight. All the furniture had found a place – all the old paraphernalia, as she expressed it. Even the photographs were on the mantelpiece and the medicine bottles on the shelf above the washstand. Her clothes lay across a chair – her outdoor things, a purple cape and a round hat with a plume in it. Looking at them she wished that she was going away from this house, too. And she saw herself driving away from them all in a little buggy, driving away from everybody and not even waving.

Back came Stanley girt with a towel, glowing and slapping his thighs. He pitched the wet towel on top of her hat and cape, and standing firm in the exact centre of a square of sunlight he began to do his exercises. Deep breathing, bending and squatting like a frog and shooting out his legs. He was so delighted with his firm, obedient body that he hit himself on the chest and gave a loud 'Ah'. But this amazing vigour seemed to set him worlds away from Linda. She lay on the white tumbled bed and watched him as if from the clouds.

'Oh, damn! Oh, blast!' said Stanley, who had butted into a crisp white shirt only to find that some idiot had fastened the neck-band and he was caught. He stalked over to Linda waving his arms.

'You look like a big fat turkey,' said she.

'Fat. I like that,' said Stanley. 'I haven't a square inch of fat on me. Feel that.'

'It's rock – it's iron,' mocked she.

'You'd be surprised,' said Stanley, as though this were

intensely interesting, 'at the number of chaps at the club who have got a corporation. Young chaps, you know – men of my age.' He began parting his bushy ginger hair, his blue eyes fixed and round in the glass, his knees bent, because the dressing-table was always – confound it – a bit too low for him. 'Little Wally Bell, for instance,' and he straightened, describing upon himself an enormous curve with the hairbrush. 'I must say I've a perfect horror . . .'

'My dear, don't worry. You'll never be fat. You are far too energetic.'

'Yes, yes, I suppose that's true,' said he, comforted for the hundredth time, and taking a pearl penknife out of his pocket he began to pare his nails.

'Breakfast, Stanley.' Beryl was at the door. 'Oh, Linda, Mother says you are not to get up yet.' She popped her head in at the door. She had a big piece of syringa stuck through her hair.

'Everything we left on the veranda last night is simply sopping this morning. You should see poor dear Mother wringing out the tables and the chairs. However, there is no harm done –' this with the faintest glance at Stanley.

'Have you told Pat to have the buggy round in time? It's a good six and a half miles to the office.'

'I can imagine what this early start for the office will be like,' thought Linda. 'It will be very high pressure indeed.'

'Pat, Pat.' She heard the servant girl calling. But Pat was evidently hard to find; the silly voice went baa-baaing through the garden.

Linda did not rest again until the final slam of the front door told her that Stanley was really gone.

Later she heard her children playing in the garden.

Prelude

Lottie's stolid, compact little voice cried: 'Ke-zia. Isabel.' She was always getting lost or losing people only to find them again, to her great surprise, round the next tree or the next corner. 'Oh, there you are after all.' They had been turned out after breakfast and told not to come back to the house until they were called. Isabel wheeled a neat pramload of prim dolls and Lottie was allowed for a great treat to walk beside her holding the doll's parasol over the face of the wax one.

'Where are you going to, Kezia?' asked Isabel, who longed to find some light and menial duty that Kezia might perform and so be roped in under her government.

'Oh, just away,' said Kezia. . . .

Then she did not hear them any more. What a glare there was in the room. She hated blinds pulled up to the top at any time, but in the morning it was intolerable. She turned over to the wall and idly, with one finger, she traced a poppy on the wallpaper with a leaf and a stem and a fat bursting bud. In the quiet, and under her tracing finger, the poppy seemed to come alive. She could feel the sticky, silky petals, the stem, hairy like a gooseberry skin, the rough leaf and the tight glazed bud. Things had a habit of coming alive like that. Not only large substantial things like furniture but curtains and the patterns of stuffs and the fringes of quilts and cushions. How often she had seen the tassel fringe of her quilt change into a funny procession of dancers with priests attending. . . . For there were some tassels that did not dance at all but walked stately, bent forward as if praying or chanting. How often the medicine bottles had turned into a row of little men with brown top-hats on; and the washstand jug had a way of sitting in the basin like a fat bird in a round nest.

Katherine Mansfield

'I dreamed about birds last night,' thought Linda. What was it? She had forgotten. But the strangest part of this coming alive of things was what they did. They listened, they seemed to swell out with some mysterious important content, and when they were full she felt that they smiled. But it was not for her, only, their sly secret smile; they were members of a secret society and they smiled among themselves. Sometimes, when she had fallen asleep in the daytime, she woke and could not lift a finger, could not even turn her eyes to left or right because THEY were there; sometimes when she went out of a room and left it empty, she knew as she clicked the door to that THEY were filling it. And there were times in the evenings when she was upstairs, perhaps, and everybody else was down, when she could hardly escape from them. Then she could not hurry, she could not hum a tune; if she tried to say ever so carelessly – 'Bother that old thimble' – THEY were not deceived. THEY knew how frightened she was; THEY saw how she turned her head away as she passed the mirror. What Linda always felt was that THEY wanted something of her, and she knew that if she gave herself up and was quiet, more than quiet, silent, motionless, something would really happen.

'It's very quiet now,' she thought. She opened her eyes wide, and she heard the silence spinning its soft endless web. How lightly she breathed; she scarcely had to breathe at all.

Yes, everything had come alive down to the minutest, tiniest particle, and she did not feel her bed, she floated, held up in the air. Only she seemed to be listening with her wide open watchful eyes, waiting for someone to come who just did not come, watching for something to happen that just did not happen.

Prelude

VI

In the kitchen at the long deal table under the two windows old Mrs Fairfield was washing the breakfast dishes. The kitchen window looked out on to a big grass patch that led down to the vegetable garden and the rhubarb beds. On one side the grass patch was bordered by the scullery and wash-house and over this whitewashed lean-to there grew a knotted vine. She had noticed yesterday that a few tiny corkscrew tendrils had come right through some cracks in the scullery ceiling and all the windows of the lean-to had a thick frill of ruffled green.

'I am very fond of a grape vine,' declared Mrs Fairfield, 'but I do not think that the grapes will ripen here. It takes Australian sun.' And she remembered how Beryl when she was a baby had been picking some white grapes from the vine on the back veranda of the Tasmanian house and she had been stung on the leg by a huge red ant. She saw Beryl in a little plaid dress with red ribbon tie-ups on the shoulders screaming so dreadfully that half the street rushed in. And how the child's leg had swelled! 'T-t-t-t!' Mrs Fairfield caught her breath remembering. 'Poor child, how terrifying it was.' And she set her lips tight and went over to the stove for some more hot water. The water frothed up in the big soapy bowl with pink and blue bubbles on top of the foam. Old Mrs Fairfield's arms were bare to the elbow and stained a bright pink. She wore a grey foulard dress patterned with large purple pansies, a white linen apron and a high cap shaped like a jelly mould of white muslin. At her throat there was a silver crescent moon with five little owls seated on it, and round her neck she wore a watch-guard made of black beads.

Katherine Mansfield

It was hard to believe that she had not been in that kitchen for years; she was so much a part of it. She put the crocks away with a sure, precise touch, moving leisurely and ample from the stove to the dresser, looking into the pantry and the larder as though there were not an unfamiliar corner. When she had finished, everything in the kitchen had become part of a series of patterns. She stood in the middle of the room wiping her hands on a check cloth; a smile beamed on her lips; she thought it looked very nice, very satisfactory.

'Mother! Mother! Are you there?' called Beryl.

'Yes, dear. Do you want me?'

'No. I'm coming,' and Beryl rushed in, very flushed, dragging with her two big pictures.

'Mother, whatever can I do with these awful hideous Chinese paintings that Chung Wah gave Stanley when he went bankrupt? It's absurd to say that they are valuable, because they were hanging in Chung Wah's fruit shop for months before. I can't make out why Stanley wants them kept. I'm sure he thinks them just as hideous as we do, but it's because of the frames,' she said spitefully. 'I suppose he thinks the frames might fetch something some day or other.'

'Why don't you hang them in the passage?' suggested Mrs Fairfield; 'they would not be much seen there.'

'I can't. There is no room. I've hung all the photographs of his office there before and after building, and the signed photos of his business friends, and that awful enlargement of Isabel lying on the mat in her singlet.' Her angry glance swept the placid kitchen. 'I know what I'll do. I'll hang them here. I will tell Stanley they got a little damp in the moving so I have put them in here for the time being.'

She dragged a chair forward, jumped on it, took a

Prelude

hammer and a big nail out of her pinafore pocket and banged away.

'There! That is enough! Hand me the picture, Mother.'

'One moment, child.' Her mother was wiping over the carved ebony frame.

'Oh, Mother, really you need not dust them. It would take years to dust all those little holes.' And she frowned at the top of her mother's head and bit her lip with impatience. Mother's deliberate way of doing things was simply maddening. It was old age, she supposed, loftily.

At last the two pictures were hung side by side. She jumped off the chair, stowing away the little hammer.

'They don't look so bad there, do they?' said she. 'And at any rate nobody need gaze at them except Pat and the servant girl – have I got a spider's web on my face, Mother? I've been poking into that cupboard under the stairs and now something keeps tickling my nose.'

But before Mrs Fairfield had time to look Beryl had turned away. Someone tapped on the window: Linda was there, nodding and smiling. They heard the latch of the scullery door lift and she came in. She had no hat on; her hair stood upon her head in curling rings and she was wrapped up in an old cashmere shawl.

'I'm so hungry,' said Linda. 'Where can I get something to eat, Mother? This is the first time I've been in the kitchen. It says "Mother" all over; everything is in pairs.'

'I will make you some tea,' said Mrs Fairfield, spreading a clean napkin over a corner of the table, 'and Beryl can have a cup with you.'

'Beryl, do you want half my gingerbread?' Linda waved the knife at her. 'Beryl, do you like the house now that we are here?'

'Oh yes, I like the house immensely and the garden is beautiful, but it feels very far away from everything to me. I can't imagine people coming out from town to see us in that dreadful jolting bus, and I am sure there is not anyone here to come and call. Of course it does not matter to you because –'

'But there's the buggy,' said Linda. 'Pat can drive you into town whenever you like.'

That was a consolation, certainly, but there was something at the back of Beryl's mind, something she did not even put into words for herself.

'Oh, well, at any rate it won't kill us,' she said drily, putting down her empty cup and standing up and stretching. 'I am going to hang curtains.' And she ran away singing:

> 'How many thousand birds I see
> That sing aloud from every tree . . .

'. . . birds I see That sing aloud from every tree . . .' But when she reached the dining-room she stopped singing, her face changed; it became gloomy and sullen.

'One may as well rot here as anywhere else,' she muttered savagely, digging the stiff brass safety-pins into the red serge curtains.

The two left in the kitchen were quiet for a little. Linda leaned her cheek on her fingers and watched her mother. She thought her mother looked wonderfully beautiful with her back to the leafy window. There was something comforting in the sight of her that Linda felt she could never do without. She needed the sweet smell of her flesh, and the soft feel of her cheeks and her arms and shoulders still softer. She loved the way her hair curled, silver at her forehead, lighter at her neck and bright brown still in the big coil under the muslin cap.

Prelude

Exquisite were her mother's hands, and the two rings she wore seemed to melt into her creamy skin. And she was always so fresh, so delicious. The old woman could bear nothing but linen next to her body and she bathed in cold water winter and summer.

'Isn't there anything for me to do?' asked Linda.

'No, darling. I wish you would go into the garden and give an eye to your children; but that I know you will not do.'

'Of course I will, but you know Isabel is much more grown up than any of us.'

'Yes, but Kezia is not,' said Mrs Fairfield.

'Oh, Kezia has been tossed by a bull hours ago,' said Linda, winding herself up in her shawl again.

But no, Kezia had seen a bull through a hole in a knot of wood in the paling that separated the tennis lawn from the paddock. But she had not liked the bull frightfully, so she had walked away back through the orchard, up the grassy slope, along the path by the lace-bark tree and so into the spread tangled garden. She did not believe that she would ever not get lost in this garden. Twice she had found her way back to the big iron gates they had driven through the night before, and then had turned to walk up the drive that led to the house, but there were so many little paths on either side. On one side they all led into a tangle of tall dark trees and strange bushes with flat velvet leaves and feathery cream flowers that buzzed with flies when you shook them – this was the frightening side, and no garden at all. The little paths here were wet and clayey with tree roots spanned across them like the marks of big fowls' feet.

But on the other side of the drive there was a high box border and the paths had box edges and all of them led into a deeper and deeper tangle of flowers. The camellias were in bloom, white and crimson and pink and white striped with flashing leaves. You could not see a leaf on the syringa bushes for the white clusters. The roses were in flower – gentlemen's button-hole roses, little white ones, but far too full of insects to hold under anyone's nose, pink monthly roses with a ring of fallen petals round the bushes, cabbage roses on thick stalks, moss roses, always in bud, pink smooth beauties opening curl on curl, red ones so dark they seemed to turn back as they fell, and a certain exquisite cream kind with a slender red stem and bright scarlet leaves.

There were clumps of fairy bells, and all kinds of geraniums, and there were little trees of verbena and bluish lavender bushes and a bed of pelargoniums with velvet eyes and leaves like moths' wings. There was a bed of nothing but mignonette and another of nothing but pansies – borders of double and single daisies and all kinds of little tufty plants she had never seen before.

The red-hot pokers were taller than she; the Japanese sunflowers grew in a tiny jungle. She sat down on one of the box borders. By pressing hard at first it made a nice seat. But how dusty it was inside! Kezia bent down to look and sneezed and rubbed her nose.

And then she found herself at the top of the rolling grassy slope that led down to the orchard.... She looked down at the slope a moment; then she lay down on her back, gave a squeak and rolled over and over into the thick flowery orchard grass. As she lay waiting for things to stop spinning, she decided to go up to the house and ask the servant girl for an empty matchbox. She wanted to make a surprise for the grandmother.... First she would put a leaf inside with a big violet lying on it, then she would put a very small white picotee, perhaps, on

Prelude

each side of the violet, and then she would sprinkle some lavender on the top, but not to cover their heads.

She often made these surprises for the grandmother, and they were always most successful.

'Do you want a match, my granny?'

'Why, yes, child, I believe a match is just what I'm looking for.'

The grandmother slowly opened the box and came upon the picture inside.

'Good gracious, child! How you astonished me!'

'I can make her one every day here,' she thought, scrambling up the grass on her slippery shoes.

But on her way back to the house she came to that island that lay in the middle of the drive, dividing the drive into two arms that met in front of the house. The island was made of grass banked up high. Nothing grew on the top except one huge plant with thick, grey-green, thorny leaves, and out of the middle there sprang up a tall stout stem. Some of the leaves of the plant were so old that they curled up in the air no longer; they turned back, they were split and broken; some of them lay flat and withered on the ground.

Whatever could it be? She had never seen anything like it before. She stood and stared. And then she saw her mother coming down the path.

'Mother, what is it?'

Linda looked up at the fat swelling plant with its cruel leaves and fleshy stem. High above them, as though becalmed in the air, and yet holding so fast to the earth it grew from, it might have had claws instead of roots. The curving leaves seemed to be hiding something; the blind stem cut into the air as if no wind could ever shake it.

'That is an aloe, Kezia,' said her mother.

'Does it ever have any flowers?'

'Yes, Kezia,' and Linda smiled down at her, and half shut her eyes. 'Once every hundred years.'

VII

On his way home from the office Stanley Burnell stopped the buggy at the Bodega, got out and bought a large bottle of oysters. At the Chinaman's shop next door he bought a pineapple in the pink of condition, and noticing a basket of fresh black cherries he told John to put him in a pound of those as well. The oysters and the pine he stowed away in the box under the front seat, but the cherries he kept in his hand.

Pat, the handy-man, leapt off the box and tucked him up again in the brown rug.

'Lift yer feet, Mr Burnell, while I give yer a fold under,' said he.

'Right! Right! First rate!' said Stanley. 'You can make straight for home now.'

Pat gave the grey mare a touch and the buggy sprang forward.

'I believe this man is a first-rate chap,' thought Stanley. He liked the look of him sitting up there in his neat brown coat and brown bowler. He liked the way Pat had tucked him in, and he liked his eyes. There was nothing servile about him – and if there was one thing he hated more than another it was servility. And he looked as if he was pleased with his job – happy and contented already.

The grey mare went very well; Burnell was impatient to be out of the town. He wanted to be home. Ah, it was splendid to live in the country – to get right out of that hole of a town once the office was closed; and this drive

Prelude

in the fresh warm air, knowing all the while that his own house was at the other end, with its garden and paddocks, its three tip-top cows and enough fowls and ducks to keep them in poultry, was splendid too.

As they left the town finally and bowled away up the deserted road his heart beat hard for joy. He rooted in the bag and began to eat the cherries, three or four at a time, chucking the stones over the side of the buggy. They were delicious, so plump and cold, without a spot or bruise on them.

Look at those two, now – black one side and white the other – perfect! A perfect little pair of Siamese twins. And he stuck them in his button-hole. . . . By Jove, he wouldn't mind giving that chap up there a handful – but no, better not. Better wait until he had been with him a bit longer.

He began to plan what he would do with his Saturday afternoons and his Sundays. He wouldn't go to the club for lunch on Saturday. No, cut away from the office as soon as possible and get them to give him a couple of slices of cold meat and half a lettuce when he got home. And then he'd get a few chaps out from town to play tennis in the afternoon. Not too many – three at most. Beryl was a good player, too. . . . He stretched out his right arm and slowly bent it, feeling the muscle. . . . A bath, a good rub-down, a cigar on the veranda after dinner. . . .

On Sunday morning they would go to church – children and all. Which reminded him that he must hire a pew, in the sun if possible and well forward so as to be out of the draught from the door. In fancy he heard himself intoning extremely well: 'When thou did overcome the *Sharp*ness of Death Though didst open the *King*dom of heaven to *all* Believers.' And he saw the neat brass-edged card on the corner of the pew – Mr Stanley Burnell and family. . . . The rest of the day he'd loaf about with Linda. . . . Now they were walking about the garden; she was on his arm, and he was explaining to her at length what he intended doing at the office the week following. He heard her saying: 'My dear, I think that is most wise. . . .' Talking things over with Linda was a wonderful help even though they were apt to drift away from the point.

Hang it all! They weren't getting along very fast. Pat had put the brake on again. Ugh! What a brute of a thing it was. He could feel it in the pit of his stomach.

A sort of panic overtook Burnell whenever he approached near home. Before he was well inside the gate he would shout to anyone within sight: 'Is everything all right?' And then he did not believe it was until he heard Linda say: 'Hullo! Are you home again?' That was the worst of living in the country – it took the deuce of a long time to get back. . . . But now they weren't far off. They were on the top of the last hill; it was a gentle slope all the way now and not more than half a mile.

Pat trailed the whip over the mare's back and he coaxed her: 'Goop now. Goop now.'

It wanted a few minutes to sunset. Everything stood motionless bathed in bright, metallic light and from the paddocks on either side there streamed the milky scent of ripe grass. The iron gates were open. They dashed through and up the drive and round the island, stopping at the exact middle of the veranda.

'Did she satisfy yer, sir?' said Pat, getting off the box and grinning at his master.

'Very well indeed, Pat,' said Stanley.

Linda came out of the glass door; her voice rang in the shadowy quiet. 'Hullo! Are you home again?'

Prelude

At the sound of her his heart beat so hard that he could hardly stop himself dashing up the steps and catching her in his arms.

'Yes, I'm home again. Is everything all right?'

Pat began to lead the buggy round to the side gate that opened into the courtyard.

'Here, half a moment,' said Burnell. 'Hand me those two parcels.' And he said to Linda, 'I've brought you back a bottle of oysters and a pineapple,' as though he had brought her back all the harvest of the earth.

They all went into the hall; Linda carried the oysters in one hand and the pineapple in the other. Burnell shut the glass door, threw his hat down, put his arms round her and strained her to him, kissing the top of her head, her ears, her lips, her eyes.

'Oh, dear! Oh, dear!' said she. 'Wait a moment. Let me put down these silly things,' and she put the bottle of oysters and the pine on a little carved chair. 'What have you got in your button-hole – cherries?' She took them out and hung them over his ear.

'Don't do that, darling. They are for you.'

So she took them off his ear again. 'You don't mind if I save them. They'd spoil my appetite for dinner. Come and see your children. They are having tea.'

The lamp was lighted on the nursery table. Mrs Fairfield was cutting and spreading bread and butter. The three little girls sat up to table wearing large bibs embroidered with their names. They wiped their mouths as their father came in ready to be kissed. The windows were open; a jar of wild flowers stood on the mantelpiece, and the lamp made a big soft bubble of light on the ceiling.

'You seem pretty snug, Mother,' said Burnell, blinking at the light. Isabel and Lottie sat one on either side of the table, Kezia at the bottom – the place at the top was empty.

'That's where my boy ought to sit,' thought Stanley. He tightened his arm round Linda's shoulder. By God, he was a perfect fool to feel as happy as this!

'We are, Stanley. We are very snug,' said Mrs Fairfield, cutting Kezia's bread into fingers.

'Like it better than town – eh, children?' asked Burnell.

'Oh, yes,' said the three little girls, and Isabel added as an afterthought: 'Thank you very much indeed, Father dear.'

'Come upstairs,' said Linda. 'I'll bring your slippers.'

But the stairs were too narrow for them to go up arm in arm. It was quite dark in the room. He heard her ring tapping on the marble mantelpiece as she felt for the matches.

'I've got some, darling. I'll light the candles.'

But instead he came up behind her and again he put his arms round her and pressed her head into his shoulder.

'I'm so confoundedly happy,' he said.

'Are you?' She turned and put her hands on his breast and looked up at him.

'I don't know what has come over me,' he protested.

It was quite dark outside now and heavy dew was falling. When Linda shut the window the cold dew touched her finger tips. Far away a dog barked. 'I believe there is going to be a moon,' she said.

At the words, and with the cold wet dew on her fingers, she felt as though the moon had risen – that she was being strangely discovered in a flood of cold light. She shivered; she came away from the window and sat down upon the box ottoman beside Stanley.

*

Prelude

In the dining-room, by the flicker of a wood fire, Beryl sat on a hassock playing the guitar. She had bathed and changed all her clothes. Now she wore a white muslin dress with black spots on it and in her hair she had pinned a black silk rose.

> 'Nature has gone to her rest, love,
> See, we are alone.
> Give me your hand to press, love,
> Lightly within my own.'

She played and sang half to herself, for she was watching herself playing and singing. The firelight gleamed on her shoes, on the ruddy belly of the guitar, and on her white fingers. . . .

'If I were outside the window and looked in and saw myself I really would be rather struck,' thought she. Still more softly she played the accompaniment – not singing now but listening.

'. . . The first time that I ever saw you, little girl – oh, you had no idea that you were not alone – you were sitting with your little feet upon a hassock, playing the guitar. God, I can never forget. . . .' Beryl flung up her head and began to sing again:

> 'Even the moon is aweary . . .'

But there came a loud bang at the door. The servant girl's crimson face popped through.

'Please, Miss Beryl, I've got to come and lay.'

'Certainly, Alice,' said Beryl, in a voice of ice. She put the guitar in a corner. Alice lunged in with a heavy black iron tray.

'Well, I have had a job with that oving,' said she. 'I can't get nothing to brown.'

'Really!' said Beryl.

But no, she could not stand that fool of a girl. She ran into the dark drawing-room and began walking up and down. ... Oh, she was restless, restless. There was a mirror over the mantel. She leaned her arms along and looked at her pale shadow in it. How beautiful she looked, but there was nobody to see, nobody.

'Why must you suffer so?' said the face in the mirror. 'You were not made for suffering. ... Smile!'

Beryl smiled, and really her smile was so adorable that she smiled again – but this time because she could not help it.

VIII

'Good morning, Mrs Jones.'

'Oh, good morning, Mrs Smith. I'm so glad to see you. Have you brought your children?'

'Yes, I've brought both my twins. I have had another baby since I saw you last, but she came so suddenly that I haven't had time to make her any clothes yet. So I left her. ... How is your husband?'

'Oh, he is very well, thank you. At least he had an awful cold but Queen Victoria – she's my godmother, you know – sent him a case of pineapples and that cured it im-mediately. Is that your new servant?'

'Yes, her name's Gwen. I've only had her two days. Oh, Gwen, this is my friend, Mrs Smith.'

'Good morning, Mrs Smith. Dinner won't be ready for about ten minutes.'

'I don't think you ought to introduce me to the servant. I think I ought to just begin talking to her.'

'Well, she's more of a lady-help than a servant and you

Prelude

do introduce lady-helps, I know, because Mrs Samuel Josephs had one.'

'Oh, well, it doesn't matter,' said the servant carelessly, beating up a chocolate custard with half a broken clothes peg. The dinner was baking beautifully on a concrete step. She began to lay the cloth on a pink garden seat. In front of each person she put two geranium leaf plates, a pine-needle fork and a twig knife. There were three daisy heads on a laurel leaf for poached eggs, some slices of fuchsia petal cold beef, some lovely little rissoles made of earth and water and dandelion seeds, and the chocolate custard which she had decided to serve in the pawa shell she had cooked it in.

'You needn't trouble about my children,' said Mrs Smith graciously. 'If you'll just take this bottle and fill it at the tap – I mean at the dairy.'

'Oh, all right,' said Gwen, and she whispered to Mrs Jones: 'Shall I go and ask Alice for a little bit of real milk?'

But someone called from the front of the house and the luncheon party melted away, leaving the charming table, leaving the rissoles and the poached eggs to the ants and to an old snail who pushed his quivering horns over the edge of the garden seat and began to nibble a geranium plate.

'Come round to the front, children. Pip and Rags have come.'

The Trout boys were the cousins Kezia had mentioned to the storeman. They lived about a mile away in a house called Monkey Tree Cottage. Pip was tall for his age, with lank black hair and a white face, but Rags was very small and so thin that when he was undressed his shoulder blades stuck out like two little wings. They had a mongrel dog with pale blue eyes and a long tail turned up at the end who followed them everywhere; he was called Snooker. They spent half their time combing and brushing Snooker and dosing him with various awful mixtures concocted by Pip, and kept secretly by him in a broken jug covered with an old kettle lid. Even faithful little Rags was not allowed to know the full secret of these mixtures. ... Take some carbolic tooth powder and a pinch of sulphur powdered up fine, and perhaps a bit of starch to stiffen up Snooker's coat. ... But that was not all; Rags privately thought that the rest was gun-powder. ... And he never was allowed to help with the mixing because of the danger. ... 'Why, if a spot of this flew in your eye, you would be blinded for life,' Pip would say, stirring the mixture with an iron spoon. 'And there's always the chance – just the chance, mind you – of it exploding if you whack it hard enough. ... Two spoons of this in a kerosene tin will be enough to kill thousands of fleas.' But Snooker spent all his spare time biting and snuffling, and he stank abominably.

'It's because he is such a grand fighting dog,' Pip would say. 'All fighting dogs smell.'

The Trout boys had often spent the day with the Burnells in town, but now that they lived in this fine house and boncer garden they were inclined to be very friendly. Besides, both of them liked playing with girls – Pip, because he could fox them so, and because Lottie was so easily frightened, and Rags for a shameful reason. He adored dolls. How he would look at a doll as it lay asleep, speaking in a whisper and smiling timidly, and what a treat it was to him to be allowed to hold one. ...

'Curve your arms round her. Don't keep them stiff like that. You'll drop her,' Isabel would say sternly.

Prelude

Now they were standing on the veranda and holding back Snooker, who wanted to go into the house but wasn't allowed to because Aunt Linda hated decent dogs.

'We came over in the bus with Mum,' they said, 'and we're going to spend the afternoon with you. We brought over a batch of our gingerbread for Aunt Linda. Our Minnie made it. It's all over nuts.'

'I skinned the almonds,' said Pip. 'I just stuck my hand into a saucepan of boiling water and grabbed them out and gave them a kind of pinch and the nuts flew out of the skins, some of them as high as the ceiling. Didn't they, Rags?'

Rags nodded. 'When they make cakes at our place,' said Pip, 'we always stay in the kitchen, Rags and me, and I get the bowl and he gets the spoon and the egg-beater. Sponge cake's the best. It's all frothy stuff, then.'

He ran down the veranda steps to the lawn, planted his hands on the grass, bent forward, and just did not stand on his head.

'That lawn's all bumpy,' he said. 'You have to have a flat place for standing on your head. I can walk round the monkey tree on my head at our place. Can't I, Rags?'

'Nearly,' said Rags faintly.

'Stand on your head on the veranda. That's quite flat,' said Kezia.

'No, smarty,' said Pip. 'You have to do it on something soft. Because if you give a jerk and fall over, something in your neck goes click, and it breaks off. Dad told me.'

'Oh, do let's play something,' said Kezia.

'Very well,' said Isabel quickly, 'we'll play hospitals.

I will be the nurse and Pip can be the doctor and you and Lottie and Rags can be the sick people.'

Lottie didn't want to play that, because last time Pip had squeezed something down her throat and it hurt awfully.

'Pooh,' scoffed Pip. 'It was only the juice out of a bit of mandarin peel.'

'Well, let's play ladies,' said Isabel. 'Pip can be the father and you can be all our dear little children.'

'I hate playing ladies,' said Kezia. 'You always make us go to church hand in hand and come home and go to bed.'

Suddenly Pip took a filthy handkerchief out of his pocket. 'Snooker! Here, sir,' he called. But Snooker, as usual, tried to sneak away, his tail between his legs. Pip leapt on top of him, and pressed him between his knees.

'Keep his head firm, Rags,' he said, and he tied the handkerchief round Snooker's head with a funny knot sticking up at the top.

'Whatever is that for?' asked Lottie.

'It's to train his ears to grow more close to his head – see?' said Pip. 'All fighting dogs have ears that lie back. But Snooker's ears are a bit too soft.'

'I know,' said Kezia. 'They are always turning inside out. I hate that.'

Snooker lay down, made one feeble effort with his paw to get the handkerchief off, but finding he could not, trailed after the children, shivering with misery.

IX

Pat came swinging along; in his hand he held a little tomahawk that winked in the sun.

Prelude

'Come with me,' he said to the children, 'and I'll show you how the kings of Ireland chop the head off a duck.'

They drew back – they didn't believe him, and besides, the Trout boys had never seen Pat before.

'Come on now,' he coaxed, smiling and holding out his hand to Kezia

'Is it a real duck's head? One from the paddock?'

'It is,' said Pat. She put her hand in his hard dry one, and he stuck the tomahawk in his belt and held out the other to Rags. He loved little children.

'I'd better keep hold of Snooker's head if there's going to be any blood about,' said Pip, 'because the sight of blood makes him awfully wild.' He ran ahead dragging Snooker by the handkerchief.

'Do you think we ought to go?' whispered Isabel. 'We haven't asked or anything. Have we?'

At the bottom of the orchard a gate was set in the paling fence. On the other side a steep bank led down to a bridge that spanned the creek, and once up the bank on the other side you were on the fringe of the paddocks. A little old stable in the first paddock had been turned into a fowl-house. The fowls had strayed far away across the paddock down to a dumping ground in a hollow, but the ducks kept close to that part of the creek that flowed under the bridge.

Tall bushes overhung the stream with red leaves and yellow flowers and clusters of blackberries. At some places the stream was wide and shallow, but at others it tumbled into deep little pools with foam at the edges and quivering bubbles. It was in these pools that the big white ducks had made themselves at home, swimming and guzzling along the weedy banks.

Up and down they swam, preening their dazzling

breasts, and other ducks with the same dazzling breasts and yellow bills swam upside down with them.

'There is the little Irish navy,' said Pat, 'and look at the old admiral there with the green neck and the grand little flag-staff on his tail.'

He pulled a handful of grain from his pocket and began to walk towards the fowl-house, lazy, his straw hat with the broken crown pulled over his eyes.

'Lid. Lid—lid—lid—lid—' he called.

'Qua. Qua—qua—qua—qua—' answered the ducks, making for land, and flapping and scrambling up the bank they streamed after him in a long waddling line. He coaxed them, pretending to throw the grain, shaking it in his hands and calling to them until they swept round him in a white ring.

From far away the fowls heard the clamour and they too came running across the paddock, their heads thrust forward, their wings spread, turning in their feet in the silly way fowls run and scolding as they came.

Then Pat scattered the grain and the greedy ducks began to gobble. Quickly he stooped, seized two, one under each arm, and strode across to the children. Their darting heads and round eyes frightened the children – all except Pip.

'Come on, sillies,' he cried, 'they can't bite. They haven't any teeth. They've only got those two little holes in their beaks for breathing through.'

'Will you hold one while I finish with the other?' asked Pat. Pip let go of Snooker. 'Won't I? Won't I? Give us one. I don't mind how much he kicks.'

He nearly sobbed with delight when Pat gave the white lump into his arms.

There was an old stump beside the door of the fowl-house. Pat grabbed the duck by the legs, laid it flat

Prelude

across the stump, and almost at the same moment down came the little tomahawk and the duck's head flew off the stump. Up the blood spurted over the white feathers and over his hand.

When the children saw the blood they were frightened no longer. They crowded round him and began to scream. Even Isabel leaped about crying: 'The blood! The blood!' Pip forgot all about his duck. He simply threw it away from him and shouted, 'I saw it. I saw it,' and jumped round the wood block.

Rags, with cheeks as white as paper, ran up to the little head, put out a finger as if he wanted to touch it, shrank back again and then again put out a finger. He was shivering all over.

Even Lottie, frightened little Lottie, began to laugh and pointed at the duck and shrieked: 'Look, Kezia, look.'

'Watch it!' shouted Pat. He put down the body and it began to waddle – with only a long spurt of blood where the head had been; it began to pad away without a sound towards the steep bank that led to the stream. . . . That was the crowning wonder.

'Do you see that? Do you see that?' yelled Pip. He ran among the little girls tugging at their pinafores.

'It's like a little engine. It's like a funny little railway engine,' squealed Isabel.

But Kezia suddenly rushed at Pat and flung her arms round his legs and butted her head as hard as she could against his knees.

'Put head back! Put head back!' she screamed.

When he stooped to move her she would not let go or take her head away. She held on as hard as she could and sobbed: 'Head back! Head back!' until it sounded like a loud strange hiccup.

'It's stopped. It's tumbled over. It's dead,' said Pip.

Pat dragged Kezia up into his arms. Her sun-bonnet had fallen back, but she would not let him look at her face. No, she pressed her face into a bone in his shoulder and clasped her arms round his neck.

The children stopped screaming as suddenly as they had begun. They stood round the dead duck. Rags was not frightened of the head any more. He knelt down and stroked it now.

'I don't think the head is quite dead yet,' he said. 'Do you think it would keep alive if I gave it something to drink?'

But Pip got very cross: 'Bah! You baby.' He whistled to Snooker and went off.

When Isabel went up to Lottie, Lottie snatched away. 'What are you always touching me for, Isabel?'

'There now,' said Pat to Kezia. 'There's the grand little girl.'

She put up her hands and touched his ears. She felt something. Slowly she raised her quivering face and looked. Pat wore little round gold ear-rings. She never knew that men wore ear-rings. She was very much surprised.

'Do they come on and off?' she asked huskily.

X

Up in the house, in the warm tidy kitchen, Alice, the servant girl, was getting the afternoon tea. She was 'dressed'. She had on a black stuff dress that smelt under the arms, a white apron like a large sheet of paper, and a lace bow pinned on to her hair with two jetty pins. Also her comfortable carpet slippers were changed for a

Prelude

pair of black leather ones that pinched her corn on her little toe something dreadful. . . .

It was warm in the kitchen. A blowfly buzzed, a fan of whity steam came out of the kettle, and the lid kept up a rattling jig as the water bubbled. The clock ticked in the warm air, slow and deliberate, like the click of an old woman's knitting needle, and sometimes – for no reason at all, for there wasn't any breeze – the blind swung out and back, tapping the window.

Alice was making watercress sandwiches. She had a lump of butter on the table, a barracouta loaf, and the cresses tumbled in a white cloth.

But propped against the butter dish there was a dirty, greasy little book, half unstitched, with curled edges, and while she mashed the butter she read:

> To dream of black-beetles drawing a hearse is bad. Signifies death of one you hold near or dear, either father, husband, brother, son, or intended. If beetles crawl backwards as you watch them it means death from fire or from great height such as flight of stairs, scaffolding, etc.
>
> Spiders. To dream of spiders creeping over you is good. Signifies large sum of money in near future. Should party be in family way an easy confinement may be expected. But care should be taken in sixth month to avoid eating of probable present of shellfish. . . .

'How many thousand birds I see.'

Oh, life. There was Miss Beryl. Alice dropped the knife and slipped the *Dream Book* under the butter dish. But she hadn't time to hide it quite, for Beryl ran into the kitchen and up to the table, and the first thing her eye lighted on were those greasy edges. Alice saw Miss Beryl's meaning little smile and the way she raised her eyebrows and screwed up her eyes as though she were not quite sure what that could be. She decided to answer if Miss Beryl should ask her: 'Nothing as belongs to you, Miss.' But she knew Miss Beryl would not ask her.

Alice was a mild creature in reality, but she had the most marvellous retorts ready for questions that she knew would never be put to her. The composing of them and the turning of them over and over in her mind comforted her just as much as if they'd been expressed. Really, they kept her alive in places where she'd been that chivvied she'd been afraid to go to bed at night with a box of matches on the chair in case she bit the tops off in her sleep, as you might say.

'Oh, Alice,' said Miss Beryl. 'There's one extra to tea, so heat a plate of yesterday's scones, please. And put on the Victoria sandwich as well as the coffee cake. And don't forget to put little doyleys under the plates – will you? You did yesterday, you know, and the tea looked so ugly and common. And, Alice, don't put that dreadful old pink and green cosy on the afternoon teapot again. That is only for the mornings. Really, I think it ought to be kept for the kitchen – it's so shabby, and quite smelly. Put on the Japanese one. You quite understand, don't you?'

Miss Beryl had finished.

'That sing aloud from every tree . . .'

she sang as she left the kitchen, very pleased with her firm handling of Alice.

Oh, Alice was wild. She wasn't one to mind being told, but there was something in the way Miss Beryl had of speaking to her that she couldn't stand. Oh, that she couldn't. It made her curl up inside, as you might say, and she fair trembled. But what Alice really hated Miss Beryl for was that she made her feel low. She talked to Alice in a special voice as though she wasn't quite all there; and she never lost her temper with her – never. Even when Alice dropped anything or forgot anything important Miss Beryl seemed to have expected it to happen.

'If you please, Mrs Burnell,' said an imaginary Alice, as she buttered the scones, 'I'd rather not take my orders from Miss Beryl. I may be only a common servant girl as doesn't know how to play the guitar, but . . .'

This last thrust pleased her so much that she quite recovered her temper.

'The only thing to do,' she heard, as she opened the dining-room door, 'is to cut the sleeves out entirely and just have a broad band of black velvet over the shoulders instead. . . .'

XI

The white duck did not look as if it had ever had a head when Alice placed it in front of Stanley Burnell that night. It lay, in beautifully basted resignation, on a blue dish – its legs tied together with a piece of string and a wreath of little balls of stuffing round it.

It was hard to say which of the two, Alice or the duck, looked the better basted; they were both such a rich colour and they both had the same air of gloss and strain. But Alice was fiery red and the duck a Spanish mahogany.

Burnell ran his eye along the edge of the carving knife. He prided himself very much upon his carving, upon making a first-class job of it. He hated seeing a woman carve; they were always too slow and they never seemed to care what the meat looked like afterwards. Now he did; he took a real pride in cutting delicate shaves of cold beef, little wads of mutton, just the right thickness, and in dividing a chicken or a duck with nice precision. . . .

'Is this the first of the home products?' he asked, knowing perfectly well that it was.

'Yes, the butcher did not come. We have found out that he only calls twice a week.'

But there was no need to apologize. It was a superb bird. It wasn't meat at all, but a kind of very superior jelly. 'My father would say,' said Burnell, 'this must have been one of those birds whose mother played to it in infancy upon the German flute. And the sweet strains of the dulcet instrument acted with such effect upon the infant mind . . . Have some more, Beryl? You and I are the only ones in this house with a real feeling for food. I'm perfectly willing to state, in a court of law, if necessary, that I love good food.'

Tea was served in the drawing-room, and Beryl, who for some reason had been very charming to Stanley ever since he came home, suggested a game of crib. They sat at a little table near one of the open windows. Mrs Fairfield disappeared, and Linda lay in a rocking-chair, her arms above her head, rocking to and fro.

'You don't want the light – do you, Linda?' said Beryl. She moved the tall lamp so that she sat under its soft light.

How remote they looked, those two, from where Linda sat and rocked. The green table, the polished cards, Stanley's big hands and Beryl's tiny ones, all seemed to be part of one mysterious movement. Stanley himself, big and solid, in his dark suit, took his ease, and Beryl

Prelude

tossed her bright head and pouted. Round her throat she wore an unfamiliar velvet ribbon. It changed her, somehow – altered the shape of her face – but it was charming, Linda decided. The room smelled of lilies; there were two big jars of arums in the fireplace.

'Fifteen two – fifteen four – and a pair is six and a run of three is nine,' said Stanley, so deliberately, he might have been counting sheep.

'I've nothing but two pairs,' said Beryl, exaggerating her woe because she knew how he loved winning.

The cribbage pegs were like two little people going up the road together, turning round the sharp corner, and coming down the road again. They were pursuing each other. They did not so much want to get ahead as to keep near enough to talk – to keep near, perhaps that was all.

But no, there was always one who was impatient and hopped away as the other came up, and would not listen. Perhaps the white peg was frightened of the red one, or perhaps he was cruel and would not give the red one a chance to speak. . . .

In the front of her dress Beryl wore a bunch of pansies, and once when the little pegs were side by side, she bent over and the pansies dropped out and covered them.

'What a shame,' said she, picking up the pansies. 'Just as they had a chance to fly into each other's arms.'

'Farewell, my girl,' laughed Stanley, and away the red peg hopped.

The drawing-room was long and narrow with glass doors that gave on to the veranda. It had a cream paper with a pattern of gilt roses, and the furniture, which had belonged to old Mrs Fairfield, was dark and plain. A little piano stood against the wall with yellow pleated silk let into the carved front. Above it hung an oil painting by Beryl of a large cluster of surprised-looking clematis. Each flower was the size of a small saucer, with a centre like an astonished eye fringed in black. But the room was not finished yet. Stanley had set his heart on a Chesterfield and two decent chairs. Linda liked it best as it was. . . .

Two big moths flew in through the window and round and round the circle of lamplight.

'Fly away before it is too late. Fly out again.'

Round and round they flew; they seemed to bring the silence and the moonlight in with them on their silent wings. . . .

'I've two kings,' said Stanley. 'Any good?'

'Quite good,' said Beryl.

Linda stopped rocking and got up. Stanley looked across. 'Anything the matter, darling?'

'No, nothing. I'm going to find Mother.'

She went out of the room and standing at the foot of the stairs she called, but her mother's voice answered her from the veranda.

The moon that Lottie and Kezia had seen from the storeman's wagon was full, and the house, the garden, the old woman and Linda – all were bathed in dazzling light.

'I have been looking at the aloe,' said Mrs Fairfield. 'I believe it is going to flower this year. Look at the top there. Are those buds or is it only an effect of light?'

As they stood on the steps, the high grassy bank on which the aloe rested rose up like a wave, and the aloe seemed to ride upon it like a ship with the oars lifted. Bright moonlight hung upon the lifted oars like water, and on the green wave glittered the dew.

'Do you feel it, too,' said Linda, and she spoke to her

Prelude

mother with the special voice that women use at night to each other as though they spoke in their sleep or from some hollow cave – 'Don't you feel that it is coming towards us?'

She dreamed that she was caught up out of the cold water into the ship with the lifted oars and the budding mast. Now the oars fell striking quickly, quickly. They rowed far away over the top of the garden trees, the paddocks and the dark bush beyond. Ah, she heard herself cry: 'Faster! Faster!' to those who were rowing.

How much more real this dream was than that they should go back to the house where the sleeping children lay and where Stanley and Beryl played cribbage.

'I believe those are buds,' said she. 'Let us go down into the garden, Mother. I like that aloe. I like it more than anything here. And I am sure I shall remember it long after I've forgotten all the other things.'

She put her hand on her mother's arm and they walked down the steps, round the island and on to the main drive that led to the front gates.

Looking at it from below she could see the long sharp thorns that edged the aloe leaves, and at the sight of them her heart grew hard. . . . She particularly liked the long sharp thorns. . . . Nobody would dare to come near the ship or to follow after.

'Not even my Newfoundland dog,' thought she, 'that I'm so fond of in the daytime.'

For she really was fond of him; she loved and admired and respected him tremendously. Oh, better than anyone else in the world. She knew him through and through. He was the soul of truth and decency, and for all his practical experience he was awfully simple, easily pleased and easily hurt. . . .

If only he wouldn't jump at her so, and bark so loudly,

and watch her with such eager, loving eyes. He was too strong for her; she had always hated things that rush at her, from a child. There were times when he was frightening – really frightening. When she just had not screamed at the top of her voice, 'You are killing me.' And at those times she had longed to say the most coarse, hateful things. . . .

'You know I'm very delicate. You know as well as I do that my heart is affected, and the doctor has told you I may die any moment. I have had three great lumps of children already. . . .'

Yes, yes, it was true. Linda snatched her hand from her mother's arm. For all her love and respect and admiration she hated him. And how tender he always was after times like those, how submissive, how thoughtful. He would do anything for her; he longed to serve her. . . . Linda heard herself saying in a weak voice, 'Stanley, would you light a candle?'

And she heard his joyful voice answer, 'Of course I will, my darling.' And he leapt out of bed as though he were going to leap at the moon for her.

It had never been so plain to her as it was at this moment. There were all her feelings for him, sharp and defined, one as true as the other. And there was this other, this hatred, just as real as the rest. She could have done her feelings up in little packets and given them to Stanley. She longed to hand him that last one, for a surprise. She could see his eyes as he opened that. . . .

She hugged her folded arms and began to laugh silently. How absurd life was – it was laughable, simply laughable. And why this mania of hers to keep alive at all? For it really was a mania, she thought, mocking and laughing.

'What am I guarding myself for so preciously? I shall

Prelude

go on having children and Stanley will go on making money and the children and the gardens will grow bigger and bigger, with whole fleets of aloes in them for me to choose from.'

She had been walking with her head bent, looking at nothing. Now she looked up and about her. They were standing by the red and white camellia trees. Beautiful were the rich dark leaves spangled with light and the round flowers that perch among them like red and white birds. Linda pulled a piece of verbena and crumpled it, and held her hands to her mother.

'Delicious,' said the old woman. 'Are you cold, child? Are you trembling? Yes, your hands are cold. We had better go back to the house.'

'What have you been thinking about?' said Linda. 'Tell me.'

'I haven't really been thinking of anything. I wondered as we passed the orchard what the fruit trees were like and whether we should be able to make much jam this autumn. There are splendid healthy currant bushes in the vegetable garden. I noticed them today. I should like to see those pantry shelves thoroughly well stocked with our own jam. . . .'

XII

My darling Nan,

Don't think me a piggy wig because I haven't written before. I haven't had a moment, dear, and even now I feel so exhausted that I can hardly hold a pen.

Well, the dreadful deed is done. We have actually left the giddy whirl of town, and I can't see how we shall ever go back again, for my brother-in-law has bought this house "lock, stock and barrel", to use his own words.

In a way, of course, it is an awful relief, for he has been threatening to take a place in the country ever since I've lived with them – and I must say the house and garden are awfully nice – a million times better than that awful cubby-hole in town.

But buried, my dear. Buried isn't the word.

We have got neighbours, but they are only farmers – big louts of boys who seem to be milking all day, and two dreadful females with rabbit teeth who brought us some scones when we were moving and said they would be pleased to help. But my sister who lives a mile away doesn't know a soul here, so I am sure we never shall. It's pretty certain nobody will ever come out from town to see us, because though there is a bus it's an awful old rattling thing with black leather sides that any decent person would rather die than ride in for six miles.

Such a life. It's a sad ending for poor little B. I'll get to be a most awful frump in a year or two and come and see you in a mackintosh and a sailor hat tied on with a white china silk motor veil. So pretty.

Stanley says that now we are settled – for after the most awful week of my life we really are settled – he is going to bring out a couple of men from the club on Saturday afternoons for tennis. In fact, two are promised as a great treat today. But, my dear, if you could see Stanley's men from the club . . . rather fattish, the type who look frighfully indecent without waistcoats – always with toes that turn in rather – so conspicuous when you are walking about a court in white shoes. And they are pulling up their trousers every minute – don't you know – and whacking at imaginary things with their rackets.

Prelude

I used to play with them at the club last summer, and I am sure you will know the type when I tell you that after I'd been there about three times they all called me Miss Beryl. It's a dreary world. Of course Mother simply loves the place, but then I suppose when I am Mother's age I shall be content to sit in the sun and shell peas into a basin. But I'm not – not – not.

What Linda thinks about the whole affair, per usual, I haven't the slightest idea. Mysterious as ever. . . .

My dear, you know that white satin dress of mine. I have taken the sleeves out entirely, put bands of black velvet across the shoulders and two big red poppies off my dear sister's *chapeau*. It is a great success, though when I shall wear it I do not know.'

Beryl sat writing this letter at a little table in her room. In a way, of course, it was all perfectly true, but in another way it was all the greatest rubbish and she didn't believe a word of it. No, that wasn't true. She felt all those things, but she didn't really feel them like that.

It was her other self who had written that letter. It not only bored, it rather disgusted her real self.

'Flippant and silly,' said her real self. Yet she knew that she'd send it and she'd always write that kind of twaddle to Nan Pym. In fact, it was a very mild example of the kind of letter she generally wrote.

Beryl leaned her elbows on the table and read it through again. The voice of the letter seemed to come up to her from the page. It was faint already, like a voice heard over the telephone, high, gushing, with something bitter in the sound. Oh, she detested it today.

'You've always got so much animation,' said Nan Pym. 'That's why men are so keen on you.' And she had added, rather mournfully, for men were not at all keen on Nan, who was a solid kind of girl, with fat hips and a high colour – 'I can't understand how you can keep it up. But it is your nature, I suppose.'

What rot. What nonsense. It wasn't her nature at all. Good heavens, if she had ever been her real self with Nan Pym, Nannie would have jumped out of the window with surprise. . . . My dear, you know that white satin of mine. . . . Beryl slammed the letter-case to.

She jumped up and half unconsciously, half consciously she drifted over to the looking-glass.

There stood a slim girl in white – a white serge skirt, a white silk blouse, and a leather belt drawn in very tightly at her tiny waist.

Her face was heart-shaped, wide at the brows and with a pointed chin – but not too pointed. Her eyes, her eyes were perhaps her best feature; they were such a strange uncommon colour – greeny blue with little gold points in them.

She had fine black eyebrows and long lashes – so long, that when they lay on her cheeks you positively caught the light in them, someone or other had told her.

Her mouth was rather large. Too large? No, not really. Her underlip protruded a little; she had a way of sucking it in that somebody else had told her was awfully fascinating.

Her nose was her least satisfactory feature. Not that it was really ugly. But it was not half as fine as Linda's. Linda really had a perfect little nose. Hers spread rather – not badly. And in all probability she exaggerated the spreadiness of it just because it was her nose, and she was so awfully critical of herself. She pinched it with a thumb and first finger and made a little face. . . .

Lovely, lovely hair. And such a mass of it. It had the colour of fresh fallen leaves, brown and red with a glint

Prelude

of yellow. When she did it in a long plait she felt it on her backbone like a long snake. She loved to feel the weight of it dragging her head back, and she loved to feel it loose, covering her bare arms. 'Yes, my dear, there is no doubt about it, you really are a lovely little thing.'

At the words her bosom lifted; she took a long breath of delight, half closing her eyes.

But even as she looked the smile faded from her lips and eyes. Oh, God, there she was, back again, playing the same old game. False – false as ever. False as when she'd written to Nan Pym. False even when she was alone with herself, now.

What had that creature in the glass to do with her, and why was she staring? She dropped down to one side of her bed and buried her face in her arms.

'Oh,' she cried, 'I am so miserable – so frightfully miserable. I know that I'm silly and spiteful and vain; I'm always acting a part. I'm never my real self for a moment.' And plainly, plainly, she saw her false self running up and down the stairs, laughing a special trilling laugh if they had visitors, standing under the lamp if a man came to dinner, so that he should see the light on her hair, pouting and pretending to be a little girl when she was asked to play the guitar. Why? She even kept it up for Stanley's benefit. Only last night when he was reading the paper her false self had stood beside him and leaned against his shoulder on purpose. Hadn't she put her hand over his, pointing out something so that he should see how white her hand was beside his brown one.

How despicable! Despicable! Her heart was cold with rage. 'It's marvellous how you keep it up,' said she to the false self. But then it was only because she was so miserable – so miserable. If she had been happy and leading her own life, her false life would cease to be. She saw the real Beryl – a shadow . . . a shadow. Faint and unsubstantial she shone. What was there of her except the radiance? And for what tiny moments she was really she. Beryl could almost remember every one of them. At those times she had felt: 'Life is rich and mysterious and good, and I am rich and mysterious and good, too.' Shall I ever be that Beryl for ever? Shall I? How can I? And was there ever a time when I did not have a false self? . . . But just as she had got that far she heard the sound of little steps running along the passage; the door handle rattled. Kezia came in.

'Aunt Beryl, Mother says will you please come down? Father is home with a man and lunch is ready.'

Botheration! How she had crumpled her skirt, kneeling in that idiotic way.

'Very well, Kezia.' She went over to the dressing-table and powdered her nose.

Kezia crossed too, and unscrewed a little pot of cream and sniffed it. Under her arm she carried a very dirty calico cat.

When Aunt Beryl ran out of the room she sat the cat up on the dressing-table and stuck the top of the cream jar over its ear.

'Now look at yourself,' she said sternly.

The calico cat was so overcome by the sight that it toppled over backwards and bumped and bumped on to the floor. And the top of the cream jar flew through the air and rolled like a penny in a round on the linoleum – and did not break.

But for Kezia it had broken the moment it flew through the air, and she picked it up, hot all over, and put it back on the dressing-table.

Then she tiptoed away, far too quickly and airily. . . .

Alice Munro
Miles City, Montana

My father came across the field carrying the body of the boy who had been drowned. There were several men together, returning from the search, but he was the one carrying the body. The men were muddy and exhausted, and walked with their heads down, as if they were ashamed. Even the dogs were dispirited, dripping from the cold river. When they all set out, hours before, the dogs were nervy and yelping, the men tense and determined, and there was a constrained, unspeakable excitement about the whole scene. It was understood that they might find something horrible.

The boy's name was Steve Gauley. He was eight years old. His hair and clothes were mud-coloured now and carried some bits of dead leaves, twigs and grass. He was like a heap of refuse that had been left out all winter. His face was turned in to my father's chest, but I could see a nostril, an ear, plugged up with greenish mud.

I don't think so. I don't think I really saw all this. Perhaps I saw my father carrying him, and the other men following along, and the dogs, but I would not have been allowed to get close enough to see something like mud in his nostril. I must have heard someone talking about that and imagined that I saw it. I see his face unaltered except for the mud – Steve Gauley's familiar, sharp-honed, sneaky-looking face – and it wouldn't have been like that; it would have been bloated and changed and perhaps muddied all over after so many hours in the water.

To have to bring back such news, such evidence, to a waiting family, particularly a mother, would have made searchers move heavily, but what was happening here was worse. It seemed a worse shame (to hear people talk) that there was no mother, no woman at all – no grandmother or aunt, or even a sister – to receive Steve Gauley and give him his due of grief. His father was a hired man, a drinker but not a drunk, an erratic man without being entertaining, not friendly but not exactly a troublemaker. His fatherhood seemed accidental, and the fact that the child had been left with him when the mother went away, and that they continued living together, seemed accidental. They lived in a steep-roofed, grey-shingled hillbilly sort of house that was just a bit better than a shack – the father fixed the roof and put supports under the porch, just enough and just in time – and their life was held together in a similar manner; that is, just well enough to keep the Children's Aid at bay. They didn't eat meals together or cook for each other, but there was food. Sometimes the father would give Steve money to buy food at the store, and Steve was seen to buy quite sensible things, such as pancake mix and macaroni dinner.

I had known Steve Gauley fairly well. I had not liked him more often than I had liked him. He was two years older than I was. He would hang around our place on Saturdays, scornful of whatever I was doing but unable to leave me alone. I couldn't be on the swing without him wanting to try it, and if I wouldn't give it up he came and pushed me so that I went crooked. He teased the dog. He got me into trouble – deliberately and maliciously, it seemed to me afterward – by daring me to do things I wouldn't have thought of on my own: digging up the potatoes to see how big they were when they were still only the size of marbles, and pushing over the stacked firewood to make a pile we could jump off. At shool, we never spoke to each other. He was solitary, though not tormented. But on Saturday mornings, when I saw his thin, self-possessed figure sliding through the cedar hedge, I knew I was in for something and he would decide what. Sometimes it was all right. We pretended we were cowboys who had to tame wild horses. We played in the pasture by the river, not far from the place where Steve drowned. We were horses and riders both, screaming and neighing and bucking and waving whips of tree branches beside a little nameless river that flows into the Saugeen in southern Ontario.

The funeral was held in our house. There was not enough room at Steve's father's place for the large crowd that was expected because of the circumstances. I have a memory of the crowded room but no picture of Steve in his coffin, or of the minister, or of wreaths of flowers. I remember that I was holding one flower, a white narcissus, which must have come from a pot somebody forced indoors, because it was too early for even the forsythia bush or the trilliums and marsh marigolds in the woods. I stood in a row of children, each of us holding a narcissus. We sang a children's hymn, which somebody played on our piano: 'When He Cometh, When He Cometh, To Make Up His Jewels.' I was wearing white ribbed stockings, which were disgustingly itchy, and wrinkled at the knees and ankles. The feeling of these stockings on my legs is mixed up with another feeling in my memory. It is hard to describe. It had to do with my parents. Adults in general but my parents in particular. My father, who had carried Steve's body from the river, and my mother, who must have done most of the arranging of this funeral. My father in his dark-blue suit and my mother in her brown velvet dress with the creamy satin collar. They stood side by side opening and closing their mouths for the hymn, and I stood removed from them, in the row of children, watching. I felt a furious and sickening disgust. Children sometimes have an access of disgust concerning adults. The size, the lumpy shapes, the bloated power. The breath, the coarseness, the hairiness, the horrid secretions. But this was more. And the accompanying anger had nothing sharp and self-respecting about it. There was no release, as when I would finally bend and pick up a stone and throw it at Steve Gauley. It could not be understood or expressed, though it died down after a while into a heaviness, then just a taste, an occasional taste – a thin, familiar misgiving.

Twenty years or so later, in 1961, my husband, Andrew, and I got a brand-new car, our first – that is, our first brand-new. It was a Morris Oxford, oyster-coloured (the dealer had some fancier name for the colour) – a big small car, with plenty of room for us and our two children. Cynthia was six and Meg three and a half.

Andrew took a picture of me standing beside the car. I was wearing white pants, a black turtleneck, and sunglasses. I lounged against the car door, canting my hips to make myself look slim

'Wonderful,' Andrew said. 'Great. You look like Jackie

Miles City, Montana

Kennedy.' All over this continent probably, dark-haired, reasonably slender young women were told, when they were stylishly dressed or getting their pictures taken, that they looked like Jackie Kennedy.

Andrew took a lot of pictures of me, and of the children, our house, our garden, our excursions and possessions. He got copies made, labelled them carefully, and sent them back to his mother and his aunt and uncle in Ontario. He got copies for me to send to my father, who also lived in Ontario, and I did so, but less regularly than he sent his. When he saw pictures he thought I had already sent lying around the house, Andrew was perplexed and annoyed. He liked to have this record go forth.

That summer, we were presenting ourselves, not pictures. We were driving back from Vancouver, where we lived, to Ontario, which we still called 'home', in our new car. Five days to get there, ten days there, five days back. For the first time, Andrew had three weeks' holiday. He worked in the legal department at B.C. Hydro.

On a Satuday morning, we loaded suitcases, two thermos bottles – one filled with coffee and one with lemonade – some fruit and sandwiches, picture books and colouring books, crayons, drawing pads, insect repellent, sweaters (in case it got cold in the mountains), and our two children into the car. Andrew locked the house, and Cynthia said ceremoniously, 'Goodbye, house.'

Meg said, 'Goodbye, house.' Then she said, 'Where will we live now?'

'It's not goodbye forever,' said Cynthia. 'We're coming back. Mother! Meg thought we weren't ever coming back!'

'I did not,' said Meg, kicking the back of my seat.

Andrew and I put on our sunglasses, and we drove away, over the Lions Gate Bridge and through the main part of Vancouver. We shed our house, the neighbourhood, the city, and — at the crossing point between Washington and British Columbia — our country. We were driving east across the United States, taking the most northerly route, and would cross into Canada again at Sarnia, Ontario. I don't know if we chose this route because the Trans-Canada Highway was not completely finished at the time or if we just wanted the feeling of driving through a foreign, a very slightly foreign, country — that extra bit of interest and adventure.

We were both in high spirits. Andrew congratulated the car several times. He said he felt so much better driving it than our old car, a 1951 Austin that slowed down dismally on the hills and had a fussy-old-lady image. So Andrew said now.

'What kind of image does this one have?' said Cynthia. She listened to us carefully and liked to try out new words such as 'image'. Usually she got them right.

'Lively,' I said. 'Slightly sporty. It's not show-off.'

'It's sensible, but it has class,' Andrew said. 'Like my image.'

Cynthia thought that over and said with a cautious pride, 'That means like you think you want to be, Daddy?'

As for me, I was happy because of the shedding. I loved taking off. In my own house, I seemed to be often looking for a place to hide — sometimes from the children but more often from the jobs to be done and the phone ringing and the sociability of the neighbourhood. I wanted to hide so that I could get busy at my real work, which was a sort of wooing of distant parts of

Miles City, Montana

myself. I lived in a state of siege, always losing just what I wanted to hold on to. But on trips there was no difficulty. I could be talking to Andrew, talking to the children and looking at whatever they wanted me to look at – a pig on a sign, a pony in a field, a Volkswagen on a revolving stand – and pouring lemonade into plastic cups, and all the time those bits and pieces would be flying together inside me. The essential composition would be achieved. This made me hopeful and light-hearted. It was being a watcher that did it. A watcher, not a keeper.

We turned east at Everett and climbed into the Cascades. I showed Cynthia our route on the map. First I showed her the map of the whole United States, which showed also the bottom part of Canada. Then I turned to the separate maps of each of the states we were going to pass through. Washington, Idaho, Montana, North Dakota, Minnesota, Wisconsin. I showed her the dotted line across Lake Michigan, which was the route of the ferry we would take. Then we would drive across Michigan to the bridge that linked the United States and Canada at Sarnia, Ontario. Home.

Meg wanted to see, too.

'You won't understand,' said Cynthia. But she took the road atlas into the back seat.

'Sit back,' she said to Meg. 'Sit still. I'll show you.'

I could hear her tracing the route for Meg, very accurately, just as I had done it for her. She looked up all the states' maps, knowing how to find them in alphabetical order.

'You know what that line is?' she said. 'It's the road. That line is the road we're driving on. We're going right along this line.'

Meg did not say anything.

'Mother, show me where we are right this minute,' said Cynthia.

I took the atlas and pointed out the road through the mountains, and she took it back and showed it to Meg. 'See where the road is all wiggly?' she said. 'It's wiggly because there are so many turns in it. The wiggles are the turns.' She flipped some pages and waited a moment. 'Now,' she said, 'show me where we are.' Then she called to me, 'Mother, she understands! She pointed to it! Meg understands maps!'

It seems to me now that we invented characters for our children. We had them firmly set to play their parts. Cynthia was bright and diligent, sensitive, courteous, watchful. Sometimes we teased her for being too conscientious, too eager to be what we in fact depended on her to be. Any reproach or failure, any rebuff, went terribly deep with her. She was fair-haired, fair-skinned, easily showing the effects of the sun, raw winds, pride, or humiliation. Meg was more solidly built, more reticent – not rebellious but stubborn sometimes, mysterious. Her silences seemed to us to show her strength of character, and her negatives were taken as signs of an imperturbable independence. Her hair was brown, and we cut it in straight bangs. Her eyes were a light hazel, clear and dazzling.

We were entirely pleased with these characters, enjoying the contradictions as well as the confirmations of them. We disliked the heavy, the uninventive, approach to being parents. I had a dread of turning into a certain kind of mother – the kind whose body sagged, who moved in a woolly-smelling, milky-smelling fog, solemn with trivial burdens. I believed that all the attention these mothers paid, their need to be burdened, was the cause of colic, bed-wetting, asthma. I favoured another approach – the mock desperation, the inflated irony of the professional mothers who wrote for magazines. In those magazine pieces, the children were splendidly self-willed, hard-edged, perverse, indomitable. So were the mothers, through their wit, indomitable. The real-life mothers I warmed to were the sort who would phone up and say, 'Is my embryo Hitler by any chance over at your house?' They cackled clear above the milky fog.

We saw a dead deer strapped across the front of a pickup truck.

'Somebody shot it,' Cynthia said. 'Hunters shoot the deer.'

'It's not hunting season yet,' Andrew said. 'They may have hit it on the road. See the sign for deer crossing?'

'I would cry if we hit one,' Cynthia said sternly.

I had made peanut-butter-and-marmalade sandwiches for the children and salmon-and-mayonnaise for us. But I had not put any lettuce in, and Andrew was disappointed.

'I didn't have any,' I said.

'Couldn't you have got some?'

'I'd have had to buy a whole head of lettuce just to get enough for sandwiches, and I decided it wasn't worth it.'

This was a lie. I had forgotten.

'They're a lot better with lettuce.'

'I didn't think it made that much difference.' After a silence, I said, 'Don't be mad.'

'I'm not mad. I like lettuce on sandwiches.'

'I just didn't think it mattered that much.'

'How would it be if I didn't bother to fill up the gas tank?'

'That's not the same thing.'

'Sing a song,' said Cynthia. She started to sing:

> 'Five little ducks went out one day,
> Over the hills and far away.
> One little duck went
> "Quack-quack-quack."
> Four little ducks came swimming
> back.'

Andrew squeezed my hand and said, 'Let's not fight.'

'You're right. I should have got lettuce.'

'It doesn't matter that much.'

I wished that I could get my feelings about Andrew to come together into a serviceable and dependable feeling. I had even tried writing two lists, one of things I liked about him, one of things I disliked – in the cauldron of intimate life, things I loved and things I hated – as if I hoped by this to prove something, to come to a conclusion one way or the other. But I gave it up when I saw that all it proved was what I already knew – that I had violent contradictions. Sometimes the very sound of his footsteps seemed to me tyrannical, the set of his mouth smug and mean, his hard, straight body a barrier interposed – quite consciously, even dutifully, and with a nasty pleasure in its masculine authority – between me and whatever joy or lightness I could get in life. Then, with not much warning, he became my good friend and most essential companion. I felt the sweetness of his light bones and serious ideas, the vulnerability of his love, which I imagined to be much purer and more straightforward than my own. I could be greatly moved by an inflexibility, a harsh propriety, that at other times I scorned. I would think how humble he was, really, taking on such a ready-made role of husband, father,

Miles City, Montana

breadwinner, and how I myself in comparison was really a secret monster of egotism. Not so secret, either – not from him.

At the bottom of our fights, we served up what we thought were the ugliest truths. 'I know there is something basically selfish and basically untrustworthy about you,' Andrew once said. 'I've always known it. I also know that that is why I fell in love with you.'

'Yes,' I said, feeling sorrowful but complacent.

'I know that I'd be better off without you.'

'Yes. You would.'

'You'd be happier without me.'

'Yes.'

And finally – finally – racked and purged, we clasped hands and laughed, laughed at those two benighted people, ourselves. Their grudges, their grievances, their self-justification. We leap-frogged over them. We declared them liars. We would have wine with dinner, or decide to give a party.

I haven't seen Andrew for years, don't know if he is still thin, has gone completely grey, insists on lettuce, tells the truth, or is hearty and disappointed.

We stayed the night in Wenatchee, Washington, where it hadn't rained for weeks. We ate dinner in a restaurant built about a tree – not a sapling in a tub but a tall, sturdy cottonwood. In the early morning light, we climbed out of the irrigated valley, up dry, rocky, very steep hillsides that would seem to lead to more hills, and there on the top was a wide plateau, cut by the great Spokane and Columbia rivers. Grainland and grassland, mile after mile. There were straight roads here, and little farming towns with grain elevators. In fact, there was a sign announcing that this county we were going through, Douglas County, had the second-highest wheat yield of any county in the United States. The towns had planted shade trees. At least, I thought they had been planted, because there were no such big trees in the countryside.

All this was marvellously welcome to me. 'Why do I love it so much?' I said to Andrew. 'Is it because it isn't scenery?'

'It reminds you of home,' said Andrew. 'A bout of severe nostalgia.' But he said this kindly.

When we said 'home' and meant Ontario, we had very different places in mind. My home was a turkey farm, where my father lived as a widower, and though it was the same house my mother had lived in, had papered, painted, cleaned, furnished, it showed the effects now of neglect and of some wild sociability. A life went on in it that my mother could not have predicted or condoned. There were parties for the turkey crew, the gutters and pluckers, and sometimes one or two of the young men would be living there temporarily, inviting their own friends and having their own impromptu parties. This life, I thought, was better for my father than being lonely, and I did not disapprove, had certainly no right to disapprove. Andrew did not like to go there, naturally enough, because he was not the sort who could sit around the kitchen table with the turkey crew, telling jokes. They were intimidated by him and contemptuous of him, and it seemed to me that my father, when they were around, had to be on their side. And it wasn't only Andrew who had trouble. I could manage those jokes, but it was an effort.

I wished for the days when I was little, before we had the turkeys. We had cows, and sold the milk to the cheese factory. A turkey farm is nothing like as

Miles City, Montana

pretty as a dairy farm or a sheep farm. You can see that the turkeys are on a straight path to becoming frozen carcasses and table meat. They don't have the pretence of a life of their own, a browsing idyll, that cattle have, or pigs in the dappled orchard. Turkey barns are long, efficient buildings – tin sheds. No beams or hay or warm stables. Even the smell of guano seems thinner and more offensive than the usual smell of stable manure. No hints there of hay coils and rail fences and songbirds and the flowering hawthorn. The turkeys were all let out into one long field, which they picked clean. They didn't look like great birds there but like fluttering laundry.

Once, shortly after my mother died, and after I was married – in fact, I was packing to join Andrew in Vancouver – I was at home alone for a couple of days with my father. There was a freakishly heavy rain all night. In the early light, we saw that the turkey field was flooded. At least, the low-lying parts of it were flooded – it was like a lake with many islands. The turkeys were huddled on these islands. Turkeys are very stupid. (My father would say, 'You know a chicken? You know how stupid a chicken is? Well, a chicken is an Einstein compared with a turkey.') But they had managed to crowd to higher ground and avoid drowning. Now they might push each other off, suffocate each other, get cold and die. We couldn't wait for the water to go down. We went out in an old rowboat we had. I rowed and my father pulled the heavy, wet turkeys into the boat and we took them to the barn. It was still raining a little. The job was difficult and absurd and very uncomfortable. We were laughing. I was happy to be working with my father. I felt close to all hard, repetitive, appalling work, in which the body is finally worn out, the mind sunk (though sometimes the spirit can stay marvellously light), and

I was homesick in advance for this life and this place. I thought that if Andrew could see me there in the rain, red-handed, muddy, trying to hold on to turkey legs and row the boat at the same time, he would only want to get me out of there and make me forget about it. This raw life angered him. My attachment to it angered him. I thought that I shouldn't have married him. But who else? One of the turkey crew?

And I didn't want to stay there. I might feel bad about leaving, but I would feel worse if somebody made me stay.

Andrew's mother lived in Toronto, in an apartment building looking out on Muir Park. When Andrew and his sister were both at home, his mother slept in the living room. Her husband, a doctor, had died when the children were still too young to go to school. She took a secretarial course and sold her house at Depression prices, moved to this apartment, managed to raise her children, with some help from relatives – her sister Caroline, her brother-in-law Roger. Andrew and his sister went to private schools and to camp in the summer.

'I suppose that was courtesy of the Fresh Air fund?' I said once, scornful of his claim that he had been poor. To my mind, Andrew's urban life had been sheltered and fussy. His mother came home with a headache from working all day in the noise, the harsh light of a department-store office, but it did not occur to me that hers was a hard or admirable life. I don't think she herself believed that she was admirable – only unlucky. She worried about her work in the office, her clothes, her cooking, her children. She worried most of all about what Roger and Caroline would think.

Caroline and Roger lived on the east side of the park, in a handsome stone house. Roger was a tall man with a

Miles City, Montana

bald, freckled head, a fat, firm stomach. Some operation on his throat had deprived him of his voice – he spoke in a rough whisper. But everybody paid attention. At dinner once in the stone house – where all the dining-room furniture was enormous, darkly glowing, palatial – I asked him a question. I think it had to do with Whittaker Chambers, whose story was then appearing in the *Saturday Evening Post*. The question was mild in tone, but he guessed its subversive intent and took to calling me Mrs Gromyko, referring to what he alleged to be my 'sympathies'. Perhaps he really craved an adversary, and could not find one. At that dinner, I saw Andrew's hand tremble as he lit his mother's cigarette. His Uncle Roger had paid for Andrew's education, and was on the board of directors of several companies.

'He is just an opinionated old man,' Andrew said to me later. 'What is the point of arguing with him?'

Before we left Vancouver, Andrew's mother had written, 'Roger seems quite intrigued by the idea of your buying a small car!' Her exclamation mark showed apprehension. At that time, particularly in Ontario, the choice of a small European car over a large American car could be seen as some sort of declaration – a declaration of tendencies Roger had been sniffing after all along.

'It isn't that small a car,' said Andrew huffily.

'That's not the point,' I said. 'The point is, it isn't any of his business!'

We spent the second night in Missoula. We had been told in Spokane, at a gas station, that there was a lot of repair work going on along Highway 2, and that we were in for a very hot, dusty drive, with long waits, so we turned on to the interstate and drove through Coeur d'Alene and Kellogg into Montana. After Missoula, we turned south toward Butte, but detoured to see Helena, the state capital. In the car, we played Who Am I?

Cynthia was somebody dead, and an American, and a girl. Possibly a lady. She was not in a story. She had not been seen on television. Cynthia had not read about her in a book. She was not anybody who had come to the kindergarten, or a relative of any of Cynthia's friends.

'Is she human?' said Andrew, with a sudden shrewdness.

'No! That's what you forgot to ask!'

'An animal,' I said reflectively.

'Is that a question? Sixteen questions!'

'No, it is not a question. I'm thinking. A dead animal.'

'It's the deer,' said Meg, who hadn't been playing.

'That's not fair!' said Cynthia. 'She's not playing!'

'What deer?' said Andrew.

I said, 'Yesterday.'

'The day before,' said Cynthia. 'Meg wasn't playing. Nobody got it.'

'The deer on the truck,' said Andrew.

'It was a lady deer, because it didn't have antlers, and it was an American and it was dead,' Cynthia said.

Andrew said, 'I think it's kind of morbid, being a dead deer.'

'I got it,' said Meg.

Cynthia said, 'I think I know what morbid is. It's depressing.'

Helena, an old silver-mining town, looked forlorn to us even in the morning sunlight. Then Bozeman and Billings, not forlorn in the slightest – energetic, strung-out towns, with miles of blinding tinsel fluttering over used-car lots. We got too tired and hot even to play Who Am I? These busy, prosaic cities reminded me of

Miles City, Montana

similar places in Ontario, and I thought about what was really waiting there – the great tombstone furniture of Roger and Caroline's dining-room, the dinners for which I must iron the children's dresses and warn them about forks, and then the other table a hundred miles away, the jokes of my father's crew. The pleasures I had been thinking of – looking at the countryside or drinking a Coke in an old-fashioned drugstore with fans and a high, pressed-tin ceiling – would have to be snatched in between.

'Meg's asleep,' Cynthia said. 'She's so hot. She makes me hot in the same seat with her.'

'I hope she isn't feverish,' I said, not turning around.

What are we doing this for, I thought, and the answer came – to show off. To give Andrew's mother and my father the pleasure of seeing their grandchildren. That was our duty. But beyond that we wanted to show them something. What strenuous children we were, Andrew and I, what relentless seekers of approbation. It was as if at some point we had received an unforgettable, indigestible message – that we were far from satisfactory, and that the most commonplace success in life was probably beyond us. Roger dealt out such messages, of course – that was his style – but Andrew's mother, my own mother and father couldn't have meant to do so. All they meant to tell us was 'Watch out. Get along.' My father, when I was in high school, teased me that I was getting to think I was so smart I would never find a boyfriend. He would have forgotten that in a week. I never forgot it. Andrew and I didn't forget things. We took umbrage.

'I wish there was a beach,' said Cynthia.

'There probably is one,' Andrew said. 'Right around the next curve.'

'There isn't any curve,' she said, sounding insulted.
'That's what I mean.'
'I wish there was some more lemonade.'
'I will just wave my magic wand and produce some,' I said. 'Okay, Cynthia? Would you rather have grape juice? Will I do a beach while I'm at it?'

She was silent, and soon I felt repentant. 'Maybe in the next town there might be a pool,' I said. I looked at the map. 'In Miles City. Anyway, there'll be something cool to drink.'

'How far is it?' Andrew said.

'Not so far,' I said. 'Thirty miles, about.'

'In Miles City,' said Cynthia, in the tones of an incantation, 'there is a beautiful blue swimming pool for children, and a park with lovely trees.'

Andrew said to me, 'You could have started something.'

But there was a pool. There was a park, too, though not quite the oasis of Cynthia's fantasy. Prairie trees with thin leaves – cottonwoods and poplars – worn grass, and a high wire fence around the pool. Within this fence, a wall, not yet completed, of cement blocks. There were no shouts or splashes; over the entrance I saw a sign that said the pool was closed every day from noon until two o'clock. It was then twenty-five after twelve.

Nevertheless I called out, 'Is anybody there?' I thought somebody must be around, because there was a small truck parked near the entrance. On the side of the truck were these words: 'We have Brains, to fix your Drains. (We have Roto-Rooter too.)'

A girl came out, wearing a red lifeguard's shirt over her bathing suit. 'Sorry, we're closed.'

'We were just driving through,' I said.

Miles City, Montana

'We close every day from twelve until two. It's on the sign.' She was eating a sandwich.

'I saw the sign,' I said. 'But this is the first water we've seen for so long, and the children are awfully hot, and I wondered if they could just dip in and out – just five minutes. We'd watch them.'

A boy came into sight behind her. He was wearing jeans and a T-shirt with the words 'Roto-Rooter' on it.

I was going to say that we were driving from British Columbia to Ontario, but I remembered that Canadian place names usually meant nothing to Americans. 'We're driving right across the country,' I said. 'We haven't time to wait for the pool to open. We were just hoping the children could get cooled off.'

Cynthia came running up barefoot behind me. 'Mother. Mother, where is my bathing suit?' Then she stopped, sensing the serious adult negotiations. Meg was climbing out of the car – just wakened, with her top pulled up and her shorts pulled down, showing her pink stomach.

'Is it just those two?' the girl said.

'Just the two. We'll watch them.'

'I can't let any adults in. If it's just the two, I guess I could watch them. I'm having my lunch.' She said to Cynthia, 'Do you want to come in the pool?'

'Yes, please,' said Cynthia firmly.

Meg looked at the ground.

'Just a short time, because the pool is really closed,' I said. 'We appreciate this very much,' I said to the girl.

'Well, I can eat my lunch out there, if it's just the two of them.' She looked toward the car as if she thought I might try to spring some more children on her.

When I found Cynthia's bathing suit, she took it into the changing room. She would not permit anybody, even Meg, to see her naked. I changed Meg, who stood on the front seat of the car. She had a pink cotton bathing suit with straps that crossed and buttoned. There were ruffles across the bottom.

'She *is* hot,' I said. 'But I don't think she's feverish.'

I loved helping Meg to dress or undress, because her body still had the solid unself-consciousness, the sweet indifference, something of the milky smell, of a baby's body. Cynthia's body had long ago been pared down, shaped and altered, into Cynthia. We all liked to hug Meg, press and nuzzle her. Sometimes she would scowl and beat us off, and this forthright independence, this ferocious bashfulness, simply made her more appealing, more apt to be tormented and tickled in the way of family love.

Andrew and I sat in the car with the windows open. I could hear a radio playing, and thought it must belong to the girl or her boyfriend. I was thirsty, and got out of the car to look for a concession stand, or perhaps a soft-drink machine, somewhere in the park. I was wearing shorts, and the backs of my legs were slick with sweat. I saw a drinking fountain at the other side of the park and was walking toward it in a roundabout way, keeping to the shade of the trees. No place became real till you got out of the car. Dazed with the heat, with the sun on the blistered houses, the pavement, the burned grass, I walked slowly. I paid attention to a squashed leaf, ground a Popsicle stick under the heel of my sandal, squinted at a trash can strapped to a tree. This is the way you look at the poorest details of the world resurfaced, after you've been driving for a long time – you feel their singleness and precise location and the forlorn coincidence of your being there to see them.

Where are the children?

I turned around and moved quickly, not quite running,

to a part of the fence beyond which the cement wall was not completed. I could see some of the pool. I saw Cynthia, standing about waist-deep in the water, fluttering her hands on the surface and discreetly watching something at the end of the pool, which I could not see. I thought by her pose, her discretion, the look on her face, that she must be watching some byplay between the lifeguard and her boyfriend. I couldn't see Meg. But I thought she must be playing in the shallow water – both the shallow and deep ends of the pool were out of my sight.

'Cynthia!' I had to call twice before she knew where my voice was coming from. 'Cynthia! Where's Meg?'

It always seems to me, when I recall this scene, that Cynthia turns very gracefully toward me, then turns all around in the water – making me think of a ballerina on point – and spreads her arms in a gesture of the stage. 'Dis-ap-peared!'

Cynthia was naturally graceful, and she did take dancing lessons, so these movements may have been as I have described. She did say 'Disappeared' after looking all around the pool, but the strangely artificial style of speech and gesture, the lack of urgency, is more like my invention. The fear I felt instantly when I couldn't see Meg – even while I was telling myself she must be in the shallower water – must have made Cynthia's movements seem unbearably slow and inappropriate to me, and the tone in which she could say 'Disappeared' before the implications struck her (or was she covering, at once, some ever-ready guilt?) was heard by me as quite exquisitely, monstrously self-possessed.

I cried out for Andrew, and the lifeguard came into view. She was pointing toward the deep end of the pool, saying, 'What's that?'

There, just within my view, a cluster of pink ruffles appeared, a bouquet, beneath the surface of the water. Why would a lifeguard stop and point, why would she ask what that was, why didn't she just dive into the water and swim to it? She didn't swim; she ran all the way around the edge of the pool. But by that time Andrew was over the fence. So many things seemed not quite plausible – Cynthia's behaviour, then the lifeguard's – and now I had the impression that Andrew jumped with one bound over this fence, which seemed about seven feet high. He must have climbed it very quickly, getting a grip on the wire.

I could not jump or climb it, so I ran to the entrance, where there was a sort of lattice gate, locked. It was not very high, and I did pull myself over it. I ran through the cement corridors, through the disinfectant pool for your feet, and came out on the edge of the pool.

The drama was over.

Andrew had got to Meg first, and had pulled her out of the water. He just had to reach over and grab her, because she was swimming somehow, with her head underwater – she was moving toward the edge of the pool. He was carrying her now, and the lifeguard was trotting along behind. Cynthia had climbed out of the water and was running to meet them. The only person aloof from the situation was the boyfriend, who had stayed on the bench at the shallow end, drinking a milkshake. He smiled at me, and I thought that unfeeling of him, even though the danger was past. He may have meant it kindly. I noticed that he had not turned the radio off, just down.

Meg had not swallowed any water. She hadn't even scared herself. Her hair was plastered to her head and her eyes were wide open, golden with amazement.

'I was getting the comb,' she said. 'I didn't know it was deep.'

Andrew said, 'She was swimming! She was swimming by herself. I saw her bathing suit in the water and then I saw her swimming.'

'She nearly drowned,' Cynthia said. 'Didn't she? Meg nearly drowned.'

'I don't know how it could have happened,' said the lifeguard. 'One moment she was there, and the next she wasn't.'

What had happened was that Meg had climbed out of the water at the shallow end and run along the edge of the pool toward the deep end. She saw a comb that somebody had dropped lying on the bottom. She crouched down and reached in to pick it up, quite deceived about the depth of the water. She went over the edge and slipped into the pool, making such a light splash that nobody heard – not the lifeguard, who was kissing her boyfriend, or Cynthia, who was watching them. That must have been the moment under the trees when I thought, Where are the children? It must have been the same moment. At that moment, Meg was slipping, surprised, into the treacherously clear blue water.

'It's okay,' I said to the lifeguard, who was nearly crying. 'She can move pretty fast.' (Though that wasn't what we usually said about Meg at all. We said she thought everything over and took her time.)

'You swam, Meg,' said Cynthia, in a congratulatory way. (She told us about the kissing later.)

'I didn't know it was deep,' Meg said. 'I didn't drown.'

We had lunch at a take-out place, eating hamburgers and fries at a picnic table not far from the highway. In my excitement, I forgot to get Meg a plain hamburger, and had to scrape off the relish and mustard with plastic spoons, then wipe the meat with a paper napkin, before she would eat it. I took advantage of the trash can there to clean out the car. Then we resumed driving east, with the car windows open in front. Cynthia and Meg fell asleep in the back seat.

Andrew and I talked quietly about what had happened. Suppose I hadn't had the impulse just at that moment to check on the children? Suppose we had gone uptown to get drinks, as we had thought of doing? How had Andrew got over the fence? Did he jump or climb? (He couldn't remember.) How had he reached Meg so quickly? And think of the lifeguard not watching. And Cynthia, taken up with the kissing. Not seeing anything else. Not seeing Meg drop over the edge.

Disappeared.

But she swam. She held her breath and came up swimming.

What a chain of lucky links.

That was all we spoke about – luck. But I was compelled to picture the opposite. At this moment, we could have been filling out forms. Meg removed from us, Meg's body being prepared for shipment. To Vancouver – where we had never noticed such a thing as a graveyard – or to Ontario? The scribbled drawings she had made this morning would still be in the back seat of the car. How could this be borne all at once, how did people bear it? The plump, sweet shoulders and hands and feet, the fine brown hair, the rather satisfied, secretive expression – all exactly the same as when she had been alive. The most ordinary tragedy. A child drowned in a swimming pool at noon on a sunny day. Things tidied up quickly. The pool opens as usual at two o'clock. The lifeguard is a bit shaken up and gets the

Miles City, Montana

afternoon off. She drives away with her boyfriend in the Roto-Rooter truck. The body sealed away in some kind of shipping coffin. Sedatives, phone calls, arrangements. Such a sudden vacancy, a blind sinking and shifting. Waking up groggy from the pills, thinking for a moment it wasn't true. Thinking if only we hadn't stopped, if only we hadn't taken this route, if only they hadn't let us use the pool. Probably no one would ever have known about the comb.

There's something trashy about this kind of imagining, isn't there? Something shameful. Laying your finger on the wire to get the safe shock, feeling a bit of what it's like, then pulling back. I believed that Andrew was more scrupulous than I about such things, and that at this moment he was really trying to think about something else.

When I stood apart from my parents at Steve Gauley's funeral and watched them, and had this new, unpleasant feeling about them, I thought that I was understanding something about them for the first time. It was deadly serious thing. I was understanding that they were implicated. Their big, stiff, dressed-up bodies did not stand between me and sudden death, or any kind of death. They gave consent. So it seemed. They gave consent to the death of children and to my death not by anything they said or thought but by the very fact that they had made children – they had made me. They had made me, and for that reason my death – however grieved they were, however they carried on – would seem to them anything but impossible or unnatural. This was a fact, and even then I knew they were not to blame.

But I did blame them. I charged them with effrontery, hypocrisy. On Steve Gauley's behalf, and on behalf of all children, who knew that by rights they should have sprung up free, to live a new, superior kind of life, not to be caught in the snares of vanquished grown-ups, with their sex and funerals.

Steve Gauley drowned, people said, because he was next thing to an orphan and was let run free. If he had been warned enough and given chores to do and kept in check, he wouldn't have fallen from an untrustworthy tree branch into a spring pond, a full gravel pit near the river – he wouldn't have drowned. He was neglected, he was free, so he drowned. And his father took it as an accident, such as might happen to a dog. He didn't have a good suit for the funeral, and he didn't bow his head for the prayers. But he was the only grown-up that I let off the hook. He was the only one I didn't see giving consent. He couldn't prevent anything, but he wasn't implicated in anything, either – not like the others, saying the Lord's Prayer in their unnaturally weighted voices, oozing religion and dishonour.

At Glendive, not far from the North Dakota border, we had a choice – either to continue on the interstate or head north-east, toward Williston, taking Route 16, then some secondary roads that would get us back to Highway 2.

We agreed that the interstate would be faster, and that it was important for us not to spend too much time – that is, money – on the road. Nevertheless we decided to cut back to Highway 2.

'I just like the idea of it better,' I said.

Andrew said, 'That's because it's what we planned to do in the beginning.'

'We missed seeing Kalispell and Havre. And Wolf Point. I like the name.'

'We'll see them on the way back.'

Miles City, Montana

Andrew's saying 'on the way back' was a surprising pleasure to me. Of course, I had believed that we would be coming back, with our car and our lives and our family intact, having covered all that distance, having dealt somehow with those loyalties and problems, held ourselves up for inspection in such a foolhardy way. But it was a relief to hear him say it.

'What I can't get over,' said Andrew, 'is how you got the signal. It's got to be some kind of extra sense that mothers have.'

Partly I wanted to believe that, to bask in my extra sense. Partly I wanted to warn him – to warn everybody – never to count on it.

'What I can't understand,' I said, 'is how you got over the fence.'

'Neither can I.'

So we went on, with the two in the back seat trusting us, because of no choice, and we ourselves trusting to be forgiven, in time, for everything that had first to be seen and condemned by those children: whatever was flippant, arbitrary, careless, callous – all our natural, and particular, mistakes.

Iris Murdoch

extract from

The Bell

The lay religious community at Imber Court is well-intentioned if also self-deceiving. Dora and Toby, both outsiders, are young enough to withstand the moral pressures brought to bear by their elders — Dora's husband Paul, Toby's mentor Michael. Nevertheless, the two visitors resent the roles being forced upon them by the group and their extraordinary plan to raise the medieval bell sunk in Imber lake proves most effective in re-establishing their true identities and in exposing the unconscious and somewhat predatory motives of those around them.

By the time Dora arrived back at Imber she felt considerably more subdued. She had caught a train at once, but it was a slow one. She was vastly hungry again. She was afraid of Paul's anger. She tried to keep on believing that something good had happened to her; but now it seemed that this good thing had after all nothing whatever to do with her present troubles. It had been a treat and now it was over. At any rate, Dora was tired and couldn't think any more and felt discouraged, frightened, and resentful. The village taxi took her most of the way down the drive; she would not let it come right up to the house as she wanted the fact of her return to dawn quietly on the brotherhood. She was also afraid that, unless she could first see him alone, Paul would make a public scene. She saw from a distance the lights of the Court and they looked to her hostile and censorious.

It was well after ten o'clock. As Dora approached along the last part of the drive, stepping as quietly as possible on the gravel, she saw that there were lights on in the hall and the common-room. She could not see the window of her and Paul's room, which faced the other reach of the lake. The Court loomed darkly over her, blotting out the stars; and then she heard a sound of music. She stopped. Quite clearly on the soft and quiet warm night air there came the sharp sound of a piano. Dora listened, puzzled. Surely there was no piano at Imber. Then she thought, of course, a gramophone record, the Bach recital. This was the night for it and the community must all be gathered in the common-room listening. She wondered if Paul would be there. Leaning carefully on the balustrade so as to step more lightly she glided up the steps on to the balcony.

The lights from the hall and from the modern French windows of the common-room made a brightly illuminated area in the space at the top of the steps. Dora could see the flagstones clearly revealed. The music was now very loud and it was plain that no one could have heard her approaching. Dora stood for a moment or two, well out of the beam of light, attending to the music. Yes, that was Bach all right. Dora disliked any music in which she could not participate herself by singing or dancing. Paul had given up taking her to concerts since she could not keep her feet still. She listened now with distaste to the hard patterns of sound which plucked at her emotions without satisfying them and which demanded in an arrogant way to be contemplated. Dora refused to contemplate them.

She slithered round, still well in the darkness, until she reached a place from which she could see into the common-room. She trusted that the sharp contrast of light and dark would curtain her from the observation of those within. She found, with something of a shock, that she could see in quite clearly and that by moving round she could inspect the whole room. The music had seemed to make, like a waterfall, some enormous barrier, and it was strange now to find so many people so close to her. They were, however, people under a spell; and she felt she could survey them as an enchanter surveys his victims.

The Bell

The community were gathered in a semi-circle and seated in the uncomfortable wooden-armed common-room chairs, except for Mrs Mark who was sitting on the floor cross-legged, her skirt well tucked in under her ankles. She was leaning back against the leg of her husband's chair. Mark Strafford, his hand arrested in the act of stroking his beard, was turned towards the corner where the gramophone was, and looked like someone acting Michelangelo's Moses in a charade. Next to him sat Catherine, her hands clasped, the palms moving slightly against each other. Her head was inclined forward, her eyes brooding, the heavy expanse between the lashes and the high curved eyebrows slumberously revealed. Her gipsy hair was thrust carelessly behind her ears. Dora wondered if she was really listening to the music. Toby sat in the centre, opposite to the window, curled gracefully in the chair, one long leg under him, the other hooked over the arm, a hand dangling. He looked absent-minded and rather worried. Next to him was Michael who was leaning his elbows on his knees, his face hidden in his hands, his faded yellow hair spurting through his fingers. Beside him James sat with head thrown back in shameless almost smiling enjoyment of the music. In the corner was Paul, sitting rigid and wearing that somewhat military air which his moustache sometimes gave him and which went so ill with the rest of his personality. He looked tense, concentrated, as if he were about to bark out an order.

Dora was sorry to find Paul at the recital. With any luck he might have been more easily accosted, moping upstairs; as indeed he ought to be, she reflected resentfully, with the mystery of his wife's disappearance still unsolved. Dora watched him for a while, nervously, and then returned to scanning the whole group. Seeing them all together like that she felt excluded and aggressive, and Noel's exhortations came back to her. They had a secure complacent look about them: the spiritual ruling class; and she wished suddenly that she might grow as large and fierce as a gorilla and shake the flimsy doors off their hinges, drowning the repulsive music in a savage carnivorous yell.

Dora had now watched for so long that she felt herself invisible. She moved slightly, about to withdraw, and as she did so she saw that Toby was looking straight out of the window towards her. She wasn't sure for a moment whether he had seen her and she stood quite still. Then a change in his expression, a widening and focusing of his eyes, a slight tensing of his body told her that she had been observed. Dora waited, wondering what Toby would do. To her surprise he did nothing. He sat for a moment giving her a look of intense concentration; and then he dropped his eyes again. Dora slid quietly back into the darkness. No one else in the room had noticed anything.

She stood at the far corner of the balcony dejected, apprehensive, wondering what to do. She supposed she ought to go up to their bedroom and wait for Paul; but the prospect of this gloomy vigil was so appalling that she could not bring herself to mount the stairs. She wandered down again to the terrace and began to walk slowly along the path that led to the causeway. The moon was just rising and there was enough light to see where she was going. The silhouette of the Abbey trees and the tower could be seen, as on her first night at Imber. She reached the lake which seemed to glimmer blackly, not yet fully struck by the rays of the moon.

As she looked back towards the house she was alarmed to see that there was a dark figure following her down the

The Bell

path. She felt sure it must be Paul, and her old deep fear of him suddenly made the whole night scene terrifying. She was ready to run; but she stood still, her hand at her breast, as if to take a physical shock. The figure came nearer, hurrying soundlessly along the grassy track. When it was quite near she saw it was Toby.

'Oh, Toby,' said Dora with relief. 'Hello. You came out of the music.'

'Yes,' said Toby. He seemed breathless. 'I came out before the last movement.'

'Do you like that music?' said Dora.

'Not terribly, actually,' said Toby. 'I was going to come out anyway. Then I saw you through the window.'

'Did you say I was back?' said Dora.

'No, I thought I'd better not talk between the movements. I just slipped out. They're good for another three-quarters of an hour in there,' he added.

'Ah well,' said Dora. 'It's a nice night.'

'Let's walk along a bit,' said Toby.

He seemed pleased to see her. Thank heaven somebody was. They walked along the path beside the lake opposite the Abbey walls. The moon, risen further, was spreading a golden fan across the surface of the water. Dora looked at Toby and found that he was looking at her. Dora was glad to be with Toby. She felt a natural complicity with him which convinced her of the abiding strength and wholeness of her youth. Here was one who was not concerned to enclose or judge her. The rest of them, however, she gloomily reflected, Paul in one way and the brotherhood in another, would make her play their role. A few hours ago she had felt free and she had come back to Imber of her own free will, performing a real action. Yet *they* would make of it the guilty enforced return of an escaped prisoner. Contemplating the inevitability, whose nature she scarcely understood, of *their* superiority over her, and the impossibility of ever getting even with them, Dora was beginning to regret that she had come back.

They walked on, exchanging a word or two about the moonlight, until the path entered the wood. The cavern of darkened foliage covered them, illuminated here and there by glimpses of the gilded water. Toby plunged on confidently and Dora followed, finding silence easy in his company. She had decided to let the three-quarters of an hour which Toby had said they were 'good for' elapse, and then a little more time, to allow the company to disperse to their rooms; then she could be sure of finding Paul alone.

'Why, here we are!' said Toby.

'Where?' said Dora. She came up beside him. The trees stood back from the water and the moonlight clearly showed a grassy space and a sloping stone ramp leading down into the lake.

'Oh, just a place I know,' said Toby. 'I swam here once or twice. No one comes here but me.'

'It's nice,' said Dora. She sat down on the stones at the top of the ramp. The lake seemed quite still and yet made strange liquid noises in the silence that followed. The Abbey wall with its battlement of trees could be seen on the other side, some distance away to the left. But opposite there was only the dark wood, the continuation across the water of the wood that lay behind. It seemed to Dora that the wide moonlit circle at the edge of which she sat was apprehensive, inhabited. An owl called. She looked up at Toby. She was glad she was not there alone.

Toby was standing quite near at the head of the ramp, looking down at her. Dora forgot what she was going to

The Bell

say. The darkness, the silence, and their proximity made her quite suddenly physically aware of Toby's presence. She felt a line of force between his body and hers. She wondered if at this moment he felt it too. She remembered how she had seen him naked, and she smiled. The moon revealed her smile and Toby smiled back.

'Tell me something, Toby,' said Dora.

Toby, seeming a little startled, came down the ramp and squatted beside her. The cool weedy smell of the water was in their nostrils. 'What?' he said.

'Oh, nothing in particular,' said Dora. 'Just tell me something, anything.'

Toby sat back on the stones. After a pause he said, 'I'll tell you something very strange.'

'Go on,' said Dora.

'There's a huge bell down there in the water.'

'*What?*' said Dora. She half rose, amazed, scarcely understanding him.

'Yes,' said Toby, pleased with the effect he had produced. 'Isn't it odd? I found it when I was swimming underwater. I wasn't sure at first, but I came back a second time. I'm certain it's a bell.'

'You saw it, touched it?'

'I touched it, I felt it all over. It's only half buried in the mud. It's too dark to see.'

'Had it carvings on it?' said Dora.

'Carvings?' said Toby. 'Well, it was sort of fretted and worked on the outside. But that might have been anything. Why do you ask?'

'Good God!' said Dora. She stood up. Her hand covered her mouth.

Toby got up too. He was quite alarmed. 'Why, what is it?'

'Have you told anyone else?' said Dora.

'No. I don't know why, but I thought I'd keep it a secret till I'd visited it once again.'

'Well, look,' said Dora, 'don't tell anyone. Let it be *our* secret now, will you?' Dora, who felt no doubts either about Toby's story or about the identity of the object, was suddenly filled with the uneasy elation of one to whom great power has been given which he does not yet know how to use. She clutched her discovery as an Arab boy might clutch a papyrus. What it was she did not know, but she was determined to sell it dear.

'All right,' said Toby, rather gratified. 'I won't utter a word. I suppose it is very odd, isn't it? I don't know why I wasn't more thrilled about it. At first I wasn't sure – and, well, a lot of other things distracted me since. Anyway, I *might* be wrong. But you seem so specially excited about it.'

'I'm sure you're not wrong,' said Dora. Then she told him the legend which Paul had told her, and which had so much seized upon her imagination, of the erring nun and the bishop's curse.

By the end of the tale Toby was as agitated as she was. 'But something like that *couldn't* be true,' he said.

'Well, no,' said Dora, 'but Paul said there's usually *some* truth in those old stories. The bell probably did get into the lake somehow, and there it is.' She pointed at the smooth surface of the water. 'If it is the medieval bell it's very important for art and history and so on. Could we pull it out?'

'We, you mean you and me?' said Toby amazed. 'We couldn't possibly. It's a huge thing, it must weigh an immense amount. And anyway, it's sunk in the mud.'

'You said only half sunk,' said Dora. 'You're an engineer. Couldn't we do it with a pulley or something?'

'We might rig up a pulley,' said Toby, 'but we haven't

The Bell

any power. At least, I suppose we might use the tractor. But what do you want to do?'

'I don't know yet,' said Dora. Her face was cupped in her hands, her eyes shining. 'Surprise everybody. Make a miracle. James said the age of miracles wasn't over.'

Toby looked dubious. 'If it's important,' he said, 'oughtn't we just to tell the others?'

'They'll know soon enough,' said Dora. 'We won't do any harm. But it would be such a marvellous surprise. Suppose – oh, well, I wonder – suppose, suppose we were to substitute the old bell for the new bell somehow, you know, when the new bell arrives next week? They're going to have the bell veiled, and unveil it at the Abbey gate. Think of the sensation when they find the medieval bell underneath the veil! Why, it would be wonderful, it would be like a real miracle, the sort of thing that makes people go on pilgrimages!'

'But it would be just a trick,' said Toby. 'And besides, the bell may be all broken and damaged. And anyway it's too difficult.'

'Nothing is too difficult,' said Dora. 'I feel this was meant for us. I should like to shake everybody up a bit. They'd get a colossal surprise – and then they'd be so pleased at having the bell, it would be like an unexpected present. Don't you think?'

'Wouldn't it be – somehow in bad taste?' said Toby.

'When something's fantastic enough and marvellous enough it can't be in bad taste,' said Dora. 'In the end, it would give everyone a lift. It would certainly give me a lift! Are you game?'

Toby began to laugh. He said, 'It's a most extraordinary idea. But I'm sure we couldn't manage it.'

'With an engineer to help me,' said Dora, 'I can do

anything.' And indeed as she stood there in the moonlight, looking at the quiet water, she felt as if by the sheer force of her will she could make the great bell rise. After all, and after her own fashion, she would fight. In this holy community she would play the witch.

* * *

'The chief requirement of the good life,' said Michael, 'is that one should have some conception of one's capacities. One must know oneself sufficiently to know what is the next thing. One must study carefully how best to use such strength as one has.'

It was Sunday, and Michael's turn to give the address. Although the idea of preaching was at this moment intensely distasteful to him, he forced himself dourly to the task, thinking it best to maintain as steadily as possible the normal pattern of his life. He spoke fluently, having thought out what he wanted to say beforehand and uttering it now without hesitations or consulting of notes. He found his present role abysmally ludicrous, but he was not at a loss for words. He stood upon the dais looking out over his tiny congregation. It was a familiar scene. Father Bob sat in the front row as usual, his hands folded, his bright bulging eyes intent upon Michael, devouring him with attention. Mark Strafford, his eyes ambiguously screwed up, sat in the second row with his wife and Catherine. Pete Topglass sat in the third row, busy polishing his spectacles on a silk handkerchief. Every now and then he peered at them and then, unsatisfied, went on polishing. He was always nervous when Michael spoke. Next to him was Patchway, who usually turned up to hear Michael, and

The Bell

who had removed his hat to reveal a bald spot which although so rarely uncovered contrived to be sunburnt. Paul and Dora were not present, having gone out for a walk looking irritable and obviously in the middle of a quarrel. Toby sat at the back, his head bowed so low in his hands that Michael could see the ruff of hair at the back of his neck.

Michael was aware now, when the knowledge was too late to do him any good, that it had been a great mistake to see Toby. The meeting, the clasp of the hands, had had an intensity, and indeed a delightfulness, which he had not foreseen – or had not cared to foresee – and which now made, with the earlier incident, something which had the weight and momentum of a story. There had been a development; there was an expectancy. Michael knew that he ought to have managed the interview with Toby differently, yet, that, being himself, he could not have done so: and since this was the case he ought to have written Toby a letter, or better still done nothing whatsoever and let the boy think of him what ill he pleased. He was ready to measure *now* how far the interview had been necessary to him in order that he might somehow refurbish Toby's conception of him, so rudely shaken by what had occurred.

The trouble was, as Michael now saw, that he had performed the action which belonged by right to a better person; and yet too, by an austere paradox, a better person would not have been in the situation that required that action. It would have been possible to conduct the meeting with Toby in an unemotional way which left the matter completely closed; it was only not possible for Michael. He remembered his prayers, and how he had taken the thing almost as a test of his faith. It was true that a person of great faith could with impunity have acted boldly: it was only that Michael was not that person. What he had failed to do was accurately to estimate his own resources, his own spiritual level: and it was indeed from his later reflections on this matter that he had, with a certain bitterness, drawn the text for his sermon. One must perform the lower act which one can manage and sustain: not the higher act which one bungles.

Michael was aware that to overestimate the importance of what was going on was itself a danger. He sighed for some robust common sense which would envisage his action as deplorable but now at least completed without disastrous consequences. He felt, rather pusillanimously, that a sturdy, even cynical, confidant could have helped him to reduce the power which the situation had over him, by seeing it in a more ordinary and less dramatic proportion. But he had no possible confidant; and he remained continually and miserably aware of one consequence which his action had had. He had completely destroyed Toby's peace of mind. He had turned the boy from an open, cheerful hard-working youth into someone anxious, secretive, and evasive. The change in Toby's conduct seemed to Michael so marked that he was surprised that no one else seemed to have noticed it.

He had also destroyed his own peace of mind. An unhealthy excitement consumed him. He worked steadily, but his work was bad. He found now that he awoke each morning with a feeling of curiosity and expectation. He could not prevent himself from continually observing Toby. Toby, on his part, avoided Michael, while being obviously extremely aware of him. Michael guessed on general grounds, and then read in the boy's behaviour, that a reaction had set in. When he had spoken with

The Bell

Toby in the nightjar alley he knew that the emotion which he had felt had received an echo: the memory of this moved him still. The sense that Toby's feelings were now ebbing, that he was perhaps deliberately hardening his heart and regarding with disgust that impulse of affection drove Michael to a sort of frenzy. He longed to speak to Toby, to question him, once more to explain; and he could not help hoping that Toby would sooner or later force such a tête-à-tête upon him. He wished that somehow he could pull out of this mess the atom of good which was in it, crystallizing out his harmless goodwill for Toby, Toby's for him. But he knew, and knew it very well, that this was impossible. In this world, it was almost certain, Toby and he could never now be friends: and hardening of the heart was perhaps indeed the best solution. He prayed constantly for Toby, but found that his prayers drifted into fantasies. He was tormented by vague physical desires and by the memory of Toby's body, warm and relaxed against his in the van; and his dreams were haunted by an ambiguous and elusive figure who was sometimes Toby and sometimes Nick.

The thought, when he let his mind dwell upon it, that Nick and Toby were together at the Lodge, added another dimension to Michael's unrest. He returned, fruitlessly, again and again, to the question of whether Nick could possibly have seen him embracing Toby. On each occasion he decided that it was impossible, but then found himself wondering afresh. Such a cloud of distress surrounded this subject that he was not sure what it was, here, that he was regretting: the damage to his own reputation, the possible damage to Nick, or something far more primitive, the loss of Nick's affection, which after all he had no reason to think he still retained and certainly no right to wish to hold.

The only result of these agitations was that it became more impossible than ever to 'do anything' about Nick himself; though he was still resolved to speak to Catherine. When his imagination, with its cursed visual agility, conjured up possible scenes at the Lodge, he was tormented by a two-way jealousy which also prevented him from reconsidering his plan, so desirable from many points of view, of moving Nick or Toby or both up to the Court. His motives, he felt, would be so evident, at any rate in the quarters which at present concerned him most, nor could he bring himself to act on such motives, even though supported by other good reasons. His only consolation was that Toby would be leaving Imber in any case in another couple of weeks; and Nick would probably leave when Catherine had entered the Abbey. It was a matter of hanging on. Afterwards he would, with God's help, set his mind in order and return to his tasks and his plans, which he was determined should not be altered by this nightmarish interlude.

Michael was continuing with his address. He went on, 'It is the positive thing that saves. Can we doubt that God requires of us that we know ourselves? Remember the parable of the talents. In each of us there are different talents, different propensities, many of them capable of good or evil use. We must endeavour to know our possibilities and use what energy we really possess in the doing of God's will. As spiritual beings, in our imperfection and also in the possibility of our perfection, we differ profoundly one from another. How different we are from each other is something which it may take a long time to find out; and certain differences may never appear at all. Each one of us has his own way of apprehending God. I am sure you will know what I mean when I say that one finds God, as it were, in certain places; one has, where

The Bell

God is concerned, a sense of direction, a sense that *here* is what is most real, most good, most true. This sense of reality and weight attaches itself to certain experiences in our lives – and for different people these experiences may be different. God speaks to us in various tongues. To this, we must be attentive.

'You will remember that last week James spoke to us about innocence. I would add this to what he so excellently said. We have been told to be, not only as harmless as doves, but also as wise as serpents. To live in innocence, or having fallen to return to the way, we need all the strength that we can muster – and to use our strength we must know where it lies. We must not, for instance, perform an act because abstractly it seems to be a good act if in fact it is so contrary to our instinctive apprehensions of spiritual reality that we cannot carry it through, that is, cannot really perform it. Each one of us apprehends a certain kind and degree of reality and from this springs our power to live as spiritual beings: and by using and enjoying what we already know we can hope to know more. Self-knowledge will lead us to avoid occasions of temptation rather than to rely on naked strength to overcome them. We must not arrogate to ourselves actions which belong to those whose spiritual vision is higher or other than ours. From this attempt, only disaster will come, and we shall find that the action which we have performed is after all not the high action which we intended, but something else.

'I would use here, again following the example of James, the image of the bell. The bell is subject to the force of gravity. The swing that takes it down must also take it up. So we too must learn to understand the mechanism of our spiritual energy, and find out where, for us, are the hiding places of our strength. This is what

I meant by saying that it is the positive thing that saves. We must work, from inside outwards, through outwards, through our strength, and by understanding and using exactly that energy which we have, acquire more. This is the wisdom of the serpent. This is the struggle, pleasing surely in the sight of God, to become more fully and deeply the person that we are; and by exploring and hallowing every corner of our being, to bring into existence that one and perfect individual which God in creating us entrusted to our care.'

Michael returned to his seat, his eyes glazed, feeling like a sleep-walker in the alarming silence which followed his words. He fell on his knees with the others and prayed the prayer for quietness of mind, which was at such moments all that he could compass. Laboriously he followed the petitions of Father Bob Joyce; and when the service was over he slipped quickly out of the Long Room and took temporary refuge in his office. He wondered how obvious it had been that he was saying the exact opposite of what James had been saying last week. This led him to reflect on how little, in all the drama of the previous days, he had dwelt upon the simple fact of having broken a rule. He recalled James's words: sodomy is not deplorable, it is forbidden. Michael knew that for himself it was just the how and why of it being deplorable that engaged his attention. He did not in fact believe that it was *just* forbidden. God had created men and women with these tendencies, and made these tendencies to run so deep that they were, in many cases, the very core of the personality. Whether in some other, and possibly better, society it could ever be morally permissible to have homosexual relations was, Michael felt, no business of his. He felt pretty sure that in any world in which he would live he would judge it,

The Bell

for various reasons, to be wrong. But this did not make him feel that he could sweep, as James did, the whole subject aside. It was complicated. For himself, God had made him so and he did not think that God had made him a monster.

It was complicated; it was *interesting*: and there was the rub. He realized that in this matter, as in many others, he was always engaged in performing what James had called the second best act: the act which goes with exploring one's personality and estimating the consequences rather than austerely following the rules. And indeed his sermon this very day had been a commendation of the second best act. But the danger here was the very danger which James had pointed out: that if one departs from a simple apprehension of certain definite commandments one may become absorbed in the excitement of a spiritual drama for its own sake.

Michael looked at his watch. He remembered now that he had arranged to see Catherine before lunch, having nerved himself at last to make the appointment. It was already time to go and find her. He knew that he must endeavour now to say something to her about Nick, to ask her to give him definite advice on how to make her brother participate more in the activities of the community. He did not look forward to raising this topic, or indeed to seeing Catherine at all, but at least it was something ordinary and patently sensible to do. He found himself hoping that Catherine might strongly advise the removal of Nick from the Lodge. He descended the stairs and glanced round the hall and put his head into the common-room.

Catherine was not to be seen; nor was she on the balcony or the terrace. Mark Strafford was sunning himself on the steps. Michael called, 'Seen Catherine anywhere?'

'She's in the stable yard with her delightful twin,' said Mark. 'Brother Nick has at last decided to mend the lorry. *Deo gratias.*'

Michael disliked this information. He was a little tempted to postpone the interview, but decided quickly that he must not do so. Catherine might be waiting for him to, as it were, release her from Nick; and since he had at last, and with such difficulty, made up his mind to talk to her about her brother he had better not let his decision become stale. It would be a relief, anyway, to get that talk over, not least because he could then feel that, to some wretchedly small degree, he had 'done something' about Nick. He set off for the stable yard.

The big gates that led on to the drive were shut. Michael noticed gloomily, and not for the first time, that they needed a coat of paint and one gate post was rotting. He entered by a little gate in the wall. The yard, one of William Kent's minor triumphs, was composed on three sides of loose boxes surmounted by a second storey lit by alternate circular and rectangular windows under a dentil cornice. It gave somewhat the impression of a small residential square. The stone-tiled roof was surmounted opposite the gates by a slender clock tower. The clock no longer went. On the right side a part of the building had been gutted by fire, and corrugated iron, contributed by Michael's grandfather, still filled the gaping holes in the lower story. The yard sloped markedly towards the lake and was divided from the drive by a high wall. Now, in the heat of the day, it was enclosed, dusty, stifling, rather dazzling in the sunshine. It reminded Michael of an arena.

The fifteen-hundredweight lorry was standing in the middle of the yard just beyond the shadow of the wall, its nose towards the lake. The bonnet was open and from underneath the vehicle a pair of feet could be seen sticking out. Nearby, regardless of the dust, Catherine Fawley was sitting on the ground. Her skirt was hitched up towards her waist and her two long legs, crossed at the ankle, were exposed almost completely to the sun. Michael was surprised to see her in this pose and surprised too that she did not, on seeing him, get up, or at least pull her skirt down. Instead she looked up at him without smiling. Michael, for the first time since he had met her, conjectured that she might positively dislike him.

Nick came edging out from underneath the lorry, his feet disappearing on one side, his head appearing on the other. He lay supine, half emerged, his head resting in the dust. He swivelled his eyes back towards Michael who, from where he was standing, saw his face upside down. He seemed to be smiling, but his inverted face looked so odd it was hard to tell.

'The big chief,' said Nick.

'Hello,' said Michael. 'Very good of you to fix the lorry. Will it be all right?'

'What drivel,' said Nick. 'It's not very good of me to fix the lorry. It's shocking of me not to have done it earlier. Why don't you say what you mean? It was only a blocked petrol feed. It should be all right now.' He continued to lie there, his strange face of a bearded demon looking up at Michael.

Michael, still conscious of Catherine's stare, fumbled for words. 'I was just looking for your sister,' he said.

'I was just talking to my sister,' said Nick. 'We were discussing our childhood. We spent our childhood together, you know.'

'Ah,' said Michael idiotically. Somehow, he could not deal with both of them, and it occurred to him that this was one of the very few occasions when he had seen them together.

'I know it's wicked to chat and reminisce,' said Nick, 'but you must forgive us two, since it's our last chance. Isn't it, Cathie?'

Catherine said nothing.

Michael mumbled, 'Well, I'll be off. I can easily see Catherine another time.'

'All shall be well and all shall be well and all manner of bloody thing shall be well,' said Nick. 'Isn't that so, Cathie?'

Michael realized he was a bit drunk. He turned to go. 'Wait a minute,' said Nick. 'You're always "off", confound you, like the bloody milk by the time it reaches me at the Lodge. If you want all manner of thing to be well there's a little service you could perform for me. Will you?'

'Certainly,' said Michael. 'What is it?'

'Just get into the lorry and put the gear lever in neutral and release the hand-brake.'

Michael, moving instinctively toward the vehicle, checked himself. 'Nick,' he said, 'don't be an imbecile, that's not funny. And do get out from under that thing. You know the slope makes it dangerous, anyway. You ought to have put the lorry sideways.'

Nick pulled himself slowly out and stood up, dusting his clothes and grinning. Seeing him now in overalls and apparently doing a job of work Michael saw how much thinner and tougher he looked than when he had arrived: handsomer too, and considerably more alert. Michael also realized that these words were the first real words which he had addressed to Nick since the day of his arrival. Nick, who had obviously angled for them, was looking pleased.

The Bell

Michael was about to utter some excuse and go when the wooden door from the drive was heard creaking open once again. They all turned. It was Toby. He stood blinking at the enclosed scene, Catherine still sitting bare-legged and Michael and Nick close to each other beside the lorry. He hesitated with the air of one interrupting an intimate talk, and then since retreat was obviously impossible, came on into the yard and closed the door. Michael's immediate thought was that Toby was looking for him. He felt as if he were blushing.

'Why, here's my understudy,' said Nick. 'You might have had a lesson. But it's all over now.' Then turning his back on Toby he said to Catherine, 'Cathie, would you mind starting her up?'

To Michael's surprise, who had never associated her with engines of any kind, Catherine got up slowly, shook out her skirts, and climbed into the lorry. Watching her he had the feeling, which he had never had before, that she was acting a part. She started the engine. Nick, peering into the bonnet, surveyed the results. They seemed satisfactory. He closed the bonnet and stood for a moment grinning at Michael. Then he said, raising his voice in the continuing din of the engine, 'I think we'll take her for a little spin to make sure she's all right. Catherine shall drive. Come along, Toby.'

Toby, who had been standing uneasily near the gate, looked startled and came forward.

'Come along, quickly,' said Nick, holding open the door of the driving cabin, 'you're coming too.'

Toby got in.

'How about you, Michael?' said Nick. 'It would be rather a squeeze, but I expect someone could sit on someone's knee.'

Michael shook his head.

'Then would you mind opening the gates for us?' said Nick. He was sitting in the middle between Toby and Catherine, his arms spread out along the back of the seat so that he embraced the boy and his sister.

As in a dream Michael went to the big wooden gates and dragged them open. Catherine let in the clutch smoothly and the lorry swept past him in a cloud of dust and disappeared into the drive. A few moments later, as he still stood exasperated and wretched in the empty yard, he saw it reappear far off on the other side of the lake, roar up towards the Lodge, and vanish on to the main road.

* * *

Toby rose from his bed and picked up his shoes. He had not undressed, and had not dared to go to sleep for fear of oversleeping. His rendezvous with Dora was for two-thirty a.m. It was now just after two. He opened the door of his room and listened. The door of Nick's room was open, but snores could be heard from within. Toby glided down the stairs and reached the outer door. A movement behind him gave him a momentary shock, but it was only Murphy who had evidently followed him downstairs. The dog snuffled against his trouser leg, looking up at him interrogatively. He patted him, half guiltily, and slipped out of the door alone, closing it firmly behind him. On this particular expedition even Murphy was not to be trusted.

This was the night when Toby and Dora were to attempt to raise the bell. Since its apparently crazy inception this plan had grown in substance and complication; and Toby, who had at first regarded it as a dream,

The Bell

had now become its business-like and enthusiastic manager. Just why Dora was so keen on something so dotty had not at first been clear to Toby. It was still not clear to him, but now he no longer troubled about anything except to please Dora: and also to overcome certain technical problems whose fascination had become evident to his mechanical mind.

On the day after his first conversation with Dora about the bell he had gone for another solitary swim. He had dived a large number of times investigating the shape and position of the object in detail. He had now no doubts, fired by Dora's certainty and confirmed by his own findings, that this was indeed *the* bell. Two colossal problems now faced him. The first was how to get the bell out of the water, and the second was how to effect the substitution of the old bell for the new which was to constitute Dora's miracle: both these tasks to be performed undiscovered and with no helper but Dora. It was a tall order.

Dora, who had clearly got no conception of how large and how heavy the bell was, seemed to think it all perfectly possible, and relied upon Toby's skill with an *insouciance* which both exasperated and melted him. Even though he knew it to be based on ignorance, her confidence infected him: he was infected too by her curious vision, her grotesque imagination of the return to life of the medieval bell. It was as if, for her, this was to be a magical act of shattering significance, a sort of rite of power and liberation; and although it was not an act which Toby could understand, or which in any other circumstance he would have had any taste for, he was prepared to catch her enthusiasm and to be, for this occasion, the sorcerer's apprentice.

It was the apprentice, however, who had to contrive

the details of the sorcery. He had discussed various plans with Dora, whose ignorance of dynamics turned out to be staggering. The fact was, after some suggestions involving cart-horses had been set aside, that the only motive power available to them which could have even a chance of doing the job was the tractor. Even then, as Toby tried to impress upon Dora, it was possible that they would be simply unable to shift the bell. The amount of muddy ooze inside it alone would double its weight; and the lower part of it might turn out to be thoroughly jammed in the thicker mud of the floor of the lake. Toby had attempted to dig the ooze away from it on his last diving expedition, but with only partial success. It was a bore that Dora could neither swim nor drive the tractor, since this meant that the bell could not be given an extra helping hand from below while it was being pulled from above.

'I'm afraid I'm perfectly useless!' said Dora, her hands about her knees, her large eyes glowing at him with submissive admiration as they sat in the wood having their final conference. Toby found her perfectly captivating.

The official plan for the new bell was as follows. It was arriving at the Court on Thursday morning. It would then be placed upon one of the iron trolleys which were sometimes used to bring logs from the wood, and it would thereon be attired with white garments and surrounded with flowers. So apparelled it would be blessed and 'baptized' by the Bishop at a little service planned to take place immediately after the latter's arrival on Thursday evening, and at which only the brotherhood would be present. The bell would spend the night of Thursday to Friday in the stable yard. On Friday morning shortly before seven o'clock, the time at which postulants were customarily admitted to the

Abbey, the bell would be the centre of a little country festival, whose details had been lovingly designed by Mrs Mark, during which it would be danced to by the local Morris, serenaded by a recorder band from the village school, and sung in solemn procession across the causeway by the choir from the local church, who had for some time now been studying ambitious pieces in its honour, one indeed composed for the occasion by the choirmaster. The procession, whose form and order was still under dispute, would consist of the performers, the brotherhood, and any villagers who cared to attend; and as interest was rather unexpectedly running high in the village quite a number of people seemed likely to come in spite of the earliness of the hour. The great gate of the Abbey would be opened as the procession approached and as its attendants fanned out on either side of it on the opposite bank the bell would be unveiled during a final burst of song. After it had stood for a suitable interval, revealed to the general admiration, it would be wheeled into the Abbey by specially selected workmen who had a dispensation to enter the enclosure for the purpose of erecting the bell. The closing of the gates behind the bell would end the ceremony as far as the outside world was concerned.

Toby and Dora's plan was as follows. On Wednesday night they would endeavour to raise the old bell. For this purpose they would use the tractor which as good fortune would have it Toby was now being permitted sometimes to drive. The ploughing up of the pastureland had commenced, and since the beginning of the week Toby had been working on the pasture with Patchway. The evening departure of the latter usually took place with unashamed punctuality; it would be an easy matter for Toby, about whose activities at that hour nobody would be bothering, instead of putting the tractor away, to drive it into the wood near the old barn. He had already cleared the branches and larger obstacles from the path that led through the barn to the lakeside, so that the tractor could be taken right through and almost to the water's edge. There it would be left until some time after midnight when Toby and Dora would meet at the ramp.

The tractor possessed a winch and a stout steel hawser with a hook at the end, used for hauling logs. With the hawser attached to the great ring which formed part of the head of the bell Toby hoped to be able to raise the bell, first by the winch and then by towing, and drag it into the barn. He had taken the precaution of sinking some stones and gravel at the foot of the ramp in case the bell should catch on the edge of the ramp where it ended under the level of the ooze. The danger at this point, apart from the unpredictability of the bell's behaviour, was that the sound of the tractor might be heard; but Toby judged that, with the south-west wind blowing as it had now been for some time, the noise was not likely to be audible at the Court, or if heard would not be recognizable. It might pass for a car or a distant aeroplane.

The next stage of the operation was no less complex. The large iron trolley on which the new bell was to rest had, fortunately, a twin brother. It was indeed the existence of this twin which made the plan feasible at all. Once the bell was inside the barn, the steel hawser would be passed over one of the large beams and the winch used to raise it from the ground. From this position it could be lowered onto the second trolley and made fast. The trolley could then, on Thursday night, without undue difficulty, be propelled along the concrete road

The Bell

which led beside the wood, sloping slightly down in the direction of the Court. The road led directly via the market-garden to the stable yard where the wood store was; and where the new bell would be, apparelled for its trip on the morrow. Here it should be possible for the bells to change clothes. The flowers and other garnishings of the trolley would conceal any small differences of shape which a sharp eye might notice between the two twins. If the bells turned out to be of vastly different sizes this would certainly be a snag: but Toby, who had slyly discovered the dimensions of the new bell, and who had taken what measurements he could of the old, was confident that they were roughly of a size. The new bell, disrobed, would then be wheeled into one of the empty loose-boxes into which no one ever peered, and the operation would be complete. The most perilous, as opposed to difficult, part of it would be the last; but as the stable yard was a little distant from the house, and as none of the brotherhood slept on the side nearest the yard, it was to be hoped that no one would hear anything.

There was one final annoyance. The second iron trolley, which would convey the old bell, was in daily use in the packing sheds. Mrs Mark used it as a table on which she arranged her goods, before pushing it up to the back of the van for loading. If Toby were to remove it on Wednesday night its absence would be noted on Thursday. It must therefore be removed on Thursday night. A minimum of operations at the barn would, however, be left for Thursday. On Wednesday the bell would be lifted, by the hawser passing over the beam, to a point, measured by Toby, a fraction higher than the level of the trolley. A second hawser, which Toby had discovered in the store room, would then be brought into action, hooked into the bell at one end, thrown over the beam, and made fast in the fork of a nearby tree by means of a crowbar passed through the ring in which the hawser ended. The first hawser, which was attached to the tractor, could then be released and the bell left hanging. The tractor would be taken back to the ploughing very early on Thursday morning. The bell would spend Thursday hanging in the barn. Dora had collected a quantity of green boughs and creepers with which it might be disguised; but in fact discovery during that day was exceedingly unlikely. On Thursday night the trolley would be brought and passed under the bell. If Toby's measurements, including the allowance he had made for sagging in the hawser, were exact enough the two surfaces would meet without interval; if his measurements were not quite exact the trolley could be lifted a little on earth and stones, or else dug into the floor of the barn, to take the rim of the bell. The hawser would then be removed and the bell would be resting on the trolley. This ingenious arrangement made it unnecessary to have the tractor in attendance on the second night.

 The mechanical details of the plan aroused in Toby a sort of ecstasy. It was all so difficult and yet so exquisitely possible and he brooded over it as over a work of art. It was also his homage to Dora and his proof to himself that he was in love. Ever since the moment in the chapel when Dora's image had so obligingly filled out that blank form of femininity towards which Toby interrogatively turned his inclinations he had been, he felt, under her domination, indeed as he almost precisely put it, under her orders. The fact that Dora was married troubled Toby very little. He had no intention of making any declaration to Dora or revealing by any word or gesture what was his state of mind. He took a proud

The Bell

satisfaction in this reticence, and felt rather like a medieval knight who sighs and suffers for a lady whom he has scarcely seen and will never possess. This conception of her remoteness made the vitality of her presence and the easy friendliness with which, in their curious enterprise, she treated him, all the more delightful. She had for him a radiance and an authority, and the freshness of the emotion which she aroused gave him a sense almost of the renewal of innocence.

Strangely co-existent with the revelation of himself which, with daily additions, Dora was unconsciously bringing about, there was a dark continuing twisted concern about Michael. Toby avoided Michael but watched him and could not keep his thoughts from him; and his feelings veered between resentment and guilt. He had a sense of having been plunged into something unclean; and at the same time a miserable awareness that he was hurting Michael. Yet how could he not? His imagination dwelt vaguely upon some momentous interview which he would have with Michael before he left Imber; and there were many moments when he was strongly tempted to go and knock on the door of Michael's office. He had little conception of what he would do or say inside, but cherished, partly with embarrassment and partly with satisfaction, the view that Michael was in need of his forgiveness, and in need more simply of a kind word. Toby had, altogether, where this matter was concerned, a strong sense of unfinished business.

He made his way cautiously along the path beside the lake. The moon had not failed them and was high in the sky and almost full and the wide glimmering scene of trees and water was attentive, significant, as if aware of a great deed which was to be done. The lake, so soon to yield up its treasure, was serene, almost inviting, and the air was warm. He walked faster now, watching out for the figure of Dora ahead of him, almost breathless with anticipation and excitement. They had agreed to meet at the barn. He knew very well that there were a hundred things which could go wrong; but he burned with confidence and with the hope of delighting Dora and with a sheer feverish desire to get at the bell.

He reached the open space by the ramp and stopped. After the soft swishing sound of his footsteps there was an eerie silence. Then Dora emerged, taking shape in the moonlight, from the path leading to the barn. He spoke her name.

'Thank God,' said Dora in a low voice. 'I've been absolutely scared stiff in this place. There were such funny noises, I kept thinking the drowned nun was after me.'

A clear sound arose quite near them suddenly in the reeds and they both jumped. It was a harsh yet sweet trilling cry which rose several notes and then died bubbling away.

'Whatever was that?' said Dora.

'The sedge warbler,' said Toby. 'The poor man's nightingale, Peter Topglass calls him. He won't bother us. Now, Dora, quickly to work.'

'I think we're perfectly mad,' said Dora. 'Why did we ever have this insane idea? Why did you encourage me?' She was half serious.

'Everything will be all right,' said Toby. Dora's flutter made him calm and decisive. He paused, breathing deeply. The sedge warbler sang again, a little farther off. The lake was brittle and motionless, the reeds and grasses moving very slightly in the warm breeze, the moon as bright as it could be. It seemed then to Toby fantastic that in a moment there would be the roar of the tractor, the breaking into the lake. He felt as an army

The Bell

commander might feel just before launching a surprise attack.

He took a few steps into the wood. The tractor was there where he had left it, just outside the barn on the lake side. It was lucky that the barn had large doors opening both ways so that it had been possible to drive the tractor straight through. He had not dared to bring it any nearer to the water for fear its polished red radiator might be visible during daylight from the causeway. He quickly took off his clothes, and dressed only in his bathing trunks approached the tractor, shining his torch on it and checking the hawser and the winch. The winch had not been in use lately, but Toby had given it a good oiling and it seemed to be perfectly sound. He unwound a good length of hawser and looped it loosely round the drum. All this while Dora was hovering about behind him. At such a moment, attached as he was to her, he envied his medieval prototype who at least did not have to deal with both his lady and his adventure at the same time. For most of the operation Dora was useless.

'Just stand by near the water, would you,' said Toby, 'and do what I tell you.' He took a deep breath. He felt himself magnificent. He started the engine of the tractor.

A shattering roar broke the expectant moonlit silence of the wood. Toby could hear Dora's exclamations of dismay. He wasted no time but jumped on to the seat of the tractor, released the clutch, and let the great thing amble slowly in reverse toward the water. He felt love for the tractor, delight and confidence in its strength. He stopped it in the space near the top of the ramp and jumped off. He put the brake well on and began to drag a large log of wood across under the wheels. Dora rushed to help. He left the engine running, judging that a distant sound which continues is less likely to attract attention than an intermittent one. Then holding the end of the hawser, with its stout hook, he began to walk down the ramp.

The water was cold and its chilly touch shocked Toby, making him aware for a moment how completely he was entranced. He gasped, but plunged on till his feet left the stones and he was swimming, holding the hook in one hand. He now knew by heart the geography of the lake floor beyond the ramp. He felt he could almost see the bell. With the rhythmical sound of the tractor in his ears he dived. The hawser was heavy and helped to take him to the bottom, and his hand immediately encountered the mouth of the bell. Trailing the hook on the lake floor, the hawser running loosely through his fingers, he began to fumble towards the other end of the bell to find its great eye. As he did so a sudden consciousness of what he was doing came over him. He made as if to open his mouth and in a moment of panic shot up to the surface letting the hawser drop below him into the mud. Gasping, restored to the now terrifying scene of the moonlit lake and the roar of the engine, he swam back to the ramp.

Dora was standing with her feet in the water. She said something inaudible to him in frantic tones. Toby ignored her and began to drag the hawser in from the bottom. It came slowly, muddily. At last he had the hook in his hand again, and breathing steadily he swam out once more and dived. He grasped the rim of the bell and pulled himself towards it. With his next clutch he had his hand on the eye, his fingers slipping into the wide hole. Clinging on to the bell with one hand he approached the large hook with the other. With a sense of desperate joy he felt the hook pass through the hole.

The Bell

Then he rose, directing himself towards the ramp, and holding the hawser as taut as possible in his hand. He scrambled out. There was not much slack, he had judged the length needed very well. He pushed Dora out of the way and mounted the tractor. He geared the engine on to the winch and let it turn at a slow pace, first taking in the slack, and ready to switch off hastily if at any moment the bell seemed likely to pull the tractor into the lake. The hawser became taut, and he could feel the direct pull beginning between the tractor and the bell.

The winch came to a standstill. The engine roared, but the power was of no avail. Thinking quickly, Toby switched the power off the winch, moved the tractor a little away from the water, letting the hawser unwind, and brought it back to the tree-trunk in a new position. He switched over again to the winch and the hawser tightened. A heaving struggle began. Although the winch did not yet begin to move, he could feel a colossal agitation at the other end of the line. This was the moment at which the hawser was most likely to break. Toby sent up a prayer. Then he saw with incredulity and wild delight that very slowly the drum was beginning to turn. A fearful dragging could be heard, or perhaps felt, in that pandemonium it was hard to say which, upon the floor of the lake. Enormous muddy bubbles were breaking the surface. The movement was continuous now. The tractor was drawing the bell somewhat jerkily but steadily towards it as the strong winch turned. Toby could feel the great arching wheels braced against the tree-trunk. Like a live thing the tractor pulled. Then a grinding sound was to be heard: the bell must have reached the stony pile at the bottom of the ramp. Holding his breath Toby kept his eyes fixed on the point at which the thin line of the hawser, silvered by the moonlight, broke the heaving surface of the water. He felt a shock, which was probably the rim of the bell passing over the bottom edge of the ramp, and almost at the same moment, and sooner than he had expected, the hook came into view. Behind it an immense bulk rose slowly from the lake.

Hardly believing his eyes, yet chill with determined concentration, Toby waited until the bell lay upon the ramp, clear of the water, stranded like a terrible fish. He switched the power off the winch, and let the hawser fall slack, making sure that the bell was lodged securely on the gentle slope. Then he jumped down and began to pull the log away from under the wheels. A pale flurry seen from the corner of his eye was Dora still trying to help. He got back on to the roaring tractor, slipped the engine back into its normal gear, and very slowly released the clutch. The tractor bucked for a moment and then the great wheels began to turn and Toby saw the foliage moving past his head. He turned back to look at the bell. The rim was scraping hard on the stone and the upper end just clearing the ground. It jolted over the head of the ramp and the rim bit into the softer surface of the earth. Gathering beneath it a pile of earth and stones it followed the tractor into the darkness of the wood. Already Toby sensed the blackness of the barn roof above him, and he steadied the tractor across the floor and out through the wide door on the opposite side. When he judged that the bell had reached the middle of the barn he stopped the tractor and switched off the engine.

An appalling almost stunning silence followed. Toby sat quite still on the seat of the tractor. Then he breathed out slowly and rubbed his hands over his face and brows. He felt rather as if he would like now to crawl away somewhere and go to sleep. The last few minutes had been too crammed with experience. He began to climb from his seat and was mildly surprised to find that the extreme tension of his muscles had made him stiff. He got down and leaned over to rub his leg. He was amazed to find himself naked except for the bathing trunks.

'Toby, you were marvellous!' said Dora's voice beside him. 'You're an absolute hero. Are you all right? Toby, we've succeeded!'

Toby was in no mood for transports. He sneezed, and said, 'Yes, yes, I'm O.K. Let's look at the thing now. It'll probably turn out to be an old bedstead or something.' He stumbled past the dark shape in the middle of the floor and found his torch. Then he played the light upon it.

The bell lay upon its side, the black hole of its mouth still jagged with mud. Its outer surface, much encrusted with watery growths and shell-like incrustations, was a brilliant green. It lay there, gaping and enormous, and they looked at it in silence. It was a thing from another world.

'Well, good heavens,' said Dora at last. She spoke in a low voice as if awed by the presence of the bell. She reached out cautiously and touched it. The metal was thick, rough, and curiously warm. The thing was monstrous, lying there stranded upon the floor. She said, 'I had no idea it would be so huge.'

'Is it *the* one?' said Toby. He was amazed as he looked at it to think that it had been possible to make so large and inert an object obey his will. It was weird too that a thing so brightly coloured should have come out of so dark a place. He touched it too, almost humbly.

'Bring the torch closer,' said Dora. 'Paul said there were scenes of the life of Christ.'

They bent over the bell together, playing the light closely upon the vivid uneven surface. A little way from the rim it seemed to be divided into sections. Toby clawed with his fingers in the circle of light, pulling off encrusted mud and algae. Something was appearing. 'My God,' said Toby. Eyes stared at them out of square faces and a scene of squat figures was revealed.

'It must be!' said Dora. 'But I don't recognize that. Go on scraping. How grotesque they are. Yes, there's another scene. Why, it's the nativity for sure! Do you see the ox and the ass? And there are people catching fish. And all those men at the table must be having the Last Supper. And here's the crucifixion.'

'And the resurrection,' said Toby.

'There's something written,' said Dora.

Toby turned the light on to the rim of the bell. The words, interspersed with strangely shaped crosses, stood out clearly in the green metal. After a moment he said, 'Yes, it's Latin.'

'Read it out,' said Dora.

Toby read out, *'Vox ego sum Amoris. Gabriel vocor.* "I am the voice of Love. I am called Gabriel."'

'Gabriel!' cried Dora. 'Why, that was its name! Paul told me. It *is* the bell!' She looked up at Toby from where she was kneeling near its mouth. Toby turned the torch on to her. Her hair was wet with lake water and her cheeks were smudged with mud. A dark trickle was finding its way into the bosom of her hastily buttoned dress. Her hands laid upon the bell she blinked in the light, smiling up at Toby.

'Dora!' said Toby. He dropped the torch on the ground where its curtailed arc of light continued to shine. Naked as a fish, Toby felt a miraculous strength twisting inside him. He, and he alone, had pulled the bell from the lake.

The Bell

He was a hero, he was a king. He fell upon Dora, his two hands reaching for her shoulders, his body collapsing upon hers. He heard her gasp and then relax, receiving his weight, her arms passing round his neck. Clumsily, passionately, Toby's hard lips sought her in the darkness. Struggling together they rolled into the mouth of the bell.

As they did so the clapper, moving within the dark metal hollow, struck violently against the side, and a muted boom arose and echoed away across the lake whose waters had now once again subsided to rest.

* * *

Michael Meade was awakened by a strange hollow booming sound which seemed to come from the direction of the lake. He lay rigid for a moment listening anxiously to the silence that succeeded the sound, and then got out of bed and went to the open window. It was a bright moonlight night and the moon, full and risen high, cast a brilliance which was almost golden on the tranquil expanse of the water. Michael rubbed his eyes, amazed at the speed of his reaction, and still wondering whether he was awake or dreaming. He stood a while watching the quiet scene. Then he turned the light on and looked at his watch which said ten past three. He felt wide awake now and anxious. He sat on the edge of his bed, tense, listening. He had again that strange sense of impending evil. He sniffed, wondering if there were in fact some nauseating smell pervading the room. He remembered that just before he woke he had been dreaming of Nick.

He was too uneasy to sleep again. The noise he had

heard – he was sure this time that he had really heard it – unnerved him. He had vague memories of stories heard in childhood of noises coming out of the sea to portend disaster. He got dressed, intending to make a tour round the house to see that everything was all right. Strange visions afflicted him of finding that the Court was on fire. He turned the light on in the corridor and walked about a bit. Everything was as usual and no one else seemed to be stirring. He went out on to the balcony and looked round him in the splendid night. He saw at once in the distance that there was a light on in the Lodge. Nick at least was up. Or Toby. He scanned the banks of the lake as far as he could see in either direction. All seemed quiet.

Then he noticed something moving, and saw that a figure was walking along the path that led from the causeway to the ferry. He was clearly revealed now, with a long shadow, the figure of a man walking purposefully. Michael felt an immediate thrill of alarm and apprehension. He watched for a moment and then hurried down the steps and across the terrace to intercept the night wanderer, whoever he might be. The man, seeing Michael coming, stopped abruptly and waited for him to come nearer. Straining his eyes in the moonlight, and almost running now, Michael approached; and then recognized the figure, with mingled disappointment and relief, as Paul Greenfield.

'Oh, it's you,' said Paul.

'Hello,' said Michael. 'Anything the matter?'

'Dora's vanished,' said Paul. 'I woke up and found her gone. Then when she didn't come back I thought I'd go and look for her.'

'Did you hear an extraordinary sound just now?' said Michael.

The Bell

'Yes,' said Paul. 'I was just falling into a gorse bush at the time. What was it?'

'I don't know,' said Michael. 'It sounded like a bell.'

'A *bell*?' said Paul.

'I see there's a light on in the Lodge,' said Michael.

'That's just where I'm going now,' said Paul. 'I thought Dora might be there. Or if she isn't, I'd be interested to know whether Master Gashe is in his bed. Have you noticed those two rushing round together like a pair of conspirators?'

Michael who had indeed on his own account noticed this said, 'No, I noticed nothing.' They began to walk towards the ferry.

'Do you mind if I come with you?' said Michael. He too felt an intense desire to know what was going on at the Lodge.

Paul seemed to have no objection. They crossed in the boat and began to hurry along the path to the avenue. The light beaconed out clearly now. They passed out of the moonlight into the darkness of the trees and felt the firm gravel of the drive underfoot.

As they neared the Lodge they saw that the door was open. The light from the living-room, through the door and the uncurtained windows, revealed the gravel, the tall grasses, the iron rails of the gate. Paul, beginning to run, reached the doorway before Michael. He pushed his way in without knocking. Michael hastened after him, looking over his shoulder.

The scene in the living-room was peaceful and indeed familiar. The usual litter of newspapers covered the floor and the table. The stove was lit and Murphy was lying stretched out beside it. Behind the table, in his usual place, sat Nick. On the table there was a bottle of whisky and a glass. There was no one else to be seen.

Paul seemed nonplussed. He said to Nick, 'Oh, good evening, Fawley.' Paul was the only person who addressed Nick in this manner. 'I was just wondering if my wife was here.'

Nick, who had shown a little surprise, Michael thought, at his own arrival, was now smiling in his characteristic grimacing manner. With his greasy curling hair and his grimy white shirt, unbuttoned, and his long legs sticking straight out under the table he looked like some minor Dickensian rake. He reached for the bottle, and raised his eyebrows, possibly to express the slightly patronizing amazement, which Michael had often felt, too, at the frankness with which Paul revealed his matrimonial difficulties.

'Good morning, Greenfield,' said Nick. 'No, she ain't here. Why should she be? Have a drink?'

Paul said irritably, 'Thank you, no, I never take whisky.'

'Michael?' said Nick.

Michael jumped at his name, and took a moment to realize what Nick meant. He shook his head.

'Is Toby upstairs?' said Paul.

Nick went on smiling at him and kept him waiting for the answer. Then he said, 'No. He ain't here either.'

'Do you mind if I look upstairs?' said Paul. He pushed through the room.

Michael, who was just beginning to realize that Paul was in fact in a frantic state, found himself left alone with Nick. He cast a glance at him without smiling. He was fairly frantic himself.

Nick smiled. 'One of the deadly sins,' he said.

'What?' said Michael.

'Jealousy,' said Nick.

The Bell

Paul's feet were heard on the stairs. He came blundering back into the living-room.

'Satisfied?' said Nick.

Paul did not reply to this, but stood in the middle of the room, his face wrinkled up with anxiety. He said to Nick.

'Do you know where he is?'

'Gashe?' said Nick. 'No. I am not Gashe's keeper.'

Paul stood irresolutely for a moment, and then turned to go. As he passed Michael he paused. 'It was odd what you said about a bell.'

'Why?' said Michael.

'Because there's a legend about this place. I meant to tell you. The sound of a bell portends a death.'

'Did you hear that strange sound a little while ago?' Michael asked Nick.

'I heard nothing,' said Nick.

Paul stumped out of the door and began walking back along the drive.

Michael stayed where he was. He felt very tired and confused. If Nick would only have stayed quiet he would like to have sat with him for a while in silence. But those were all mad thoughts.

'Have a drink?' said Nick.

'No thanks, Nick,' said Michael. He found it very hard not to look at Nick. A solemn face seemed hostile and a smiling face provocative. He cast a rather twisted smile in his direction and then looked away.

Nick got up and came towards Michael. Michael stiffened as he approached. For a moment he thought Nick was going to come right up to him and touch him. But he stopped about two feet away, still smiling. Michael looked at him fully now. He wished he could drive that smile off his face. He had a strong impulse to reach out and put his two hands on Nick's shoulders. The sound that had awakened him, the moonlight, the madness of the night, made him feel suddenly that communication between them was now permitted. His whole body was aware, almost to trembling, of the proximity of his friend. Perhaps after all this was the moment at which he should in some way remove the barrier which he had set up between them. No good had come of it. And the fact remained, as he deeply realized in this moment, for whatever it meant and whatever it was worth, that he loved Nick. Some good might yet come of that.

'Nick,' Michael began.

Speaking almost at the same time Nick said, 'Don't you want to know where Toby is?'

Michael flinched at the question. He hoped his face was without expression. He said, 'Well, where is he?'

'He's in the wood making love to Dora,' said Nick.

'How do you know?'

'I saw them.'

'I don't believe you,' said Michael. But he did believe. He added, 'Anyway, it's no business of mine.' That was foolish, since on any view of the matter it was his business.

Nick stepped back to sit in a leisurely way on the table, watching Michael and still smiling.

Michael turned and went out, banging the door behind him.

* * *

'Well, and what happened then?' said James Tayper Pace.

The Bell

It was the next morning, and James and Michael were in the greenhouse picking tomatoes. The good weather was breaking, and although the sun still shone, a strong wind, which had arisen towards dawn, was sweeping across the kitchen garden. The tall lines of runner-beans swayed dangerously and Patchway went about his work with one hand clutching his hat. Inside the greenhouse however all was quiet and the warm soil-scented air and the firm red bunches of fruit made an almost tropical peace. Today all routines were altered because of the arrival of the bell, which was due to be delivered some time during the morning. The Bishop was to make his appearance during the afternoon, and after the baptism service would partake of tea with the community, a meal which, in the form of a stand-up buffet, was being planned on a grand scale by Margaret Strafford. He would then stay the night and officiate at the more elaborate rites on the following morning.

'Nothing happened,' said Michael. 'After I met Paul I went with him to the Lodge. Toby wasn't there. We came away again and I went back to bed and Paul wandered off to do some more searching. When I saw him this morning he said that he went back to his room about three-quarters of an hour later and found Dora there. She said it was such a hot night she'd been for a walk round the lake.'

James laughed his gruff booming laugh and lined another box with newspaper. 'I'm afraid,' he said, 'that Mrs Greenfield is what is popularly called a bitch. I'm sorry to say so, but one must call things by their names. Only endless trouble comes from not doing so.'

'You say you didn't hear any noise in the night?' said Michael.

'Not a sound. But I'm so dead tired these days I sleep

like the proverbial log. The last trump wouldn't wake me. They'd have to send a special messenger!'

Michael was silent. Nimbly he fingered the glowing tomatoes, warm with the sun and firm with ripeness. The boxes were filling fast.

James went on, 'One oughtn't to laugh, of course. I can't believe anything serious happened last night. Paul is a dreadful alarmist and a chronically jealous man. All the same, we ought to keep an eye on things; and I think it's regrettable that they've gone as far as they have.'

'Yes,' said Michael.

'I'm sure Toby and Dora have done nothing but run around together like a couple of youngsters,' said James. 'Dora is just about his mental age anyway. But with a woman like that you can't be sure that there wouldn't be some gesture, some word that might upset him. After all, he's not like my young East-enders. He's been a very sheltered child. A boy's first intimations of sex are so important, don't you think? And tampering with the young's a serious matter.'

'Quite,' said Michael.

'It's a pity,' said James, 'that we seem to have made so little impression on Mrs G. I wish she'd have a talk with Mother Clare. I'm sure it'd straighten her out a bit. That girl's just a great emotional mess at present. I feel we've let Paul down rather.'

'Possibly,' said Michael.

'And you know, we're fully responsible for the boy,' said James. 'He came here, after all, as a sort of retreat, a preparation for Oxford. Of course there's nothing seriously amiss in his rampaging around with Dora in a companionable way – but I think someone ought to put in a word.'

'Who to?' said Michael.

The Bell

'To Dora, I'd say,' said James. 'Appealing to Dora's better nature may turn out to be a difficult operation. I fear that girl is a blunt instrument at the best of times – and also resembles the *jeune homme de Dijon qui n'avait aucune religion!* But even if she doesn't care about her husband's blood pressure she ought to show some respect for the boy. She should see *that* point. Suppose you gave her a little kindly admonition, Michael?'

'Not me,' said Michael.

'Well, how about Margaret?' said James. 'Margaret is such a motherly soul and Dora seems to like her – and maybe that sort of advice would come better from a woman. Why, here is Margaret!'

Michael looked up sharply. Margaret Strafford could be seen running along the concrete path towards them her full skirt flapping in the wind. Michael interpreted her portentous haste immediately and his heart sank.

Margaret threw open the door, letting in a great blast of chill air. 'Michael,' she cried, delighted with her commission, 'the Abbess wants to see you at once!'

'I say, you *are* in luck!' said James. Their two bright amiable faces looked at him enviously.

Michael washed his hands at the tap in the corner of the greenhouse and dried them on his handkerchief. 'Sorry to leave you with the job,' he said to James. 'Excuse me if I dash.'

He set off at a run down the path which led along behind the house to the lake. It was customary to run when summoned by the Abbess. As he turned to the left towards the causeway the full blast of the wind caught him. It was almost blowing a gale. Then he saw, looking across the other reach of the lake, that an enormous lorry had just emerged from the trees of the avenue and was proceeding at a slow pace along the open part of the drive. It must be the bell. He should have been interested, excited, pleased. He noted its arrival coldly and forgot it at once. He turned on to the causeway. He felt certain that the Abbess must know all about Toby. It was irrational to think this. How could she possibly have found out? Yet it was astonishing what she knew. Breathlessly, as he reached the wooden section in the centre of the causeway, he slowed down. His footsteps echoed hollow upon the wood. He had not expected this summons. He felt as if he were about to undergo some sort of spiritual violence. He felt closed, secretive, unresponsive, almost irritated.

At the corner of the parlour building Sister Ursula was waiting. She always acted watchdog to audiences with the Abbess. Her large commanding face beamed approval at Michael from some way off. She saw the summons as a sign of special grace. After all, interviews with the Abbess were coveted by all and granted only to a few.

'In the first parlour,' she said to Michael, as he passed her mumbling a salutation.

Michael burst into the narrow corridor and paused a moment to get his breath before opening the first door. The gauze panel was drawn across on his side in front of the grille and there was silence beyond. It was usual for the person summoned to arrive first. Michael pulled back the panel on his side to reveal the grille and the second gauze panel on the far side which screened the opposite parlour inside the enclosure. Then he straightened his shirt collar – he was wearing no tie – buttoned up his shirt, smoothed down his hair, and made a strenuous effort to become calm. He stood, he could not bring himself to sit down, looking at the blank face of the inner panel.

The Bell

After a minute or two during which he could feel the uncomfortable violence of his heart he heard a movement and saw a dim shadow upon the gauze. Then the panel was pulled open and he saw the tall figure of the Abbess opposite to him, and behind her another little room exactly similar to his. He genuflected in the accustomed way and waited for her to sit down. Slightly smiling she sat, and motioned him to be seated too. Michael pulled his chair well up to the grille and sat down on the edge of it sideways so that their two heads were close together.

'Well, my dear son, I'm glad to see you,' said the Abbess in the brisk voice with which she always opened an audience. 'I hope I haven't chosen the most dreadfully inconvenient time? You must be so busy today.'

'It's perfectly all right,' said Michael, 'it's a good time for me.' He smiled at her through the bars. His irritation, at least, was gone, overwhelmed by the profound affection which, mingled with respect and awe, he felt for the Abbess. Her bright, gentle, authoritative, exceedingly intelligent face, its long dry wrinkles as if marked with a fine tool, the ivory light from her wimple reflected upon it, reminiscent of some Dutch painting, reminded him of his mother, so long ago dead.

'I'm in a dreadful rush myself,' said the Abbess. 'I just felt I wanted to see you. It's been ages now, hasn't it? And there are one or two little business details. I won't keep you long.'

Michael felt relieved by this exordium. He had been afraid of being in some way hauled over the coals: and this was not the moment at which he wanted an intimate talk with the Abbess. In his present state he felt that any pressure from her would tip him over into a morass of profitless self-accusation. Taking courage from her business-like tone he said, 'I think everything's in train for tonight and tomorrow. Margaret Strafford has been doing marvels.'

'Bless her!' said the Abbess. 'We're all so excited, we can hardly wait for tomorrow morning. I believe the Bishop is arriving this afternoon? I hope I shall catch a glimpse of him before he goes. He's such a busy man. So good of him to give us his time.'

'I hope he won't think we're a lot of ineffectual muddlers,' said Michael. 'I'm afraid the procession tomorrow may be a bit wild and impromptu. There's plenty of goodwill, but not much spit and polish!'

'So much the better!' said the Abbess. 'When I was a girl I often saw religious processions in Italy and they were usually quite chaotic, even the grand ones. But it seemed to make them all the more spontaneous and alive. I'm sure the Bishop doesn't want a drill display. No, I've no doubt tomorrow will be splendid. What I really wanted to ask you about was the financial question.'

'We've drafted the appeal,' said Michael, 'and we've made a list of possible Friends of Imber. I'd be very grateful if you'd cast your eye over both documents. I thought, subject to your views, we'd send the appeal out about a fortnight from now. We can cyclostyle it ourselves at the Court.'

'That's right,' said the Abbess. 'I think, for a cause of this kind, not a printed appeal. After all, it's something quite domestic, isn't it? There are times when money calls to money, but this isn't one of them. We're only writing to our friends. I'd like to see what you've done, if you'd send it in today by Sister Ursula. We can probably add some names to the list. I wonder what sort of publicity our bell will get? That might help in some

The Bell

quarters, mightn't it? I see no harm in the world being reminded, very occasionally, that we exist!'

Michael smiled. 'I thought of that too,' he said. 'That's why I don't want the appeal delayed. We won't have any journalists present of course. Not that any have shown signs of wanting to turn up. But I've prepared a hand-out for the local press, and a shorter one for the national press. I talked the wording over with Mother Clare. And I've asked Peter to take some photographs which we might send along as well.'

'Well done,' said the Abbess. 'I just can't think how you find the time to do all the things you do do. I hope you aren't overworking. You look rather pale.'

'I'm in excellent health,' said Michael. 'There'll be a let-up in a week or two anyway. I'm sure the others are working far harder than I am. James and Margaret simply never stop.'

'I'm worried about your young friend at the Lodge,' said the Abbess.

Michael breathed in deeply. That was it after all. He could feel a hot blush spreading up into his face. He kept his eyes away from the Abbess, fixing them on one of the bars beyond her head. 'Yes?' he said.

'I know it's very difficult,' said the Abbess, 'and of course I know very little about it, but I feel he's not exactly getting what he came to Imber to get.'

'You may be right,' said Michael tonelessly, waiting for the direct attack.

'I expect it's largely his own fault,' said the Abbess, 'but he is dreadfully out of things, isn't he? And will be more so when Catherine is in with us.'

Michael realized with a shock of relief that the Abbess was speaking of Nick, not of Toby. He turned to look at her. Her eyes were sharp. 'I know,' he said. 'It's been very much on my mind. I ought to have done more about it. I'll see to it that something *is* done. I'll put someone, perhaps James, quite seriously on his tail. We'll move him up to the house and just make him join in somehow. But as you say, it's not easy. He doesn't want to work. I'm afraid he's only putting in a little time here. He'll soon be off to London.'

'He's a *mauvais sujet* to be sure,' said the Abbess, 'and that's all the more reason for us to take trouble. But a man like that does not come to a place like this for fun. Of course he came to be near Catherine. But the fact that he wants to be near her *now*, and the fact that he wants to stay in the community and not in the village, are at least suggestive. We cannot be certain that there is not some genuine grain of hope for better things. And if I may say so, the person who ought to be, as you express it, on his tail, is not James, but you.'

Michael sustained her gaze which was quizzical rather than accusing. 'I find him difficult to deal with,' he said. 'But I'll think carefully about it.' He felt an increased determination not to be frank with the Abbess.

The Abbess studied his face. 'I confess to you,' she said, 'that I feel worried and I'm not quite sure why. I feel worried about him and I feel worried about you. I wonder if there's anything you'd like to tell me?'

Michael held on to his chair. From behind her the spiritual force of the place seemed to blow upon him like a gale. It was ironical, he reflected, that when he had wanted to tell the Abbess all about it she had not let him and now when she wanted to know he would not tell her. The fact was, he wanted her advice but not her absolution; and he could not ask the one without seeming to ask the other. Not that the Abbess would be tolerant. But he shied away almost with disgust from the idea of revealing to her his pitiable state of confusion. The story of Nick she almost certainly knew already in outline; what she wanted was to understand his present state of mind, and that would inevitably involve the story of Toby. If he began to tell the whole tale he knew that he could not tell it, now, without an absurd degree of emotion and without indulging in that particular brand of self-pity which he had been used to mistake for penitence. Silence was cleaner, better, in such a case. Looking down he saw, laid along the ledge of the grille, quite near to him like a deliberate temptation, infinitely wrinkled and pale, her hand, which had been covered with the tears of better men than himself. If he were to reach out to that hand he was lost. He averted his eyes and said, 'I don't think so.'

The Abbess went on looking at him for a little while, while he, feeling shrivelled and small and dry, looked at the corner of the room behind her. She said, 'You are most constantly in our prayers. And your friend too. I know how much you grieve over those who are under your care: those you try to help and fail, those you cannot help. Have faith in God and remember that He will in His own way and in His own time complete what we so poorly attempt. Often we do not achieve for others the good that we intend; but we achieve something, something that goes on from our effort. Good is an overflow. Where we generously and sincerely intend it, we are engaged in a work of creation which may be mysterious even to ourselves – and because it is mysterious we may be afraid of it. But this should not make us draw back. God can always show us, if we will, a higher and a better way; and we can only learn to love by loving. Remember that all our failures are ultimately failures in love. Imperfect love must not be condemned and rejected, but made perfect. The way is always forward, never back.'

Michael, facing her now, nodded slightly. He could not trust himself to utter any words after this speech. She turned her hand over, opening the palm towards him. He took it, feeling her cool dry grip.

'Well, I've kept you too long, dear child,' said the Abbess. 'I'd like to see you again in a little while, when this hurly-burly's done. Try not to overwork, won't you?'

Michael bent over her hand. Closing his eyes he kissed it and pressed it to his cheek. Then he raised a calm face to her. He felt obscurely that by his silence he had won a spiritual victory. He felt that he merited her approval. They both rose, and as Michael bowed to her again she closed the gauze panel and was gone.

He stood a while in the silent room looking at the bars of the grille and at the blank shut door of the panel behind them. Then he closed the panel on his side. How well she knew his heart. But her exhortations seemed to him a marvel rather than a practical inspiration. He was too tarnished an instrument to do the work that needed doing. Love. He shook his head. Perhaps only those who had given up the world had the right to use that word.

Edna O'Brien

extract from

Girl With Green Eyes

Caithleen's family invoke everything from the Virgin Mary to their own questionable assumptions concerning their daughter's mental instability in an effort to break off her relationship with a married man. But the attraction between the young Irish girl and the older, cosmopolitan Eugene is only strengthened by opposition.

At tea-time a wind began to rise, and rattled the shutters. Anna rushed out to bring in napkins which she had spread on one of the thorny bushes. A galvanized bucket rolled along the cobbled yard.

I had felt afraid all day, knowing that they were bound to come – but if a mountain storm blew up, it might keep them away. By the morrow I'd be gone.

After tea we sat in the study with a map of London spread on both our knees while he marked various streets and sights for me. I was to go early next morning and he had sent a telegram to Ginger, so that she could meet me.

'We ought to lock the doors,' I said, unnerved by the rattling of shutters.

'All right,' he said, 'we'll lock everything.' And I carried the big flashlamp around while he locked the potting-shed door, the back door, and another side door. The keys had rusted in their locks and he had to tap the bolts with a block of wood to loosen them. Anna and Denis had gone backstairs to their own apartments, and we could hear dance music from their radio.

'Tell them if there's a knock, not to answer it,' I suggested.

'Nonsense,' he said, 'they never come down once they've

gone up at night. They go to bed after the nine-o'clock news.' He was very proud and did not wish to share his troubles with anyone.

'Now the hall door,' I said. We opened it for a minute and looked out at the windy night and listened to the trees groaning.

'Go away from the window, bogy man,' he said as we came in and sat on the couch in front of the study fire. The oak box was stocked with logs and he said that we were perfectly safe and that no one could harm us.

There was a shot-gun in the corner of the hall, and I thought that maybe he should get it to be on the safe side.

'Nonsense,' he said. 'You just want some melodrama. . . .'

I could hear the wind and I imagined that I heard a car driving up to the house; I heard it all the time, but it was only in my imagination. I rubbed his hair and massaged the muscles at the back of his neck, and he said that it was very nice and very comforting.

'We get on well together, you and I,' he said.

'Yes,' I said, and thought how easy it would be, if he said then, I love you, or I could love, or I'm falling in love with you, but he didn't; he just said that we got on well together.

'We only know each other a couple of months,' he said to the fire, as if he had sensed my disappointment. I knew that he believed in the slow, invisible processes of growth, the thing which had to take root first in the lonely, dark part of one, away from the light. He liked to plant trees and watch them grow; he liked our friendship to take its course; he was not ready for me.

'Do you believe in God?' I said abruptly. I don't know why I said it.

'Not when I'm sitting at my own fire. I may do when I'm driving eighty miles an hour. It varies.' I thought it a very peculiar answer, altogether.

'What things are you afraid of?' I wished that somehow he would make some deep confession to me and engross me in his fears so that I could forget my own, or that we could play I-spy-with-my-little-eye, or something.

'Just bombs,' he said, and I thought that a peculiar answer too.

'But not hell?' I said, naming my second greatest fear.

'They'll give me a job making fires in hell, I'm good at fires.' I wondered how his voice could be so calm, his face so still. Sometimes I rubbed his neck and then again I rested my arm and sat very close to him, wondering how I could live without him in London for the while – until things blew over, he said.

'The best thing you can do about hell . . .' he began, but I never heard the end of the sentence, because just then the dog barked in the yard outside. She barked steadily for a few seconds and then let out a low, warning howl that was almost human-sounding. I jumped up.

'Sssh, ssh,' he said, as I stumbled over a tray of tea-things that was on the floor. He ran across and lowered the Tilley lamp; then we waited. Nothing happened, no footsteps, no car, nothing but the wind and the beating rain. Yet, I knew they were coming and that in a moment they would knock on the door.

'Must have been a badger or a fox.' He poured me a drink from the whisky bottle on the gun bureau.

'You look as white as a sheet,' he said, sipping the whisky. Then the dog barked again, loudly and continuously, and I knew by her hysterical sounds that she was trying to leap the double doors in the back yard. We had not locked them. My whole body began to shake and tremble.

'It's them,' I said, going cold all over. We heard boots on the gravel and men talking, and suddenly great banging and tapping on the hall door. The dog continued to bark hysterically, and above the noise of banging fists and wind blowing I heard the beating of my own heart. Knuckles rapped on the window, the shutters rattled, and at the same time the stiff knocker boomed. I clutched Eugene's sleeve and prayed.

'Oh God,' I said to him.

'Open up,' a man's voice shouted.

'They'll break down the door,' I said. Five or six of them seemed to be pounding on it, all at once. I thought that my heart would burst.

'How dare they abuse my door like that,' he said as he moved towards the hall.

'Don't, don't!' I stood in his way and told him not to be mad. 'We won't answer,' I said, but I had spoken too late. One of my people had gone around the back of the house, and we heard the metallic click of the back-door latch being raised impatiently. Then the bold was drawn and I heard Anna say, 'What'n the name of God do you want at this hour of night?'

I suppose that she must have been half asleep and had tumbled down thinking that we had been locked out or that the police had come for me.

I heard the Ferret's voice speak my name. 'We've come to take that girl out of here.'

'I don't know anything about it. Wait outside,' Anna said insolently, and then he must have walked straight past her because she shouted: 'How dare you!' and the sheepdog ran up the passage from the kitchen, yelping. The others were still knocking at the front of the house.

'This is beyond endurance,' Eugene said, and as he went to open the hall door, I ran back into the study, and looked around for somewhere to hide. I crawled under the spare bed hoping that he would bring them to the sitting-room, because he did not like people in the study where he worked. I heard him say:

'I can't answer you that, I'm afraid.'

'Deliver her out,' a voice demanded.

I had to think, to recall who it was.

'Come on now.' It was Andy, my father's cousin, a cattle-dealer. I recalled strange cattle – making the noises which cows make in unfamiliar places – being driven into our front field on the evenings preceding a fair day. Then cousin Andy would come up to the house for tea, and sitting in the kitchen in his double-breasted brown suit he'd discuss the price of heifers with my father. Once he gave me a threepenny bit which was so old and worn that the King had been rubbed off.

'Where is my only child?' my father cried.

She's under the bed, she's suffocating, I said to myself, praying that I would be there only for a second, while Eugene picked up the lamp and brought them across to the sitting-room. Could I then hide in the barn – and take the torch to ward off rats!

'My only child,' my father cried again.

For two pins I'd come out and tell him a thing or two about his only child!

'Who are you looking for?' Eugene said. 'We'll confer in the other room.'

But my father had noticed the fire, and with a sinking feeling I heard them all troop into the study. Someone sat on the bed; the spring touched my back, and smelling cow-dung from his boots, I guessed that it was cousin Andy. I recognized two other voices – Jack Holland's and the Ferret's.

'Don't you think it is a little late in the day for social calls?' Eugene said.

'We want that poor, innocent girl,' cousin Andy said – he, the famed bachelor, who had spoken only to cows and bullocks all his life, bullying them along the road to country fairs. 'Hand the girl over, and by God if there's a hair astray on her, you'll pay dear for it,' he shouted, and I imagined how he looked with his miser's face and a mean little mouth framed by a red moustache. He always had to carry stomach mixture with him everywhere, and had once raised his hand to my mother because she hinted about all the free grazing he took from Dada. On that occasion my father in his one known act of chivalry said, 'If you lay a finger on my missus, I'll lay you out.'

'This is outrageous,' Eugene said.

Various matches were struck – they were settling in.

'Allow me,' Jack Holland said, proceeding to make introductions, but he was shouted down by my father.

'A divorced man. Old enough to be her father. Carrying off my little daughter.'

'To set the record straight I did not bring her here, she came,' Eugene said.

I thought, he's going to let me down, he's going to send me away with them; my mother was right, 'Weep and you weep alone.'

'You got her with dope. Everyone knows that,' my father said.

Eugene laughed. I thought how odd, and immoral, he

must look to them, in his corduroy trousers and his old check shirt. I hoped that all his buttons were done up. My nose began to itch with the dust.

'You're her father?' Eugene said.

'Allow me,' Jack Holland said again, and this time he performed the introductions. I wondered if it was *he* who had betrayed me.

'Yes, I'm her father,' Dada said, in a doleful voice.

'Go on now and get the girl,' Andy shouted.

I began to tremble anew. I couldn't breathe. I would suffocate under those rusty springs. I would die while they sat there deciding my life. I would die – with Andy's dungy boots under my nose. It was ironic. My mother used to scrub the rungs of the chair after his visits to our house. I said short prayers and multiplication-tables and the irregular plural of Latin nouns – anything that I knew by heart – to distract myself. I thought of a line from *Julius Caesar* which I had once recited, wearing a red nightdress, at a school concert – 'I see thee still and on thy blade and dudgeon gouts of blood. . . .'

'Are you a Catholic?' the Ferret asked, in a policeman's voice.

'I'm not a Catholic,' Eugene answered.

'D'you go to Mass?' my father asked.

'But, my dear man –' Eugene began.

'There's no "my dear man". Cut it out. Do you go to Mass or don't you? D'you eat meat on Fridays?'

'God help Ireland,' Eugene said, and I imagined him throwing his hands up in his customary gesture of impatience.

'None of that blasphemy,' cousin Andy shouted, making a noise as he struck his fist into his palm.

'What about a drink to calm us down?' Eugene suggested, and then, sniffing, he added, 'Perhaps better not – you seem to have brought enough alcohol with you.'

I could smell their drink from under the bed now, and I guessed that they had stopped at every pub along the way to brace themselves for the occasion. Probably my father had paid for most of it.

'Well . . . a sip of port wine all round might be conducive to negotiation,' Jack Holland suggested in his soft, mannerly way.

'Could I have a drink of water – to take an aspirin?' my father said.

'Good idea. I'll join you in an aspirin,' Eugene said, and I thought for a second that things were going to be all right. Water was poured. I closed my eyes to pray, dropped my forehead on to the back of my hand, and gasped. My face was damp with cold sweat.

'I would like you to realize that your daughter is escaping from *you*. I'm not abducting her. *I'm* not forcing her – she is running away from you and your way of living . . .' Eugene began.

'What the hell is he talking about?' Andy said.

'The tragic history of our fair land,' Jack Holland exclaimed. 'Alien power sapped our will to resist.'

'They get girls with dope,' the Ferret said. 'Many an Irish girl ends up in the white-slave traffic in Piccadilly. Foreigners run it. All foreigners.'

'Where's your wife, Mister? Would you answer that?' Andy said.

'And what are you doing with my daughter?' my father asked fiercely, as if recollecting what they had come for.

'I'm not *doing* anything with her,' Eugene said, and I thought, he has shed all responsibility for me, he does not love me.

'You're a foreigner,' Andy said contemptuously.

'Not at all,' Eugene said pleasantly. 'Not at all as foreign as *your* tiny, blue, Germanic eyes, my friend.'

'What are your intentions?' my father asked abruptly. And then he must have drawn the anonymous letter from his pocket, because he said, 'There's a few things here would make your hair stand on end.'

'He hasn't much hair, he's near bald,' the Ferret said.

'I haven't any *intentions*; I suppose in time I would like to marry her and have children. . . . Who knows?'

'Ah, the patter of little feet,' said Jack Holland idiotically, and Dada told him to shut up and stop making a fool of himself.

He doesn't really want me, I thought as I took short, quick breaths and said an Act of Contrition, thinking that I was near my end. I don't know why I stayed under there, it was stifling.

'Would you turn?' my father said, and of course Eugene did not know what he meant by that.

'Turn?' he asked, in a puzzled voice.

'Be a Catholic,' the Ferret said. And then Eugene sighed and said, 'Why don't we all have a cup of tea?' And Dada said, 'Yes, yes.'

It will go on all night and I'll be found dead under this bed, I thought as I wished more and more that I could scratch a place between my shoulder-blades which itched terribly.

When he opened the door to fetch some tea he must have found Anna listening at the keyhole, because I heard him say to her, 'Oh Anna, you're here, can you bring us a tray of tea, please?' And then he seemed to go out of the room, because suddenly they were all talking at once.

'She could have got out the back way,' my father said.

'Get tough, boy, get tough,' Andy said. 'Follow him out, you fool, before he makes a run for it.'

'Poor Brady,' the Ferret said when Dada had apparently gone out, 'that's the thanks he gets for sending that little snotty-nose to a convent and giving her a fine education.'

'She was never right, that one,' cousin Andy said, 'reading books and talking to trees. Her mother spoilt her. . . .'

'Ah, her dear mother,' said Jack Holland, and while he raved on about Mama being a lady, the other two passed remarks about the portrait of Eugene over the fire.

'Look at the nose of him – you know what he is? They'll be running this bloody country soon,' Andy said.

'God 'tis a bloody shame, ruining a girl like that,' Andy said, and I thought how baffled they'd be if they had known that I was not seduced yet, even though I had slept in his bed for two whole nights.

I heard the rattle of cups as Eugene and my father came back.

'How much money do you earn in a year?' my father asked, and I knew how they would sneer if they heard that he made poky little films about rats, and sewerage.

'I earn lots of money,' Eugene lied.

'You're old enough to be her father,' Dada said. 'You're nearly as old as myself.'

'Look,' Eugene said after a minute, 'where is all this ill-temper going to get us? Why don't you go down to the village and stay in the hotel for the night, then come up in the morning and discuss it with Caithleen. She won't be so frightened in the morning and I will try and get her to agree to seeing you.'

'Not on your bloody life,' cousin Andy said.

'We'll not go without her,' my father added threateningly, and I lost heart then and knew that there was no escape. They would find me and pull me forth. We would go out in the wind and sit in the Ferret's car and drive all night, while they abused me. If only Baba was there, she'd find a way. . . .

'She's over twenty-one, you can't force her,' Eugene said, 'not even in Ireland.'

'Can't we? We won our fight for freedom. It's our country now,' Andy said.

'We can have her put away. She's not all there,' my father said.

'Mental,' the Ferret added.

'What about that, Mister?' cousin Andy shouted. 'A very serious offence having to do with a mentally affected girl. You could get twenty years for that.'

I gritted my teeth, my head boiled – why was I such a coward as to stay under there? They'd make a goat ashamed. Tears of rage and shame ran over the back of my hand and I wanted to scream, I disown them, they're nothing to do with me, don't connect me with them, but I said nothing – just waited.

'Go and get her,' my father said. *'Now!'* And I imagined the spits that shot out of his mouth in anger.

'You heard what Mr Brady said,' cousin Andy shouted, and he must have risen from the bed because the springs lifted. I knew how ratty he must look with his small blue eyes, his red moustache, his stomach ulcer.

'Very well then,' Eugene said, 'she's in my legal care. A guest in my house. When she leaves she will do so of her own free will. Leave my house or I'll telephone for the police.' I wondered if they'd notice that there *was* no phone.

'You heard me,' Eugene said, and I thought, oh God he'll get hit. Didn't he know how things ended – 'Man in hospital with fifty-seven penknife wounds'. I started to struggle out, to give myself up.

I heard the first smack of their fists and then they must have knocked him over because the Tilley lamp crashed and the globe broke into smithereens.

I screamed as I got out and staggered up. Flames from the wood fire gave enough light for me to see by. Eugene was on the floor, trying to struggle up and Andy and the Ferret were hitting and kicking him. Jack Holland tried to hold them back, and my father, hardly knowing what he was doing, held the back of Jack Holland's coat, saying, 'Now Jack, now Jack, God save us, now Jack – oh Jack –'

My father saw me suddenly and must have thought that I had risen up from the ground – my hair was all tossed and there was fluff and dust on me. He opened his mouth so wide that his loose dental-plate dropped on to his tongue. They were cheap teeth that he had made by a dental mechanic.

'I didn't do it, I didn't do it, Maura,' he whispered, and backed away from me clutching his teeth. Long after, I realized that he thought I was Mama risen from her grave in the Shannon lake. I must have looked like a ghost; my face daubed with tears and grey dust, my hair hanging in my eyes.

I shouted at the Ferret to stop, when the door burst open and the room lit up with a great red and yellow flash, as Anna had fired the shot-gun at the ceiling. The thunder-clap made me stagger back against the bed with my head numb and singing. I tried to stay still, waiting to die. I thought I'd been shot, but it was only the shock of the explosion in my ears. The black smoke of gunpowder entered our throats and made me cough. Jack Holland was on his knees, praying and coughing, while Andy and the Ferret were turned to the door with their hands to their ears. My father leaned over a chair gasping, and Eugene moaned on the floor and put his hand to his bleeding nose. Shattered plaster fell down all over the carpet and the white dust mixed with gun smoke. The smell was awful.

'There's another one in it, I'll blow your brains out,' Anna said. She stood at the study door, in her nightdress, holding Eugene's shot-gun. Denis stood beside her with a lighted Christmas candle.

'Out you get,' she said to them, holding the gun steadily up.

'By God, I'm getting out of this,' the Ferret said. 'These people would kill you!' I went to Eugene, who was still sitting on the floor with blood coming from his nose. I put my handkerchief to it.

'Dangerous savages,' my father said, his face white, holding his teeth in one hand. 'She might have killed us.'

'I'll blow your feet off if you don't clear out of here,' Anna said in a quivering voice.

'Get out,' Eugene said to them as he stood up. His shirt was torn. 'Get out. Go. Leave. Never come inside my gates again.'

'Have you a drop of whisky?' my father said, shakily, putting his hand to his heart.

'No,' Eugene said. 'Leave my house, immediately.'

'A pretty night's work, a pretty night's work,' Jack Holland said sadly, as they left. Anna stood to one side to let them pass and Denis opened the hall door. The last thing I saw was the Ferret's hooked iron hand being shaken back at us.

Eugene slammed the door and Denis bolted it. I collapsed on to the bed, trembling.

'That's the way to handle them,' Anna said, as she put the gun on the table.

'You saved my life,' Eugene said, and he sat on the couch and drew up the leg of his trousers. There was blood on his shin, where he had been kicked. His nose also was bleeding.

'I'm sorry, I'm sorry,' I said between sobs.

'Oh tough men, tough men,' Denis said solemnly as we heard them outside arguing, and the dog barking from the back yard.

'Get some iodine,' Eugene said. I went upstairs but couldn't find it, so Anna had to go and get it, along with a clean towel and a basin of water. He lay back on the armchair, and I opened his shoe-laces and took off his shoes.

'Wh'ist,' Denis said. We heard the car drive away.

Anna washed the cuts on Eugene's face and legs. He squirmed with pain as she swabbed on iodine.

'I shouldn't have hidden,' I said, handing him a clean handkerchief from the top drawer of his desk, where he kept them. 'Oh, I shouldn't have come here.'

Through the handkerchief he said, 'Go get yourself a drink. It will help you to stop shaking. Get me one too.'

After a while the nose-bleed stopped and he raised his head and looked at me. His upper lip had swollen.

'It was terrible,' I said.

'It was,' he said, 'ridiculous. Like this country.'

'Only for me where would we be?' Anna said.

'What about a cup of tea?' he said in a sad voice, and I knew that he would never forget what had happened and that some of their conduct had rubbed off on to me.

*

Girl With Green Eyes

We went to bed late. His shin ached and a cut over his eye throbbed a lot. It was an hour before he went to sleep. I lay for most of the night, looking at the moonlit wall, thinking. Near dawn I found him awake, and looking at me.

'I love you,' I said suddenly. I had not prepared it or anything, it just fell out of my mouth.

'Love!' he said, as if it were a meaningless word, and he moved his head on the pillow to face me. He smiled and closed his eyes, going back to sleep again. What could I do to make up? I wasn't any good in bed, never mind not being able to fire a gun. I'd go back to Baba. I cried a bit, and later got up to make some tea.

Anna was in the kitchen putting on her good shoes and silk stockings, preparing to go to Mass.

'I'm not over it yet,' she said.

'I'll never be over it,' I said, and to myself, they've ruined, and ruined, and ruined me. He'll never look at me again. I'll have to go away.

* * *

She came back from Mass, bubbling over with news.

'They think in the village that you must be a film star,' she said as she took a long hatpin out of her blue hat, removed the hat and stuck the pin through it for the next Sunday. She said that I was the topic of conversation in the three shops. My father and his friends had stopped at the hotel for drinks on the way up.

As she put the frying-pan on the range, I noticed the tracks of mice in the cold fat.

'I expect you'll be leaving today,' she said.

'I expect so.'

It was after ten so I made Eugene's tea and carried it upstairs. Standing for a moment in the doorway with the tray I felt suddenly privileged to be in his room while he slept. The hollows of his cheeks were more pronounced in sleep and his face bore a slight look of pain. He had a nice gentle mouth, his lips handsomely shaped.

I drew back the curtains.

'You'll break the curtain rings,' he said, sitting up. His startled eyes looked twice their normal size.

'Oh, hello,' he said, surprised to see me and then rubbed his lids and probably remembered everything. I put a pullover across his shoulders and knotted the two sleeves under his chin.

'Nice tea,' he said as he lay there, like a Christ, sipping tea; his head resting on the mahogany bedhead.

Anna tapped on the door and burst in, before he had time to cry halt.

'I handed in the telegram – it will go first thing in the morning,' she said. It was to his solicitor.

She told me that my black pudding, below on the range, would be dried up if I didn't go down and eat.

'Black pudding!' he groaned.

'Your nose is a nice sight,' she said to him.

'Probably broken,' he said, without a smile.

'Oh – not broken!' I said.

'Lucky I don't earn my living with my nose,' he said. 'Or make love with it.'

'Hmmmh,' Anna said as she stood in the middle of the room, hands on hips, surveying the tossed bed and my nightdress on a chair.

'All right,' he said to us both, 'trot off,' and I went but she stayed there. I listened outside the door:

'I saved your life, didn't I?'

'You did. I am very grateful to you, Anna. Remind me to strike you a leather medal.'

'Will you loan me fifty pounds?' she asked. 'I want to get a sewing-machine and a few things for the baba. If I had a sewing-machine we could mend all your shirts.'

'We could?' he said, mockingly.

'Will you loan me it?'

'Why don't you say "give me fifty pounds". I know that word "loan" has no meaning here.'

'That's not a nice thing to say.' She sounded offended.

'Anna, I'll give it to you,' he said. 'A reward.'

'Good man. Keep it to yourself, not a word to Denis. If he knew I had fifty pounds he'd buy a bull or something.'

She came out of the room beaming, and I ran away, ashamed at having been caught listening.

'Tell-tale-tattle,' she said as I hurried guiltily along the carpeted passage. 'Come on, I'll race you down the stairs,' and we ran the whole way to the kitchen.

She read the Sunday papers.

'She's the image of Laura,' she said, pointing to an heiress who was reported as being in love with a barber.

'Fitter changes sex,' she read aloud. 'Mother of God, I don't understand people at all. Do they never look at themselves when they're taking their clothes off!'

She read our horoscopes – Denis's, the baby's, Eugene's, mine, and Laura's. She included Laura in everything, so that by the time she went out after lunch with Denis and the baby, I had the feeling that Laura was due back any minute. It was with this unsettling feeling that I made my first tour of the house. Eugene had gone down the fields to look at the ram pump.

There were five bedrooms. The mattresses were folded over and the wardrobes empty, except for wooden hangers. The furniture was old, dark, unmatching, and in lockers beside the beds there were chamber-pots with pink china roses on the insides of them.

In the top drawer of a linen chest I found a silver evening bag with a diary of Laura's inside. The diary had no entries, just names and telephone numbers. There was also a purple evening glove that smelt of stale but wonderful perfume. I fitted on the glove and for some reason my heart began to pound. There was nothing in any of the other drawers, just chalk marks stating the number of each drawer.

Nearing dusk I came downstairs and raised the wick of the hanging lamp which Anna had lit for me before she went out. The rabbit was on the table, as she had left it, skinned and ready to be cooked. Denis had caught it the day before.

'The dinner,' I said aloud, as I got a cookery book and looked up the index under R.

Radishes,
Ragout of Kidneys,
Raisin Bread,
Raisin Pie,
Raisin Pudding,
Rarebit,
Raspberries.

Rabbit was not mentioned. The cookery book had belonged to Laura. Her maiden name and her married name were written in strong handwriting on the fly-leaf.

'The dinner,' I said, to suppress a tear, and then I remembered how Eugene had asked, earlier in the day, 'Can you cook?'

'Sort of,' I had said.

It was a total lie. I never cooked in my whole life, except the Friday Gustav and Joanna went to a solicitor's to make a will. I brought home two fish for lunch, one for Baba, one for me. Baba laid the table while I fried the fish. I knew nothing about cleaning them. I just put the grey, podgy little fish on the big frying-pan and lit the gas under it. Nothing happened for a few minutes and then the side of one fish burst.

'There's a hell of a stink out there,' Baba called from the dining-room.

'It's just the fish,' I said. Both fish had burst by then.

'It's just what?' she said, rushing into the kitchen, holding her nose.

When she saw the mess she simply took hold of the pan and ran down the garden to dump it on Gustav's compost heap.

'Phew,' she said, coming back in to the house. 'You should have been alive when they ate raw cows and bones and things. A bloody savage.' And she put the pan into the sink and ran the tap on it.

We went out to lunch to Woolworths. It was a big thrill being able to march around with a tray, helping ourselves to whatever we fancied – chips, sausages, trifle topped with custard, coffee, a little jug of cream, and lemon meringue pie.

Sitting in the big flagged kitchen I thought of Baba and cried. I missed her. I had never been alone before in my whole life, alone and dependent on my own resources. I thought with longing of all the evenings we went out together, reeking with vanilla essence and good humour. Usually we ended up in the cinema, thrilled by the darkness, and the big screen, with perhaps a choc ice to keep us going.

'Oh God,' I said, remembering Baba, my father, everyone; and I buried my face in my hands and cried, not knowing what I cried for.

Three or four times, I went around the corner of the front drive and leaned on the wet, white gate to see if there was a sign of anybody coming. Nobody came, except a policeman who cycled down the by-road, stood at the gate-lodge for a minute, relieved himself, and cycled off again. He was probably keeping an eye out for poachers.

By the time Eugene came back I had dried my eyes; and I wondered if perhaps he expected me to have left discreetly while he was out.

'I'm still here,' I said.

'I'm glad,' he said as he kissed me. It was dusk and we proceeded to light the Tilley lamps.

As we sat by the study fire he said, 'Ah you poor little lonely bud, it's not a nice honeymoon for you, is it? Think of nice things . . . sunshine, mountain rivers, fuchsia, birds flying . . .'

I lay in his arms and could think only about what would happen next. He had put a record on the wind-up gramophone, and music filled the room. Outside, rain spattered against the window, and the water had lodged on the inner ledge of the window frame. It was very quiet except for the music and the rain. His eyes were closed, as he listened to the music. Music had a strange effect on him: his face softened, his whole spirit responded to it.

'That's Mahler,' he said, just when I expected him to say, 'You can stay or you can go.'

Girl With Green Eyes

'I like songs that have words,' I said to clarify my position. But his eyes were closed and I did not think that he heard me at all. The music still reminded me of birds, birds wheeling out of a bush and startling the mellow hush of a summer evening; crows above an old slate quarry at home, multiplied by their own shadows and by their screaming and cawing. I wondered about my father then, and felt that they would come again, that night.

'But this music has words,' Eugene said, unexpectedly. So he had heard me. 'Words of a more perfect order, this music says things about people, people's lives, progress, wars, hunger, revolution. . . . Music can express with as simple instruments as reeds, the grey bodiless pain of living.'

I thought he must be a little mad to talk like that, especially when I worried about my father coming; and feeling very apart from him, I jumped up, on the excuse that I must look at the dinner. We had put on the rabbit.

It simmered very slowly and the white meat was falling away from the bone, gradually. I thickened the gravy with cornflour but it lumped a lot. Little beads of the flour floated on the surface.

''Twill have to do, I thought, as I went away to put some more powder on my face – the steam of the dinner had reddened my cheeks. When I came back to the room he was reading.

I sat opposite him and stared up at the circle of wrecked plaster – the result of Anna's shot. I thought, when I leave here tomorrow it is this that I will remember, I will always remember it.

'I'll go tomorrow,' I said suddenly. The yellow lamplight shone on his forehead and the reflection of a vase showed in the top part of his lenses. He had put on horn-rimmed glasses.

'*Go?*' he said, raising his eyes from the paper which rested on his knee. 'Where will you go?'

'I might go to London.'

'Do you want to?'

'No.'

'Then why are you going?'

'What else can I do?'

'You can stay.'

'That wouldn't be right,' I said, pleased that it was he who suggested it, and not me.

'Why not?'

'Because it would be throwing myself at you,' I said. 'I'll go away, and then when I'm gone you can write to me, and maybe I'll come back.'

'Supposing I don't want you to go away, then what?' he asked.

'I wouldn't believe it,' I said, and he raised his eyes to the ceiling, in mild irritation. I kept thinking that he asked me to stay because he pitied me, or maybe he was lonely.

'Why do you want me to stay?' I asked.

'Because I like you. I've lived like a hermit for so long, I mean, sometimes I feel lonely.' And he stopped himself suddenly, because he saw my eyes fill with tears.

'Caithleen,' he said softly – he usually said Kate, or Katie – 'Caithleen, stay,' and he put out his hand for mine.

'I'll stay for a week or two,' I said, and he kissed me and said how pleased he was.

We closed the shutters and had dinner. The rabbit meat and potatoes were crushed in the flour-thickened sauce, and the meal tasted very nice. He said that he would buy me a marriage ring, so that Anna and the neighbours would not bother me with questions.

'We can't actually get married, I'm not divorced and there is the child,' he said as he looked away from me, towards the crooked ink on the graph paper of the barograph. I followed his gaze – the jagged ink line suggested to me the jagged lines of all our lives, and I said, to hide my disappointment:

'I don't ever intend to get married, anyhow.'

'We'll see,' he said, and laughed, and then to cheer me up he told me all about his family.

He began – 'My mother is a hypochondriac' – he seemed to have forgotten that I met her – 'and she married my father in those fortunate days when women's legs were covered in long skirts. I say fortunate because her legs are like match-sticks. They met going down Grafton Street. He was a visiting musician – tall, dark, foreign, on his way to buy a French-English dictionary – and very courteously he asked the lady if she could direct him to a bookshop. I' – he tapped his chest – 'am the product of that accidental encounter.'

I laughed and thought how odd that his mother should have charmed the stranger so quickly. He went on to tell me that his father had left them when he was about five. He remembered his father dimly as a man who came home from work with a fiddle and oranges; his mother had worked as a waitress to feed them both, and like nine-tenths of the human race he had had a hard life and an unhappy childhood.

'Your turn,' he said, making an elegant gesture in my direction.

Fragments of my childhood came to mind – eating bread and sugar on the stone step of the back kitchen, and drinking hot jelly which had been put aside to cool.

Sometimes one word can recall a whole span of life. I said, 'Mama was in America when she was young, so she had American words for everything – "apple-sauce", "sweater", "greenhorn", and "dessert".'

I thought of incidental things – of the tinker woman stealing Mama's good shoes from the back-kitchen window, and of Mama having to go to court to give evidence and later regretting it because the tinker woman got a month in jail; of the dog having fits, and of a hundred day-old chickens being killed once by a weasel. In talking of it I could see the place again, the fields green and peaceful, rolling out from the solid cut-stone house; and in summertime, meadowsweet, creamy-white along the headlands, and Hickey humming 'How can you buy Killarney' as he sat like an emperor on the rusted mowing machine, swearing to me that dried cow-dung was sold in the shops as tobacco. I watched the grease settle on the dinner plates and still I sat there talking to Eugene as I had never talked before. He was a good listener. I did not tell him about Dada drinking.

We went to bed long after midnight. He limped upstairs while I followed behind with the Tilley lamp and wondered foolishly if I were likely to drop it and set fire to the turkey-red carpet.

'So we both need a father,' he said. 'We have a common bond.'

He did not make love to me that night. We had talked too much and anyhow he was stiff from having been kicked.

'There's no hurry,' I said.

He petted my stomach and we said warm, comforting things to lull each other to sleep.

Girl With Green Eyes

* * *

On Monday afternoon Eugene's solicitor drove out from Dublin. We had a fire in the sitting-room as we were expecting him. He was an austere, red-haired man with red eyebrows and pale blue eyes.

'And you say these people assaulted Mr Gaillard?' he asked.

'Yes. They did.'

'Did you witness this?'

'No, I was under the bed.'

'The bed?' He raised his sandy eyebrows and looked at me with cold disapproval.

'She's getting it all garbled, she means the spare bed in my study,' Eugene explained quickly. 'She hid under it when they came, because she was afraid.'

'Yes, a bed,' I said, annoyed with both of them.

'I see,' the lawyer said coldly as he wrote something down.

'Are you married, Miss Ah. . .?'

'No,' I said, and caught Eugene smiling at me, as much as to say, You will be.

Then the solicitor asked me what was my father's Christian name and surname, and the names of the others and their proper addresses. I felt badly about being the cause of sending them solicitors' letters but Eugene said that it had to be.

'It is just routine,' the solicitor said. 'We will warn them that they cannot come here again and molest Mr Gaillard. You are quite certain that you are over twenty-one?'

'I am quite certain,' I said, adopting his language.

Then he questioned Eugene, while I sat there looping and unlooping my hanky around my finger. Eugene had made notes of the whole scene which led up to their attacking him. He was very methodical like that.

I brought tea, and fresh scones with apple jelly and cream; but even that did not cheer the solicitor up. He talked to Eugene about dupress trees.

He left shortly after four and I waved to the moving motor-car, out of habit. It was getting dark and the air was full of those soft noises that come at evening – cows lowing, the trees rustling, the hens wandering around, crowing happily, availing themselves of the last few minutes before being shut up for the night.

'Well, that's that,' Eugene said as we came back in to the room, and he felt the teapot to see if the tea had gone cold.

'They won't trouble us again,' he said, pouring a half-cup of strong tea.

'They'll trouble us always,' I said. Recounting the whole incident had saddened me again.

'They'll have to accept it,' he said; but two mornings later I had a wretched letter from my aunt.

Dear Caithleen;
   None of us has slept a wink since, nor eaten a morsel. We are out of our minds to know what's happening to you. If you have any pity in you, write to me, and tell me what are you doing. I pray for you, night and day! You know that you always have a welcome here, when you come back. Write by return and may God and His Blessed Mother watch over you and keep you pure and safe. Your father does nothing but cry. Write to him.
                                   Your aunt Molly

'Don't answer it,' Eugene said. 'Do nothing.'

Girl With Green Eyes

'But I can't leave them worrying like that.'

'Look,' he said, 'this sentimentality will get you nowhere; once you make a decision you must stick to it. You've got to be hard on people, you've got to be hard on yourself.'

It was early morning and we had vowed never to begin an argument before lunch. In the mornings he was usually testy, and he liked to walk alone for an hour or two before talking to me.

'It's cruel,' I said.

'Yes,' he said. 'Kicking me with hobnailed boots is cruel. If you write to them,' he warned, 'they will come here and this time I leave *You* to deal with them.' His mouth was bitter, but that did not stop me from loving him.

'All right,' I said and I went away to think about it. Out in the woods everything was damp; the trees dripped and brooded, the house brooded, the brown mountain hung above me, deep in sullen recollection. It was a lonely place.

In the end I did nothing but have a cry, and by afternoon he was in better humour.

That night, he said, 'We're going into town tomorrow.' And taking a spare wallet from a drawer, he put notes in it and gave it to me. His initials were in gold on the beige-coloured leather, and he said it had been a present from someone.

'We'll buy you a ring and one or two other things,' he said; and then as he had his back to me, hefting a big log on to the fire, I peeped into the wallet and counted the number of notes he had given me. There were twenty in all.

Next day, walking down Grafton Street in a bitter wind,

I felt as if people were going to accuse me of my sin in public.

'Bang, bang,' he said, shooting our imaginary enemies, but I was still afraid, and glad to escape into a jeweller's shop.

We bought a wide gold ring and he put it on me in the shop – 'With this expensive ring, I thee bed,' he said, and I gave a little shiver and laughed.

We bought groceries and wine and two paperback novels and some note-paper. I asked him in the bookshop if he were very rich.

'Not very,' he said. 'The money is nearly gone, but I'll get your dowry or I'll work. . . .' There was some talk about his going to South America in the spring to do a documentary film on irrigation for a chemical company. And already I worried about whether he would bring me or not.

He had a haircut in a place that was attached to a hotel. He left me in the lounge, sipping a whisky and soda, but the minute he was out of sight I gulped the drink down and fled to the cloakroom in case anyone should recognize me. I washed my hands a few times and put on more make-up and each time I washed my hands the attendant rushed over with a clean towel for me. I suppose she thought that I was mad, washing my hands so often, but it passed the time. My ring shone beautifully after washing and I could see myself in it, when I brought my hand close to my face.

I must stop biting my nails, I thought, as I pressed the cuticles back, and remembered the time when I was young and bit my nails and thought foolishly that once I became seventeen I would grow up quite suddenly and be a lady and have long painted nails and no problems.

I gave the grey-haired attendant five shillings and she got very flustered and asked if I wanted change.

'It's all right,' I said. 'I got married today.' I had to say it to someone. She shook my hand and tears filled her kind eyes as she wished me a long life of happiness. I cried a bit myself, to keep her company. She was motherly; I longed to stay there and tell her the truth and have her assurances that I had done the right thing, but that would have been ridiculous, so I came away.

Fortunately I was back in the lounge, sitting in one of the armchairs, when I saw him return. Even after such a short absence as that, I thought when I saw him, how beautiful he is with his olive skin and his prominent jawbones.

'That's done,' he said as he bent down and brushed his cheek against mine. He had had a shave too.

I had put on a lot of perfume and he said how opulent I smelled. Then, as a celebration, we crossed the hall to the empty dining-room and were the first to be served with dinner that night. He ordered a half-bottle of champagne, but when the waiter brought it in a tub of ice it looked so miserable that he sent it back again and got a full bottle. I asked to be given the cork and I still have it. It is the only possession I have which I regard as mine, that cork with its round silvered top.

We touched glasses and he said, 'To us,' and I drank, hoping that I would stay young always.

That night was pleasant. His face looked young and boyish because of the haircut, and I had a new black dress, bought with the money he gave me. In certain lights and at certain moments, most women look beautiful – that light and that moment were mine, and in the wall mirror I saw myself, fleetingly beautiful.

'I could eat you,' he said, 'like an ice-cream,' and later when we were home in bed, he re-said it, as he turned to make love to me. He twisted the wedding ring round and round my finger:

'It's a bit big for you, we'll get a clip on it,' he said.

"Twill do,' I said, being lazy and feeling mellow just then from champagne and the reassurance of his voice in my ear, as he smelled the warm scent of my hair.

'That ring has to last you a long time,' he said.

'How long?'

'As long as you keep your girlish laughter.'

I noticed with momentary regret that he never used dangerous words like 'for ever and ever'.

'Knock, knock, let me in,' he said, coaxing his way gently into my body.

'I am not afraid, I am not afraid,' I said. For days he had told me to say this to myself, to persuade myself that I was not afraid. The first thrust pained, but the pain inspired me and I lay there astonished with myself, as I licked his bare shoulder.

I let out a moan but he kissed it silent and I lay quiet, caressing his buttocks with the soles of my feet. It was very strange, being part of something so odd, so comic: and then I thought of how Baba and I used to hint about this particular situation and wonder about it and be appalled by our own curiosity. I thought of Baba and Martha and my aunt and all the people who regarded me as a child and I knew that I had now passed – inescapably – into womanhood.

I felt no pleasure, just some strange satisfaction that I had done what I was born to do. My mind dwelt on foolish, incidental things. I thought to myself, so this is it; the secret I dreaded, and longed for. . . . All the perfume, and sighs, and purple brassières, and curling-pins in bed, and gin-and-it, and necklaces, had all been for this. I saw it as something comic, and beautiful. The growing excitement of his body enthralled me – like the rhythm of the sea. So did the love words that he whispered to me. Little moans and kisses; kisses and little cries that he put into my body, until at last he expired on me and washed me with his love.

Then it was quiet; such quietness; quietness and softness and the tender limp thing like a wet flower between my legs. And all the time the moon shining in on the old brown carpet. We had not bothered to draw the curtains.

He lay still, holding me in his arms; then tears slowly filled my eyes and ran down my cheeks, and I moved my face sideways so that he should not mistake the tears because he had been so happy.

'You're a ruined woman now,' he said, after some time. His voice seemed to come from a great distance, because in hearing his half-articulated words of love I had forgotten that his speaking voice was so crisp.

'Ruined!' I said, re-echoing his words with a queer thrill.

I felt different from Baba now and from every other girl I knew. I wondered if Baba had experienced this, and if she had been afraid, or if she had liked it. I thought of Mama and of how she used to blow on hot soup before she gave it to me and of the rubber bands she put inside the turn-down of my ankle-socks, to keep them from falling.

He moved over and lay on his back and I felt lonely, without the weight of his body. He lit a candle and from it he lit himself a cigarette.

'Well, a new incumbent, more responsibility, more trouble.'

'I'm sorry for coming like this, without being asked,' I said, thinking that 'incumbent' was an insulting word; I mixed it up with 'encumbrance'.

'It's all right; I wouldn't throw a nice girl like you out of my bed,' he joked, and I wondered what he really thought of me. I was not sophisticated and I couldn't talk very well nor drive a car.

'I'll try and get sophisticated,' I said. I would cut my hair, buy tight skirts and a corset.

'I don't want you sophisticated,' he said, 'I just want to give you nice babies.'

'Babies –' I nearly died when he said that and I sat up and said anxiously, 'but you said that we wouldn't have babies.'

'Not now,' he said, shocked by the sudden change in my voice. Babies terrified me – I remembered the day Baba first told me about breast feeding and I felt sick again, just as I had done that day walking across the field eating a packet of sherbet. I got sick then and hid it with dock leaves while Baba finished the sherbet.

'Don't worry,' he said, easing me back on to the bed, 'don't worry about things like that. It will come out all right in the end. Don't think about it, this is your honeymoon.'

'The bed is all tossed,' I said, in an effort to get my mind on to something simple. But we were too comfortable to get up and rearrange it. He reached to the end of the bed for his shirt and his undervest which was inside it. I helped him put it on and kissed the hollow between his shoulder-blades, recalling their apricot colour in daylight.

'Are you hungry?' I asked, when he lay down. I was wide awake and wanted to prolong the happiness of the night.

Girl With Green Eyes

'No, just sleepy,' he yawned, and lay on the side nearest to me.

'I was a good girl,' I said as he put his hand on my stomach.

'You were a marvellous girl.'

'It's not so terrible.'

'No more old chat out of you,' he said, 'go to sleep.' I could feel my stomach rising and falling gently under the weight of his hand.

'What's your diaphragm?' I asked.

'Meet you outside Jacobs at nine tomorrow night, Miss Potbelly.' He was asleep almost as he spoke, and slowly his hand slid down off my stomach.

I did not expect to sleep but somehow I did.

When I wakened the room was bright and I saw him staring at me.

'Hello,' I said, blinking because of the bright sunshine.

'Kate,' he said, 'you look so peaceful in your sleep. I've been looking at you for the past half-hour. You're like a doll.'

I moved my head over on to his pillow so that our faces were close together.

'Oh,' I said with happiness, and stretched my feet. Our toes stuck out at the end of the tossed bed. He said that we ought to have another little moment before we got up and washed ourselves; and he made love to me very quickly that time, and it did not seem so strange any more.

In the bathroom we washed together. We couldn't have a bath because the range had not been lit and the water was cold. It was freezing cold water which came from a tank up in the woods and I gasped with the cold of it, and the pleasure of it, as he dabbed a wet sponge on my body.

'Don't, don't,' I begged, but he said that it was good for the circulation.

He washed that part of himself without taking off his clothes again; he just rained the rubber tube that was fixed to the end of the cold tap on it, saying that it had had a monk's life.

'Have to make up for lost time,' he said as I dabbed it dry with a clean towel and asked, unwisely, if he loved me.

'Lucky you don't snore,' he said, 'or I'd send you back.'

'Do you love me?' I asked again.

'Ask me that in ten years' time, when I know you better,' he said as he linked me down to breakfast and told Anna that we had got married.

'That's great news,' she said, but I knew that she knew we were lying.

Kathy Page

The Ancient Siddanese

Our guide steps from the shadows to greet us. He looks cool in his loose white suit and dark glasses; we, fresh from the dark-windowed hoverbug, are reeling in the desert heat.

'Ladies and gentlemen, I don't believe in false modesty so I can tell you that you're fortunate to have me as your official guide for today! Do come inside, out of this terrible heat . . .' He makes a little bow as he greets us. We eye the perspex dome behind him suspiciously: the walls of pinkish stone beneath it look squat, plain and, frankly, ugly. It all seems terribly small, set in such an unremitting expanse of space.

'I have spent twenty-three years studying these ruins,' our guide continues as we wipe our brows and sigh in the shade of the reception area. He gives the faintest of smiles, 'And I'm personally responsible for several of the discoveries which have at last made a definitive interpretation of the site possible. Furthermore, I'm one of the few people who can claim to be descended from the ancient Siddanese themselves . . .'

Sidda, I've read in the monograph, has been open to the public for over a hundred years, though even now when everyone travels so incessantly, few people arrive here, it being so remote. That's part of the attraction, I suppose. We're an odd group, about fifteen, all different in our ages, nationalities and states of health. But we're all pilgrims of a kind: the couple bent with age, the father with his two sons, the photographer, the three girls, the woman with the baby and the sun-resistant clothes she has designed herself and constantly recommends to the rest of us.

'Everything covered!' she declares proudly. 'Even the face. No need for all those chemical creams which are probably as bad for you as the sun itself.' She is an optimist, she told me on the way out: 'There's always a way.'

I suspect I am not the only one who wishes that the fat man with the peppering of dark growths creeping across his face and the backs of his hands would wear her outfit – would tuck the thin silvery veil into his collar, sit his hat back on top, slide his hands into the stretch gloves you can't even feel, and let us all forget. Not that it's easy:

'Before we move out on to the site, I must ask you to change into the soft shoes provided, and warn you about the light here. Despite the dome erected over the site to prevent wind-damage and cut out some of the glare, no one should venture outside without some kind of extra protection, particularly on their head and shoulders. The shading and air conditioning are efficient, but deceptive.'

Obediently we re-cream our faces and hands, search for hats and sunglasses in our bags. Except, that is, for Mr Melanoma, who stands defiant and tries unsuccessfully to catch the guide's eye, as if to say man to man – what a silly pointless fuss, shutting the stable door, eh? – and the veiled woman, of course, who quickly checks her baby's layers of protection, then waits – serene, I suppose, though, hidden beneath that silvery curtain, she could be weeping for all I really know.

The Ancient Siddanese

'Terrible thing to do,' someone mutters, poking me in the side, 'exposing a child like that.' I smile and shrug. I don't want to be distracted. I want to get what I came for. Our guide waits, unmoving, until we are finished.

'Despite the discomfort, what you are to see today is certainly absolutely unique and you'll all thank yourselves for having made the effort. Thank you.' He makes his bow again. 'Come over to the observation panel please.'

There is something about our guide that I like. I'm hopeful. It's a great responsibility, I think, watching how he stands, turning his head smoothly from us to the observation panel and back, telling us of the recent history of the site – as great a responsibility, if not greater, than that of the pilot who bore me safely from home to here, speeding between the sun and the too-bright sea. A careless or malicious guide can ruin a trip like this, can leave you with nightmares and a very bitter taste in your mouth.

'Let's begin with an overview –'

The party falls silent. Through the tinted pane that makes all colours seem richer than they are, lending the desert an almost damp appearance, a tempting succulence, we gaze at the pinkish stones that are Sidda. Before this one, there have been other guides here, official and unofficial, and before them of course came explorers, those first archaeologists who sought such places out, and they in turn had guides of their own. Now there is him. It is his job to make Sidda complete for us, to add something to the things we can read in books.

'Sidney Carbourne,' he begins, 'is credited with the discovery of Sidda . . .'

*

Two men, crossing the desert. Both wearing cloths draped over their heads then wrapped around their necks according to the local custom, but one of them a European: Mr Sidney Carbourne, gentleman. Behind the two men, three imported camels, heavily laden – not only with the necessities of life: tents, water, food, but also with notebooks, ink, pens and many lumps of stone.

'What is that, in the distance to the left?' Mr Carbourne asks, gesturing at a small eminence, indistinct and pinkish in the haze of heat.

'To the left, sir?' The other man does not look up; although he knows the desert better than anyone alive, he has never seen it, for he was born blind. Besides, he is old and each journey he makes tires him more. This one he thinks – almost hopes – will be his last.

'That will be the old city of Sidda,' he says. 'I don't recommend we stop: it's little more than a heap of stones.'

'Aha!' Mr Carbourne's voice is always loud, and now it is jubilant as well. Since they set out he has continually suspected his guide of laziness and of trying to cheat him: were the man's eyes not so obviously useless, seamed shut as if by tiny stitches, he would suspect him of counterfeiting his blindness itself. 'But that could be said of many sites. You people are so used to the ancient wonders of your land that you often fail to appreciate them. Let us go to Sidda. Perhaps we can camp there for the night.'

'It's a long way,' the old man says.

'Nonsense!' Mr Carbourne smiles broadly. They have been together four months now. Sometimes he relieves his irritation by making faces at the other man, secure in the knowledge that his rudeness won't be detected. He straightens his back. 'Sidda, by nightfall!' he cries.

'It is further than you think,' the old man replies

The Ancient Siddanese

quietly, 'and I need to rest.' Nonetheless, he alters direction. Mr Carbourne begins to whistle a marching song.

By the time it is dark they are perhaps halfway there.

'I presume,' Mr Carbourne says, 'you can find our way just as well in the dark?'

'Please give me some water,' the old man replies. 'Yes. Besides, we are going the right way. Our mounts will take us there.'

After many hours, through most of which Mr Carbourne has slept, something alerts him to a change and he wakes. The moon has emerged, and they are riding through a walled square. He stops, dismounts, then grabs the halter of his guide's beast.

'Wake up, you!' he shouts at the figure slumped in the saddle. 'There's work to be done! I know your game!' He waits for the figure to start and straighten, but when the camel stamps, it slips further down in the seat. The old man has died, leaving Mr Carbourne to tend the camels, tie them to a crude statue standing in the centre of the square, light a dung fire, unpack blankets and sleep alone till dawn.

When it is light he heaves the body, rigid but very light, from the camel, and carries it to the corner of the square: the death was obviously from the most natural cause of all, and not in any way his fault; the man he tells himself, is too old to have anyone waiting for his return. Then he wanders round the ruins of Sidda . . .

'Immediately,' says our guide, gesturing gracefully through the panel, 'immediately, you are struck by the central feature: a square of open ground a hundred metres across, bordered by four very thick walls roughly two metres high. Even from here you can see that these walls are in fact even thicker at their base than at the top, and that they're built from irregular but precisely interlocking pieces of pinkish stone. There is no mortar. These stones were mined, shaped and assembled here without the use of any tools other than other pieces of stone. You'll notice that this isn't strictly speaking a square at all, because the four walls do not join at the corners and show no sign of ever having done so. In the centre of the square, where the paths that pass through these openings meet, exactly where it was found, is a large statue made of similar stone but of a greenish hue.

'Beyond the confines of the square you'll notice the seemingly irregular disposition of thirty-nine circular holes surmounted with low stonework rims. I don't want anyone to try and get inside these holes – they are very deep indeed and do provide a cool resting place for several types of snake. Bear in mind that these rims were originally several metres high, but that early explorers of the site were driven to knock them down in order to make them conform to their mistaken notions about the purpose of the pits. Over there to the left of the site you can see one of the pit mouths which is in the slow process of painstaking reconstruction, and far out on the edge of the site that mound is where the stones so dishonestly removed were hidden. Many of these stones were used to construct the base for the protective dome so as to be in harmony with the site it protects and also as an experiment to calculate how long it would have taken to construct Sidda. Our low wall took a team of twenty men fifteen years to build, using the interlocking method. Sidda was not built in a day!

'Leading up to each of the square's open corners are what look like narrow roads or paths – these lead due

The Ancient Siddanese

north, south, east and west, and appear to peter out just beyond the limits of the site as defined by our dome, though it's my view that proper exploration would show them to lead straight on for very many miles. The paths are made from millions of brittle pottery shards, and amongst these have been found many which bear finely preserved examples of the letters of an ancient alphabet.

'Outside the north, south, west and east walls of the square you can see the remains of three hexagonal structures. In the southern hexagon were found the only human remains the site has yielded, and these can now be seen in the site museum. Now, let us go outside, and I'll tell you a little about the people who constructed Sidda, and the way they lived . . .'

We follow him out into the tinted dome. You can tell he is right about the sun, for though it is cooler than outside, thin shadows trail behind us and the dry walls are hot to touch. We are a unique generation, skipping as we do from shadow to shadow, our skins screened to escape the fire that once created us. A generation of greedy travellers, living in the last days and wanting to see it all, the world as onion, layer on layer going back beneath today's crisp dry skin.

Sidney Carbourne lived in a different world and saw different things. He missed the interlocking stones entirely, had not the slightest thought of alphabets. He stepped out protected only by a cotton cloth wrapped over his head. He examined the numerous circular holes in the ground: wells, he thought, now gone dry, and the reason, probably, for the city being abandoned. The hexagonal structures he judged to be fortifications. If the old man had still been with him, he would have pretended a greater interest than he felt, but, alone, he could admit that the city was indeed little more than a heap of stones piled together to form a courtyard – without ornament other than the crude statue. He was disappointed, but there was no point in staying.

It was only as he walked back to the square that he was struck by the enormous thickness of its walls and noticed also that, whereas their inner surface seemed roughly perpendicular, the outer one sloped ever so slightly inwards towards the top. He stood back, shielded his eyes and projected this angle into the sky. Suddenly the stones of Sidda leapt to life. He saw the place, as new. He stood, filled with it, a great smile carving up his sunburnt face.

In a fever of excitement he returned to unload his drawing and measuring instruments. If only he had taken the risk of bringing a whole team out! If only he had more water! If only his guide had not chosen such a moment to die! All day he worked, recording Sidda in plan, section and elevations, all to scale, on fine cartridge paper, his ink drying instantaneously in the heat. Here and there he embellished the scene with a scrubby tree, a lizard or some imaginary birds wheeling in the sky, for it was all rather plain. He drew until dark came, suddenly as it does in these latitudes, then wandered restlessly around the ruins in the dark, feeling the stones, collecting handfuls of pottery shards. It would take him two months to organise a proper expedition: he felt he would be unable to sleep until he returned.

In the morning he spent an hour with his maps and a compass. Sidda was unmarked, which gladdened his heart, but also made his way on perilous, a matter of estimating degrees and times and speeds. As a precaution, he composed a letter to his fellow enthusiast,

The Ancient Siddanese

Dr Fellows, and fixed it to his bundle of drawings and notes before packing them safely away:

... Here my esteemed friend and fellow enthusiast, and quite unexpectedly, I have at last made a real Discovery! I believe this ruined city of Sidda to be indeed the cradle of civilization, a crude thing, but of immense scientific importance. It would seem to me that the courtyard walls – so immensely thick – were meant to support some further construction, since disappeared. From the evidence of the numerous wells, one can conjecture that this land was not always so dry, not always such a perfect desert as it is now. Many years before the birth of Christ, I think it quite reasonable to assume that some kind of trees may have grown here in reasonable abundance. Hence I conclude that the structure erected above these four walls was made of timber, and that has disappeared due to the action of the voracious ants and termites found in these parts. Projecting the angle of the walls skywards (see drawing numbered 14), you will see that we have a pyramidical edifice – not one such as is found in Egypt based on the equilateral triangle, but rather one that conforms exactly to the rule of isosceles. I have sketched out the possible method of construction for such a Pyramid, using only short lengths of timber such as might have been available. It is my conviction that Sidda became subject to prolonged drought and was gradually abandoned. Some few of the inhabitants may well have taken the long route by sea to Egypt itself, and there, in the course of many years, refined their original structure.

This desert is an inhospitable place for any man

and if by any chance, mishap should befall me on my return to the capital I wish to entrust you, my esteemed friend, with the discovery of this inestimable treasure. I beg of you in the name of our long association and our common love of science to publish my findings as well as you can, and then make your way with all haste here to continue my work. I have no doubt but that items of immense value and beauty are to be found in the sand beneath the tombs. Your affectionate friend . . .

Not forty years ago – when the man standing before us today with a small ironic smile playing about his lips was still in the deep shade of his mother's womb – before we passed the millennium, before the shady dome was built – another guide, a short, fattish man not half so elegant, though just as perfectly spoken as ours, would have been much preoccupied with the story of Sidney Carbourne . . .

'It was only after Dr Fellows' death,' he says, 'that this letter was found, plunging his family into disgrace. His daughter was so ashamed that she committed suicide. He even passed off the drawings, which Carbourne had neglected to sign, as his own!'

There is more than a suspicion of military background about this other guide, and an angry passion about the eyes. His party, larger than ours, obey his every instruction with alacrity: eyes right, eyes left, marching forth on the sand hot as coals. Yet they are freer than us in their dress: the women, hatless, in low-cut tops and calf-length dresses or baggy shorts, the men with blazers off, short-sleeved shirts undone at the neck and stained

The Ancient Siddanese

beneath the arms. Their skins are deeply tanned, even red and flaking here and there, but they do not care. They want to soak it all up, history and sunshine alike.

'I'm afraid the early history of archaeology is full of such unscrupulousness. These were colonial times. Foreigners came with their heads full of nonsense and everyone believed them.' He laughs bitterly. Some of the party smile, but uncertainly – they are foreigners too and feel his contempt. 'Nowadays we are much more scrupulous. Carbourne's theory, though correct in some respects, is largely a fairy tale fuelled by his consuming jealousy of a friend of his who had made his reputation and fortune by means of a discovery in Egypt. It was a minor one compared to what was to come – but considered important at the time. Sidney Carbourne dreamed of addressing the Royal Society back in England, but he never did. Some say that he wasn't even the first to discover Sidda: the remains of a single human skeleton of recent origin were found buried in a shallow grave.

'Carbourne's Pyramid is clearly a ridiculous hypothesis easily disproved by a few calculations' – forceful and intense, this other guide jabs contemptuously at the glass case containing Sidney's last written words, and a piece of pink stone he collected and marked with indian ink – 'and in seeing Sidda merely as a precursor of Egyptian civilization he severely underestimated it. Nowadays' – he stands a little straighter – 'we value it as the first emergence of that ingenuity and fortitude we like to think of as an essential feature of our national character. Follow me!

'You have to imagine these surrounding lands, as Carbourne suggested, far greener than they are today. There was water in relative abundance, for beneath this sand is a thick band of rock and beneath that there were at the time underground streams. Here and there, a fault in the bed of rock allowed water to seep upwards, creating fertile patches of land. This area was particularly rich in such secret wells, and the Siddanese took a vital first step when they decided to dig down and search beneath the sand for the source of the damp. They found that as they went down the dampness increased, and that with much labour they could in the end tap the source of water itself. This was sufficient to turn them from a nomadic to a settled people. With the stones they had brought up from beneath the sand they began to build, and with the water they irrigated the land round about. By the second century of its existence Sidda had fifteen functioning wells. They can still be distinguished: the larger ones, clustered together to your left. Imagine how Sidda must have appeared to the traveller: a shimmering oasis of green on the horizon, scarcely believable in its beauty. As the land began to yield a surplus and trade developed, a class system began to emerge, with an upper tier of landowners and a lower of manual workers, employed year in year out with the cutting and carrying of stone and the transport of water. Above both of these were the four well guardians or priests, who ensured that life was lived so as to please the gods responsible for their city's good fortune. These four hexagonal towers were the priest houses. Follow me inside the courtyard!

'Imagine this sculpture in its full glory: beneath it was a powerful natural spring, forcing water upwards like a fountain. See how it's built from many stones, leaving cracks and fissures between which the water gushed out, then flowed down into the sand. If you will excuse the gesture – see how a little saliva brings out the rich green of the rock, so like the green of healthy leaves.

The Ancient Siddanese

This we think was the centre of the water ceremonies, in which celebrants approached from the four corners of the square along these paths, watched by the priests in their towers . . .' Nowadays, this guide's story would not excite us. We'd know what was to come, and we'd turn away: 'Then disaster struck –' Who wants to hear of such things? Who wants to see Mr Melanoma's face? But back then it was different, they felt quite safe, and liked to hear of catastrophe:

'One by one the fifteen wells ran dry. Twenty-four new ones were dug in an increasingly desperate search for water, making the number up to thirty-nine. If you look at the path you're standing beside, you will see many fragments of pottery. Pick one up – you hold in your hand a pattern of lines and dots in which we can read the story of the end of Sidda. The marks are arranged in units ranging from fifteen to seventy-eight, which is twice thirty-nine. Each dot is a well still functioning, each line is a dry one. Thus we have a record of the fluctuating fortunes of the city, and indeed the main work of the Institute is now to arrange them chronologically so as to piece together a history of each well. Each fragment is part of a water bowl, and these, we think, were brought before the statue of the water god, filled, and then smashed on the way back out of the square as a gesture of homage and propitiation. Please put the pieces back.

'Gather round. I can show you here – an exact replica from the last days – look: all lines. Empty, empty, empty. No water. Sidda was destroyed by the very forces of nature that had brought it into being in the first place, its inhabitants forced to take up again the harsh nomadic life of times before. Yet, naturally, we hope that one day the desert will flower again, and even now plans are afoot to bring a team of international scientists into the desert north of here in the hope of discovering underground waters. Then we could grow barley and tomatoes, avocado, watermelon, even strawberries, and you visitors would not see so many starving children begging in the street.

'Ladies and gentlemen, you will leave in ten minutes. Please ask me questions if you wish, or take a cold drink in the café by the car-park. Nowadays, I'm afraid the water comes many miles by road in glass bottles! Thank you.' He salutes them at the end, looking over the tops of their heads at his imaginary oasis, of which there is now no trace.

'Where did you learn your English?' a woman with white skin baked brown but for the thin marks of swimsuit straps would have asked.

'In Oxford.' He would have smiled. 'I have read all your literature.'

'What's your view of the dreadful bombings last week?' That would be the woman's husband, standing stiffly beside her. 'I understand several tourists were killed.'

'You must understand' – then that other guide's face would have grown dark – 'that we are struggling hard to establish ourselves as a nation in our own right, and no one is helping us. You might say we are trying to recreate, in hostile circumstances, a beautiful garden, such as once flourished here. Violence ... such things are unpleasant, I think, but inevitable.'

'Where would you be without tourism? It's crazy, blowing people up.'

And a thin boy with very short hair would have asked, scratching at his scalp, red from the sun, 'Where did the people live? Why aren't there any houses?'

The Ancient Siddanese

'Because,' that other guide would have declared, smiling again, 'they were built of wood. And I expect you have seen the ants and termites in the grounds of your hotel? In two weeks one colony of termites can devour four tons of timber. The homes of the ancient Siddanese are nothing but dust blowing in the wind. Of course, now everything is painted with preservative.'

We can't blame these other guides – times change – nor must we forget them: they are part of the picture too.
'But,' says our guide now, and I feel as if behind those thick dark lenses he is staring straight at me, 'they were telling – if we are charitable – half-truths. Sidda is the most misunderstood archaeological site on the face of the earth. Today, I will tell you facts.
'How many people do you think occupied this site? Five hundred? A thousand? The answer is none. "City" isn't really the appropriate term for Sidda. We think of cities as bustling centres of trade, places on a crossroads where people gather and live in close proximity. Sidda was indeed a busy place, but no one lived here. It was the creation of many people who lived scattered about in the surrounding lands, but not their home.
'It was one of the fundamental beliefs of the ancient Siddanese that *individuals* should leave nothing behind them. When a house fell into disuse, such materials as could not be reused were burned and the ashes scattered to the winds. And when a person died, their body was taken to a lonely place and left unguarded on the sand so that ants and vultures could feast upon the flesh. A year later, the bones were buried, without marking, deep in the desert sand. This way, please . . .'
A trickle of sweat runs down between my shoulderblades, and somehow sand has slipped inside my shoes:

I can feel the tiny grains pressing in. We gather quietly round our guide without him having to ask, and wait for the two old ones to catch us up, inching forward on the uneven ground.

'The only memorial allowed the dead can in fact be seen right at your feet: these countless pottery shards, which are all fragments of decorated bowls, some large, some small. The day of the bowl came after the day of the bones, and on it the dead person's relatives carried his or her drinking bowl to the city of Sidda and once within the confines of the city' – he holds up an imaginary bowl, then brings his hands suddenly down – 'smashed it on the ground. Every night the day's shards were swept into the four sunken paths, gradually filling them, until, as you can see, they are almost level with the rest of the ground.'

The pottery fragments are dry, reddish and open-pored. As people shift on their feet I can hear them crunch and snap.

'But Sidda isn't simply a city of remembrance. It's also a monument. Two contradictory impulses were behind its painstaking creation: on the one hand a desire to honour the Siddanese way of life – obsession might be a better word, for it was long before they were in any danger of extinction that building commenced – and on the other the urge to hide it from other peoples' understanding and, in particular, that of those coming after them. Sidda was built to impress, but not to inform. And largely, until now, it has succeeded.' He beckons; we draw more closely round and watch him reach into his pocket.

'Consider the alphabet. Here are examples of some of the commonest symbols. They consist of collections of dots and lines, up to thirty-nine of each per unit, which can be enclosed in a circle or a rectangle and arranged

The Ancient Siddanese

either horizontally or vertically in various orders. This is not a picture alphabet, but a phonetic one. Each unit represents a sound. A rectangle or a circular enclosure implies a stressed or unstressed sound – syllable is not the correct term, for the language of Sidda was composed literally of strings of sounds, each discrete. Now, please pass these around . . .'

The piece I hold is roughly triangular, but slightly curved. The inside is smooth, and a slightly darker red. I turn it over: there they are, the ridges and the dots, carefully traced, perhaps with a twig –

'Close your eyes,' our guide says, 'and touch it lightly with your fingertips . . . Yes. Can you feel the difference between the bumps and the holes? The ridges and the lines? I think you'll find that if you run your fingernail across, it's quite easy to count them rapidly.' We do so. The sound, like the buzz of tiny crickets, is all around me and continues as he speaks.

'You understand? This is an alphabet of the blind. But not, like our braille, a second-hand thing, representing another alphabet, representing in turn a language spoken and invented by the sighted, that is, an alphabet *for* not *of* the blind. No. This alphabet represents a language created and spoken by the sightless, and the city around you was built entirely by a race of people who could not see.' I open my eyes briefly, am dazzled by the light, close them again.

'There are several theories. My colleague, Professor Nielsen, has recently published his theory that the Siddanese blinded their own offspring at birth, much as in some cultures the foreskin is automatically removed. And I believe Mossinsky has argued that the Siddanese were in fact a community of outcasts from the surrounding regions, where it is well known that many tribes expelled those with mental or physical abnormalities. The sightless, he argues, continued this custom in their own way by keeping themselves apart and developing a culture so arcane as to be impenetrable to the other groups and the tribes that had expelled them. Intriguing as both these hypotheses are, they do in the end seem over-elaborate to me. It seems far more likely that these people were, like myself, born sightless –' Everyone opens their eyes wide at this. 'Or else victims of a progressive dulling of their sight due to disease or perhaps even the fearful intensity of the desert light.' One and all we stare at our elegant guide, peer at his close-fitting glasses, so very dark. Is he really telling the truth? But we don't dare ask, and anyway, he reads our minds.

'Indeed. I find my way around this city by memory, the feel of the ground under my feet, the sense of where shadows fall – and something more than any of these – a feeling that I have always known the city of Sidda. Outside I carry a stick, but here it has never seemed necessary.

'To return to the alphabet. Whilst it has so far been impossible to decode more than a handful of words, we have learned the way in which it was written: not left to right, right to left or up and down, but starting always with the first symbol enclosed in a square centrally positioned in the available space. The next would be to the top left corner, top right corner, bottom right, bottom left; those following would be positioned between the top right of the outer top left symbol and the top left of the outer top right symbol and so on, forming a regular pattern like checks – or a honeycomb – of symbols and space. We think, for instance, that these symbols make up the word for her or his, and these make up the word

The Ancient Siddanese

for bowl. Perhaps this one is bone. Of course, we have no idea as to which sound a given letter represents. It's my view the alphabet will never be fully understood.' Mr Melanoma holds his piece of pottery out to give it back. I slip mine in my bag: it'll do no harm, I think, there are plenty more.

The thick pink walls cut off our view of the desert; the path that snaps like brittle bones beneath our feet leads straight as a die to the sculpture where Sidney Carbourne tied his camel.

'It's the only pictorial image of any kind the Siddanese left in their city,' our guide says. 'The stone is of uniform colour, but see how the texture varies' – he reaches out – 'here porous, here almost as smooth as glass, with the smoothest pieces of all used for the face and arms. Notice the intricacy of the work on the face – no less than forty pieces, carefully chosen to indicate the ears, nose and mouth. The space beneath the brows is blank – and what other reason could there be for this than that the Siddanese knew how they differed from others? This sculpture could rank alongside any of the great pieces in the world – above, I say, for consider how it was made without sight and without tools, other than perhaps another stone to knock a corner off here and there: what judgement and patience, what philosophy, must have gone into its construction!

'Around this statue, ladies and gentlemen, the Siddanese gathered to produce and appreciate their culture. They travelled many miles from their flimsy homes, going always on foot. They sang and played instruments, they told stories and riddles, and drank an intoxicant brewed from moulds cultivated inside the mouths of the thirty-nine pits beyond the square. Traces of this mould have been found on the concave surfaces of the pottery fragments we have discussed, and inside the hexagonal towers which we deduce to be public kitchens. Under the influence of this drink, they became convinced that they could read the future. They saw or guessed how their own demise would come, and how the sighted world would inevitably misunderstand their achievements. Consider these people, blind, scattered, knowing themselves to be unique in their peaceful and economical culture – proud, and justifiably so, but also vulnerable, afraid and alone. Perhaps it's not surprising that they wanted to build a city such as this, itself a riddle that could be unlocked only by the knowing touch of those, like them, free of the distraction of sight.

'Ladies and gentlemen, you have here a moving testimony as to the diversity of the human species. For almost two thousand years the Siddanese lived here, in a completely different manner from the other peoples of the world. Navigating in their inner darkness across the desert, they built a city without the use of tools; they refrained from eating meat or using animals as beasts of burden, they avoided trade and eschewed science: developing not astronomy like the Egyptians or geometry like the Greeks but their own austere metaphysics and philosophy. Whilst all the other peoples of the globe were slaves to superstition, the Siddanese pondered the problems of communication and interpretation, fitting one stone carefully on top of the next. Whilst others looked back to the origins of the gods and sought to bend nature to their will, the Siddanese felt their way forward to the future and guessed what was to come. But I like to think of them as a deeply sensual as well as a serious people, rather as I like to see myself.' He smiles at us properly for the first time.

'We are lucky, I think, that such a people lived. You

The Ancient Siddanese

may take photographs if you wish, though remember, this place is not designed to appeal to the eyes! There are various publications on sale by the entrance, and some small-scale replicas of the statue – an intriguing puzzle which you can try to assemble yourselves . . . But what I suggest is that in the few remaining minutes you close your eyes and explore Sidda by touch, for it's only in darkness that its full beauty can be appreciated.'

Nowadays, no one asks questions of a guide. It either works or it does not. He moves to wait in the shade for the next group. Gratefully, I close my eyes again and wander, arms outstretched, blundering unpractised until my fingers touch Sidda's walls. I can feel the sun's fatal heat on my back as I trace the border between one stone and the next. I slip my fingernail into the gap between. I feel how in these last hot days and years the world is full of parables, prefiguration and correspondence. Even half-truths or outright lies hide lessons and examples; and somewhere, beneath one of these dry stones, curled like a bug, is hope. I can hear other people on the path, and the cry of the veiled woman's child, but apart from that it is quiet under the dome. I press against the wall, opening myself to its roughness and accumulated warmth. I have come to my last site. I want to touch our guide, to take his hand in mine – it would be dry and warm, like old stone – with my eyes still closed.

I know that there may be yet other guides. I know that they may even come in shapes different than ours – limbless, green-skinned, minute, extra-sensory, photosynthetic, mechanic, invisible: 'We're nearing the end of our tour. Just one more thing – below is the planet earth. Mostly desert now, though once it was uniquely fertile and inhabited by many forms of life, one of which came to dominate, and, we guess, was responsible for the change. We're passing now over one of the smaller sites they occupied: you can see the form of a circle, and inside that a square, with several smaller circles scattered about. These beings left their mark, but they had no culture to speak of, and have often been compared, in their compulsion to build and multiply without thought, to the blue beetles which caused such havoc on our planet some years ago.'

'But on what evidence do we make such statements about their culture?' says one of these beings, maybe not through lips and teeth with air, but somehow, somehow. 'No one's troubled to go and look, have they?' Already it's gone, passed from view; but the shape of Sidda and the idea of those earth-beetles long ago move her, and she decides she will return one day to vindicate their name . . .

That's hope! I walk slowly beside the wall, just grazing it with my fingertips. I sense where it ends just before my fingers slip into air. I believe the blind man who waits in the shade; I must. I have closed my eyes and touched one of the wonders of the world, forgotten for a moment the terrible heat and the fearful sound of a wind blowing full of sand.

Sylvia Plath

extract from

The Bell Jar

Sylvia Plath's novel was first published under the pseudonym Victoria Lucas, which suggests that it was important for her as a writer to distance herself from the strong autobiographical elements in the book. It describes the breakdown of a nineteen-year-old college star, Esther Greenwood; her unhappy introduction to New York life and her return to her mother's home in Connecticut for the summer. Treated for depression with ECT (electric shock treatment) she finds herself drawn increasingly to the idea of suicide.

'Of course his mother killed him.'

I looked at the mouth of the boy Jody had wanted me to meet. His lips were thick and pink and a baby face nestled under the silk of white-blond hair. His name was Cal, which I thought must be short for something, but I couldn't think what it would be short for, unless it was California.

'How can you be sure she killed him?' I said.

Cal was supposed to be very intelligent, and Jody had said over the phone that he was cute and I would like him. I wondered, if I'd been my old self, if I would have liked him.

It was impossible to tell.

'Well, first she says No no no, and then she says Yes.'

'But then she says No no again.'

Cal and I lay side by side on an orange and green striped towel on a mucky beach across the swamps from Lynn. Jody and Mark, the boy she was pinned to, were swimming. Cal hadn't wanted to swim, he had wanted to talk, and we were arguing about this play where a young man finds out he has a brain disease, on account of his father fooling around with unclean women, and in the end his brain, which has been softening all along, snaps completely, and his mother is debating whether to kill him or not.

I had a suspicion that my mother had called Jody and begged her to ask me out, so I wouldn't sit around in my room all day with the shades drawn. I didn't want to go at first, because I thought Jody would notice the change in me, and that anybody with half an eye would see I didn't have a brain in my head.

But all during the drive north, and then east, Jody had joked and laughed and chattered and not seemed to mind that I only said 'My' or 'Gosh' or 'You don't say'.

We browned hotdogs on the public grills at the beach, and by watching Jody and Mark and Cal very carefully I managed to cook my hotdog just the right amount of time and didn't burn it or drop it into the fire, the way I was afraid of doing. Then, when nobody was looking, I buried it in the sand.

After we ate, Jody and Mark ran down to the water hand-in-hand, and I lay back, staring into the sky, while Cal went on and on about this play.

The only reason I remembered this play was because it had a mad person in it, and everything I had ever read about mad people stuck in my mind, while everything else flew out.

'But it's the Yes that matters,' Cal said. 'It's the Yes she'll come back to in the end.'

I lifted my head and squinted out at the bright blue plate of the sea – a bright blue plate with a dirty rim. A big round grey rock, like the upper half of an egg, poked out of the water about a mile from the stony headland.

'What was she going to kill him with? I forget.'

I hadn't forgotten. I remembered perfectly well, but I wanted to hear what Cal would say.

'Morphia powders.'

The Bell Jar

'Do you suppose they have morphia powders in America?'

Cal considered a minute. Then he said, 'I wouldn't think so. They sound awfully old-fashioned.'

I rolled over on to my stomach and squinted at the view in the other direction, towards Lynn. A glassy haze rippled up from the fires in the grills and the heat on the road, and through the haze, as through a curtain of clear water, I could make out a smudgy skyline of gas tanks and factory stacks and derricks and bridges.

It looked one hell of a mess.

I rolled on to my back again and made my voice casual. 'If you were going to kill yourself, how would you do it?'

Cal seemed pleased. 'I've often thought of that. I'd blow my brains out with a gun.'

I was disappointed. It was just like a man to do it with a gun. A fat chance I had of laying my hands on a gun. And even if I did, I wouldn't have a clue as to what part of me to shoot at.

I'd already read in the papers about people who'd tried to shoot themselves, only they ended up shooting an important nerve and getting paralysed, or blasting their face off, but being saved, by surgeons and a sort of miracle, from dying outright.

The risks of a gun seemed great.

'What kind of a gun?'

'My father's shotgun. He keeps it loaded. I'd just have to walk into his study one day and,' Cal pointed a finger to his temple and made a comical, screwed-up face, 'click!' He widened his pale grey eyes and looked at me.

'Does your father happen to live near Boston?' I asked idly.

'Nope. In Clacton-on-Sea. He's English.'

Jody and Mark ran up hand-in-hand, dripping and shaking off water drops like two loving puppies. I thought there would be too many people, so I stood up and pretended to yawn.

'I guess I'll go for a swim.'

Being with Jody and Mark and Cal was beginning to weigh on my nerves, like a dull wooden block on the strings of a piano. I was afraid that at any moment my control would snap, and I would start babbling about how I couldn't read and couldn't write and how I must be just about the only person who had stayed awake for a solid month without dropping dead of exhaustion.

A smoke seemed to be going up from my nerves like the smoke from the grills and the sun-saturated road. The whole landscape – beach and headland and sea and rock – quavered in front of my eyes like a stage backcloth.

I wondered at what point in space the silly, sham blue of the sky turned black.

'You swim too, Cal.'

Jody gave Cal a playful little push.

'Ohhh,' Cal hid his face in the towel. 'It's too cold.'

I started to walk towards the water.

Somehow, in the broad, shadowless light of noon, the water looked amiable and welcoming.

I thought drowning must be the kindest way to die, and burning the worst. Some of those babies in the jars that Buddy Willard showed me had gills, he said. They went through a stage where they were just like fish.

A little, rubbishy wavelet, full of candy wrappers and orange peel and seaweed, folded over my foot.

I heard the sand thud behind me, and Cal came up.

'Let's swim to that rock out there.' I pointed at it.

'Are you crazy? That's a mile out.'

'What are you?' I said. 'Chicken?'

Cal took me by the elbow and jostled me into the water. When we were waist high, he pushed me under. I surfaced, splashing, my eyes seared with salt. Underneath, the water was green and semi-opaque as a hunk of quartz.

I started to swim, a modified dogpaddle, keeping my face towards the rock. Cal did a slow crawl. After a while he put his head up and treaded water.

'Can't make it.' He was panting heavily.

'Okay. You go back.'

I thought I would swim out until I was too tired to swim back. As I paddled on, my heartbeat boomed like a dull motor in my ears.

I am I am I am.

That morning I had tried to hang myself.

I had taken the silk cord of my mother's yellow bathrobe as soon as she left for work, and, in the amber shade of the bedroom, fashioned it into a knot that slipped up and down on itself. It took me a long time to do this, because I was poor at knots and had no idea how to make a proper one.

Then I hunted around for a place to attach the rope.

The trouble was, our house had the wrong kind of ceilings. The ceilings were low, white and smoothly plastered, without a light fixture or a wood beam in sight. I thought with longing of the house my grandmother had before she sold it to come and live with us, and then with my Aunt Libby.

My grandmother's house was built in the fine, nineteenth-century style, with lofty rooms and sturdy chandelier brackets and high closets with stout rails across them, and an attic where nobody ever went, full of trunks and parrot cages and dressmaker's dummies and overhead beams thick as a ship's timbers.

But it was an old house, and she'd sold it, and I didn't know anybody else with a house like that.

After a discouraging time of walking about with the silk cord dangling from my neck like a yellow cat's tail and finding no place to fasten it, I sat on the edge of my mother's bed and tried pulling the cord tight.

But each time I would get the cord so tight I could feel a rushing in my ears and a flush of blood in my face, my hands would weaken and let go, and I would be all right again.

Then I saw that my body had all sorts of little tricks, such as making my hands go limp at the crucial second, which would save it, time and again, whereas if I had the whole say, I would be dead in a flash.

I would simply have to ambush it with whatever sense I had left, or it would trap me in its stupid cage for fifty years without any sense at all. And when people found out my mind had gone, as they would have to, sooner or later, in spite of my mother's guarded tongue, they would persuade her to put me into an asylum where I could be cured.

Only my case was incurable.

I had bought a few paperbacks on abnormal psychology at the drug store and compared my symptoms with the symptoms in the books, and sure enough, my symptoms tallied with the most hopeless cases.

The only thing I could read, beside the scandal sheets, were these abnormal psychology books. It was as if some slim opening had been left, so I could learn all I needed to know about my case to end it in the proper way.

I wondered, after the hanging fiasco, if I shouldn't just give it up and turn myself over to the doctors, but

The Bell Jar

then I remembered Doctor Gordon and his private shock machine. Once I was locked up they could use that on me all the time.

And I thought of how my mother and brother and friends would visit me, day after day, hoping I would be better. Then their visits would slacken off, and they would give up hope. They would grow old. They would forget me.

They would be poor, too.

They would want me to have the best of care at first, so they would sink all their money in a private hospital like Doctor Gordon's. Finally, when the money was used up, I would be moved to a state hospital, with hundreds of people like me, in a big cage in the basement.

The more hopeless you were, the further away they hid you.

Cal had turned around and was swimming in.

As I watched, he dragged himself slowly out of the neck-deep sea. Against the khaki-coloured sand and the green shore wavelets, his body was bisected for a moment, like a white worm. Then it crawled completely out of the green and on to the khaki and lost itself among dozens and dozens of other worms that were wriggling or just lolling about between the sea and the sky.

I paddled my hands in the water and kicked my feet. The egg-shaped rock didn't seem to be any nearer than it had been when Cal and I had looked at it from the shore.

Then I saw it would be pointless to swim as far as the rock, because my body would take that excuse to climb out and lie in the sun, gathering strength to swim back.

The only thing to do was to drown myself then and there.

So I stopped.

I brought my hands to my breast, ducked my head, and dived, using my hands to push the water aside. The water pressed in on my eardrums and on my heart. I fanned myself down, but before I knew where I was, the water had spat me up into the sun, and the world was sparkling all about me like blue and green and yellow semi-precious stones.

I dashed the water from my eyes.

I was panting, as after a strenuous exertion, but floating, without effort.

I dived, and dived again, and each time popped up like a cork.

The grey rock mocked me, bobbing on the water easy as a lifebuoy.

I knew when I was beaten.

I turned back.

The flowers nodded like bright, knowledgeable children as I trundled them down the hall.

I felt silly in my sage-green volunteer's uniform, and superfluous, unlike the white-uniformed doctors and nurses, or even the brown-uniformed scrubwomen with their mops and their buckets of grimy water, who passed me without a word.

If I had been getting paid, no matter how little, I could at least count this a proper job, but all I got for a morning of pushing round magazines and candy and flowers was a free lunch.

My mother said the cure for thinking too much about yourself was helping somebody who was worse off than you, so Teresa had arranged for me to sign on as a volunteer at our local hospital. It was difficult to be a volunteer at this hospital, because that's what all the

Junior League women wanted to do, but luckily for me, a lot of them were away on vacation.

I had hoped they would send me to a ward with some really gruesome cases, who would see through my numb, dumb face to how I meant well, and be grateful. But the head of the volunteers, a society lady at our church, took one look at me and said, 'You're on maternity.'

So I rode the elevator up three flights to the maternity ward and reported to the head nurse. She gave me the trolley of flowers. I was supposed to put the right vases at the right beds in the right rooms.

But before I came to the door of the first room I noticed that a lot of the flowers were droopy and brown at the edges. I thought it would be discouraging for a woman who'd just had a baby to see somebody plonk down a big bouquet of dead flowers in front of her, so I steered the trolley to a wash-basin in an alcove in the hall and began to pick out all the flowers that were dead.

Then I picked out all those that were dying.

There was no waste-basket in sight, so I crumpled the flowers up and laid them in the deep white basin. The basin felt cold as a tomb. I smiled. This must be how they laid the bodies away in the hospital morgue. My gesture, in its small way, echoed the larger gesture of the doctors and nurses.

I swung the door of the first room open and walked in, dragging my trolley. A couple of nurses jumped up, and I had a confused impression of shelves and medicine cabinets.

'What do you want?' one of the nurses demanded sternly. I couldn't tell one from the other, they all looked just alike.

'I'm taking the flowers round.'

The nurse who had spoken put a hand on my shoulder

and led me out of the room, manoeuvring the trolley with her free, expert hand. She flung open the swinging doors of the room next to that one and bowed me in. Then she disappeared.

I could hear giggles in the distance till a door shut and cut them off.

There were six beds in the room, and each bed had a woman in it. The women were all sitting up and knitting or riffling through magazines or putting their hair in pincurls and chattering like parrots in a parrot house.

I had thought they would be sleeping, or lying quiet and pale, so I could tiptoe round without any trouble and match the bed numbers to the numbers inked on adhesive tape on the vases, but before I had a chance to get my bearings, a bright, jazzy blonde with a sharp, triangular face beckoned to me.

I approached her, leaving the trolley in the middle of the floor, but then she made an impatient gesture, and I saw she wanted me to bring the trolley too.

I wheeled the trolley over to her bedside with a helpful smile.

'Hey, where's my larkspur?' A large, flabby lady from across the ward raked me with an eagle eye.

The sharp-faced blonde bent over the trolley. 'Here are my yellow roses,' she said, 'but they're all mixed up with some lousy iris.'

Other voices joined the voices of the first two women. They sounded cross and loud and full of complaint.

I was opening my mouth to explain that I had thrown a bunch of dead larkspur in the sink, and that some of the vases I had weeded out looked skimpy, there were so few flowers left, so I had joined a few of the bouquets together to fill them out, when the swinging door flew open and a nurse stalked in to see what the commotion was.

'Listen, nurse, I had this big bunch of larkspur Larry brought last night.'

'She's loused up my yellow roses.'

Unbuttoning the green uniform as I ran, I stuffed it, in passing, into the washbasin with the rubbish of dead flowers. Then I took the deserted side steps down to the street two at a time, without meeting another soul.

'Which way is the graveyard?'

The Italian in the black leather jacket stopped and pointed down an alley behind the white Methodist church. I remembered the Methodist church. I had been a Methodist for the first nine years of my life, before my father died and we moved and turned Unitarian.

My mother had been a Catholic before she was a Methodist. My grandmother and my grandfather and my Aunt Libby were all still Catholics. My Aunt Libby had broken away from the Catholic Church at the same time my mother did, but then she'd fallen in love with an Italian Catholic, so she'd gone back again.

Lately I had considered going into the Catholic Church myself. I knew that Catholics thought killing yourself was an awful sin. But perhaps, if this was so, they might have a good way to persuade me out of it.

Of course, I didn't believe in life after death or the virgin birth or the Inquisition or the infallibility of that little monkey-faced Pope or anything, but I didn't have to let the priest see this, I could just concentrate on my sin, and he would help me repent.

The only trouble was, Church, even the Catholic Church, didn't take up the whole of your life. No matter how much you knelt and prayed, you still had to eat three meals a day and have a job and live in the world.

I thought I might see how long you had to be a Catholic before you became a nun, so I asked my mother, thinking she'd know the best way to go about it.

My mother had laughed at me. 'Do you think they'll take somebody like you, right off the bat? Why you've got to know all these catechisms and credos and believe in them, lock, stock and barrel. A girl with your sense!'

Still, I imagined myself going to some Boston priest – it would have to be Boston, because I didn't want any priest in my home town to know I'd thought of killing myself. Priests were terrible gossips.

I would be in black, with my dead white face, and I would throw myself at this priest's feet and say, 'O Father, help me.'

But that was before people had begun to look at me in a funny way, like those nurses in the hospital.

I was pretty sure the Catholics wouldn't take in any crazy nuns. My Aunt Libby's husband had made a joke once, about a nun that a nunnery sent to Teresa for a check-up. This nun kept hearing harp notes in her ears and a voice saying over and over, 'Alleluia!' Only she wasn't sure, on being closely questioned, whether the voice was saying Alleluia or Arizona. The nun had been born in Arizona. I think she ended up in some asylum.

I tugged my black veil down to my chin and strode in through the wrought-iron gates. I thought it odd that in all the time my father had been buried in this graveyard, none of us had ever visited him. My mother hadn't let us come to his funeral because we were only children then, and he had died in hospital, so the graveyard and even his death, had always seemed unreal to me.

I had a great yearning, lately, to pay my father back

for all the years of neglect, and start tending his grave. I had always been my father's favourite, and it seemed fitting I should take on a mourning my mother had never bothered with.

I thought that if my father hadn't died, he would have taught me all about insects, which was his speciality at the university. He would also have taught me German and Greek and Latin, which he knew, and perhaps I would be a Lutheran. My father had been a Lutheran in Wisconsin, but they were out of style in New England, so he had become a lapsed Lutheran and then, my mother said, a bitter atheist.

The graveyard disappointed me. It lay at the outskirts of the town, on low ground, like a rubbish dump, and as I walked up and down the gravel paths, I could smell the stagnant salt marshes in the distance.

The old part of the graveyard was all right, with its worn, flat stones and lichen-bitten monuments, but I soon saw my father must be buried in the modern part with dates in the 1940s.

The stones in the modern part were crude and cheap, and here and there a grave was rimmed with marble, like an oblong bath-tub full of dirt, and rusty metal containers stuck up about where the person's navel would be, full of plastic flowers.

A fine drizzle started drifting down from the grey sky, and I grew very depressed.

I couldn't find my father anywhere.

Low, shaggy clouds scudded over that part of the horizon where the sea lay, behind the marshes and the beach shanty settlements, and raindrops darkened the black mackintosh I had bought that morning. A clammy dampness sank through to my skin.

I had asked the salesgirl, 'Is it water-repellent?'

And she had said, 'No raincoat is ever water-*repellent*. It's showerproofed.'

And when I asked her what showerproofed was, she told me I had better buy an umbrella.

But I hadn't enough money for an umbrella. What with bus fare in and out of Boston and peanuts and newspapers and abnormal psychology books and trips to my old home town by the sea, my New York fund was almost exhausted.

I had decided that when there was no more money in my bank account I would do it, and that morning I'd spent the last of it on the black raincoat.

Then I saw my father's gravestone.

It was crowded right up by another gravestone, head to head, the way people are crowded in a charity ward when there isn't enough space. The stone was of a mottled pink marble, like tinned salmon, and all there was on it was my father's name and, under it, two dates, separated by a little dash.

At the foot of the stone I arranged the rainy armful of azaleas I had picked from a bush at the gateway of the graveyard. Then my legs folded under me, and I sat down in the sopping grass. I couldn't understand why I was crying so hard.

Then I remembered that I had never cried for my father's death.

My mother hadn't cried either. She had just smiled and said what a merciful thing it was for him he had died, because if he had lived he would have been crippled and an invalid for life, and he couldn't have stood that, he would rather have died than had that happen.

I laid my face to the smooth face of the marble and howled my loss into the cold salt rain.

*

I knew just how to go about it.

The minute the car tyres crunched off down the drive and the sound of the motor faded, I jumped out of bed and hurried into my white blouse and green figured skirt and black raincoat. The raincoat felt damp still, from the day before, but that would soon cease to matter.

I went downstairs and picked up a pale blue envelope from the dining-room table and scrawled on the back, in large, painstaking letters: *I am going for a long walk.*

I propped the message where my mother would see it the minute she came in.

Then I laughed.

I had forgotten the most important thing.

I ran upstairs and dragged a chair into my mother's closet. Then I climbed up and reached for the small green strongbox on the top shelf. I could have torn the metal cover off with my bare hands, the lock was so feeble, but I wanted to do things in a calm, orderly way.

I pulled out my mother's upper right-hand bureau drawer and slipped the blue jewellery box from its hiding-place under the scented Irish linen handkerchiefs. I unpinned the little key from the dark velvet. Then I unlocked the strongbox and took out the bottle of new pills. There were more than I had hoped.

There were at least fifty.

If I had waited until my mother doled them out to me, night by night, it would have taken me fifty nights to save up enough. And in fifty nights, college would have opened, and my brother would have come back from Germany, and it would be too late.

I pinned the key back in the jewellery box among the clutter of inexpensive chains and rings, put the jewellery box back in the drawer under the handkerchiefs, returned the strongbox to the closet shelf and set the chair on the rug in the exact spot I had dragged it from.

Then I went downstairs and into the kitchen. I turned on the tap and poured myself a tall glass of water. Then I took the glass of water and the bottle of pills and went down into the cellar.

A dim, undersea light filtered through the slits of the cellar windows. Behind the oil burner, a dark gap showed in the wall at about shoulder height and ran back under the breezeway, out of sight. The breezeway had been added to the house after the cellar was dug, and built out over this secret, earth-bottomed crevice.

A few old, rotting fireplace logs blocked the hole mouth. I shoved them back a bit. Then I set the glass of water and the bottle of pills side by side on the flat surface of one of the logs and started to heave myself up.

It took me a good while to heft my body into the gap, but at last, after many tries, I managed it, and crouched at the mouth of the darkness, like a troll.

The earth seemed friendly under my bare feet, but cold. I wondered how long it had been since this particular square of soil had seen the sun.

Then, one after the other, I lugged the heavy, dust-covered logs across the hole mouth. The dark felt thick as velvet. I reached for the glass and bottle, and carefully, on my knees, with bent head, crawled to the farthest wall.

Cobwebs touched my face with the softness of moths. Wrapping my black coat round me like my own sweet shadow, I unscrewed the bottle of pills and started taking them swiftly, between gulps of water, one by one by one.

At first nothing happened, but as I approached the

bottom of the bottle, red and blue lights began to flash before my eyes. The bottle slid from my fingers and I lay down.

The silence drew off, baring the pebbles and shells and all the tatty wreckage of my life. Then, at the rim of vision, it gathered itself, and in one sweeping tide, rushed me to sleep.

*   *   *

It was completely dark.

I felt the darkness, but nothing else, and my head rose, feeling it, like the head of a worm. Someone was moaning. Then a great, hard weight smashed against my cheek like a stone wall and the moaning stopped.

The silence surged back, smoothing itself as black water smooths to its old surface calm over a dropped stone.

A cool wind rushed by. I was being transported at enormous speed down a tunnel into the earth. Then the wind stopped. There was a rumbling, as of many voices, protesting and disagreeing in the distance. Then the voices stopped.

A chisel cracked down on my eye, and a slit of light opened, like a mouth or a wound, till the darkness clamped shut on it again. I tried to roll away from the direction of the light, but hands wrapped round my limbs like mummy bands, and I couldn't move.

I began to think I must be in an underground chamber, lit by blinding lights, and that the chamber was full of people who for some reason were holding me down.

Then the chisel struck again, and the light leapt into

my head, and through the thick, warm, furry dark, a voice cried, 'Mother!'

Air breathed and played over my face.

I felt the shape of a room around me, a big room with open windows. A pillow moulded itself under my head, and my body floated, without pressure, between thin sheets.

Then I felt warmth, like a hand on my face. I must be lying in the sun. If I opened my eyes, I would see colours and shapes bending in upon me like nurses.

I opened my eyes.

It was completely dark.

Somebody was breathing beside me.

'I can't see,' I said.

A cheery voice spoke out of the dark. 'There are lots of blind people in the world. You'll marry a nice blind man some day.'

The man with the chisel had come back.

'Why do you bother?' I said. 'It's no use.'

'You mustn't talk like that.' His fingers probed at the great, aching boss over my left eye. Then he loosened something, and a ragged gap of light appeared, like the hole in a wall. A man's head peered round the edge of it.

'Can you see me?'

'Yes.'

'Can you see anything else?'

Then I remembered. 'I can't see anything.' The gap narrowed and went dark. 'I'm blind.'

'Nonsense! Who told you that?'

'The nurse.'

The man snorted. He finished taping the bandage

back over my eye. 'You are a very lucky girl. Your sight is perfectly intact.'

'Somebody to see you.'

The nurse beamed and disappeared.

My mother came smiling round the foot of the bed. She was wearing a dress with purple cartwheels on it and she looked awful.

A big tall boy followed her. At first I couldn't make out who it was, because my eye only opened a short way, but then I saw it was my brother.

'They said you wanted to see me.'

My mother perched on the edge of the bed and laid a hand on my leg. She looked loving and reproachful, and I wanted her to go away.

'I didn't think I said anything.'

'They said you called for me.' She seemed ready to cry. Her face puckered up and quivered like a pale jelly.

'How are you?' my brother said.

I looked my mother in the eye.

'The same,' I said.

'You have a visitor.'

'I don't want a visitor.'

The nurse bustled out and whispered to somebody in the hall. Then she came back. 'He'd very much like to see you.'

I looked down at the yellow legs sticking out of the unfamiliar white silk pyjamas they had dressed me in. The skin shook flabbily when I moved, as if there wasn't a muscle in it, and it was covered with a short, thick stubble of black hair.

'Who is it?'

'Somebody you know.'

'What's his name?'
'George Bakewell.'
'I don't know any George Bakewell.'
'He says he knows you.'

Then the nurse went out, and a very familiar boy came in and said, 'Mind if I sit on the edge of your bed?'

He was wearing a white coat, and I could see a stethoscope poking out of his pocket. I thought it must be somebody I knew dressed up as a doctor.

I had meant to cover my legs if anybody came in, but now I saw it was too late, so I let them stick out, just as they were, disgusting and ugly.

'That's me,' I thought. 'That's what I am.'

'You remember me, don't you, Esther?'

I squinted at the boy's face through the crack of my good eye. The other eye hadn't opened yet, but the eye doctor said it would be all right in a few days.

The boy looked at me as if I were some exciting new zoo animal and he was about to burst out laughing.

'You remember me, don't you, Esther?' He spoke slowly, the way one speaks to a dull child. 'I'm George Bakewell. I go to your church. You dated my room-mate once at Amherst.'

I thought I placed the boy's face then. It hovered dimly at the rim of memory – the sort of face to which I would never bother to attach a name.

'What are you doing here?'

'I'm houseman at this hospital.'

How could this George Bakewell have become a doctor so suddenly? I wondered. He didn't really know me, either. He just wanted to see what a girl who was crazy enough to kill herself looked like.

I turned my face to the wall.

'Get out,' I said. 'Get the hell out and don't come back.'

'I want to see a mirror.'

The nurse hummed busily as she opened one drawer after another, stuffing the new underclothes and blouses and skirts and pyjamas my mother had bought me into the black patent leather overnight case.

'Why can't I see a mirror?'

I had been dressed in a sheath, striped grey and white, like mattress ticking, with a wide, shiny red belt, and they had propped me up in an armchair.

'Why can't I?'

'Because you better not.' The nurse shut the lid of the overnight case with a little snap.

'Why?'

'Because you don't look very pretty.'

'Oh, just let me see.'

The nurse sighed and opened the top bureau drawer. She took out a large mirror in a wooden frame that matched the wood of the bureau and handed it to me.

At first I didn't see what the trouble was. It wasn't a mirror at all, but a picture.

You couldn't tell whether the person in the picture was a man or a woman, because their hair was shaved off and sprouted in bristly chicken-feather tufts all over their head. One side of the person's face was purple, and bulged out in a shapeless way, shading to green along the edges, and then to a sallow yellow. The person's mouth was pale brown, with a rose-coloured sore at either corner.

The most startling thing about the face was its supernatural conglomeration of bright colours.

I smiled.

The mouth in the mirror cracked into a grin.

A minute after the crash another nurse ran in. She took one look at the broken mirror, and at me, standing over the blind, white pieces, and hustled the young nurse out of the room.

'Didn't I *tell* you,' I could hear her say.

'But I only . . .'

'Didn't I *tell* you!'

I listened with mild interest. Anybody could drop a mirror. I didn't see why they should get so stirred up.

The other, older nurse came back into the room. She stood there, arms folded, staring hard at me.

'Seven years' bad luck.'

'What?'

'I said,' the nurse raised her voice, as if speaking to a deaf person, *'seven years' bad luck.'*

The young nurse returned with a dustpan and brush and began to sweep up the glittery splinters.

'That's only a superstition,' I said then.

'Huh!' The second nurse addressed herself to the nurse on her hands and knees as if I wasn't there. 'At you-know-where they'll take care of *her*!'

From the back window of the ambulance I could see street after familiar street funnelling off into a summery green distance. My mother sat on one side of me, and my brother on the other.

I had pretended I didn't know why they were moving me from the hospital in my home town to a city hospital, to see what they would say.

'They want you to be in a special ward,' my mother said. 'They don't have that sort of ward at our hospital.'

The Bell Jar

'I liked it where I was.'

My mother's mouth tightened. 'You should have behaved better, then.'

'What?'

'You shouldn't have broken that mirror. Then maybe they'd have let you stay.'

But of course I knew the mirror had nothing to do with it.

I sat in bed with the covers up to my neck.

'Why can't I get up? I'm not sick.'

'Ward rounds,' the nurse said. 'You can get up after ward rounds.' She shoved the bed-curtains back and revealed a fat young Italian woman in the next bed.

The Italian woman had a mass of tight black curls, starting at her forehead, that rose in a mountainous pompadour and cascaded down her back. Whenever she moved, the huge arrangement of hair moved with her, as if made of stiff black paper.

The woman looked at me and giggled. 'Why are you here?' She didn't wait for an answer. 'I'm here on account of my French-Canadian mother-in-law.' She giggled again. 'My husband knows I can't stand her, and still he said she could come and visit us, and when she came, my tongue stuck out of my head, I couldn't stop it. They ran me into Emergency and then they put me up here,' she lowered her voice, 'along with the nuts.' Then she said, 'What's the matter with you?'

I turned her my full face, with the bulging purple and green eye. 'I tried to kill myself.'

The woman stared at me. Then, hastily, she snatched up a movie magazine from her bed-table and pretended to be reading.

The swinging door opposite my bed flew open, and a whole troop of young boys and girls in white coats came in, with an older, grey-haired man. They were all smiling with bright, artificial smiles. They grouped themselves at the foot of my bed.

'And how are you feeling this morning, Miss Greenwood?'

I tried to decide which one of them had spoken. I hate saying anything to a group of people. When I talk to a group of people I always have to single out one and talk to him, and all the while I am talking I feel the others are peering at me and taking unfair advantage. I also hate people to ask cheerfully how you are when they know you're feeling like hell and expect you to say 'Fine'.

'I feel lousy.'

'Lousy. Hmm,' somebody said, and a boy ducked his head with a little smile. Somebody else scribbled something on a clipboard. Then somebody pulled a straight, solemn face and said, 'And why do you feel lousy?'

I thought some of the boys and girls in that bright group might well be friends of Buddy Willard. They would know I knew him, and they would be curious to see me, and afterwards they would gossip about me among themselves. I wanted to be where nobody I knew could ever come.

'I can't sleep . . .'

They interrupted me. 'But the nurse says you slept last night.' I looked round the crescent of fresh, strange faces.

'I can't read.' I raised my voice. 'I can't eat.' It occurred to me I'd been eating ravenously ever since I came to.

The people in the group had turned from me and

were murmuring in low voices to each other. Finally, the grey-haired man stepped out.

'Thank you, Miss Greenwood. You will be seen by one of the staff doctors presently.'

Then the group moved on to the bed of the Italian woman.

'And how are you feeling today, Mrs . . .' somebody said, and the name sounded long and full of l's, like Mrs Tomolillo.

Mrs Tomolillo giggled. 'Oh, I'm fine, doctor. I'm just fine.' Then she lowered her voice and whispered something I couldn't hear. One or two people in the group glanced in my direction. Then somebody said, 'All right, Mrs Tomolillo,' and somebody stepped out and pulled the bed-curtain between us like a white wall.

I sat on one end of a wooden bench in the grassy square between the four brick walls of the hospital. My mother, in her purple cartwheel dress, sat at the other end. She had her head propped in her hand, index finger on her cheek, and thumb under her chin.

Mrs Tomolillo was sitting with some dark-haired, laughing Italians on the next bench down. Every time my mother moved, Mrs Tomolillo imitated her. Now Mrs Tomolillo was sitting with her index finger on her cheek and her thumb under her chin, and her head tilted wistfully to one side.

'Don't move,' I told my mother in a low voice. 'That woman's imitating you.'

My mother turned to glance round, but quick as a wink, Mrs Tomolillo dropped her fat white hands in her lap and started talking vigorously to her friends.

'Why no, she's not,' my mother said. 'She's not even paying any attention to us.'

But the minute my mother turned round to me again, Mrs Tomolillo matched the tips of her fingers together the way my mother had just done and cast a black, mocking look at me.

The lawn was white with doctors.

All the time my mother and I had been sitting there, in the narrow cone of sun that shone down between the tall brick walls, doctors had been coming up to me and introducing themselves. 'I'm Doctor Soandso, I'm Doctor Soandso.'

Some of them looked so young I knew they couldn't be proper doctors, and one of them had a queer name that sounded just like Doctor Syphilis, so I began to look out for suspicious, fake names, and sure enough, a dark-haired fellow who looked very like Doctor Gordon, except that he had black skin where Doctor Gordon's skin was white, came up and said, 'I'm Doctor Pancreas,' and shook my hand.

After introducing themselves, the doctors all stood within listening distance, only I couldn't tell my mother that they were taking down every word we said without their hearing me, so I leaned over and whispered into her ear.

My mother drew back sharply.

'Oh, Esther, I wish you would co-operate. They say you don't co-operate. They say you won't talk to any of the doctors or make anything in Occupational Therapy . . .'

'I've got to get out of here,' I told her meaningly. 'Then I'd be all right. You got me in here,' I said. 'You get me out.'

'I thought if only I could persuade my mother to get me out of the hospital I could work on her sympathies, like that boy with brain disease in the play, and convince her what was the best thing to do.

To my surprise, my mother said, 'All right, I'll try to get you out – even if only to a better place. If I try to get you out,' she laid a hand on my knee, 'promise you'll be good?'

I spun round and glared straight at Doctor Syphilis, who stood at my elbow taking notes on a tiny, almost invisible pad. 'I promise,' I said in a loud, conspicuous voice.

The negro wheeled the food cart into the patients' dining-room. The Psychiatric Ward at the hospital was very small – just two corridors in an L-shape, lined with rooms, and an alcove of beds behind the OT shop, where I was, and a little area with a table and a few seats by a window in the corner of the L, which was our lounge and dining-room.

Usually it was a shrunken old white man that brought our food, but today it was a negro. The negro was with a woman in blue stiletto heels, and she was telling him what to do. The negro kept grinning and chuckling in a silly way.

Then he carried a tray over to our table with three lidded tin tureens on it, and started banging the tureens down. The woman left the room locking the door behind her. All the time the negro was banging down the tureens and then the dinted silver and the thick, white china plates, he gawped at us with big, rolling eyes.

I could tell we were his first crazy people.

Nobody at the table made a move to take the lids off the tin tureens, and the nurse stood back to see if any of us would take the lids off before she came to do it. Usually Mrs Tomolillo had taken the lids off and dished out everybody's food like a little mother, but then they sent her home, and nobody seemed to want to take her place.

I was starving, so I lifted the lid off the first bowl.

'That's very nice of you, Esther,' the nurse said pleasantly. 'Would you like to take some beans and pass them round to the others?'

I dished myself out a helping of green string beans and turned to pass the tureen to the enormous red-headed woman at my right. This was the first time the red-headed woman had been allowed up to the table. I had seen her once, at the very end of the L-shaped corridor, standing in front of an open door with bars on the square, inset window.

She had been yelling and laughing in a rude way and slapping her thighs at the passing doctors, and the white-jacketed attendant who took care of the people in that end of the ward was leaning against the hall radiator, laughing himself sick.

The red-headed woman snatched the tureen from me and upended it on her plate. Beans mountained up in front of her and scattered over on to her lap and on to the floor like stiff, green straws.

'Oh, Mrs Mole!' the nurse said in a sad voice. 'I think you better eat in your room today.'

And she returned most of the beans to the tureen and gave it to the person next to Mrs Mole and led Mrs Mole off. All the way down the hall to her room, Mrs Mole kept turning round and making leering faces at us, and ugly, oinking noises.

The negro had come back and was starting to collect the empty plates of people who hadn't dished out any beans yet.

'We're not done,' I told him. 'You can just wait.'

'Mah, mah!' The negro widened his eyes in mock wonder. He glanced round. The nurse had not yet returned from locking up Mrs Mole. The negro made me an insolent bow. 'Miss Mucky-Muck,' he said under his breath.

I lifted the lid off the second tureen and uncovered a wodge of macaroni, stone-cold and stuck together in a gluey paste. The third and last tureen was chock-full of baked beans.

Now I knew perfectly well you didn't serve two kinds of beans together at a meal. Beans and carrots, or beans and peas, maybe, but never beans and beans. The negro was just trying to see how much we would take.

The nurse came back, and the negro edged off at a distance. I ate as much as I could of the baked beans. Then I rose from the table, passing round to the side where the nurse couldn't see me below the waist, and behind the negro, who was clearing the dirty plates. I drew my foot back and gave him a sharp, hard kick on the calf of the leg.

The negro leapt away with a yelp and rolled his eyes at me. 'Oh Miz, oh Miz,' he moaned, rubbing his leg. 'You shouldn't of done that, you shouldn't, you reely shouldn't.'

'That's what *you* get,' I said, and stared him in the eye.

'Don't you want to get up today?'

'No.' I huddled down more deeply in the bed and pulled the sheet up over my head. Then I lifted a corner of the sheet and peered out. The nurse was shaking down the thermometer she had just removed from my mouth.

'You *see*, it's normal.' I had looked at the thermometer before she came to collect it, the way I always did. 'You *see*, it's normal, what do you keep taking it for?'

I wanted to tell her that if only something were wrong with my body it would be fine, I would rather have anything wrong with my body than something wrong with my head, but the idea seemed so involved and wearisome that I didn't say anything. I only burrowed down further in the bed.

Then, through the sheet, I felt a slight, annoying pressure on my leg. I peeped out. The nurse had set her tray of thermometers on my bed while she turned her back and took the pulse of the person who lay next to me, in Mrs Tomolillo's place.

A heavy naughtiness pricked through my veins, irritating and attractive as the hurt of a loose tooth. I yawned and stirred, as if about to turn over, and edged my foot under the box.

'Oh!' The nurse's cry sounded like a cry for help, and another nurse came running. 'Look what you've done!'

I poked my head out of the covers and stared over the edge of the bed. Around the overturned enamel tray, a star of thermometer shards glittered, and balls of mercury trembled like celestial dew.

'I'm sorry,' I said. 'It was an accident.'

The second nurse fixed me with a baleful eye. 'You did it on purpose. I *saw* you.'

Then she hurried off, and almost immediately two attendants came and wheeled me, bed and all, down to Mrs Mole's old room, but not before I had scooped up a ball of mercury.

Soon after they had locked the door, I could see the negro's face, a molasses-coloured moon, risen at the window grating, but I pretended not to notice.

I opened my fingers a crack, like a child with a secret and smiled at the silver globe cupped in my palm. If I dropped it, it would break into a million little replicas of itself, and if I pushed them near each other, they would fuse, without a crack, into one whole again.

I smiled and smiled at the small silver ball.

I couldn't imagine what they had done with Mrs Mole.

Jean Rhys

extract from

Wide Sargasso Sea

Antoinette Bertha Cosway, known by her stepfather's name, Mason, first appeared in Charlotte Brontë's Jane Eyre. *She was the Creole heiress whom Mr Rochester married on his father's orders, and who was later to haunt Miss Eyre as the mad woman kept hidden in the attics of Thornfield Hall. Jean Rhys also found herself haunted by Antoinette. In* Wide Sargasso Sea, *her best novel, she invents a childhood for this tragic character as the daughter of a Jamaican family ruined by the emancipation of the slaves.*

They say when trouble comes close ranks, and so the white people did. But we were not in their ranks. The Jamaican ladies had never approved of my mother, 'because she pretty like pretty self' Christophine said. She was my father's second wife, far too young for him they thought, and, worse still, a Martinique girl. When I asked her why so few people came to see us, she told me that the road from Spanish Town to Coulibri Estate where we lived was very bad and that road repairing was now a thing of the past. (My father, visitors, horses, feeling safe in bed – all belonged to the past.)

Another day I heard her talking to Mr Luttrell, our neighbour and her only friend. 'Of course they have their own misfortunes. Still waiting for this compensation the English promised when the Emancipation Act was passed. Some will wait for a long time.'

How could she know that Mr Luttrell would be the first who grew tired of waiting? One calm evening he shot his dog, swam out to sea and was gone for always. No agent came from England to look after his property – Nelson's Rest it was called – and strangers from Spanish Town rode up to gossip and discuss the tragedy.

'Live at Nelson's Rest? Not for love or money. An unlucky place.'

Mr Luttrell's house was left empty, shutters banging

in the wind. Soon the black people said it was haunted, they wouldn't go near it. And no one came near us.

I got used to a solitary life, but my mother still planned and hoped — perhaps she had to hope every time she passed a looking glass.

She still rode about every morning not caring that the black people stood about in groups to jeer at her, especially after her riding clothes grew shabby (they notice clothes, they know about money).

Then, one day, very early I saw her horse lying down under the frangipani tree. I went up to him but he was not sick, he was dead and his eyes were black with flies. I ran away and did not speak of it for I thought if I told no one it might not be true. But later that day, Godfrey found him, he had been poisoned. 'Now we are marooned,' my mother said, 'now what will become of us?'

Godfrey said, 'I can't watch the horse night and day. I too old now. When the old time go, let it go. No use to grab at it. The Lord make no distinction between black and white, black and white the same for Him. Rest yourself in peace for the righteous are not forsaken.' But she couldn't. She was young. How could she not try for all the things that had gone so suddenly, so without warning. 'You're blind when you want to be blind,' she said ferociously, 'and you're deaf when you want to be deaf. The old hypocrite,' she kept saying. 'He knew what they were going to do.' 'The devil prince of this world,' Godfrey said, 'but this world don't last so long for mortal man.'

She persuaded a Spanish Town doctor to visit my younger brother Pierre who staggered when he walked and couldn't speak distinctly. I don't know what the doctor told her or what she said to him but he never came again and after that she changed. Suddenly, not gradually. She grew thin and silent, and at last she refused to leave the house at all.

Our garden was large and beautiful as that garden in the Bible – the tree of life grew there. But it had gone wild. The paths were overgrown and a smell of dead flowers mixed with the fresh living smell. Underneath the tree ferns, tall as forest tree ferns, the light was green. Orchids flourished out of reach or for some reason not to be touched. One was snaky looking, another like an octopus with long thin brown tentacles bare of leaves hanging from a twisted root. Twice a year the octopus orchid flowered – then not an inch of tentacle showed. It was a bell-shaped mass of white, mauve, deep purples, wonderful to see. The scent was very sweet and strong. I never went near it.

All Coulibri Estate had gone wild like the garden, gone to bush. No more slavery – why should *anybody* work? This never saddened me. I did not remember the place when it was prosperous.

My mother usually walked up and down the *glacis*, a paved roofed-in terrace which ran the length of the house and sloped upwards to a clump of bamboos. Standing by the bamboos she had a clear view to the sea, but anyone passing could stare at her. They stared, sometimes they laughed. Long after the sound was far away and faint she kept her eyes shut and her hands clenched. A frown came between her black eyebrows, deep – it might have been cut with a knife. I hated this frown and once I touched her forehead trying to smooth it. But she pushed me away, not roughly but calmly, coldly, without a word, as if she had decided once and for all that I was useless to her. She wanted to sit with Pierre or walk where she pleased without being pestered, she wanted peace and quiet. I was old enough to look after myself. 'Oh, let me alone,' she would say, 'let me alone,' and after I knew that she talked aloud to herself I was a little afraid of her.

So I spent most of my time in the kitchen which was in an outbuilding some way off. Christophine slept in the little room next to it.

When evening came she sang to me if she was in the mood. I couldn't always understand her patois songs – she also came from Martinique – but she taught me the one that meant 'The little ones grow old, the children leave us, will they come back?' and the one about the cedar tree flowers which only last for a day.

The music was gay but the words were sad and her voice often quavered and broke on the high note. 'Adieu.' Not adieu as we said it, but *à dieu*, which made more sense after all. The loving man was lonely, the girl was deserted, the children never came back. Adieu.

Her songs were not like Jamaican songs, and she was not like the other women.

She was much blacker – blue-black with a thin face and straight features. She wore a black dress, heavy gold earrings and a yellow handkerchief – carefully tied with the two high points in front. No other negro woman wore black, or tied her handkerchief Martinique fashion. She had a quiet voice and a quiet laugh (when she did laugh), and though she could speak good English if she wanted to, and French as well as patois, she took care to talk as they talked. But they would have nothing to do with her and she never saw her son who worked in Spanish Town. She had only one friend – a woman called Maillotte, and Maillotte was not a Jamaican.

The girls from the bayside who sometimes helped

with the washing and cleaning were terrified of her. That, I soon discovered, was why they came at all – for she never paid them. Yet they brought presents of fruit and vegetables and after dark I often heard low voices from the kitchen.

So I asked about Christophine. Was she very old? Had she always been with us?

'She was your father's wedding present to me – one of his presents. He thought I would be pleased with a Martinique girl. I don't know how old she was when they brought her to Jamaica, quite young. I don't know how old she is now. Does it matter? Why do you pester and bother me about all these things that happened long ago? Christophine stayed with me because she wanted to stay. She had her own very good reasons you may be sure. I dare say we would have died if she'd turned against us and that would have been a better fate. To die and be forgotten and at peace. Not to know that one is abandoned, lied about, helpless. All the ones who died – who says a good word for them now?'

'Godfrey stayed too,' I said. 'And Sass.'

'They stayed,' she said angrily, 'because they wanted somewhere to sleep and something to eat. That boy Sass! When his mother pranced off and left him here – a great deal *she* cared – why he was a little skeleton. Now he's growing into a big strong boy and away he goes. We shan't see him again. Godfrey is a rascal. These new ones aren't too kind to old people and he knows it. That's why he stays. Doesn't do a thing but eat enough for a couple of horses. Pretends he's deaf. He isn't deaf – he doesn't want to hear. What a devil he is!'

'Why don't you tell him to find somewhere else to live?' I said and she laughed.

'He wouldn't go. He'd probably try to force us out. I've learned to let sleeping curs lie,' she said.

'Would Christophine go if you told her to?' I thought. But I didn't say it. I was afraid to say it.

It was too hot that afternoon. I could see the beads of perspiration on her upper lip and the dark circles under her eyes. I started to fan her, but she turned her head away. She might rest if I left her alone, she said.

Once I would have gone back quietly to watch her asleep on the blue sofa – once I made excuses to be near her when she brushed her hair, a soft black cloak to cover me, hide me, keep me safe.

But not any longer. Not any more.

These were all the people in my life – my mother and Pierre, Christophine, Godfrey, and Sass who had left us.

I never looked at any strange negro. They hated us. They called us white cockroaches. Let sleeping dogs lie. One day a little girl followed me singing, 'Go away white cockroach, go away, go away.' I walked fast, but she walked faster. 'White cockroach, go away, go away. Nobody want you. Go away.'

When I was safely home I sat close to the old wall at the end of the garden. It was covered with green moss soft as velvet and I never wanted to move again. Everything would be worse if I moved. Christophine found me there when it was nearly dark, and I was so stiff she had to help me to get up. She said nothing, but next morning Tia was in the kitchen with her mother Maillotte, Christophine's friend. Soon Tia was my friend and I met her nearly every morning at the turn of the road to the river.

Sometimes we left the bathing pool at midday, sometimes we stayed till late afternoon. Then Tia would

Wide Sargasso Sea

light a fire (fires always lit for her, sharp stones did not hurt her bare feet, I never saw her cry). We boiled green bananas in an old iron pot and ate them with our fingers out of a calabash and after we had eaten she slept at once. I could not sleep, but I wasn't quite awake as I lay in the shade looking at the pool – deep and dark green under the trees, brown-green if it had rained, but a bright sparkling green in the sun. The water was so clear that you could see the pebbles at the bottom of the shallow part. Blue and white and striped red. Very pretty. Late or early we parted at the turn of the road. My mother never asked me where I had been or what I had done.

Christophine had given me some new pennies which I kept in the pocket of my dress. They dropped out one morning so I put them on a stone. They shone like gold in the sun and Tia stared. She had small eyes, very black, set deep in her head.

Then she bet me three of the pennies that I couldn't turn a somersault under water 'like you say you can'.

'Of course I can.'

'I never see you do it,' she said. 'Only talk.'

'Bet you all the money I can,' I said.

But after one somersault I still turned and came up choking. Tia laughed and told me that it certainly look like I drown dead that time. Then she picked up the money.

'I did do it,' I said when I could speak, but she shook her head. I hadn't done it good and besides pennies didn't buy much. Why did I look at her like that?

'Keep them then, you cheating nigger,' I said, for I was tired, and the water I had swallowed made me feel sick. 'I can get more if I want to.'

That's not what she hear, she said. She hear all we

poor like beggar. We ate salt fish – no money for fresh fish. That old house so leaky, you run with calabash to catch water when it rain. Plenty white people in Jamaica. Real white people, they got gold money. They didn't look at us, nobody see them come near us. Old time white people nothing but white nigger now, and black nigger better than white nigger.

I wrapped myself in my torn towel and sat on a stone with my back to her, shivering cold. But the sun couldn't warm me. I wanted to go home. I looked round and Tia had gone. I searched for a long time before I could believe that she had taken my dress – not my underclothes, she never wore any – but my dress, starched, ironed, clean that morning. She had left me hers and I put it on at last and walked home in the blazing sun feeling sick, hating her. I planned to get round the back of the house to the kitchen, but passing the stables I stopped to stare at three strange horses and my mother saw me and called. She was on the *glacis* with two young ladies and a gentleman. Visitors! I dragged up the steps unwillingly – I had longed for visitors once, but that was years ago.

They were very beautiful I thought and they wore such beautiful clothes that I looked away down at the flagstones and when they laughed – the gentleman laughed the loudest – I ran into the house, into my bedroom. There I stood with my back against the door and I could feel my heart all through me. I heard them talking and I heard them leave. I came out of my room and my mother was sitting on the blue sofa. She looked at me for some time before she said that I had behaved very oddly. My dress was even dirtier than usual.

'It's Tia's dress.'

'But why are you wearing Tia's dress? Tia? Which one of them is Tia?'

Christophine, who had been in the pantry listening, came at once and was told to find a clean dress for me. 'Throw away that thing. Burn it.'

Then they quarrelled.

Christophine said I had no clean dress. 'She got two dresses, wash and wear. You want clean dress to drop from heaven? Some people crazy in truth.'

'She must have another dress,' said my mother. 'Somewhere.' But Christophine told her loudly that it shameful. She run wild, she grow up worthless. And nobody care.

My mother walked over to the window. ('Marooned,' said her straight narrow back, her carefully coiled hair. 'Marooned.')

'She has an old muslin dress. Find that.'

While Christophine scrubbed my face and tied my plaits with a fresh piece of string, she told me that those were the new people at Nelson's Rest. They called themselves Luttrell, but English or not English they were not like old Mr Luttrell. 'Old Mr Luttrell spit in their face if he see how they look at you. Trouble walk into the house this day. Trouble walk in.'

The old muslin dress was found and it tore as I forced it on. She didn't notice.

No more slavery! She had to laugh! 'These new ones have Letter of the Law. Same thing. They got magistrate. They got fine. They got jail house and chain gang. They got tread machine to mash up people's feet. New ones worse than old ones – more cunning, that's all.'

All that evening my mother didn't speak to me or look at me and I thought, 'She is ashamed of me, what Tia said is true.'

I went to bed early and slept at once. I dreamed that I was walking in the forest. Not alone. Someone who hated me was with me, out of sight. I could hear heavy footsteps coming closer and though I struggled and screamed I could not move. I woke crying. The covering sheet was on the floor and my mother was looking down at me.

'Did you have a nightmare?'

'Yes, a bad dream.'

She sighed and covered me up. 'You were making such a noise. I must go to Pierre, you've frightened him.'

I lay thinking, 'I am safe. There is the corner of the bedroom door and the friendly furniture. There is the tree of life in the garden and the wall green with moss. The barrier of the cliffs and the high mountains. And the barrier of the sea. I am safe. I am safe from strangers.'

The light of the candle in Pierre's room was still there when I slept again. I woke next morning knowing that nothing would be the same. It would change and go on changing.

I don't know how she got money to buy the white muslin and the pink. Yards of muslin. She may have sold her last ring, for there was one left. I saw it in her jewel box – that, and a locket with a shamrock inside. They were mending and sewing first thing in the morning and still sewing when I went to bed. In a week she had a new dress and so had I.

The Luttrells lent her a horse, and she would ride off very early and not come back till late next day – tired out because she had been to a dance or a moonlight picnic. She was gay and laughing – younger than I had ever seen her and the house was sad when she had gone.

So I too left it and stayed away till dark. I was never long at the bathing pool, I never met Tia.

I took another road, past the old sugar works and the water-wheel that had not turned for years. I went to parts of Coulibri that I had not seen, where there was no road, no path, no track. And if the razor grass cut my legs and arms I would think, 'It's better than people.' Black ants or red ones, tall nests swarming with white ants, rain that soaked me to the skin – once I saw a snake. All better than people.

Better. Better, better than people.

Watching the red and yellow flowers in the sun thinking of nothing, it was as if a door opened and I was somewhere else, something else. Not myself any longer.

I knew the time of day when though it is hot and blue and there are no clouds, the sky can have a very black look.

I was bridesmaid when my mother married Mr Mason in Spanish Town. Christophine curled my hair. I carried a bouquet and everything I wore was new – even my beautiful slippers. But their eyes slid away from my hating face. I had heard what all these smooth smiling people said about her when she was not listening and they did not guess I was. Hiding from them in the garden when they visited Coulibri, I listened.

'A fantastic marriage and he will regret it. Why should a very wealthy man who could take his pick of all the girls in the West Indies, and many in England too probably?' 'Why *probably*?' the other voice said. '*Certainly*.' 'Then why should he marry a widow without a penny to her name and Coulibri a wreck of a place? Emancipation troubles killed old Cosway? Nonsense – the estate was going downhill for years before that. He drank himself to death. Many's the time when – well! And all those women! She never did anything to stop him – she encouraged him. Presents and smiles for the bastards every Christmas. Old customs? Some old customs are better dead and buried. Her new husband will have to spend a pretty penny before the house is fit to live in – leaks like a sieve. And what about the stables and the coach house dark as pitch, and the servants' quarters and the six-foot snake I saw with my own eyes curled up on the privy seat last time I was here. Alarmed? I screamed. Then that horrible old man she harbours came along, doubled up with laughter. As for those two children – the boy an idiot kept out of sight and mind and the girl going the same way in my opinion – a *lowering* expression.'

'Oh I agree,' the other one said, 'but Annette is such a pretty woman. And what a dancer. Reminds me of that song "light as cotton blossom on the something breeze", or is it air? I forget.'

Yes, what a dancer – that night when they came home from their honeymoon in Trinidad and they danced on the *glacis* to no music. There was no need for music when she danced. They stopped and she leaned backwards over his arm, down till her black hair touched the flagstones – still down, down. Then up again in a flash, laughing. She made it look so easy – as if anyone could do it, and he kissed her – a long kiss. I was there that time too but they had forgotten me and soon I wasn't thinking of them. I was remembering that woman saying, 'Dance! He didn't come to the West Indies to dance – he came to make money as they all do. Some of the big estates are going cheap, and one unfortunate's loss is always a clever man's gain. No, the whole thing is a mystery. It's evidently useful to keep a Martinique obeah woman on the premises.' She meant Christophine. She said it mockingly, not meaning it, but soon other people were saying it – and meaning it.

While the repairs were being done and they were in Trinidad, Pierre and I stayed with Aunt Cora in Spanish Town.

Mr Mason did not approve of Aunt Cora, an ex-slave-owner who had escaped misery, a flier in the face of Providence.

'Why did she do nothing to help you?'

I told him that her husband was English and didn't like us and he said, 'Nonsense.'

'It isn't nonsense, they lived in England and he was angry if she wrote to us. He hated the West Indies. When he died not long ago she came home, before that what could she do? *She* wasn't rich.'

'That's her story. I don't believe it. A frivolous woman. In your mother's place I'd resent her behaviour.'

'None of you understand about us,' I thought.

Coulibri looked the same when I saw it again, although it was clean and tidy, no grass between the flagstones, no leaks. But it didn't feel the same. Sass had come back and I was glad. They can *smell* money, somebody said. Mr Mason engaged new servants – I didn't like any of them excepting Mannie the groom. It was their talk about Christophine that changed Coulibri, not the repairs or the new furniture or the strange faces. Their talk about Christophine and obeah changed it.

I knew her room so well – the pictures of the Holy Family and the prayer for a happy death. She had a bright patchwork counterpane, a broken-down press for her clothes, and my mother had given her an old rocking-chair.

Yet one day when I was waiting there I was suddenly very much afraid. The door was open to the sunlight, someone was whistling near the stables, but I was afraid. I was certain that hidden in the room (behind the old black press?) there was a dead man's dried hand, white chicken feathers, a cock with its throat cut, dying slowly, slowly. Drop by drop the blood was falling into a red basin and I imagined I could hear it. No one had ever spoken to me about obeah – but I knew what I would find if I dared to look. Then Christophine came in smiling and pleased to see me. Nothing alarming ever happened and I forgot, or told myself I had forgotten.

Mr Mason would laugh if he knew how frightened I had been. He would laugh even louder than he did when my mother told him that she wished to leave Coulibri.

This began when they had been married for over a year. They always said the same things and I seldom listened to the argument now. I knew that we were hated – but to go away . . . for once I agreed with my stepfather. That was not possible.

'You must have some reason,' he would say, and she would answer, 'I need a change' or 'We could visit Richard'. (Richard, Mr Mason's son by his first marriage, was at school in Barbados. He was going to England soon and we had seen very little of him.)

'An agent could look after this place. For the time being. The people here hate us. They certainly hate me.' Straight out she said that one day and it was then he laughed so heartily.

'Annette, be reasonable. You were the widow of a slave-owner, the daughter of a slave-owner, and you had been living here alone, with two children, for nearly five years when we met. Things were at their worst then. But you were never molested, never harmed.'

'How do you know that I was not harmed?' she said. 'We were so poor then,' she told him, 'we were something to laugh at. But we are not poor now,' she said.

'You are not a poor man. Do you suppose that they don't know all about your estate in Trinidad? And the Antigua property? They talk about us without stopping. They invent stories about you, and lies about me. They try to find out what we eat every day.'

'They are curious. It's natural enough. You have lived alone far too long, Annette. You imagine enmity which doesn't exist. Always one extreme or the other. Didn't you fly at me like a little wild cat when I said nigger. Not nigger, nor even negro. Black people I must say.'

'You don't like, or even recognize, the good in them,' she said, 'and you won't believe in the other side.'

'They're too damn lazy to be dangerous,' said Mr Mason. 'I know that.'

'They are more alive than you are, lazy or not, and they can be dangerous and cruel for reasons you wouldn't understand.'

'No, I don't understand,' Mr Mason always said. 'I don't understand at all.'

But she'd speak about going away again. Persistently. Angrily.

Mr Mason pulled up near the empty huts on our way home that evening. 'All gone to one of those dances,' he said. 'Young and old. How deserted the place looks.'

'We'll hear the drums if there is a dance.' I hoped he'd ride on quickly but he stayed by the huts to watch the sun go down, the sky and the sea were on fire when we left Bertrand Bay at last. From a long way off I saw the shadow of our house high up on its stone foundations. There was a smell of ferns and river water and I felt safe again, as if I was one of the righteous. (Godfrey said that we were not righteous. One day when he was drunk he told me that we were all damned and no use praying.)

'They've chosen a very hot night for their dance,' Mr Mason said, and Aunt Cora came on to the *glacis*.
'What dance? Where?'
'There is some festivity in the neighbourhood. The huts were abandoned. A wedding perhaps?'
'Not a wedding,' I said. 'There is never a wedding.' He frowned at me but Aunt Cora smiled.

When they had gone indoors I leaned my arms on the cool *glacis* railings and thought that I would never like him very much. I still called him 'Mr Mason' in my head. 'Goodnight white pappy,' I said one evening and he was not vexed, he laughed. In some ways it was better before he came, though he'd rescued us from poverty and misery. 'Only just in time too.' The black people did not hate us quite so much when we were poor. We were white but we had not escaped and soon we would be dead for we had no money left. What was there to hate?

Now it had started up again and worse than before, my mother knows but she can't make him believe it. I wish I could tell him that out here is not at all like English people think it is. I wish ...

I could hear them talking and Aunt Cora's laugh. I was glad she was staying with us. And I could hear the bamboos shiver and creak though there was no wind. It had been hot and still and dry for days. The colours had gone from the sky, the light was blue and could not last long. The *glacis* was not a good place when night was coming, Christophine said. As I went indoors my mother was talking in an excited voice.

'Very well. As you refuse to consider it, *I* will go and take Pierre with me. You won't object to that, I hope?'

'You are perfectly right, Annette,' said Aunt Cora and that did surprise me. She seldom spoke when they argued.

Mr Mason also seemed surprised and not at all pleased.

'You talk so wildly,' he said. 'And you are so mistaken. Of course you can get away for a change if you wish it. I promise you.'

'You have promised that before,' she said. 'You don't keep your promises.'

He sighed. 'I feel very well here. However, we'll arrange something. Quite soon.'

'I will not stay at Coulibri any longer,' my mother said. 'It is not safe. It is not safe for Pierre.'

Aunt Cora nodded.

As it was late I ate with them instead of by myself as usual. Myra, one of the new servants, was standing by the sideboard, waiting to change the plates. We ate English food now, beef and mutton, pies and puddings.

I was glad to be like an English girl but I missed the taste of Christophine's cooking.

My stepfather talked about a plan to import labourers – coolies he called them – from the East Indies. When Myra had gone out Aunt Cora said, 'I shouldn't discuss that if I were you. Myra is listening.'

'But the people here won't work. They don't want to work. Look at this place – it's enough to break your heart.'

'Hearts have been broken,' she said. 'Be sure of that. I suppose you all know what you are doing.'

'Do you mean to say –'

'I said nothing, except that it would be wiser not to tell that woman your plans – necessary and merciful no doubt. I don't trust her.'

'Live here most of your life and know nothing about the people. It's astonishing. They are children – they wouldn't hurt a fly.'

'Unhappily children do hurt flies,' said Aunt Cora.

Myra came in again looking mournful as she always did though she smiled when she talked about hell. Everyone went to hell, she told me, you had to belong to her sect to be saved and even then – just as well not to be too sure. She had thin arms and big hands and feet and the handkerchief she wore round her head was always white. Never striped or a gay colour.

So I looked away from her at my favourite picture, 'The Miller's Daughter', a lovely English girl with brown curls and blue eyes and a dress slipping off her shoulders. Then I looked across the white tablecloth and the vase of yellow roses at Mr Mason, so sure of himself, so without a doubt English. And at my mother, so without a doubt not English, but no white nigger either. Not my mother. Never had been. Never could be. Yes, she would have died, I thought, if she had not met him. And for the first time I was grateful and liked him. There are more ways than one of being happy, better perhaps to be peaceful and contented and protected, as I feel now, peaceful for years and long years, and afterwards I may be saved whatever Myra says. (When I asked Christophine what happened when you died, she said, 'You want to know too much.') I remembered to kiss my stepfather goodnight. Once Aunt Cora had told me, 'He's very hurt because you never kiss him.'

'He does not look hurt,' I argued. 'Great mistake to go by looks,' she said, 'one way or the other.'

I went into Pierre's room which was next to mine, the last one in the house. The bamboos were outside his window. You could almost touch them. He still had a crib and he slept more and more, nearly all the time. He was so thin that I could lift him easily. Mr Mason had promised to take him to England later on, there he would be cured, made like other people. 'And how will you like that?' I thought, as I kissed him. 'How will you like being made exactly like other people?' He looked happy asleep. But that will be later on. Later on. Sleep now. It was then I heard the bamboos creak again and a sound like whispering. I forced myself to look out of the window. There was a full moon but I saw nobody, nothing but shadows.

I left a light on the chair by my bed and waited for Christophine, for I liked to see her last thing. But she did not come, and as the candle burned down, the safe peaceful feeling left me. I wished I had a big Cuban dog to lie by my bed and protect me, I wished I had not heard a noise by the bamboo clump, or that I were very young again, for then I believed in my stick. It was not a stick, but a long narrow piece of wood, with two nails sticking out at the end, a shingle, perhaps. I picked it up soon after they killed our horse and I thought I can fight with this, if the worst comes to the worst I can fight to the end though the best ones fall and that is another song. Christophine knocked the nails out, but she let me keep the shingle and I grew very fond of it, I believed that no one could harm me when it was near me, to lose it would be a great misfortune. All this was long ago, when I was still babyish and sure that everything was alive, not only the river or the rain, but chairs, looking-glasses, cups, saucers, everything.

I woke up and it was still night and my mother was there. She said, 'Get up and dress yourself, and come downstairs quickly.' She was dressed, but she had not put up her hair and one of her plaits was loose. 'Quickly,' she said again, then she went into Pierre's room, next door. I heard her speak to Myra and I heard Myra answer her. I lay there, half asleep, looking at the lighted candle on the chest of drawers, till I heard a noise as though a chair had fallen over in the little room, then I got up and dressed.

The house was on different levels. There were three steps down from my bedroom and Pierre's to the dining-room and then three steps from the dining-room to the rest of the house, which we called 'downstairs'. The folding doors of the dining-room were not shut and I could see that the big drawing-room was full of people. Mr Mason, my mother, Christophine and Mannie and Sass. Aunt Cora was sitting on the blue sofa in the corner now, wearing a black silk dress, her ringlets were carefully arranged. She looked very haughty, I thought. But Godfrey was not there, or Myra, or the cook, or any of the others.

'There is no reason to be alarmed,' my stepfather was saying as I came in. 'A handful of drunken negroes.' He opened the door leading to the *glacis* and walked out. 'What is all this,' he shouted. 'What do you want?' A horrible noise swelled up, like animals howling, but worse. We heard stones falling on to the *glacis*. He was pale when he came in again, but he tried to smile as he shut and bolted the door. 'More of them than I thought, and in a nasty mood too. They will repent in the morning. I foresee gifts of tamarinds in syrup and ginger sweets tomorrow.'

'Tomorrow will be too late,' said Aunt Cora, 'too late for ginger sweets or anything else.' My mother was not listening to either of them. She said, 'Pierre is asleep and Myra is with him, I thought it better to leave him in his own room, away from this horrible noise. I don't know. Perhaps.' She was twisting her hands together, her wedding ring fell off and rolled into a corner near the steps. My stepfather and Mannie both stooped for it, then Mannie straightened up and said, 'Oh, my God, they get at the back, they set fire to the back of the house.' He pointed to my bedroom door which I had shut after me, and smoke was rolling out from underneath.

I did not see my mother move she was so quick. She opened the door of my room and then again I did not see her, nothing but smoke. Mannie ran after her, so did Mr Mason but more slowly. Aunt Cora put her arms round me. She said, 'Don't be afraid, you are quite safe. We are all quite safe.' Just for a moment I shut my eyes and rested my head against her shoulder. She smelled of vanilla, I remember. Then there was another smell, of burned hair, and I looked and my mother was in the room carrying Pierre. It was her loose hair that had burned and was smelling like that.

I thought, Pierre is dead. He looked dead. He was white and he did not make a sound, but his head hung back over her arm as if he had no life at all and his eyes were rolled up so that you only saw the whites. My stepfather said, 'Annette, you are hurt – your hands . . .' But she did not even look at him. 'His crib was on fire,' she said to Aunt Cora. 'The little room is on fire and Myra was not there. She has gone. She was not there.'

'That does not surprise me at all,' said Aunt Cora. She laid Pierre on the sofa, bent over him, then lifted up her skirt, stepped out of her white petticoat and began to tear it into strips.

'She left him, she ran away and left him alone to die,' said my mother, still whispering. So it was all the more dreadful when she began to scream abuse at Mr Mason, calling him a fool, a cruel stupid fool. 'I told you,' she said, 'I told you what would happen again and again.' Her voice broke, but still she screamed, 'You would not listen, you sneered at me, you grinning hypocrite, you ought not to live either, you know so much, don't you? Why don't you go out and ask them to let you go? Say how innocent you are. Say you have always trusted them.'

I was so shocked that everything was confused. And it happened quickly. I saw Mannie and Sass staggering along with two large earthenware jars of water which were kept in the pantry. They threw the water into the bedroom and it made a black pool on the floor, but the smoke rolled over the pool. Then Christophine, who had run into my mother's bedroom for the pitcher there, came back and spoke to my aunt. 'It seems they have fired the other side of the house,' said Aunt Cora. 'They must have climbed that tree outside. This place is going to burn like tinder and there is nothing we can do to stop it. The sooner we get out the better.'

Mannie said to the boy, 'You frightened?' Sass shook his head. 'Then come on,' said Mannie. 'Out of my way,' he said and pushed Mr Mason aside. Narrow wooden stairs led down from the pantry to the outbuildings, the kitchen, the servants' rooms, the stables. That was where they were going. 'Take the child,' Aunt Cora told Christophine, 'and come.'

It was very hot on the *glacis* too, they roared as we came out, then there was another roar behind us. I had not seen any flames, only smoke and sparks, but now I saw tall flames shooting up to the sky, for the bamboos had caught. There were some tree ferns near, green and damp, one of those was smouldering too.

'Come quickly,' said Aunt Cora, and she went first, holding my hand. Christophine followed, carrying Pierre, and they were quite silent as we went down the *glacis* steps. But when I looked round for my mother I saw that Mr Mason, his face crimson with heat, seemed to be dragging her along and she was holding back, struggling. I heard him say, 'It's impossible, too late now.'

'Wants her jewel case?' Aunt Cora said.

'Jewel case? Nothing so sensible,' bawled Mr Mason. 'She wanted to go back for her damned parrot. I won't allow it.' She did not answer, only fought him silently, twisting like a cat and showing her teeth.

Our parrot was called Coco, a green parrot. He didn't talk very well, he could say *Qui est là? Qui est là?* and answer himself *Ché Coco, Ché Coco*. After Mr Mason clipped his wings he grew very bad tempered, and though he would sit quietly on my mother's shoulder, he darted at everyone who came near her and pecked their feet.

'Annette,' said Aunt Cora. 'They are laughing at you, do not allow them to laugh at you.' She stopped fighting then and he half supported, half pulled her after us, cursing loudly.

Still they were quiet and there were so many of them I could hardly see any grass or trees. There must have been many of the bay people but I recognized no one. They all looked the same, it was the same face repeated over and over, eyes gleaming, mouth half open to shout. We were past the mounting stone when they saw Mannie driving the carriage round the corner. Sass followed, riding one horse and leading another. There was a ladies' saddle on the one he was leading.

Somebody yelled, 'But look the black Englishman! Look the white niggers!' and then they were all yelling. 'Look the white niggers! Look the damn white niggers!' A stone just missed Mannie's head, he cursed back at them and they cleared away from the rearing, frightened horses. 'Come on, for God's sake,' said Mr Mason. 'Get to the carriage, get to the horses.' But we could not move for they pressed too close round us. Some of them were laughing and waving sticks, some of the ones at the back were carrying flambeaux and it was light as day. Aunt Cora held my hand very tightly and her lips moved but I could not hear because of the noise. And I was afraid, because I knew that the ones who laughed would be the worst. I shut my eyes and waited. Mr Mason stopped swearing and began to pray in a loud pious voice. The prayer ended, 'May Almighty God defend us.' And God who is indeed mysterious, who had made no sign when they burned Pierre as he slept – not a clap of thunder, not a flash of lightning – mysterious God heard Mr Mason at once and answered him. The yells stopped.

I opened my eyes, everybody was looking up and pointing at Coco on the *glacis* railings with his feathers alight. He made an effort to fly down but his clipped wings failed him and he fell screeching. He was all on fire.

I began to cry. 'Don't look,' said Aunt Cora. 'Don't look.' She stooped and put her arms round me and I hid my face, but I could feel that they were not so near. I heard someone say something about bad luck and remembered that it was very unlucky to kill a parrot, or even to see a parrot die. They began to go then, quickly, silently, and those that were left drew aside and watched us as we trailed across the grass. They were not laughing any more.

'Get to the carriage, get to the carriage,' said Mr Mason. 'Hurry!' He went first, holding my mother's arm, then Christophine carrying Pierre, and Aunt Cora was last, still with my hand in hers. None of us looked back.

Mannie had stopped the horses at the bend of the cobblestone road and as we got closer we heard him shout, 'What all you are, eh? Brute beasts?' He was speaking to a group of men and a few women who were standing round the carriage. A coloured man with a machete in his hand was holding the bridle. I did not see Sass or the other two horses. 'Get in,' said Mr Mason. 'Take no notice of him, get in.' The man with the machete said no. We would go to police and tell a lot of damn lies. A woman said to let us go. All this an accident and they had plenty witness. 'Myra she witness for us.'

'Shut your mouth,' the man said. 'You mash centipede, mash it, leave one little piece and it grow again ... What you think police believe, eh? You, or the white nigger?'

Mr Mason stared at him. He seemed not frightened, but too astounded to speak. Mannie took up the carriage whip but one of the blacker men wrenched it out of his hand, snapped it over his knee and threw it away. 'Run away, black Englishman, like the boy run. Hide in the bushes. It's better for you.' It was Aunt Cora who stepped forward and said, 'The little boy is very badly hurt. He will die if we cannot get help for him.'

The man said, 'So black and white, they burn the same, eh?'

'They do,' she said. 'Here and hereafter, as you will find out. Very shortly.'

He let the bridle go and thrust his face close to hers. He'd throw her on the fire, he said, if she put bad luck on him. Old white jumby, he called her. But she did not move an inch, she looked straight into his eyes and threatened him with eternal fire in a calm voice. 'And never a drop of sangoree to cool your burning tongue,' she said. He cursed her again but he backed away. 'Now get in,' said Mr Mason. 'You, Christophine, get in with the child.' Christophine got in. 'Now you,' he said to my mother. But she had turned and was looking back at the house and when he put his hand on her arm, she screamed.

One woman said she only come to see what happen. Another woman began to cry. The man with the cutlass said, 'You cry for her – when she ever cry for you? Tell me that.'

But now I turned too. The house was burning, the yellow-red sky was like sunset and I knew that I would never see Coulibri again. Nothing would be left, the golden ferns and the silver ferns, the orchids, the ginger lilies and the roses, the rocking-chairs and the blue sofa, the jasmine and the honeysuckle, and the picture of the Miller's Daughter. When they had finished, there would be nothing left but blackened walls and the mounting stone. That was always left. That could not be stolen or burned.

Then, not so far off, I saw Tia and her mother and I ran to her, for she was all that was left of my life as it had been. We had eaten the same food, slept side by side, bathed in the same river. As I ran, I thought, I will live with Tia and I will be like her. Not to leave Coulibri. Not to go. Not. When I was close I saw the jagged stone in her hand but I did not see her throw it. I did not feel it either, only something wet, running down my face. I looked at her and I saw her face crumple up as she began to cry. We stared at each other, blood on my face, tears on hers. It was as if I saw myself. Like in a looking-glass.

Françoise Sagan

extract from

Bonjour Tristesse

Cécile, holidaying with her widowed father, has long been accustomed to sharing his affections with a string of girlfriends and is unperturbed when the latest of these, Elsa, arrives at the villa. Although Cécile has inherited her father's charm she is too young to understand the deeper manipulations binding men and women. Her feelings towards Anne, who appears to be supplanting Elsa, reflect her own reservations concerning love.

Anne was extraordinarily kind to Elsa during the following days. In spite of the numerous silly remarks that punctuated Elsa's conversation, she never gave vent to any of those cutting phrases which were her speciality, and which would have covered the poor girl with ridicule. I was most surprised, and began to admire Anne's forbearance and generosity without realizing how subtle she was; for my father, who would soon have tired of such cruel tactics, was now filled with gratitude towards her. He used his appreciation as a pretext for drawing her, so to speak, into the family circle; by implying all the time that I was partly her responsibility, and altogether behaving towards her as if she were a second mother to me. But I noticed that his every look and gesture betrayed a secret desire for her. Whenever I caught a similar gleam in Cyril's eye, it left me undecided whether to egg him on or to run away. On that point I must have been more easily influenced than Anne, for her attitude to my father expressed such indifference and calm friendliness that I was reassured. I began to believe that I had been mistaken the first day. I did not notice that this unconcern of hers was just what provoked my father. And then there were her silences, apparently so artless and full of fine feeling, and such a contrast to Elsa's incessant chatter, that it was like light and shade. Poor Elsa! She had really no suspicions whatsoever, and although still suffering from the effects of the sun, remained her usual talkative and exuberant self.

A day came, however, when she must have intercepted a look of my father's and drawn her own conclusions from it. Before lunch I saw her whispering into his ear. For a moment he seemed rather put out, but then he nodded and smiled. After coffee Elsa walked over to the door, turned round, and striking a languorous, film-star pose, said in an affected voice, 'Are you coming, Raymond?'

My father got up and followed her, muttering something about the benefits of the siesta. Anne had not moved, her cigarette was smouldering between her fingers. I felt I ought to say something:

'People say that a siesta is restful, but I think it is the opposite . . .'

I stopped short, conscious that my words were equivocal.

'That's enough,' said Anne dryly.

There was nothing equivocal about her tone. She had of course found my remark in bad taste, but when I looked at her I saw that her face was deliberately calm and composed. It made me feel that perhaps at that moment she was passionately jealous of Elsa. While I was wondering how I could console her, a cynical idea occurred to me. Cynicism always enchanted me by producing a delicious feeling of self-assurance and of being in league with myself. I could not keep it back.

'I imagine that with Elsa's sunburn that kind of siesta can't be very exciting for either of them.'

I would have done better to say nothing.

'I detest that kind of remark. At your age it's not only stupid, but deplorable.'

I suddenly felt angry:

'I only said it as a joke, you know. I'm sure they are really quite happy.'

She turned to me with an outraged expression, and I at once apologized. She closed her eyes and began to speak in a low, patient voice.

'Your idea of love is rather primitive. It is not a series of sensations, independent of each other. . . .'

I realized how every time I had fallen in love it had been like that: a sudden emotion, roused by a face, a gesture or a kiss, which I remembered only as incoherent moments of excitement. 'It is something different,' said Anne. 'There are such things as lasting affection, sweetness, a sense of loss . . . but I suppose you wouldn't understand.'

She made an evasive gesture and took up a newspaper. If only she had been angry instead of showing that resigned indifference to my emotional irresponsibility! All the same I felt she was right: that I was governed by my instincts like an animal, swayed this way and that by other people, that I was shallow and weak. I despised myself, and it was a horribly painful sensation, all the more since I was not used to self-criticism. I went up to my room in a daze. Lying in bed on my lukewarm sheet I thought of Anne's words: 'It is something different, it's a sense of loss.' Had I ever missed anyone?

The next fortnight is rather vague in my memory because I deliberately shut my eyes to any threat to our security, but the rest of the holiday stands out all the more clearly because of the role I chose to play in it.

To go back to those first three weeks, three happy weeks after all: when exactly did my father begin to treat Anne with a new familiarity? Was it the day he reproached her for her indifference, while pretending to laugh at it? Or the time he grimly compared her subtlety with Elsa's semi-imbecility? My peace of mind was based on the stupid idea that they had known each other for fifteen years, and that if they had been going to fall in love, they would have done so earlier. And I thought also that if it had to happen, the affair would last at the most three months, and Anne would be left with her memories and perhaps a slight feeling of humiliation. Yet all the time I knew in my heart that Anne was not a woman who could be lightly abandoned.

But Cyril was there, and I was fully occupied. In the evenings we often drove to Saint-Tropez and danced in various bars to the soft music of a clarinet. At those moments we felt we were madly in love, but by the next morning it was all forgotten. During the day we went sailing. My father sometimes came with us. He thought a lot of Cyril, especially since he had been allowed to beat him in a swimming race. He called Cyril 'my boy', Cyril called him 'sir', but I sometimes wondered which of the two was the adult.

One afternoon we went to tea with Cyril's mother, a quiet smiling old lady who spoke to us of her difficulties as a widow and mother. My father sympathized with her, looked gratefully at Anne, and paid innumerable compliments. I must say he never minded wasting his time! Anne looked on at the spectacle with an amiable smile, and afterwards said she thought her charming. I broke into imprecations against old ladies of that sort. They both seemed amused, which made me furious.

'Don't you realize how self-righteous she is?' I insisted. 'That she pats herself on the back because she feels she has done her duty by leading a respectable bourgeois life?'

'But it is true,' said Anne. 'She has done her duty as a wife and mother, as they say.'

'You don't understand at all,' I said. 'She brought up her child; most likely she was faithful to her husband, and so had no worries; she has led the life of millions of other women, and she's proud of it. She glorifies herself for a negative reason, and not for having accomplished anything.'

'Your ideas are fashionable, but you don't know what you are talking about,' Anne said.

She was probably right: I believed what I said at the time, but I must admit that I was only repeating what I had heard. Nevertheless my life and my father's upheld that theory, and Anne hurt my feelings by despising it. One can be just as attached to futilities as to anything else. I suddenly felt an urgent desire to undeceive her. I did not think the opportunity would occur so soon, nor that I would be able to seize it. Anyhow it was quite likely that in a month's time I might have entirely different opinions on any given subject. What more could have been expected of me?

*   *   *

And then one day things came to a head. In the morning my father announced that he would like to go to Cannes that evening to dance at the casino, and perhaps gamble as well. I remember how pleased Elsa was. In the familiar casino atmosphere she hoped to resume her role of a 'femme fatale', slightly obscured of late by her sunburn and our semi-isolation. Contrary to my expectation Anne did not oppose our plans; she even seemed quite pleased. As soon as dinner was over I went up to my room to put on an evening frock, the only one I possessed, by the way. It had been chosen by my father, and was made of an exotic material, probably too exotic for a girl of my age, but my father, either from inclination or habit, liked to give me a veneer of sophistication. I found him downstairs, sparkling in a new dinner jacket, and I put my arms round his neck.

'You're the best-looking man I know!'

'Except Cyril,' he answered without conviction. 'And as for you, you're the prettiest girl I know.'

'After Elsa and Anne,' I replied without believing it myself.

'Since they're not down yet, and have the cheek to keep us waiting, come and dance with your rheumaticky old father!'

Once again I felt the thrill that always preceded our evenings out together. He really had nothing of an old father about him! While dancing I inhaled the warmth of his familiar perfume, eau de cologne and tobacco. He danced slowly with half-closed eyes, a happy, irrepressible little smile, like my own, on his lips.

'You must teach me the bebop,' he said, forgetting his talk of rheumatism.

He stopped dancing to welcome Elsa with polite flattery. She came slowly down the stairs in her green dress, a conventional smile on her face, her casino smile. She had made the most of her lifeless hair and scorched skin, but the result was more meretricious than brilliant. Fortunately she seemed unaware of it.

'Are we going?'

'Anne's not here yet,' I remarked.

'Go up and see if she's ready,' said my father. 'It will be midnight before we get to Cannes.'

I ran up the stairs, getting somewhat entangled with

my skirt, and knocked at Anne's door. She called to me to come in, but I stopped on the threshold. She was wearing a grey dress, a peculiar grey, almost white, which, when it caught the light, resembled the colour of the sea at dawn. She seemed to me the personification of mature charm.

'Oh Anne, what a magnificent dress!' I said.

She smiled into the mirror as one smiles at a person one is about to leave.

'This grey is a success,' she said.

'You are a success!' I answered.

She pinched my ear, her eyes were dark blue, and I saw them light up with a smile.

'You're a dear child, even though you can be tiresome at times.'

She went out in front of me without a glance at my dress. In a way I was relieved, but all the same it was mortifying. I followed her down the stairs and I saw my father coming to meet her. He stopped at the bottom, his foot on the first step, his face raised. Elsa was looking on. I remember the scene perfectly. First of all, in front of me, Anne's golden neck and perfect shoulders, a little lower down my father's fascinated face and extended hand, and, already in the distance, Elsa's silhouette.

'Anne, you are wonderful!' said my father.

She smiled as she passed him and took her coat.

'Shall we meet there?' she asked. 'Cécile, will you come with me?'

She let me drive. At night the road appeared so beautiful that I went slowly. Anne was silent; she did not even seem to notice the blaring wireless. When my father's car passed us at a bend she remained unmoved. I felt I was out of the race, watching a performance in which I could no longer intervene.

At the casino my father saw to it that we soon lost sight of each other. I found myself at the bar with Elsa and one of her acquaintances, a half-tipsy South American. He was connected with the stage and had such a passionate love for it that even in his inebriated condition he could remain amusing. I spent an agreeable hour with him, but Elsa was bored. She knew one or two big names, but that was not her world. All of a sudden she asked me where my father was, as if I had some means of knowing. She then left us. The South American seemed put out for a moment, but another whisky set him up again. My mind was a blank. I was quite light-headed, for I had been drinking with him out of politeness. It became grotesque when he wanted to dance. I was forced to hold him up and to extricate my feet from under his, which required a lot of energy. We laughed so much that when Elsa tapped me on the shoulder and I saw her Cassandra-like expression, I almost felt like telling her to go to the devil.

'I can't find them,' she said.

She looked utterly distraught. Her powder had worn off leaving her skin shiny, her features were drawn; she was a pitiable sight. I suddenly felt very angry with my father; he was being most unkind.

'Ah, I know where they are,' I said, smiling as if I referred to something quite ordinary about which she need have no anxiety. 'I'll soon be back.'

Deprived of my support, the South American fell into Elsa's arms and seemed comfortable enough there. I reflected somewhat sadly that she was more experienced than I, and that I could not very well bear her a grudge.

The casino was big, and I went all round it twice without any success. I scanned the terrace and at last thought of the car. It took me some time to find it in the car park. They were inside. I approached from behind and saw them through the rear window. Their profiles were very close together and very serious, and looked strangely beautiful in the lamplight. They were facing each other and must have been talking in low tones, for I saw their lips move. I would have liked to go away again, but the thought of Elsa made me open the door. My father had his hand on Anne's arm, and they scarcely noticed me.

'Are you having a good time?' I asked politely.

'What is the matter?' said my father irritably. 'What are you doing here?'

'And you? Elsa has been searching for you everywhere for the past hour.'

Anne turned her head slowly and reluctantly towards me.

'We're going home. Tell her I was tired and your father drove me back. When you've had enough take my car.'

I was trembling with indignation and could hardly speak.

'Had enough? But you don't realize what you're saying, it's disgusting!'

'What is disgusting?' asked my father with astonishment.

'You take a red-haired girl to the seaside, expose her to the hot sun which she can't stand, and when her skin has all peeled you abandon her. It's altogether too simple! What on earth shall I say to Elsa?'

Anne turned to him with an air of weariness. He smiled at her, obviously not listening. My exasperation knew no bounds.

'I shall tell Elsa that my father has found someone

else to sleep with, and that she had better come back some other time. Is that right?'

My father's exclamation and Anne's slap were simultaneous. I hurriedly withdrew my head from the cardoor. She had hurt me.

'Apologize at once!' said my father.

I stood motionless, with my thoughts in a whirl. Noble attitudes always occur to me too late.

'Come here,' said Anne.

She did not sound menacing, and I went closer. She put her hand against my cheek and spoke slowly and gently as if I were rather simple.

'Don't be naughty. I'm very sorry for Elsa, but you are tactful enough to arrange everything for the best. Tomorrow we'll discuss it all. Did I hurt you very much?'

'Not at all,' I said politely. Her sudden gentleness after my intemperate rage made me want to burst into tears. I watched them drive away, feeling completely deflated. My only consolation was the thought of my tactfulness.

I walked slowly back to the casino, where I found Elsa with the South American clinging to her arm.

'Anne wasn't well,' I said in an off-hand manner. 'Papa had to take her home. What about a drink?'

She looked at me without answering. I tried to find a more convincing explanation.

'She was awfully sick,' I said. 'It was ghastly, her dress is ruined.' This detail seemed to me to make my story more plausible, but Elsa began to weep quietly and sadly. I did not know what to do.

'Oh, Cécile, we were so happy!' she said, and her sobs redoubled in intensity. The South American began to cry, repeating 'We were so happy, so happy!' At that moment I heartily detested Anne and my father.

I would have done anything to stop Elsa from crying, her eye-black from running, and the South American from howling.

'Nothing is settled yet, Elsa. Come home with me now!'

'No! I'll fetch my suitcases later,' she sobbed. 'Goodbye, Cécile, we got on well together, didn't we?'

We had never talked of anything but clothes or the weather, but still it seemed to me that I was losing an old friend. I quickly turned away and ran to the car.

* * *

The following morning was wretched, probably because of the whisky I had drunk the night before. I awoke to find myself lying across my bed in the dark; my tongue heavy, my limbs unbearably damp and sticky. A single ray of sunshine filtered through the slats of the shutters and I could see a million motes dancing in it. I felt no desire to get up, nor to stay in bed. I wondered how Anne and my father would look if Elsa were to turn up that morning. I forced myself to think of them in order to be able to get out of bed without effort. At last I managed to stand up on the cool stone floor. I was giddy and aching. The mirror reflected a sad sight; I leant against it and peered at those dilated eyes and dry lips, an unknown face; mine? If I was weak and cowardly, could it be because of those lips, the particular shape of my body, these odious, arbitrary limits? And if I were limited, why had I only now become aware of it? I amused myself by detesting my reflection, hating that wolf-like face, hollow and worn by debauch. I repeated the word 'debauch' dumbly, looking into my eyes in the mirror, and suddenly I saw myself smile. What a debauch! A few unfortunate drinks, a slap in the face and some tears! I brushed my teeth and went downstairs.

My father and Anne were already on the terrace sitting beside each other in front of their breakfast tray. I sat down opposite them, muttering a vague 'good morning'. A feeling of shyness made me keep my eyes lowered, but after a time, as they remained silent I was forced to look at them. Anne appeared tired, the only sign of a night of love. They were both smiling happily, and I was very much impressed, for happiness has always seemed to me a great achievement.

'Did you sleep well?' asked my father.

'Not too badly,' I replied. 'I drank a lot of whisky last night.'

I poured out a cup of coffee, but after the first sip I quickly put it down. Their silence had a waiting quality that made me feel uneasy. I was too tired to bear it for long.

'What's the matter? You look so mysterious.'

My father lit a cigarette, making an obvious effort to seem unconcerned, and for once in her life Anne seemed embarrassed.

'I would like to ask you something,' she said at last.

'I suppose you want me to take another message to Elsa?' I said, imagining the worst.

She turned towards my father.

'Your father and I want to get married,' she said.

I stared first at her, then at my father. I half expected some sign from him, perhaps a wink, which, though I might have found it shocking, would have reassured me, but he was looking down at his hands. I said to myself 'it can't be possible!' but I already knew it was true.

'What a good idea,' I said to gain time.

I could not understand how my father, who had always set himself so obstinately against marriage and its chains, could have decided on it in a single night. We were about to lose our independence. I could visualize our future family life, a life which would suddenly be given equilibrium by Anne's intelligence and refinement; the life I had envied her. We would have clever tactful friends, and quiet pleasant evenings. . . . I found myself despising noisy dinners, South Americans and girls like Elsa. I felt proud and superior.

'It's a very, very good idea,' I repeated, and I smiled at them.

'I knew you'd be pleased, my pet,' said my father.

He was relaxed and delighted. Anne's face, subtly changed by love, seemed gentler, making her appear more accessible than she had ever been before.

'Come here, my pet,' said my father; and holding out his hands, he drew me close to them both. I was half-kneeling in front of them, while they stroked my hair and looked at me with tender emotion. But I could not stop thinking that although my life was perhaps at that very moment changing its whole course, I was in reality nothing more than a kitten to them, an affectionate little animal. I felt them above me, united by a past and a future, by ties that I did not know and which could not hold me. But I deliberately closed my eyes and went on playing my part, laying my head on their knees and laughing. For was I not happy? Anne was all right, I had no serious fault to find with her. She would guide me, relieve me of responsibility, and be at hand whenever I might need her. She would make both my father and me into paragons of virtue.

My father got up to fetch a bottle of champagne. I felt sickened. He was happy, which was the chief thing, but I had so often seen him happy on account of a woman.

'I was rather frightened of you,' said Anne.

'Why?' I asked. Her words had given me the impression that a veto from me could have prevented their marriage.

'I was afraid of your being frightened of me,' she said laughing.

I began to laugh too, because actually I was a little scared of her. She wanted me to understand that she knew it, and that it was unnecessary.

'Does the marriage of two old people like ourselves seem ridiculous to you?'

'You're not old,' I said emphatically, as my father came dancing back with a bottle in his hand.

He sat down next to Anne and put his arm round her shoulders. She moved nearer to him and I looked away in embarrassment. She was no doubt marrying him for just that; for his laughter, for the firm reassurance of his arm, for his vitality, his warmth. At forty there could be the fear of solitude, or perhaps a last upsurge of the senses. ... I had never thought of Anne as a woman, but as an entity. I had seen her as a self-assured, elegant and clever person, but never weak or sensual. I quite understood that my father felt proud, the self-satisfied, indifferent Anne Larsen was going to marry him. Did he love her, and if so, was he capable of loving her for long? Was there any difference between this new feeling and the affection he had shown Elsa? The sun was making my head spin, and I shut my eyes. We were all three on the terrace, full of reserves, of secret fears, and of happiness.

Elsa did not come back just then. A week flew by, seven happy, agreeable days, the only ones. We made elaborate plans for furnishing our home, and discussed time tables which my father and I took pleasure in cutting as fine as possible with the blind obstinacy of those who have never had any use for them. Did we ever believe in them for one moment? Did my father really think it possible to have lunch every day at the same place at 12.30 sharp, to have dinner at home, and not to go out afterwards? However, he gaily prepared to inter Bohemianism, and began to preach order, and to extol the joys of an elegant, organized bourgeois existence. No doubt for him, as well as for myself, all these plans were merely castles in the air.

How well I remember that week! Anne was relaxed, confident and very sweet; my father loved her. I saw them coming down in the mornings, leaning on each other, laughing gaily, with shadows under their eyes, and I swear that I should have like nothing better than that their happiness should last all their lives. In the evening we often drank our aperitif sitting on some café terrace by the sea. Everywhere we went we were taken for a happy, normal family, and I, who was used to going out alone with my father and seeing the knowing smiles, and malicious or pitying glances, was delighted to play a role more suitable to my age. They were to be married on our return to Paris.

Poor Cyril had witnessed the transformation in our midst with a certain amazement, but he was comforted by the thought that this time it would be legalized. We went out sailing together and kissed when we felt inclined, but sometimes during our embraces I thought of Anne's face as I saw it in the mornings, with its softened contours. I recalled the happy nonchalance, the languid grace that love imparted to her movements, and I envied her. One can grow tired of kissing, and no doubt if Cyril had not been so fond of me I would have become his mistress that week.

At six o'clock, on our return from the islands, Cyril would pull the boat on to the sand. We would go up the house through the pine wood in single file, pretending we were Indians, or run handicap races to warm ourselves up. He always caught me before we reached the house and would spring on me with a shout of victory, rolling me on the pine needles, pinning my arms down and kissing me. I can still remember those light, breathless kisses, and Cyril's heart beating against mine in rhythm with the soft thud of the waves on the sand. Four heart beats and four waves, and then gradually he would regain his breath and his kisses would become more urgent, the sound of the sea would grow dim and give way to the pulse in my ears.

One evening we were surprised by Anne's voice. Cyril was lying close to me in the red glow of the sunset. I can understand that Anne might have been misled by the sight of us there in our scanty bathing things. She called me sharply.

Cyril bounded to his feet, naturally somewhat ashamed. Keeping my eyes on Anne, I slowly got up in my turn. She faced Cyril, and looking right through him spoke in a quiet voice, 'I don't wish to see you again.'

He made no reply, but bent over and kissed my shoulder before departing. I felt surprised and touched, as if his gesture had been a sort of pledge. Anne was staring at me with the same grave and detached look, as though she were thinking of something else. Her manner infuriated me. If she was so deep in thought, why speak at all? I went up to her, feigning embarrassment for the sake of politeness. At last she seemed to notice me and mechanically removed a pine needle from my neck. I saw her face assume its beautiful mask of disdain, that expression of weariness and disapproval which became her so well, and which always frightened me a little.

'You should know that such diversions usually end up in a nursing home.'

She stood there looking straight at me as she spoke, and I was horribly ashamed. She was one of those women who can stand perfectly still while they talk; I always needed the support of a chair, or some object to hold like a cigarette, or the distraction of swinging one leg over the other and watching it move.

'You mustn't exaggerate,' I said with a smile. 'I was only kissing Cyril, and that won't lead me to any nursing home.'

'Please don't see him again,' she said, as if she did not believe me. 'Do not protest: you are seventeen and I feel a certain responsibility for you now. I'm not going to let you ruin your life. In any case you have work to do, and that will occupy your afternoons.'

She turned her back on me and walked towards the house in her nonchalant way. A paralysing sense of calamity kept me rooted to the spot. She had meant every word; what was the use of arguments or denials when she would receive them with the sort of indifference that was worse than contempt, as if I did not even exist, as if I were something to be squashed underfoot, and not myself, Cécile, whom she had always known. My only hope now was my father; surely he would say as usual: 'Well now, who's the boy? I suppose he's a handsome fellow, but beware, my girl!' If he did not react like this, my holidays would be ruined.

Dinner was a nightmare. Not for one moment had Anne suggested that she would not tell my father anything if I promised to work; it was not in her nature to bargain. I was pleased in one way, but also disappointed that she had deprived me of a chance to despise her. As usual she avoided a false move, and it was only when we had finished our soup that she seemed to remember the incident.

'I do wish you'd give your daughter some advice, Raymond. I found her in the wood with Cyril this evening, and they seemed to be going rather far.'

My father, poor man, tried to pass the whole thing off as a joke.

'What's that you say? What were they up to?'

'I was kissing him,' I said. 'And Anne thought...'

'I never thought anything at all,' she interrupted. 'But it might be a good idea for her to stop seeing him for a time and to work at her philosophy instead.'

'Poor little thing!' said my father. 'After all Cyril's a nice boy, isn't he?'

'And Cécile is a nice girl,' said Anne. 'That's why I should be heartbroken if anything should happen to her, and it seems to me inevitable that it will, if you consider what complete freedom she enjoys here, and that they are constantly together and have nothing whatever to do. Don't you agree?'

At her last words I looked up and saw that my father was very perturbed.

'You are probably right,' he said. 'After all, you ought to do some work, Cécile. You surely don't want to fail in philosophy and have to take it again?'

'What do you think I care?' I answered.

He glanced at me and then turned away. I was bewildered. I realized that procrastination can rule our lives, yet not provide us with any arguments in its defence.

'Listen,' said Anne, taking my hand across the table. 'Won't you exchange your role of a wood nymph for that of a good schoolgirl for one month? Would it be so serious?'

They both looked at me expectantly; seen in that light, the argument was simple enough. I gently withdrew my hand.

'Yes, very serious,' I said, so softly that they did not hear it, or did not want to.

The following morning I came across a phrase from Bergson:

> Whatever irrelevance one may at first find between the cause and the effects, and although a rule of guidance towards an assertion concerning the root of things may be far distant, it is always in a contact with the generative force of life that one is able to extract the power to love humanity.

I repeated the phrase, quietly at first, so as not to get agitated, then in a louder voice. I held my head in my hands and looked at the book with great attention. At last I understood it, but I felt as cold and impotent as when I had read it the first time. I could not continue. With the best will in the world I applied myself to the next lines, and suddenly something arose in me like a storm and threw me on to the bed. I thought of Cyril waiting for me down in the creek, of the swaying boat, of the pleasure of our kisses, and then I thought of Anne, but in a way that made me sit up on my bed with a fast-beating heart, telling myself that I was stupid, monstrous, nothing but a lazy, spoilt child, and had no right to have such thoughts. But all the same, in spite of myself I continued to reflect that she was dangerous, and that I must get rid of her. I thought of the lunch I had endured with clenched teeth, tortured by a feeling of resentment for which I despised and ridiculed myself. Yes, it was for this I reproached Anne: she prevented me from liking myself. I, who was so naturally meant for happiness and gaiety, had been forced by her into a world of self-criticism and guilty conscience, where, unaccustomed to introspection, I was completely lost. And what did she bring me? I took stock: she wanted my father; she had got him. She would gradually make of us the husband and step-daughter of Anne Larsen; that is to say, she would turn us into two civilized, well-behaved and happy people. For she would certainly make us happy. How easily, unstable and irresponsible as we were, we would yield to her influence, and be drawn into the attractive framework of her orderly plan of living. She was much too efficient: already my father was estranged from me. I was obsessed by his embarrassed face turning away from me at table. Tears came into my eyes at the thought of the jokes we used to have together, our gay laughter as we drove home at dawn through the empty streets of Paris. All that was over. In my turn I would be influenced, re-orientated, re-modelled by Anne. I would not even mind it, she would act with intelligence, irony and sweetness, and I would be incapable of resistance; in six months I should no longer even wish to resist.

At all costs I must take steps to regain my father and our former life. How infinitely desirable those two years suddenly appeared to me, those happy years I was so willing to renounce the other day ... the liberty to think, even to think wrongly or not at all, the freedom to choose my own life, to choose myself. I cannot say 'to be myself', for I was only soft clay, but still I could refuse to be moulded.

I realize that one might find complicated motives for

this change in me, one might endow me with spectacular complexes: such as an incestuous love for my father, or a morbid passion for Anne, but I know the true reasons were the heat, Bergson, and Cyril, or at least his absence. I dwelt on this all the afternoon in a most unpleasant mood, induced by the discovery that we were entirely at Anne's mercy. I was not used to reflection, and it made me irritable. At dinner, as in the morning, I did not open my mouth. My father thought it appropriate to chaff me.

'What I like about youth is its spontaneity, its gay conversation.'

I was trembling with rage. It was true that he loved youth; and with whom could I have talked if not with him? We had discussed everything together: love, death, music. Now he himself had disarmed and abandoned me. Looking at him I thought: 'You don't love me any more, you have betrayed me!' I tried to make him understand without words how desperate I was. He seemed suddenly alarmed; perhaps he understood that the time for joking was past, and that our relationship was in danger. I saw him stiffen, and it appeared as though he were about to ask a question. Anne turned to me.

'You don't look well. I feel sorry now for making you work.'

I did not reply. I felt too disgusted that I had got myself into a state which I could no longer control. We had finished dinner. On the terrace, in the rectangle of light projected from the dining-room window, I saw Anne's long nervous hand reach out to find my father's. I thought of Cyril. I would have liked him to take me in his arms on that moonlit terrace, alive with crickets. I would have liked to be caressed, consoled, reconciled with myself. My father and Anne were silent, they had a night of love to look forward to; I had Bergson. I tried to cry, to feel sorry for myself, but in vain; it was already Anne for whom I was sorry, as if I were certain of victory.

Ntozake Shange

extract from

*Sassafrass,
Cypress & Indigo*

Sassafrass, the eldest of three sisters, is a poet and weaver like her mother. She leaves Charleston, South Carolina and goes north to college, enjoying a bohemian life in Los Angeles and testing out her own set of values in respect of her man, her work, her evaluation of the past.

Nothing but tenor sax solos ever came out of that house. Sometimes you could hear a man and a woman arguing, but almost always some kind of music. Sassafrass and Mitch lived together in that house, sort of hidden behind untended hedges and the peeling shingles. Even though they were living in L.A., there were always some dried leaves lying all across their stoop. Sassafrass thought it was the spirits, bringing them good luck; Mitch thought it was because she didn't ever sweep. But there was still the music, and the black Great Dane, Albert, whose real name was My-Name-Is-Albert-Ayler. None of the neighbours knew the dog's full name, so Sassafrass never worried about him being stolen because he only came when someone called his whole name. Sassafrass had named him after the screenplay she had started after the album she had made, and after her lover she never met . . . Albert Ayler was found in the East River. That was one of the reasons Mitch was attracted to her, because she had named her dog so irreverently after his mentor, alto-saxist Ayler. Still, Sassafrass was so full of love she couldn't call anybody anything without bringing good vibes from a whole lot of spirits to everything she touched.

Walter Cronkite's voice could be heard through the

open window next to Sassafrass' bed. She was sitting there in a long blue and red cotton skirt, crocheting another hat for Mitch. The long walls of the fallen-down, almost Victorian house were totally covered with murals of African exploits. Every time the landlady came to repair the falling plaster on the ceiling she'd look so uncomfortable; her redneck lips would get littler than a needle and her cheeks would get all stiff. Sassafrass loved watching that old peckerwood get nervous from total blackness all through the house. The old peckerwood got $100.00 a month for the whole flat, which Sassafrass and Mitch had worked on to be a permanent monument to the indelibility of black creative innovation. She glanced up from her sixty-sixth stitch to see if there was anything else to do to the house to make it the most perfect place for her and Mitch to stay in until the black revolution, or until they moved to the black artists' and craftsmen's commune starting up just outside New Orleans, and pretty near a black nationalist settlement. Sassafrass believed it was absolutely necessary to take black arts out of the white man's hands; to take black people out of the white man's hands. But here she was in Highland Park, Los Angeles, with rednecks and Chicanos, because Mitch's parole officer refused to grant permission for them to live in any black area – and because they could only afford $100.00 a month – and because they didn't have the money to buy into the artists' commune near New Orleans anyhow: almost one thousand dollars, cash. So Sassafrass looked around to see if there was something else she could make to make them feel more like loving each other and hitting sunrise with hope, instead of the groans and crabbiness that ate through them toward the end of every poor month.

There were the exasperating patchwork curtains she

had managed to get done, and macrame hangings in every doorway – one named for each of their heroes. There was the long and knotted purple jute, hanging for Malcolm, who was a king. It had bullets woven through the ends of it, and dried sand covered twigs passing in and out of the centre. 'Bullets and land of our own,' Sassafrass had said, standing on Mitch's shoulders to hang it. Then there were the ones for Fidel, Garvey, Archie Shepp, and Coltrane. In her study, Sassafrass had sequestered a sequin-and-feather hanging shaped like a vagina, for Josephine Baker, but Mitch had made her hide it because it wasn't proper for a new Afrikan woman to make things of such a sexual nature. Just as she was remembering Mitch's tirade against her feather-work, Sassafrass felt the doors open and there he was – the cosmic lover and wonder of wonders to her: Mitch.

Mitch had to stoop a little under the doorway; he was almost seven feet tall, and long-limbed like a Watusi with Ethiopian eyes that arched like rainbows, and gold ear-rings in both ears, etched real fine because they were from Mexico (antiques). His nose was slightly hooked like Nasser's, and his presence was that of one of those Olmec gods. Mitch thought of himself as a god, and he was always telling Sassafrass not to succumb to her mortality; to live like she was one of God's stars.

That particular day Mitch was wearing his blue homespun shirt Sassafrass had made with laced cuffs, and an orange coral medallion and some copper corduroy pants that sat on his thighs like he was the hottest thing in town. But this time Mitch was serious and brusque when he spoke to Sassafrass, who was trying to push her crocheting under her skirts.

'Why aren't you writing, girl? Do you think you gonna

be some kind of writer sitting up here making me hats? I got so many damn hats I have to give some away, and you sittin' here makin' me another one. Well, if I didn't know you were being so considerate because you don't wanna deal with your writing, I'd say thanks, but you makin' me stuff and hangin' all this shit around the walls in every room so you won't haveta write nothing today.'

Sassafrass was holding her lips so tight between her teeth she could barely stand the pain, and she was making moves to get up and away from Mitch's harangue when he pushed her back on the bed.

'Look, Sassafrass, I just want you to be happy with yourself. You want to write and create new images for black folks, and you're always sittin' around making things with your hands. There's nothing wrong with that, 'cept you've known how to do that all your damn life.' Mitch began to grow fierce again, and held Sassafrass briskly by the shoulder with one hand, bringing her chin and eyes straight to his gaze with the other. And Sassafrass couldn't avoid the truth: the man she loved was not happy with her charade of homebodiness, because all this weaving and crocheting and macrameing she'd been doing all her life, and Sassafrass was supposed to be a writer. Mitch forcefully held her face close to his and continued.

'Now Sassafrass, get into yourself and find out what's holding you back. You can create whole worlds, girl. I don't wanna come and see you like this any more, listening to some white man make it easy for you to stop thinking, telling you all the white folks' news, so you think that nobody doesn't know you got to pay your dues to the spirits. Sassafrass, if another person don't tell you you're a writer, you'll know it all your life. And you better take care of it or you'll end up some kind of wino or slut, trying to fuck it away with some punk-assed schoolteacher who can't see you a jive-assed little bitch.' Mitch slowly let Sassafrass' face come into her control, and stood all the way up so Sassafrass couldn't forget who was overwhelmingly right in any situation. He straightened his shirt in his pants, and left the room to go practise horn playing.

Sassafrass was weak from Mitch's torrent. She sat so still her old fear of actually being a catatonic came back, and scared her so much she wiggled just to make sure. Mitch didn't have to say all that even if it was true; it was ridiculous for some man to come tell her she had to create. That's the same as telling her she had to have babies, and she didn't want to have babies . . . she could hardly feed herself, and Mitch didn't feed anybody. All he did was play that old horn, and look for the nearest bar that could use an 'avant-garde free-music' sax man. 'Humph.' Sassafrass caught herself focusing in on Mitch again instead of herself, because she did want to be perfected for him, like he was perfected and creating all the time. Sassafrass was running all through herself looking for some way to get into her secrets and share, like Richard Wright had done and Zora Neale Hurston had done . . . the way The Lady gave herself, every time she sang.

> Do Nothing till You Hear from Me
> Pay No Attention to What's Said

From out of the closet came Billie, The Lady, all decked out in navy crêpe and rhinestones. She was pinning a gardenia in her hair, when Sassafrass realized what was happening.

Ntozake Shange

The Lady sighed a familiar sigh. Sassafrass tried to look as calm as possible and said, 'I sure am glad to see you — why you haven't come to visit since Mama used to put me to bed singing "God Bless The Child", and you would sit right on my pillow singing with her.' The Lady smiled sort of haughty and insisted Sassafrass listen carefully to everything she was going to say.

'It's the blues, Sassafrass, that's keepin' you from your writing, and the spirits sent me because I know all about the blues . . . that's who I am: Miss Brown's Blues . . .' The Lady was holding a pearl-studded cigarette holder that dazzled Sassafrass, who could hardly believe what she was hearing. The Lady went on and on. 'Who do you love among us, Sassafrass? Ma Rainey, Mamie Smith, Big Mama Thornton, Freddie Washington, Josephine, Carmen Miranda? Don't ya know we is all sad ladies because we got the blues, and joyful women because we got our songs? Make you a song, Sassafrass, and bring it out so high all us spirits can hold it and be in your tune. We need you, Sassafrass, we need you to sing best as you can; that's our nourishment, that's how we live. But don't you get all high and mighty, 'cause all us you love so much is hussies too, and we catch on if somebody don't do us right. So make us some poems and some stories, so we can sing a liberation song. Free us from all these blues and sorry ways.'

The Lady turned to the doorway on her right and shouted, 'Come on, y'all,' and multitudes of brown-skinned dancing girls with ostrich-feather headpieces and tap shoes started doing the cake-walk all around Sassafrass, who was trying to figure out the stitching pattern on their embroidered dresses, and trying to keep from jumping up and shaking her ass when, in unison, the elaborately beaded women started swinging their hips towards her, singing: SASSAFRASS IS WHERE IT'S AT, SASSAFRASS GOTTA HIPFUL OF LOVE, A HIPFUL OF TRUTH . . . SASSAFRASS GOTTA JOB TO DO, DUES TO PAY SO SHE COULD DANCE WITH US . . . WHOOEEE!

And all of a sudden the chorus line disintegrated into a dressing-room conversation; the women started sharing secrets about lovers, managers, and children staying with their grandmas till the tour was over . . . and Sassafrass gathered all there was that was more to her than making cloth. Just as she was about to slip out of the room, Sassafrass turned to The Lady to capture just a little more of the magic, and The Lady only murmured, 'We need you to be Sassafrass 'til you can't hardly stand it . . . 'til you can't recognize yourself, and you sing all the time.'

Sassafrass closed the door on the babbling women-visitors quickly. Mitch was coming toward her, making the room reel with the craziness of his music; like he was tearing himself all up, beating and scratching through his skin. The horn rocked gently with his body, but the sounds were devastating: pure anger and revenge. He pulled the slight instrument from his mouth and licked the reed once or twice, before he slipped his hand up Sassafrass' skirts to tickle her a little.

'You gonna make me something to eat, lovely one?' Mitch grinned a Valentino grin, horn in one hand, Sassafrass on the other. She giggled distractedly and mumbled, 'Yeah, I just wanna write down a few things before I get stuck in the kitchen.'

She rubbed her temples impatiently, because for a change Mitch wasn't on her mind. She didn't want to play; she wanted to write, and Mitch was messing around, being nasty. She caught his wrist with her thumb and index finger. 'Not now, Mitch. Not now. I wanna go do something.' Mitch released her instantly. He wasn't into taking any woman who didn't want him desperately, so Sassafrass could go. And Mitch picked up his horn and tooted the melody of Looney Tune cartoons he had to watch when he was a child at the boys' reformatory in Philadelphia: dadadadada dadadadada, and then he imitated Porky Pig saying, 't-t-t-t-that's all, folks!' He smiled to himself when Sassafrass slammed the door to the kitchen and made obviously rebellious noises with every pot she handled.

Mitch had convinced Sassafrass that everything was an art, so nothing in life could be approached lightly. Creation was inherent in everything anybody ever did right; that was one of the mottos of the house. Sassafrass had made an appliquéd banner saying just that, and hung it over the stove:

CREATION IS

EVERYTHING YOU DO

MAKE SOMETHING

She sat on her personal chair to concentrate on what to create for dinner. She was busy thinking of nothing when she fixed on the idea of a rice casserole, sautéed spinach and mushrooms with sweet peppers, and broiled mackerel with red sauce. If she prepared this scrumptious meal there wouldn't be hardly enough food left to finish off the week, but since Mitch was into her being perfect today, she decided to make a perfect meal and let him perfect out the menu for later, because 'you can't cut no corners and be right' is what he always said. And Sassafrass set to work.

Sassafrass' Rice Casserole # 36

- 1 1/2 cups medium grain brown rice
- 3 ounces pimentos
- 1 cup baby green peas
- 1/2 cup fresh walnuts
- 2/3 pound smoked cheddar cheese
- 1/2 cup condensed milk
- Diced garlic to taste
- Cayenne to taste

Cook rice as usual. In an eight-inch baking dish, layer rice, cheese, pimentos, walnuts and peas. Spread garlic and cayenne as you see fit. Pour milk around side of dish so it cushions rice against the edge. Bake in oven 20–30 minutes or until all the cheese melts and the top layer has a nice brown tinge.

Sassafrass' Favourite Spinach for Mitch # 10

- 1–2 bunches Japanese spinach
- 8 good-sized mushrooms
- 2 tablespoons vegetable oil (safflower oil is very light)
- 2 tablespoons tamari
- 1/2 teaspoon finely crushed rosemary
- 4 sweet hot peppers

Wash spinach carefully in cold water. Break leaves from stem with fingers — do not cut — and set spinach in colander. Wash mushrooms. Slice vertically so each slice maintains its shape. Put oil in heavy iron skillet, heat until drop of water makes it pop. Turn flame down and lay spinach evenly in pan. Spread mushrooms; sprinkle rosemary and tamari. Simmer until leaves are soft and hot. Do not overcook. Place peppers in nice design around spinach and serve quickly.

Sassafrass: The Only Way to Broil Fish: Mackerel

Clean fish thoroughly. Dip in melted butter, add salt and pepper. Cook 4–6 minutes on each side in broiler.

Red Sauce: Sassafrass' Variation Du-Wop '59

    1 small can tomato sauce   1/2 cup finely chopped
    1 cup cooking sherry or   onion
       sangria   Garlic to taste
    1/2 cup finely chopped   Cayenne
       parsley

Mix tomato sauce and wine in saucepan. Add sautéed onions, parsley and seasonings. Spread some sauce over fish while broiling; save the rest to use on plate.

While Sassafrass cooked she usually did yoga breathing exercises or belly dance pelvic contractions as she puttered around. The movements were almost accidental: tearing the spinach she'd contract on each pull from a stem and release as soon as it hit the colander. She would breathe ten quick breaths out and ten quick ones in as she crossed the kitchen from the sink to the stove. Not wanting to waste a moment, she would do *relevés* on alternate sets of ten contractions, so it would be: contract-*relevé*-release-down. This went on for as long as it took to cook dinner, and as the mackerel came out of the oven, Sassafrass was a buoyant and contented woman.

Sassafrass made her way out of the kitchen to get Mitch for dinner. She stepped into the studio to see how his art supplies were standing up against his create-every-day saga. The acrylic paints would probably last just another week before Mitch would have only ochre left; watercolours, sufficient; oils, absolutely tubes' end. Sassafrass was figuring the actual cost or barter price some new brushes would come to, when she heard calamitous booted feet traipsing through her house, and some men's voices upsetting her resting plants. She hurriedly took an overall inventory of Mitch's drawing equipment, and copped a gracious hostess attitude for the unexpected dinner guests. Otis and Howard Goodwin-Smith, two brothers from Chicago, had been in L.A. since Korea, most of their growing-up days. They tried, sometimes, to act like they were from Chi-town, but in a couple of minutes that Southern California hip-lessness would ooze from every word. Otis was a writer, which made Sassafrass uneasy, and Howard was a painter of contorted phallic symbols dipped in Afrikan mystique and loaded with latent rapist bravado. The Goodwin-Smiths from the South Side. Sassafrass held her tongue while she greeted them; she wanted to ask why they hadn't brought their white wives. She felt her eyes sneer and her mouth smile, saying, 'Too bad

Jennie and Olga couldn't make it . . . I never see them, you know.'

Otis and Howard looked over to Mitch, who was looking at Albert the dog, to make sure Sassafrass could enjoy putting the brothers on the spot. Then Albert moved over to Howard, who was kneeling on the floor trying to get a whole idea of Mitch's new mural. Albert on his haunches was almost six feet, and he got on his haunches to try to hump the chauvinist Howard. Sassafrass saw Albert rear back and slam his front paws across Howard's back, saw his dick hanging oily-like from its fur pouch, aiming for Howard's jeans-covered backside. Howard was shocked, and steady trying to get out of Albert's way. They made circles around the room, Albert chasing Howard past the aging velvet couch, the barber's seat that doubled as a chaise longue, the driftwood coffee table, and the mural lying on the floor. Round and round they went. Sassafrass glimmered, and went to get the food. Mitch started playing the Lone Ranger's theme song. Otis was rolled over laughing, and Howard finally tore off one of his sneakers to appease Albert, who always tried to make it with small men. They ate with chopsticks, in time to Ron Carter's *Uptown Conversation*.

Otis had reconnoitred the barber's seat for himself, and from his lofty perch, began, 'I brought y'all a copy of my new book, *Ebony Cunt* . . . I autographed it special, Mitch; see here . . .'

for sassafrass . . .
I know yours is good

Sassafrass' face nearly hit the floor. She glanced at Mitch to see where he was at, and he was enjoying his clout with the fellas, because he announced: 'Sassafrass got some of the best pussy west of the Rockies, man, and I don't care who knows it, 'cause it's mine!'

They all laughed raucously, except Sassafrass was glaring from her inmost marrow and wishing there was some way to get rid of male crassness once and for all time. She called herself being kind to Mitch, because he liked his friends, while she began discreetly leaving the room. But Otis called out for a thorough reading of his new work, to Mitch's accompaniment on sax and Howard's innovative percussion with a worn-down tambourine.

THE REVUE

Otis
Sassafrass, you gotta sit in this barber chair and be the queen you are, while I read this masterpiece (*teehee*) of mine for all y'all black women all over the world.

Sassafrass
Otis, I, ah, gotta get started on something, ya know.

Otis, Mitch, Howard (in unison)
Nononono . . . you gotta hear this one, babeee!

(*Mitch picks Sassafrass off her feet and places her in the chair, squeezes her leg, and smiles*)

Mitch
Go on, Otis. We gotta celebrate this woman of mine even if she doesn't understand why we gotta have her, every morning . . . in the evenin' when the sun go down . . .

(*Mitch sings like he is Ray Charles, and shakes all around like Little Richard*)

Otis

I'ma start now. I'ma read all about it, but first I wanna say, a la Edwin Starr circa 1963:

> *extra extra reeeeeead allll about itttttt*
> *extra extra reeeeeead allll about itttttt*

(Howard, Mitch, and Otis do old Temptations Apollo routines around Sassafrass, who is enjoying this worship from the du-wop straddlers in spite of herself)

Howard

Aw right. Now Otis, get it on . . . we ready.

Otis

EBONY CUNT: for my mama and my grandma and all the women I rammed in Macon, Georgia, when I was visitin' my cousins at age sixteen:

The white man want you/the Indian run off with you Spaniards created whole nations with you/black queen-silk snatch
I wander all in your wombs & make babies in the Bronx when I come/you screammmmmmm/ jesus/ my blk man ebony cunt is worth all the gold in the world/ 15 millions of your shinin' blk bodies crossed the sea to bring all that good slick pussy to me . . .

(Sassafrass stands up like a mannequin, and gazes absolutely red-faced at Otis, Mitch and Howard, all of who stare back at her, uncomprehending)

Mitch

Sassafrass, what's wrong with you? Sit down. Otis

gotta finish the book; he isn't even done with the first page . . .

Sassafrass (standing still)
Just one god-damned minute, Mitch. You gotta mother you supposedly love so much, and a daughter by a black woman who won't see you . . . and you got me all messed up, and tryin' to make you happy . . . god damn it, I don't haveta listen to this shit. I am not interested in your sick, sick, weakly rhapsodies about all the women you fucked in all your damn lives . . . I don't like it. I am not about to sit heah and listen to a bunch of no account niggahs talk about black women; me and my sisters; like we was the same bought and sold at slave auction . . . breeding heifers the white man created 'cause y'all was fascinated by some god-damn beads he brought you on the continent . . . muthafuckahs. Yeah, that's right; muthafuckahs, don't you ever sit in my house and ask me to celebrate my inherited right to be raped. Goddamn muthafuckahs. Don't you know about anythin' besides taking women off, or is that really all you good for?

(Mitch looks at Sassafrass like she was a harlot. He puts his horn away and remains silent. Otis and Howard chuckle nervously, and get ready to split)

Otis
Look now Sassafrass, I'm sorry you took it the wrong way . . .

(He smiles. All three men leave the house. On the way out, Howard pokes his head back through the bagging-screen door)

Ntozake Shange

Howard
I don't care *what* you say, Sassafrass . . . I *know* you got good pussy!

(They all laugh jauntily on the way to the '59 Chevy two-door sedan. Sassafrass stands still in front of the barber's chair for an indefinite time)

When she moved, she went to her looms . . .

*makin cloth, bein a woman & longin
to be of the earth
a rooted blues
some ripe berries
happenin inside
spirits
walkin in a dirt road
toes dusted & free
faces movin windy
brisk like
dawn round
gingham windows &
opened eyes
reelin to days
ready-made
nature's image
i'm rejoicin
with a throat deep
shout & slow
like a river
gatherin
space*

*i am sassafrass/ a weaver's daughter/ from charleston/
i'm a woman makin cloth like all good women do/*

*the moon's daughter made cloth/ the gold array of
the sun/ the moon's daughter sat all night/ spinnin/
i have inherited fingers that change fleece to tender
garments/ i am the maker of warmth & emblems
of good spirit/ mama/ didn't ya show me how/ to
warp a loom/ to pattern stars into cotton homespun/
mama/ didn't ya name me for yr favourite natural
dye/ sassafrass/ so strong & even/ go good with deep
fertile greens/ & make tea to temper chilly evenings/
i'm a weaver with my sistahs from any earth &
fields/ we always make cloth/ love our children/
honour our men/ who protect us from our enemies/
we prepare altars & anoint candles to offer our
devotion to our guardians/ we proffer hope/ & food
to eat/ clothes to wear/ wombs to fill.*

Almost unconsciously Sassafrass had begun the laborious process of warping the four-harness table loom she had transported from Charleston. The eccentric family her family had worked for as slaves, and then as freed women weavers, had seen fit to grant Sassafrass the looms her forebears had warped and wefted thousands of times since emancipation. Sassafrass had always been proud that her mother had a craft; that all the women in her family could make something besides a baby, and shooting streams of sperm. She had grown up in a room full of spinning wheels, table and floor looms, and her mother always busy making cloth because the Fitzhugh family never wore anything but hand-woven cloth . . . until they couldn't afford it any more. Sassafrass had never wanted to weave, she just couldn't help it. There was something about the feel of raw fleece and finished threads and dainty patterned pieces that was as essential to her as dancing is to

Ntozake Shange

Carmen DeLavallade, or singing to Aretha Franklin. Her mama had done it, and her mama before that; and making cloth was the only tradition Sassafrass inherited that gave her a sense of womanhood that was rich and sensuous, not tired and stingy. She thought that if Kingfish had bought Sapphire a loom, she would never have been such a bitch. She thought that the bronze Dionysius was not saving the sad frigid women of Thebes by seducing them away from their looms, but rather he was planning, under Osiris' aegis, to wipe out Europeans before they went around the world enslaving rainbow-coloured people . . . because when women make cloth, they have time to think, and Theban women stopped thinking, and the town fell. So Sassafrass was certain of the necessity of her skill for the well-being of women everywhere, as well as for her own. As she passed the shuttle through the claret cotton warp, Sassafrass conjured images of women weaving from all time and all places: Toltecas spinning shimmering threads; East Indian women designing intricate patterns for Shakti, the impetus and destruction of creation; and Navajo women working on thick tapestries. She tried to compel an African woman to come join them – women, making cloth – and the spirits said, 'No. You cannot have her . . . in Africa men make cloth, and women . . .' Sassafrass tossed her head to the left side, and dismissed her congregation of international cloth makers while she rethreaded her shuttle. And Mitch was home . . .

* * *

Hi there Sassafrass . . .
    How's mama's favourite dumpling? Sounds to me like

you have indeed worked wonders on your little house. Just watch now that you don't overdo with too much colour. Houses are supposed to comfort us, as well as invigorate the senses. You don't get one by ignoring the other. There, you see, I do have a notion of aesthetics, black or not. They're Southern, and that's close enough. (smile)

The Wheeler girls came home from Vassar last week. They were a little behind you, I think. At any rate, they have gone completely African. Changed their names; wear these big old pieces of cloth . . . look just like mammies, to my mind. Their mother, Gertie, has refused to let them out of the house till they go round to Mrs Calhoun's and get that hair pressed. So, it's all right that you and your sisters don't come home, when I think about how you must look!

That little Shuyler boy, the one who went to Dartmouth and is now at Meharry, has wrecked two cars already, and still his father hasn't put his foot down. I can't understand loving somebody so much, you let them make you a fool, but, thank god he's no child of mine. That's that boy who kept you out all weekend when I came to visit you in New England. Don't try to act like I'm mistaken – I may not be a liberated woman, but I wasn't born yesterday. I can't see what you saw in him. For all that breeding, and the money spent on him, he acts like a natural-born hoodlum.

What else . . . oh, guess what? Your name is in the alumni magazine of the Callahan School. Seems like you are the only one, out of all those rich children, to go on ahead and be an artist. Don't be upset with me. I sent the information in myself, with samples of your work. It's the least I could do, after Mrs Fitzhugh sponsored you and all. I can't understand why you hated that place so . . . not going to your graduation, refusing to go on to college. Oh, Sassafrass, weaving is a fine craft, but with the opportunities open to Negroes your age, I just don't know why you insist on doing everything the hard way.

I hate to say this, but it follows my thoughts about your resisting the bounties our Lord has laid before you, in order to take up with the most unfortunate among us. How could you take up with a man who wasn't raised in a proper home . . . not even an orphan, just a delinquent? Even I have heard stories of the terrible conditions in the reform schools, and here my very own daughter searches far and wide, moves all the way to California, to fall in love with a man who has nothing to offer, no background, no education, no future. If you think for a minute, darling, you'll see that all the training you've had is far and away more than that boy can imagine. So what is it that you're going to learn from him? You should get down on your knees and pray for guidance. And while you're down there, thank the Lord for giving you the good sense not to compromise yourself by living in sin. You can at least still meet some more folks who are up to you, and who'll appreciate what a fine young woman you are. Truly, dear, try to get out and enjoy yourself. The race has had problems ever since we got here. You can't do anything about them by staying in your house, refusing to take part in the world you belong in.

Call cousin Loreen. I told you, her step-sons are all doctors, and mighty good-looking . . . (a word to the wise).

Love,
Mama

PS You don't have to tell Mitch everything I said about him . . . if that's an open relationship, humpf. You need a closed one!!

Elizabeth Smart

extract from

*By Grand
Central Station
I Sat Down and Wept*

A major achievement in poetic prose and a demanding, disturbing text, Elizabeth Smart's novel about the passion between a man and two women, one of them his wife, communicates its story with remarkable accessibility and candour.

I am over-run, jungled in my bed, I am infested with a menagerie of desires: my heart is eaten by a dove, a cat scrambles in the cave of my sex, hounds in my head obey a whipmaster who cries nothing but havoc as the hours test my endurance with an accumulation of tortures. Who, if I cried, would hear me among the angelic orders?

I am far, far beyond that island of days where once, it seems, I watched a flower grow, and counted the steps of the sun, and fed, if my memory serves, the smiling animal at his appointed hour. I am shot with wounds which have eyes that see a world all sorrow, always to be, panoramic and unhealable, and mouths that hang unspeakable in the sky of blood.

How can I be kind? How can I find bird-relief in the nest-building of day-to-day? Necessity supplies no velvet wing with which to escape. I am indeed and mortally pierced with the seeds of love.

Then she leans over in the pool and her damp dark hair falls like sorrow, like mercy, like the mourning-weeds of pity. Sitting nymphlike in the pool in the late afternoon her pathetic slenderness is covered over with a love as gentle as trusting as tenacious as the birds who rebuild their continually violated nests. When she clasps her hands happily at a tune she likes, it is more moving than I can bear. She is the innocent who is always the offering. She is the goddess of all things which the vigour of living destroys. Why are her arms so empty?

In the night she moans with the voice of the stream below my window, searching for the child whose touch she once felt and can never forget: the child who obeyed the laws of life better than she. But by day she obeys the voice of love as the stricken obey their god, and she walks with the light step of hope which only the naïve and the saints know. Her shoulders have always the attitude of grieving, and her thin breasts are pitiful like Virgin Shrines that have been robbed.

How can I speak to her? How can I comfort her? How can I explain to her any more than I can to the flowers that I crush with my foot when I walk in the field? He also is bent towards her in an attitude of solicitude. Can he hear his own heart while he listens for the tenderness of her sensibilities? Is there a way at all to avoid offending the lamb of god?

Under the waterfall he surprised me bathing and gave me what I could no more refuse than the earth can refuse the rain. Then he kissed me and went down to his cottage.

Absolve me, I prayed, up through the cathedral redwoods, and forgive me if this is sin. But the new moss caressed me and the water over my feet and the ferns approved me with endearments: My darling, my darling, lie down with us now for you also are earth whom nothing but love can sow.

And I lay down on the redwood needles and seemed to flow down the canyon with the thunder and confusion of the stream, in a happiness which, like birth, can afford to ignore the blood and the tearing. For nature has no time for mourning, absorbed by the turning world, and will, no matter what devastation attacks her, fulfil in underground ritual, all her proper prophecy.

Gently the woodsorrel and the dove explained the confirmation and guided my return. When I came out of the woods on to the hill, I had pine-needles in my hair for a bridal wreath, and the sea and the sky and the gold hills smiled benignly. Jupiter has been with Leda, I thought, and now nothing can avert the Trojan Wars. All legend will be born, but who will escape alive?

But what can the woodsorrel and the mourning-dove, who deal only with eternals, know of the thorny sociabilities of human living? Of how the pressure of the hours of waiting, silent and inactive, weigh upon the head with a physical force that suffocates? The simplest daily pleasantries are torture, and a samson effort is needed to avoid his glance that draws me like gravity.

For excuse, for our being together, we sit at the typewriter, pretending a necessary collaboration. He has a book to be typed, but the words I try to force out die on the air and dissolve into kisses whose chemicals are even more deadly if undelivered. My fingers cannot be martial at the touch of an instrument so much connected with him. The machine sits like a temple of love among the papers we never finish, and if I awake at night and see it outlined in the dark, I am electrified with memories of dangerous propinquity.

The frustrations of past postponement can no longer be restrained. They hang ripe to burst with the birth of any moment. The typewriter is guilty with love and flowery with shame, and to me it speaks so loudly I fear it will communicate its indecency to casual visitors.

How stationary life has become, and the hours impossibly elongated. When we sit on the gold grass of the cliff, the sun between us insists on a solution for which we search in vain, but whose urgency we feel unbearably. I never was in love with death before, nor felt grateful because the rocks below could promise certain death. But now the idea of dying violently becomes an act wrapped in attractive melancholy, and displayed with every blandishment. For there is no beauty in denying love, except perhaps by death, and towards love what way is there?

To deny love, and deceive it meanly by pretending that what is unconsummated remains eternal, or that love sublimated reaches highest to heavenly love, is repulsive, as the hypocrite's face is repulsive when placed too near the truth. Farther off from the centre of the world, of all worlds, I might be better fooled, but can I see the light of a match while burning in the arms of the sun?

No, my advocates, my angels with sadist eyes, this is the beginning of my life, or the end. So I lean affirmation across the café table, and surrender my fifty years away with an easy smile. But the surety of my love is not dismayed by any eventuality which prudence or pity can conjure up, and in the end all that we can do is to sit at the table over which our hands cross, listening to tunes from the wurlitzer, with love huge and simple between us, and nothing more to be said.

So hourly, at the slightest noise, I start, I stand ready to feel the roof cave in on my head, the thunder of God's punishment announcing the limit of his endurance.

She walks lightly, like the child whose dancing feet will touch off gigantic explosives. She knows nothing, but like autumn birds feels foreboding in the air. Her movements are nervous, there are draughts in every room, but less wise than the birds whom small signs send on three-thousand-mile flights, she only looks vaguely out to the Pacific, finding it strange that heaven has, after all, no Californian shore.

I have learned to smoke because I need something to hold on to. I dare not be without a cigarette in my hand. If I should be looking the other way when the hour of doom is struck, how shall I avoid being turned into stone unless I can remember something to do which will lead me back to the simplicity and safety of daily living?

IT is coming. The magnet of its imminent finger draws each hair of my body, the shudder of its approach disintegrates kisses, loses wishes on the disjointed air. The wet hands of the castor-tree at night brush me and I shriek, thinking that at last I am caught up with. The clouds move across the sky heavy and tubular. They gather and I am terror-struck to see them form a long black rainbow out of the mountain and disappear across the sea. The Thing is at hand. There is nothing to do but crouch and receive God's wrath.

Amy Tan

extract from

The Joy Luck Club

Sitting at what was once her mother's place at the mah-jong table, Jing-Mei Woo becomes an essential member of the Joy Luck Club, a gathering of four mothers and their first-generation Chinese-American daughters. By telling each other true stories, both groups of women come to terms with a rich and sometimes puzzling cultural heritage. One of the most moving of these accounts is the extract here, entitled 'Half and Half', related by Rose Hsu Jordan.

As proof of her faith, my mother used to carry a small leatherette Bible when she went to the First Chinese Baptist Church every Sunday. But later, after my mother lost her faith in God, that leatherette Bible wound up wedged under a too-short table leg, a way for her to correct the imbalances of life. It's been there for over twenty years.

My mother pretends that Bible isn't there. Whenever anyone asks her what it's doing there, she says, a little too loudly, 'Oh, this? I forgot.' But I know she sees it. My mother is not the best housekeeper in the world, and after all these years that Bible is still clean white.

Tonight I'm watching my mother sweep under the same kitchen table, something she does every night after dinner. She gently pokes her broom around the table leg propped up by the Bible. I watch her, sweep after sweep, waiting for the right moment to tell her about Ted and me, that we're getting divorced. When I tell her, I know she's going to say, 'This cannot be.'

And when I say that it is certainly true, that our marriage is over, I know what else she will say: 'Then you must save it.'

And even though I know it's hopeless — there's

absolutely nothing left to save – I'm afraid if I tell her that, she'll still persuade me to try.

I think it's ironic that my mother wants me to fight the divorce. Seventeen years ago she was chagrined when I started dating Ted. My older sisters had dated only Chinese boys from church before getting married.

Ted and I met in a politics of ecology class when he leaned over and offered to pay me two dollars for the last week's notes. I refused the money and accepted a cup of coffee instead. This was during my second semester at UC Berkeley, where I had enrolled as a liberal arts major and later changed to fine arts. Ted was in his third year in pre-med, his choice, he told me, ever since he dissected a fetal pig in the sixth grade.

I have to admit that what I initially found attractive in Ted were precisely the things that made him different from my brothers and the Chinese boys I had dated: his brashness; the assuredness in which he asked for things and expected to get them; his opinionated manner; his angular face and lanky body; the thickness of his arms; the fact that his parents immigrated from Tarrytown, New York, not Tientsin, China.

My mother must have noticed these same differences after Ted picked me up one evening at my parents' house. When I returned home, my mother was still up, watching television.

'He is American,' warned my mother, as if I had been too blind to notice. A *waigoren*.'

'I'm American too,' I said. 'And it's not as if I'm going to marry him or something.'

Mrs Jordan also had a few words to say. Ted had casually invited me to a family picnic, the annual clan reunion held by the polo fields in Golden Gate Park. Although we had dated only a few times in the last month – and certainly had never slept together, since both of us lived at home – Ted introduced me to all his relatives as his girlfriend, which, until then, I didn't know I was.

Later, when Ted and his father went off to play volleyball with the others, his mother took my hand, and we started walking along the grass, away from the crowd. She squeezed my palm warmly but never seemed to look at me.

'I'm so glad to meet you *finally*,' Mrs Jordan said. I wanted to tell her I wasn't really Ted's girlfriend, but she went on, 'I think it's nice that you and Ted are having such a lot of fun together. So I hope you won't misunderstand what I have to say.'

And then she spoke quietly about Ted's future, his need to concentrate on his medical studies, why it would be years before he could even think about marriage. She assured me she had nothing whatsoever against minorities; she and her husband, who owned a chain of office-supply stores, personally knew many fine people who were Oriental, Spanish, and even black. But Ted was going to be in one of those professions where he would be judged by a different standard, by patients and other doctors who might not be as understanding as the Jordans were. She said it was so unfortunate the way the rest of the world was, how unpopular the Vietnam War was.

'Mrs Jordan, I am not Vietnamese,' I said softly, even though I was on the verge of shouting. 'And I have no intention of marrying your son.'

When Ted drove me home that day, I told him I couldn't see him any more. When he asked me why,

I shrugged. When he pressed me, I told him what his mother had said, verbatim, without comment.

'And you're just going to sit there! Let my mother decide what's right?' he shouted, as if I were a co-conspirator who had turned traitor. I was touched that Ted was so upset.

'What should we do?' I asked, and I had a pained feeling I thought was the beginning of love.

In those early months, we clung to each other with a rather silly desperation, because, in spite of anything my mother or Mrs Jordan could say, there was nothing that really prevented us from seeing one another. With imagined tragedy hovering over us, we became inseparable, two halves creating the whole: yin and yang. I was victim to his hero. I was always in danger and he was always rescuing me. I would fall and he would lift me up. It was exhilarating and draining. The emotional effect of saving and being saved was addicting to both of us. And that, as much as anything we ever did in bed, was how we made love to each other: conjoined where my weaknesses needed protection.

'What should we do?' I continued to ask him. And within a year of our first meeting we were living together. The month before Ted started medical school at UCSF we were married in the Episcopal church, and Mrs Jordan sat in the front pew, crying as was expected of the groom's mother. When Ted finished his residency in dermatology, we bought a run-down three-storey Victorian with a large garden in Ashbury Heights. Ted helped me set up a studio downstairs so I could take in work as a freelance production assistant for graphic artists.

Over the years, Ted decided where we went on vacation. He decided what new furniture we should buy. He decided we should wait until we moved into a better neighbourhood before having children. We used to discuss some of these matters, but we both knew the question would boil down to my saying, 'Ted, you decide.' After a while, there were no more discussions. Ted simply decided. And I never thought of objecting. I preferred to ignore the world around me, obsessing only over what was in front of me: my T-square, my X-acto knife, my blue pencil.

But last year Ted's feelings about what he called 'decision and responsibility' changed. A new patient had come to him asking what she could do about the spidery veins on her cheeks. And when he told her he could suck the red veins out and make her beautiful again, she believed him. But instead, he accidentally sucked a nerve out, and the left side of her smile fell down and she sued him.

After he lost the malpractice lawsuit – his first, and a big shock to him I now realize – he started pushing me to make decisons. Did I think we should buy an American car or a Japanese car? Should we change from whole-life to term insurance? What did I think about that candidate who supported the contras? What about a family?

I thought about things, the pros and the cons. But in the end I would be so confused, because I never believed there was ever any one right answer, yet there were many wrong ones. So whenever I said, 'You decide,' or 'I don't care,' or 'Either way is fine with me,' Ted would say in his impatient voice, 'No *you* decide. You can't have it both ways, none of the responsibility, none of the blame.'

I could feel things changing between us. A protective veil had been lifted and Ted now started pushing me about everything. He asked me to decide on the most trivial matters, as if he were baiting me. Italian food or Thai. One appetizer or two. Which appetizer. Credit card or cash. Visa or MasterCard.

Last month, when he was leaving for a two-day dermatology course in Los Angeles, he asked if I wanted to come along and then quickly, before I could say anything, he added, 'Never mind, I'd rather go alone.'

'More time to study,' I agreed.

'No, because you can never make up your mind about anything,' he said.

And I protested, 'But it's only with things that aren't important.'

'Nothing is important to you, then,' he said in a tone of disgust.

'Ted, if you want me to go, I'll go.'

And it was as if something snapped in him. 'How the hell did we ever get married? Did you just say "I do" because the minister said "repeat after me"? What would you have done with your life if I had never married you? Did it ever occur to you?'

This was such a big leap in logic, between what I said and what he said, that I thought we were like two people standing apart on separate mountain peaks, recklessly leaning forward to throw stones at one another, unaware of the dangerous chasm that separated us.

But now I realize Ted knew what he was saying all along. He wanted to show me the rift. Because later that evening he called from Los Angeles and said he wanted a divorce.

Ever since Ted's been gone, I've been thinking, Even if I had expected it, even if I had known what I was going to do with my life, it still would have knocked the wind out of me.

When something that violent hits you, you can't help

but lose your balance and fall. And after you pick yourself up, you realize you can't trust anybody to save you — not your husband, not your mother, not God. So what can you do to stop yourself from tilting and falling all over again?

My mother believed in God's will for many years. It was as if she had turned on a celestial faucet and goodness kept pouring out. She said it was faith that kept all these good things coming our way, only I thought she said 'fate', because she couldn't pronounce that 'th' sound in 'faith'.

And later, I discovered that maybe it was fate all along, that faith was just an illusion that somehow you're in control. I found out the most *I* could have was hope, and with that I was not denying any possibility, good or bad. I was just saying, If there is a choice, dear God or whatever you are, here's where the odds should be placed.

I remember the day I started thinking this, it was such a revelation to me. It was the day my mother lost her faith in God. She found that things of unquestioned certainty could never be trusted again.

We had gone to the beach, to a secluded spot south of the city near Devil's Slide. My father had read in *Sunset* magazine that this was a good place to catch ocean perch. And although my father was not a fisherman but a pharmacist's assistant who had once been a doctor in China, he believed in his *nengkan*, his ability to do anything he put his mind to. My mother believed she had *nengkan* to cook anything my father had a mind to catch. It was this belief in their *nengkan* that had brought my parents to America. It had enabled them to have seven children and buy a house in the Sunset district with very little money. It had given them the confidence to believe their luck would never run out, that God was on their side, that the house gods had only benevolent things to report and our ancestors were pleased, that lifetime warranties meant our lucky streak would never break, that all the elements were in balance, the right amount of wind and water.

So there we were, the nine of us: my father, my mother, my two sisters, four brothers, and myself, so confident as we walked along our first beach. We marched in single file across the cool grey sand, from oldest to youngest. I was in the middle, fourteen years old. We would have made quite a sight, if anyone else had been watching, nine pairs of bare feet trudging, nine pairs of shoes in hand, nine black-haired heads turned toward the water to watch the waves tumbling in.

The wind was whipping the cotton trousers around my legs and I looked for some place where the sand wouldn't kick into my eyes. I saw we were standing in the hollow of a cove. It was like a giant bowl, cracked in half, the other half washed out to sea. My mother walked toward the right, where the beach was clean, and we all followed. On this side, the wall of the cove curved around and protected the beach from both the rough surf and the wind. And along this wall, in its shadow, was a reef ledge that started at the edge of the beach and continued out past the cove where the waters became rough. It seemed as though a person could walk out to sea on this reef, although it looked very rocky and slippery. On the other side of the cove, the wall was more jagged, eaten away by the water. It was pitted with crevices, so when the waves crashed against the wall, the water spewed out of these holes like white gulleys.

Thinking back, I remember that this beach cove was

a terrible place, full of wet shadows that chilled us and invisible specks that flew into our eyes and made it hard for us to see the dangers. We were all blind with the newness of this experience: a Chinese family trying to act like a typical American family at the beach.

My mother spread out an old striped bedspread, which flapped in the wind until nine pairs of shoes weighed it down. My father assembled his long bamboo fishing pole, a pole he had made with his own two hands, remembering its design from his childhood in China. And we children sat huddled shoulder to shoulder on the blanket, reaching into the grocery sack full of bologna sandwiches, which we hungrily ate salted with sand from our fingers.

Then my father stood up and admired his fishing pole, its grace, its strength. Satisfied, he picked up his shoes and walked to the edge of the beach and then on to the reef to the point just before it was wet. My two older sisters, Janice and Ruth, jumped up from the blanket and slapped their thighs to get the sand off. Then they slapped each other's back and raced off down the beach shrieking. I was about to get up and chase them, but my mother nodded toward my four brothers and reminded me: *'Dangsying tamende shenti,'* which means 'Take care of them,' or literally, 'Watch out for their bodies.' These bodies were the anchors of my life: Matthew, Mark, Luke and Bing. I fell back on to the sand, groaning as my throat grew tight, as I made the same lament: 'Why?' Why did *I* have to care for them?

And she gave me the same answer: *'Yiding.'*

I must. Because they were my brothers. My sisters had once taken care of me. How else could I learn responsibility? How else could I appreciate what my parents had done for me?

Matthew, Mark and Luke were twelve, ten and nine, old enough to keep themselves loudly amused. They had already buried Luke in a shallow grave of sand so that only his head stuck out. Now they were starting to pat together the outlines of a sand-castle wall on top of him.

But Bing was only four, easily excitable and easily bored and irritable. He didn't want to play with the other brothers because they had pushed him off to the side, admonishing him, 'No, Bing, you'll just wreck it.'

So Bing wandered down the beach, walking stiffly like an ousted emperor, picking up shards of rock and chunks of driftwood and flinging them with all his might into the surf. I trailed behind, imagining tidal waves and wondering what I would do if one appeared. I called to Bing every now and then, 'Don't go too close to the water. You'll get your feet wet.' And I thought how much I seemed like my mother, always worried beyond reason inside, but at the same time talking about the danger as if it were less than it really was. The worry surrounded me, like the wall of the cove, and it made me feel everything had been considered and was now safe.

My mother had a superstition, in fact, that children were predisposed to certain dangers on certain days, all depending on their Chinese birthdate. It was explained in a little Chinese book called *The Twenty-Six Malignant Gates*. There, on each page, was an illustration of some terrible danger that awaited young innocent children. In the corners was a description written in Chinese, and since I couldn't read the characters, I could only see what the picture meant.

The same little boy appeared in each picture: climbing a broken tree limb, standing by a falling gate, slipping in a wooden tub, being carried away by a snapping dog, fleeing from a bolt of lightning. And in each of these pictures stood a man who looked as if he were wearing a lizard costume. He had a big crease in his forehead, or maybe it was actually that he had two round horns. In one picture, the lizard man was standing on a curved bridge, laughing as he watched the little boy falling forward over the bridge rail, his slippered feet already in the air.

It would have been enough to think that even one of these dangers could befall a child. And even though the birthdates corresponded to only one danger, my mother worried about them all. This was because she couldn't figure out how the Chinese dates, based on the lunar calendar, translated into American dates. So by taking them all into account, she had absolute faith she could prevent every one of them.

The sun had shifted and moved over the other side of the cove wall. Everything had settled into place. My mother was busy keeping sand from blowing on to the blanket, then shaking sand out of shoes, and tacking corners of blankets back down again with the now clean shoes. My father was still standing at the end of the reef, patiently casting out, waiting for *nengkan* to manifest itself as a fish. I could see small figures farther down on the beach, and I could tell they were my sisters by their two dark heads and yellow pants. My brothers' shrieks were mixed with those of seagulls. Bing had found an empty soda bottle and was using this to dig sand next to the dark cove wall. And I sat on the sand, just where the shadows ended and the sunny part began.

Bing was pounding the soda bottle against the rock, so I called to him, 'Don't dig so hard. You'll bust a hole in the wall and fall all the way to China.' And I laughed when he looked at me as though he thought what I said was true. He stood up and started walking toward the water. He put one foot tentatively on the reef, and I warned him, 'Bing.'

'I'm gonna see Daddy,' he protested.

'Stay close to the wall, then, away from the water,' I said. 'Stay away from the mean fish.'

And I watched as he inched his way along the reef, his back hugging the bumpy cove wall. I still see him, so clearly that I almost feel I can make him stay there for ever.

I see him standing by the wall, safe, calling to my father, who looks over his shoulder toward Bing. How glad I am that my father is going to watch him for a while! Bing starts to walk over and then something tugs on my father's line and he's reeling as fast as he can.

Shouts erupt. Someone has thrown sand in Luke's face and he's jumped out of his sand grave and thrown himself on top of Mark, thrashing and kicking. My mother shouts for me to stop them. And right after I pull Luke off Mark, I look up and see Bing walking alone to the edge of the reef. In the confusion of the fight, nobody notices. I am the only one who sees what Bing is doing.

Bing walks one, two, three steps. His little body is moving so quickly, as if he spotted something wonderful by the water's edge. And I think, *He's going to fall in.* I'm expecting it. And just as I think this, his feet are already in the air, in a moment of balance, before he splashes into the sea and disappears without leaving so much as a ripple in the water.

I sank to my knees watching that spot where he disappeared, not moving, not saying anything. I couldn't make sense of it. I was thinking, Should I run to the water and try to pull him out? Should I shout to my father? Can I rise on my legs fast enough? Can I take it all back and forbid Bing from joining my father on the ledge?

And then my sisters were back, and one of them said, 'Where's Bing?' There was silence for a few seconds and then shouts and sand flying as everyone rushed past me toward the water's edge. I stood there unable to move as my sisters looked by the cove wall, as my brothers scrambled to see what lay behind pieces of driftwood. My mother and father were trying to part the waves with their hands.

We were there for many hours. I remember the search boats and the sunset when dusk came. I had never seen a sunset like that: a bright orange flame touching the water's edge and then fanning out, warming the sea. When it became dark, the boats turned their yellow orbs on and bounced up and down on the dark shiny water.

As I look back, it seems unnatural to think about the colours of the sunset and boats at a time like that. But we all had strange thoughts. My father was calculating minutes, estimating the temperature of the water, readjusting his estimate of when Bing fell. My sisters were calling, 'Bing! Bing!' as if he were hiding in some bushes high above the beach cliffs. My brothers sat in the car, quietly reading comic books. And when the boats turned off their yellow orbs, my mother went for a swim. She had never swum a stroke in her life, but her faith in her own *nengkan* convinced her that what these Americans couldn't do, she could. She could find Bing.

And when the rescue people finally pulled her out of the water, she still had her *nengkan* intact. Her hair, her clothes, they were all heavy with the cold water, but she stood quietly, calm and regal as a mermaid queen who had just arrived out of the sea. The police called off the search, put us all in our car, and sent us home to grieve.

I had expected to be beaten to death, by my father, by my mother, by my sisters and brothers. I knew it was my fault. I hadn't watched him closely enough, and yet I saw him. But as we sat in the dark living room, I heard them, one by one whispering their regrets.

'I was selfish to want to go fishing,' said my father.

'We shouldn't have gone for a walk,' said Janice, while Ruth blew her nose yet another time.

'Why'd you have to throw sand in my face?' moaned Luke. 'Why'd you have to make me start a fight?'

And my mother quietly admitted to me, 'I told you to stop their fight. I told you to take your eyes off him.'

If I had had any time at all to feel a sense of relief, it would have quickly evaporated, because my mother also said, 'So now I am telling you, we must go and find him, quickly, tomorrow morning.' And everybody's eyes looked down. But I saw it as my punishment: to go out with my mother, back to the beach, to help her find Bing's body.

Nothing prepared me for what my mother did the next day. When I woke up, it was still dark and she was already dressed. On the kitchen table was a thermos, a teacup, the white leatherette Bible, and the car keys.

'Is Daddy ready?' I asked.

'Daddy's not coming,' she said.

'Then how will we get there? Who will drive us?'

She picked up the keys and I followed her out the door to the car. I wondered the whole time as we drove to the beach how she had learned to drive overnight. She used no map. She drove smoothly ahead, turning down Geary, then the Great Highway, signalling at all the right times, getting on the Coast Highway and easily winding the car around the sharp curves that often led inexperienced drivers off and over the cliffs.

When we arrived at the beach, she walked immediately down the dirt path and over to the end of the reef ledge, where I had seen Bing disappear. She held in her hand the white Bible. And looking out over the water, she called to God, her small voice carried up by the gulls to heaven. It began with 'Dear God' and ended with 'Amen' and in between she spoke in Chinese.

'I have always believed in your blessings,' she praised God in that same tone she used for exaggerated Chinese compliments. 'We knew they would come. We did not question them. Your decisions were our decisions. You rewarded us for our faith.

'In return we have always tried to show our deepest respect. We went to your house. We brought you money. We sang your songs. You gave us more blessings. And now we have misplaced one of them. We were careless. This is true. We had so many good things, we couldn't keep them in our mind all the time.

'So maybe you hid him from us to teach us a lesson, to be more careful with your gifts in the future. I have learned this. I have put it in my memory. And now I have come to take Bing back.'

I listened quietly as my mother said these words, horrified. And I began to cry when she added, 'Forgive us for his bad manners. My daughter, this one standing here, will be sure to teach him better lessons of obedience before he visits you again.'

After her prayer, her faith was so great that she saw

him, three times, waving to her from just beyond the first wave. *'Nale!'* – There! And she would stand straight as a sentinel, until three times her eyesight failed her and Bing turned into a dark spot of churning seaweed.

My mother did not let her chin fall down. She walked back to the beach and put the Bible down. She picked up the thermos and teacup and walked to the water's edge. Then she told me that the night before she had reached back into her life, back when she was a girl in China, and this is what she had found.

'I remember a boy who lost his hand in a firecracker accident,' she said. 'I saw the shreds of this boy's arm, his tears, and then I heard his mother's claim that he would grow back another hand, better than the last. This mother said she would pay back an ancestral debt ten times over. She would use a water treatment to soothe the wrath of Chu Jung, the three-eyed god of fire. And true enough, the next week this boy was riding a bicycle, both hands steering a straight course past my astonished eyes!'

And then my mother became very quiet. She spoke again in a thoughtful, respectful manner.

'An ancestor of ours once stole water from a sacred well. Now the water is trying to steal back. We must sweeten the temper of the Coiling Dragon who lives in the sea. And then we must make him loosen his coils from Bing by giving him another treasure he can hide.'

My mother poured out tea sweetened with sugar into the teacup, and threw this into the sea. And then she opened her fist. In her palm was a ring of watery blue sapphire, a gift from her mother, who had died many years before. This ring, she told me, drew coveting stares from women and made them inattentive to the children they guarded so jealously. This would make the

Coiling Dragon forgetful of Bing. She threw the ring into the water.

But even with this, Bing did not appear right away. For an hour or so, all we saw was seaweed drifting by. And then I saw her clasp her hands to her chest, and she said in a wondrous voice, 'See, it's because we were watching the wrong direction.' And I too saw Bing trudging wearily at the far end of the beach, his shoes hanging in his hand, his dark head bent over in exhaustion. I could feel what my mother felt. The hunger in our hearts was instantly filled. And then the two of us, before we could even get to our feet, saw him light a cigarette, grow tall, and become a stranger.

'Ma, let's go,' I said as softly as possible.

'He's there,' she said firmly. She pointed to the jagged wall across the water. 'I see him. He is in a cave, sitting on a little step above the water. He is hungry and a little cold, but he has learned now not to complain too much.'

And then she stood up and started walking across the sandy beach as though it were a solid paved path, and I was trying to follow behind, struggling and stumbling in the soft mounds. She marched up the steep path to where the car was parked, and she wasn't even breathing hard as she pulled a large inner tube from the trunk. To this lifesaver, she tied the fishing line from my father's bamboo pole. She walked back and threw the tube into the sea, holding on to the pole.

'This will go where Bing is. I will bring him back,' she said fiercely. I had never heard so much *nengkan* in my mother's voice.

The tube followed her mind. It drifted out, toward the other side of the cove where it was caught by stronger waves. The line became taut and she strained to hold on tight. But the line snapped and then spiralled into the water.

We both climbed toward the end of the reef to watch. The tube had now reached the other side of the cove. A big wave smashed it into the wall. The bloated tube leapt up and then it was sucked in, under the wall and into a cavern. It popped out. Over and over again, it disappeared, emerged, glistening black, faithfully reporting it had seen Bing and was going back to try to pluck him from the cave. Over and over again, it dove and popped back up again, empty but still hopeful. And then, after a dozen or so times, it was sucked into the dark recess, and when it came out, it was torn and lifeless.

At that moment, and not until that moment, did she give up. My mother had a look on her face that I'll never forget. It was one of complete despair and horror, for losing Bing, for being so foolish as to think she could use faith to change fate. And it made me angry – so blindingly angry – that everything had failed us.

I know now that I had never expected to find Bing, just as I know now I will never find a way to save my marriage. My mother tells me, though, that I should still try.

'What's the point?' I say. 'There's no hope. There's no reason to keep trying.'

'Because you must,' she says. 'This is not hope. Not reason. This is your fate. This is your life, what you must do.'

'So what can I do?'

And my mother says, 'You must think for yourself, what you must do. If someone tells you, then you are not trying.' And then she walks out of the kitchen to let me think about this.

I think about Bing, how I knew he was in danger, how I let it happen. I think about my marriage, how I had seen the signs, really I had. But I just let it happen. And I think now that fate is shaped half by expectation, half by inattention. But somehow, when you lose something you love, faith takes over. You have to pay attention to what you lost. You have to undo the expectation.

My mother, she still pays attention to it. That Bible under the table, I know she sees it. I remember seeing her write in it before she wedged it under.

I lift the table and slide the Bible out. I put the Bible on the table, flipping quickly through the pages, because I know it's there. On the page before the New Testament begins, there's a section called 'Deaths', and that's where she wrote 'Bing Hsu' lightly, in erasable pencil.

Alice Walker

Everyday Use
for your grandmama

I will wait for her in the yard that Maggie and I made so clean and wavy yesterday afternoon. A yard like this is more comfortable than most people know. It is not just a yard. It is like an extended living-room. When the hard clay is swept clean as a floor and the fine sand around the edges lined with tiny, irregular grooves, anyone can come and sit and look up into the elm tree and wait for the breezes that never come inside the house.

Maggie will be nervous until after her sister goes: she will stand hopelessly in corners, homely and ashamed of the burn scars down her arms and legs, eyeing her sister with a mixture of envy and awe. She thinks her sister has held life always in the palm of one hand, that 'no' is a word the world never learned to say to her.

You've no doubt seen those TV shows where the child who has 'made it' is confronted, as a surprise, by her own mother and father, tottering in weakly from backstage. (A pleasant surprise, of course: what would they do if parent and child came on the show only to curse out and insult each other?) On TV mother and child embrace and smile into each other's faces. Sometimes the mother and father weep, the child wraps them in her arms and leans across the table to tell how she would not have made it without their help. I have seen these programmes.

Alice Walker

Sometimes I dream a dream in which Dee and I are suddenly brought together on a TV programme of this sort. Out of a dark and soft-seated limousine I am ushered into a bright room filled with many people. There I meet a smiling, grey, sporty man like Johnny Carson who shakes my hand and tells me what a fine girl I have. Then we are on the stage and Dee is embracing me with tears in her eyes. She pins on my dress a large orchid, even though she has told me once that she thinks orchids are tacky flowers.

In real life I am a large, big-boned woman with rough, man-working hands. In the winter I wear flannel nightgowns to bed and overalls during the day. I can kill and clean a hog as mercilessly as a man. My fat keeps me hot in zero weather. I can work outside all day, breaking ice to get water for washing; I can eat pork liver cooked over the open fire minutes after it comes steaming from the hog. One winter I knocked a bull calf straight in the brain between the eyes with a sledge hammer and had the meat hung up to chill before nightfall. But of course all this does not show on television. I am the way my daughter would want me to be: a hundred pounds lighter, my skin like an uncooked barley pancake. My hair glistens in the hot bright lights. Johnny Carson has much to do to keep up with my quick and witty tongue.

But that is a mistake. I know even before I wake up. Who ever knew a Johnson with a quick tongue? Who can even imagine me looking a strange white man in the eye? It seems to me I have talked to them always with one foot raised in flight, with my head turned in whichever way is farthest from them. Dee, though. She would always look anyone in the eye. Hesitation was no part of her nature.

*

Everyday Use

'How do I look, Mama?' Maggie says, showing just enough of her thin body enveloped in pink skirt and red blouse for me to know she's there, almost hidden by the door.

'Come out into the yard,' I say.

Have you ever seen a lame animal, perhaps a dog run over by some careless person rich enough to own a car, sidle up to someone who is ignorant enough to be kind to him? That is the way my Maggie walks. She has been like this, chin on chest, eyes on ground, feet in shuffle, ever since the fire that burned the other house to the ground.

Dee is lighter than Maggie, with nicer hair and a fuller figure. She's a woman now, though sometimes I forget. How long ago was it that the other house burned? Ten, twelve years? Sometimes I can still hear the flames and feel Maggie's arms sticking to me, her hair smoking and her dress falling off her in little black papery flakes. Her eyes seemed stretched open, blazed open by the flames reflected in them. And Dee. I see her standing off under the sweet gum tree she used to dig gum out of; a look of concentration on her face as she watched the last dingy grey board of the house fall in toward the red-hot brick chimney. Why don't you do a dance around the ashes? I'd wanted to ask her. She had hated the house that much.

I used to think she hated Maggie, too. But that was before we raised the money, the church and me, to send her to Augusta to school. She used to read to us without pity; forcing words, lies, other folks' habits, whole lives upon us two, sitting trapped and ignorant underneath her voice. She washed us in a river of make-believe, burned us with a lot of knowledge we didn't necessarily need to know. Pressed us to her with the serious way she read, to shove us away at just the moment, like dimwits, we seemed about to understand.

Dee wanted nice things. A yellow organdie dress to wear to her graduation from high school; black pumps to match a green suit she'd made from an old suit somebody gave me. She was determined to stare down any disaster in her efforts. Her eyelids would not flicker for minutes at a time. Often I fought off the temptation to shake her. At sixteen she had a style of her own: and knew what style was.

I never had an education myself. After second grade the school was closed down. Don't ask me why: in 1927 coloured asked fewer questions than they do now. Sometimes Maggie reads to me. She stumbles along good-naturedly but can't see well. She knows she is not bright. Like good looks and money, quickness passed her by. She will marry John Thomas (who has mossy teeth in an earnest face) and then I'll be free to sit here and I guess just sing church songs to myself. Although I never was a good singer. Never could carry a tune. I was always better at a man's job. I used to love to milk till I was hooked in the side in '49. Cows are soothing and slow and don't bother you, unless you try to milk them the wrong way.

I have deliberately turned my back on the house. It is three rooms, just like the one that burned, except the roof is tin; they don't make shingle roofs any more. There are no real windows, just some holes cut in the sides, like the portholes in a ship, but not round and not square, with rawhide holding the shutters up on the outside. This house is in a pasture, too, like the other one. No doubt when Dee sees it she will want to tear it down.

Everyday Use

She wrote me once that no matter where we 'choose' to live, she will manage to come see us. But she will never bring her friends. Maggie and I thought about this and Maggie asked me, 'Mama, when did Dee ever *have* any friends?'

She had a few. Furtive boys in pink shirts hanging about on wash-day after school. Nervous girls who never laughed. Impressed with her they worshipped the well-turned phrase, the cute shape, the scalding humour that erupted like bubbles in lye. She read to them.

When she was courting Jimmy T she didn't have much time to pay to us, but turned all her fault-finding power on him. He *flew* to marry a cheap city girl from a family of ignorant flashy people. She hardly had time to recompose herself.

When she comes I will meet – but there they are!

Maggie attempts to make a dash for the house, in her shuffling way, but I stay her with my hand. 'Come back here,' I say. And she stops and tries to dig a well in the sand with her toe.

It is hard to see them clearly through the strong sun. But even the first glimpse of leg out of the car tells me it is Dee. Her feet were always neat-looking, as if God himself had shaped them with a certain style. From the other side of the car comes a short, stocky man. Hair is all over his head a foot long and hanging from his chin like a kinky mule tail. I hear Maggie suck in her breath. 'Uhnnnh' is what it sounds like. Like when you see the wriggling end of a snake just in front of your foot on the road. 'Uhnnnh.'

Dee next. A dress down to the ground, in this hot weather. A dress so loud it hurts my eyes. There are yellows and oranges enough to throw back the light of the sun. I feel my whole face warming from the heat waves it throws out. Ear-rings gold, too, and hanging down to her shoulders. Bracelets dangling and making noises when she moves her arm up to shake the folds of the dress out of her armpits. The dress is loose and flows, and as she walks close, I like it. I hear Maggie go 'Uhnnnh' again. It is her sister's hair. It stands straight up like the wool on a sheep. It is black as night and around the edges are two long pigtails that rope about like small lizards disappearing behind her ears.

'Wa-su-zo-Tean-o!' she says, coming on in that gliding way the dress makes her move. The short stocky fellow with the hair to his navel is all grinning and he follows up with 'Asalamalakim, my mother and sister!' He moves to hug Maggie but she falls back, right up against the back of my chair. I feel her trembling there and when I look up I see the perspiration falling off her chin.

'Don't get up,' says Dee. Since I am stout it takes something of a push. You can see me trying to move a second or two before I make it. She turns, showing white heels through her sandals, and goes back to the car. Out she peeks next with a Polaroid. She stoops down quickly and lines up picture after picture of me sitting there in front of the house with Maggie cowering behind me. She never takes a shot without making sure the house is included. When a cow comes nibbling around the edge of the yard she snaps it and me and Maggie *and* the house. Then she puts the Polaroid in the back seat of the car, and comes up and kisses me on the forehead.

Meanwhile Asalamalakim is going through motions with Maggie's hand. Maggie's hand is as limp as a fish, and probably as cold, despite the sweat, and she keeps trying to pull it back. It looks like Asalamalakim wants

Everyday Use

to shake hands but wants to do it fancy. Or maybe he don't know how people shake hands. Anyhow, he soon gives up on Maggie.

'Well,' I say. 'Dee.'

'No, Mama,' she says. 'Not "Dee," Wangero Leewanika Kemanjo!'

'What happened to "Dee"?' I wanted to know.

'She's dead,' Wangero said. 'I couldn't bear it any longer, being named after the people who oppress me.'

'You know as well as me you was named after your aunt Dicie,' I said. Dicie is my sister. She named Dee. We called her 'Big Dee' after Dee was born.

'But who was *she* named after?' asked Wangero.

'I guess after Grandma Dee,' I said.

'And who was she named after?' asked Wangero.

'Her mother,' I said, and saw Wangero was getting tired. 'That's about as far back as I can trace it,' I said. Though, in fact, I probably could have carried it back beyond the Civil War through the branches.

'Well,' said Asalamalakim, 'there you are.'

'Uhnnnh,' I heard Maggie say.

'There I was not,' I said, 'before "Dicie" cropped up in our family, so why should I try to trace it that far back?'

He just stood there grinning, looking down on me like somebody inspecting a Model A car. Every once in a while he and Wangero sent eye signals over my head.

'How do you pronounce this name?' I asked.

'You don't have to call me by it if you don't want to,' said Wangero.

'Why shouldn't I?' I asked. 'If that's what you want us to call you, we'll call you.'

'I know it might sound awkward at first,' said Wangero.

'I'll get used to it,' I said. 'Ream it out again.'

Well, soon we got the name out of the way. Asalamalakim had a name twice as long and three times as hard. After I tripped over it two or three times he told me to just call him Hakim-a-barber. I wanted to ask him was he a barber, but I didn't really think he was, so I didn't ask.

'You must belong to those beef-cattle peoples down the road,' I said. They said 'Asalamalakim' when they met you, too, but they didn't shake hands. Always too busy: feeding the cattle, fixing the fences, putting up salt-lick shelters, throwing down hay. When the white folks poisoned some of the herd the men stayed up all night with rifles in their hands. I walked a mile and a half just to see the sight.

Hakim-a-barber said, 'I accept some of their doctrines, but farming and raising cattle is not my style.' (They didn't tell me, and I didn't ask, whether Wangero (Dee) had really gone and married him.)

We sat down to eat and right away he said he didn't eat collards and pork was unclean. Wangero, though, went on through the chitlins and corn bread, the greens and everything else. She talked a blue streak over the sweet potatoes. Everything delighted her. Even the fact that we still used the benches her daddy made for the table when we couldn't afford to buy chairs.

'Oh, Mama!' she cried. Then turned to Hakim-a-barber. 'I never knew how lovely these benches are. You can feel the rump prints,' she said, running her hands underneath her and along the bench. Then she gave a sigh and her hand closed over Grandma Dee's butter dish. 'That's it!' she said. 'I knew there was something I wanted to ask you if I could have.' She jumped up from the table and went over in the corner where the churn stood, the milk in it clabber by now. She looked at the churn and looked at it.

'This churn top is what I need,' she said. 'Didn't Uncle Buddy whittle it out of a tree you all used to have?'

'Yes,' I said.

'Uh huh,' she said happily. 'And I want the dasher, too.'

'Uncle Buddy whittle that, too?' asked the barber.

Dee (Wangero) looked up at me.

'Aunt Dee's first husband whittled the dash,' said Maggie so low you almost couldn't hear her. 'His name was Henry, but they called him Stash.'

'Maggie's brain is like an elephant's,' Wangero said, laughing. 'I can use the churn top as a centrepiece for the alcove table,' she said, sliding a plate over the churn, 'and I'll think of something artistic to do with the dasher.'

When she finished wrapping the dasher the handle stuck out. I took it for a moment in my hands. You didn't even have to look close to see where hands pushing the dasher up and down to make butter had left a kind of sink in the wood. In fact, there were a lot of small sinks; you could see where thumbs and fingers had sunk into the wood. It was beautiful light yellow wood, from a tree that grew in the yard where Big Dee and Stash had lived.

After dinner Dee (Wangero) went to the trunk at the foot of my bed and started rifling through it. Maggie hung back in the kitchen over the dishpan. Out came Wangero with two quilts. They had been pieced by Grandma Dee and then Big Dee and me had hung them on the quilt frames on the front porch and quilted them. One was in the Lone Star pattern. The other was Walk Around the Mountain. In both of them were scraps of dresses Grandma Dee had worn fifty and more years ago. Bits and pieces of Grandpa Jarrell's Paisley shirts. And one teeny faded blue piece, about the size of a penny matchbox, that was from Great Grandpa Ezra's uniform that he wore in the Civil War.

'Mama,' Wangero said sweet as a bird. 'Can I have these old quilts?'

I heard something fall in the kitchen, and a minute later the kitchen door slammed.

'Why don't you take one or two of the others?' I asked. 'These old things was just done by me and Big Dee from some tops your grandma pieced before she died.'

'No,' said Wangero. 'I don't want those. They are stitched around the borders by machine.'

'That'll make them last better,' I said.

'That's not the point,' said Wangero. 'These are all pieces of dresses Grandma used to wear. She did all this stitching by hand. Imagine!' She held the quilts securely in her arms, stroking them.

'Some of the pieces, like those lavender ones, come from old clothes her mother handed down to her,' I said, moving up to touch the quilts. Dee (Wangero) moved back just enough so that I couldn't reach the quilts. They already belonged to her.

'Imagine!' she breathed again, clutching them closely to her bosom.

'The truth is,' I said, 'I promised to give them quilts to Maggie, for when she marries John Thomas.'

She gasped like a bee had stung her.

'Maggie can't appreciate these quilts!' she said. 'She'd probably be backward enough to put them to every-day use.'

'I reckon she would,' I said. 'God knows I been saving 'em for long enough with nobody using 'em. I hope she will!' I didn't want to bring up how I had offered Dee (Wangero) a quilt when she went away to college. Then she had told me they were old-fashioned, out of style.

'But they're *priceless*!' she was saying now, furiously; for she has a temper. 'Maggie would put them on the bed and in five years they'd be in rags. Less than that!'

'She can always make some more,' I said. 'Maggie knows how to quilt.'

Dee (Wangero) looked at me with hatred. 'You just will not understand. The point is these quilts, *these* quilts!'

'Well,' I said, stumped. 'What would *you* do with them?'

'Hang them,' she said. As if that was the only thing you *could* do with quilts.

Maggie by now was standing in the door. I could almost hear the sound her feet made as they scraped over each other.

'She can have them, Mama,' she said, like somebody used to never winning anything, or having anything reserved for her. 'I can 'member Grandma Dee without the quilts.'

I looked at her hard. She had filled her bottom lip with checkerberry snuff and it gave her face a kind of dopey, hangdog look. It was Grandma Dee and Big Dee who taught her how to quilt herself. She stood there with her scarred hands hidden in the folds of her skirt. She looked at her sister with something like fear but she wasn't mad at her. This was Maggie's portion. This was the way she knew God to work.

When I looked at her like that something hit me in the top of my head and ran down to the soles of my feet. Just like when I'm in church and the spirit of God touches me and I get happy and shout. I did something I never had done before: hugged Maggie to me, then dragged her on into the room, snatched the quilts out of Miss Wangero's hands and dumped them into Maggie's lap. Maggie just sat there on my bed with her mouth open.

'Take one or two of the others,' I said to Dee.

But she turned without a word and went out to Hakim-a-barber.

'You just don't understand,' she said, as Maggie and I came out to the car.

'What don't I understand?' I wanted to know.

'Your heritage,' she said. And then she turned to Maggie, kissed her, and said, 'You ought to try to make something of yourself, too, Maggie. It's really a new day for us. But from the way you and Mama still live you'd never know it.'

She put on some sunglasses that hid everything above the tip of her nose and her chin.

Maggie smiled; maybe at the sunglasses. But a real smile, not scared. After we watched the car dust settle I asked Maggie to bring me a dip of snuff. And then the two of us sat there just enjoying, until it was time to go in the house and go to bed.

Fay Weldon

extract from

*The Hearts
and Lives of Men*

The sixties are in full swing when Clifford, young whizz-kid director of Leonardo's, the art house that isn't Sotheby's or Christie's, meets Helen, lovely daughter of the eccentric painter John Lally.

FAMILY RELATIONS

Clifford and Helen were, fortunately, innocently asleep, when John Lally burst in upon them. They lay exhausted on a rumpled bed, a hairy limb here, a smooth one there, her head on his chest, hardly comfortable to outside eyes; to lovers, real lovers, that is, perfectly comfortable, just not to those who know they'll presently have to get up and steal away before the embarrassing time for breakfast arrives. Real lovers sleep soundly, knowing that when they wake nothing has to end, but will simply continue. The conviction suffuses their sleep: they smile as they slumber. The sound of splintering wood entered their dreams and was converted there, in Helen's case, to the sound of a fluffy chicken emerging from an egg she had in the palm of her hand, and in Clifford's case, to the sound of his skis as he swept masterfully and unerringly down snowy mountain slopes. The sight of his sleeping smiling daughter, his smiling sleeping enemy, who had stolen his last treasure, inflamed John Lally the more. He roared. Clifford frowned in his sleep: chasms yawned beneath him. Helen stirred and woke. The cosy cheeping of the newborn chick had turned into a wail. She sat up. She saw her father and pulled the sheet above her breasts. Bruise marks had yet to develop.

'How did you know I was here?' she asked: it was the question of a born conspirator who feels no guilt but whose plans have gone awry. He did not deign to reply, but I will tell you.

By one of those mischances which dog the fates of lovers, Clifford's departure with Helen from the Bosch party had been the subject of a small item in a gossip column, and this had been taken up by one Harry Stephens, a *habitué* of the Appletree Pub in Lower Appleby. Now Harry had a cousin in Sotheby's, where Helen had her part-time job, restoring earthenware, and had enquired further, and thus word had got back to deepest Gloucestershire that Helen Lally had vanished into Clifford Wexford's house, and had not emerged since.

'Quite a daughter you've got there!' said Harry Stephens. John Lally was not popular in the neighbourhood. Lower Appleby forgave his eccentricity, his debts, his neglected orchard, but not the way he, a foreigner, drank cider in the pub and not shorts, and the way he treated his wife. Otherwise the subject of his daughter would not have been brought up, but tactfully ignored. As it was, John Lally finished up his cider, got in his battered Volkswagen – its top speed 25 m.p.h. – and made the journey to London through the night, through the dawn, not so much to rescue his daughter but fix Clifford Wexford once and for all as the villain he was.

'Whore!' cried John Lally now, tugging Helen out of bed, because she was nearest.

'Oh really, Dad,' she said, slipping out from under his grasp, on her feet, readjusting her slip, and then to the waking, startled Clifford, 'I'm sorry, it's my father.' She had caught her mother's habit of apologizing. She was never to lose it. Except that where her mother used the phrase, pathetically, in the hope of diverting torrents of abuse, Helen used it as a kind of bored reproach to the

The Hearts and Lives of Men

fates, with a wry lift of a delicate eyebrow. Clifford sat up, startled.

John Lally looked around the bedroom walls, at the paintings which were the sum of five years or so of his life and work: a rotten fig on a branch, a rainbow distorted by a toad, a line of washing in a cavern's mouth – I know they sound dreadful but, reader, they are not: they hang today in the world's most distinguished galleries, and no one blenches when they pass: the colours are so strong, sharp and layered, it is as if one reality is pasted on top of a whole series of others – and then at his daughter, who was half-laughing, half-crying, embarrassed, excited and angry all at once: and at Clifford's strong, naked body, with the fuzz of fair, almost white hair, along his bronzed arms and legs (Clifford and Angie had recently been on holiday, to Brazil where they had stayed at an art-collector's palace: a place of marble floors and gold-leafed taps and so on, and Tintorettos on the walls and hot, hot bleaching sun) and back to the rumpled, heated bed.

It was no doubt purity of heart and sheer self-righteousness which gave John Lally the strength of ten. He lifted Clifford Wexford, young puppy or hope of the Art World, depending on how you saw it, by a naked arm and a bare leg, and effortlessly, as if the younger man were a rag doll, raised him on high. Helen shrieked. The doll came to life just in time and with his free leg directed a sharp kick at John Lally's crotch, getting him just where it hurt most. John Lally shrieked in his turn; the cat – who had spent a warm but restless night on the end of the foam rubber bed – finally gave up and stalked off just in time, for Clifford Wexford came tumbling down just where a second ago he had been curled, as John Lally simply let him go. Clifford was no sooner down than up, hooked a young and flexible foot behind John Lally's stiff ankle and tugged it so that his beloved's father fell face down on the floor, hitting his face and making his nose bleed. Clifford, broad-shouldered, sinewy, young, stood proud and naked over his defeated foe. (He was no more ashamed of his body than Helen was. Though just as Helen felt more comfortable clothed in front of her father, no doubt, had his mother been present, Clifford would quickly have pulled on at least his underpants.)

'Your father really is a bore,' said Clifford to Helen. John Lally lay face down on the floor, his eyes open and burning into the Kelim rug. It was striped in dull oranges and muted reds; colours and pattern which were later to emerge in one of his most well known paintings – *The Scourging of St Ida*. (Painters, like writers, have the knack of putting the most distressing and extreme events to artistic good purpose.) In these days, rugs such as the one then flung so casually over Clifford's polished wood attic floor are rare and cost thousands of pounds at Liberty's. Then they could be bought for a fiver or so at any junk shop. Clifford, of course, with his knowing eye to the future, had already managed to pick up a dozen or so very fine specimens.

John Lally was not sure which was worse: the pain or the humiliation. As the former decreased, the latter intensified. His eyes watered: his nose bled: his groin ached. His fingers tingled. He had been painting obsessively for twenty-eight years, and so far as he could see to no commercial or practical purpose. Canvases stacked his studio, his garage. The only person who seemed to understand their merit was Clifford Wexford. Worse, and the artist had to acknowledge it, this blond young puppy of a man, with his meretricious view of the world,

The Hearts and Lives of Men

his easy way with women, money, society, knew exactly how to foster his talent by an encouraging word here, a moral slap there: a lift of an eyebrow as, on his periodic visits, he leafed through the stacked canvases in the Lally attic, garage, garden shed. 'Yes, that's interesting. No, no, good try but didn't quite come off, did it – Ah, yes –' and young Wexford would pick out the very ones the painter knew to be his best work and so most expected the world to disdain, and by now hoped it would disdain, the better for him to disdain and despise the world – and took them off. And a fiver or so would change hands – just enough to replace paints and brushes, though hardly enough to restock the kitchen cupboard, but that was Evelyn's problem – and they'd be whisked away and a cheque from Leonardo's would come through the letter-box every now and then, unexpected and unasked for. John Lally was torn, he was in conflict: he raged, he burned: he bled: so many passions, thought John Lally, face down, bleeding and weeping into the Kelim rug, might do me some real physical damage – that is to say, paralyse my painting hand. He calmed himself. He stopped writhing and groaning and lay still.

'Now you've stopped making a fool of yourself,' said Clifford, 'you'd better get up and get out before I lose my temper and kick you to death.'

John Lally continued to lie still. Clifford stirred his prostrate body with a casual foot.

'Don't,' said Helen.

'I'll do what I want,' said Clifford. 'Look what he's done to my door!' And he drew back his foot as if to deliver a hefty kick. He was angry, and not just because of his splintered wood, or having his privacy thus invaded, or Helen insulted, but because he realized at that moment that he actually envied and was jealous of John Lally, who could paint like an angel. And that to paint like an angel was the only thing in the world Clifford Wexford wanted. And because Clifford couldn't, everything else seemed unimportant – money, ambition, the quest for status – mere substitutes, second best. He wanted to kick John Lally to death and that was the truth of it.

'Please not,' said Helen. 'He's a bit mad. He can't help himself.'

John Lally looked up at his daughter and decided he didn't like her one bit. She was a patronizing bitch, spoilt by Evelyn, ruined by the world; she was shoddy goods, untalented, spoiled. He clambered to his feet.

'Little bitch,' he said, 'as if I cared whose bed you were in.' He was up just in time. Clifford delivered the kick and missed.

'Do what you want,' John Lally said to Helen. 'Just don't ever come near me or your mother again.'

And that, reader, was how Helen and Clifford met and how Helen gave up her family on Clifford's account.

Helen did not doubt but that presently she and Clifford would marry. They were made for each other. They were two halves of the one whole. They could tell, if only from the way their limbs seemed to fuse together, as if finding at last their natural home. Well, that's how love at first sight takes people. For good or bad, that's that.

LOOKING BACK

Clifford was proud and pleased to have discovered Helen just as she was satisfied and gratified to have found him. He looked back with amazement at his life pre-Helen:

the casual sexual encounters, his general don't-ring-me, I'll-ring-you amorous behaviour (and of course he seldom did, finding his attention and interest not fully engaged), the more decorous but still abortive marital skirmishing with a long list of more-or-less suitable girls, the frequent and ultimately tedious outings with the wrong person to the right restaurants and clubs. How had he put up with it? Why? I am sorry to say that Clifford, looking back, did not consider how many women he had wounded emotionally or socially, or both: he recalled only his own desolation and boredom.

And as for Helen, it was as if until now her life had been lived in shadow. Ah, but now! An unthought of sun illuminated her days, and sent its warm residual glow through her nights. Her eyes shone; how easily her colour came and went: she shook her head and her brown curls tossed about, as if even they were suffused with extra life. She went to her tiny workshop at Sotheby's, just sometimes, returning always not to her own little flat but to Clifford's home and bed. She was paid by the hour – poorly, but the very casualness of the job suited her. She sang as she worked; her speciality was the piecing together of early earthenware (most restorers prefer the hard sharp edges and colours of ceramics. Helen loved the challenging, tricky, melting, flaky softness of early country jugs and mugs). She forgot friends and suitors: she left her flatmate to pay the rent, and answer questions. She could not believe any more that money mattered, or reputation, or the continuing goodwill of friends. She was in love. They were in love. Clifford was rich. Clifford would protect her. Bother the detail. Bother her father's rage, her mother's distress: her employers' raised eyebrows as they totted up the hours she worked each week, and reckoned again the cost of the workshop space she took up. Clifford was all the family, the friends, she would ever need: he was the roof over her head, the cloth on her back, the sun in her sky.

Well, love can't heal everything, can it. Sometimes I see it just as a kind of ointment, which people apply to their wounded egos. True healing has to come from within: a matter of a patient, slow plod towards self-understanding, of gritting the teeth and enduring boredom and irritation, and smiling at milkmen and paying the rent, and wiping the children's faces and not showing hurt, or exhaustion, or impatience – but Helen would have none of that, reader. She was young, she was beautiful, the world was her oyster. She knew it. She let love sweep her away and swallow her up – and all she did was raise her pretty white hands to heaven and say 'I can't help it! This thing is greater than me!'

A KNIFE IN THE BACK

Clifford arrived at Leonardo's on the morning of his encounter with John Lally with a bruised fist and in a bad temper.

His first appointment that day was with Harry Blast, the ungallant young TV interviewer who had managed not to escort Angie Wellbrook home on the night of the Bosch party. It was Harry's first interview: it was to be inserted as an end piece to a programme called 'Monitor'. Harry was nervous and vulnerable. Clifford knew it.

The interview was set up in Sir Larry Patt's grand panelled office, overlooking the Thames. The BBC's cameras were large and unwieldy. The floor was a network of cables. Sir Larry Patt was as nervous as Harry Blast. Clifford was too warm from Helen's bed and his victory over the poor ruined hulk of an artist to be in the least unsure of himself. It was the first time before the cameras too but no one would ever have known it. It was, in fact, this particular interview which set Clifford on his own particular spot-lit path to art stardom. Clifford Wexford says this – Wex says that – quote the great CW and you'd be in business; if you were brave enough to ask him, that is; risk the slow put-down or the fast take-up, you could never be sure which: the quick glance of the bright blue eyes which would sum you up as okay and worth the hearing out, or dismiss you as one of the world's little people. He had the kind of even features that television cameras love – and a clear quick intelligence which cut through cant and pretension, while yet not being free of it himself – on the contrary.

'Well, now,' said Harry Blast, the interviewer, bluntly, when the cameras had stopped admiring the Jacobean panelling, County Hall across the river and the Gainsborough on the wall above the wide Georgian fireplace, and got down to business as he'd clearly prepared his question beforehand. 'It has been suggested that perhaps the Arts Council – by which of course we mean the unfortunate tax payer – has stood rather too high a proportion of the cost of the Bosch exhibition, and Leonardo's claimed rather too much of the profit. What do you say to this, Mr Wexford?'

'You mean *you* are suggesting it,' said Clifford. 'Why don't you just come out with it? Leonardo's are milking the taxpayer . . .'

'Well –' said Harry Blast, flustered, his large nose growing pinker and pinker as it did when he was stressed. A good thing colour television was yet to come, or his career might never have got under way. Stress is part of the media man's life!

'And how are we to judge these things?' asked Clifford. 'How are we to quantify, when it comes to matters of art, where profit lies? If Leonardo's brings art to an art-starved public, and governmental bodies have failed to do so, then surely we deserve, if not exactly reward, just a little encouragement? You saw those queues down the street. I hope you bothered to point your cameras. I tell you, the people of this country have been starved of beauty for too long.'

And of course it just so happened that Harry Blast had neglected to film the queues. Clifford knew it.

'As to the exact proportion of the Arts Council grant to Leonardo's funding, I think it's a matter of matching funds. Isn't that so, Sir Larry? He's king of finances round here.'

And the cameras turned, at Clifford's behest, to Sir Larry Patt, who of course didn't know without looking it up, and mumbled words to this effect instead of proclaiming ignorance loudly and clearly to the world, as he would have been better advised to do. Sir Larry had no television presence at all: his face was too old and the marks of self-indulgence written too large upon it, in the form of sloppy jowls and self-satisfied mouth. He, too, had had an upsetting morning. He had been woken by an early-morning call from Madame Bouser in Amsterdam.

'What kind of country is England?' she had demanded. 'Are you so lost to civilization that a husband can be seduced under his wife's very nose, and the husband of the woman who does it take no notice at all?'

'Madam,' said Sir Larry Patt. 'I have no idea what

you're talking about.' Nor had he. Finding his wife unattractive, it did not occur to him that other men might be attracted to her. Sir Larry belonged to a class and generation which viewed women askance; he had married one as like a boy as possible (which Clifford had once pointed out to Rowena, making her cry). He was not an unimaginative man – just one made uneasy by emotion, who reserved his rapture for art, rather than love; for paintings, rather than sex. And this, in itself, was surely a reason for self-congratulation: coming as he did from a background which prided itself on its philistinism; surely he had shown self-determination enough. He knew he had good reason to be smug. The instrument had gone dead suddenly and fortunately, as if it had been wrested out of Madame Bouser's hand. He was not surprised. She was hysterical. Women so often were. He went into Rowena's bedroom and found her sleeping peacefully, in her flat-chested way, and did not disturb her, in case she became the same. He did not feel at his best. The fact became obvious to Harry Blast that Sir Larry belonged to the past. He had to, since Clifford belonged to the future, and television believes in polarities. Good, bad, old, new, left, right, funny, tragic, Patt on the way out, Wexford on the way in. And so the interview was the beginning of Sir Larry Patt's downfall; the top of a long gentle slope down, and Clifford it was who quite wilfully, that day, nudged him on to it. Sir Larry didn't even notice. Clifford looked into a future and saw that it contained the possibility of dynasty. To make Helen his queen he would have to be King. That meant he must rule over Leonardo's, and Leonardo's itself would have to grow and change, become one of those intricate complexes of power of which the modern world was fast becoming composed. He would have to do it by stealth, by playing politics, by behaving as kings and emperors always had: by demanding loyalty, and extracting fealty, allowing no one too close to him, by playing one favourite off against another, by keeping to himself the power of life and death and using it (or hiring and firing, the modern equivalent), by giving unexpected favours, meting out unexpected punishments, by letting his smile mean munificence, his frown hardship. He would become Wexford of Leonardo's. He, the ne'er-do-well, the anxious, striving, restless son of a powerful father, would cease to be an outsider, would cease to be the moon revolving around the sun, but become the sun itself. For Helen's sake he would turn the world inside out.

He sighed and stretched; how powerful he felt! Harry Blast's cameras caught the sigh and the stretch and made the still that made the programme, and was every picture editor's favourite thereafter, whenever they ran a story on wheelings and dealings in the Art World. There was just something about it: some feeling, I dare say, of the Act of Accession – that moment which is supposed to be so important, when the Archbishop actually places the crown upon the new monarch's head – that was caught by Harry Blast's cameras, unawares.

MOTHER AND DAUGHTER

And while Clifford Wexford considered his future, and regularized, professionalized, and indeed sanctified what had so far been only a vague ambition, the girl of his dreams, Helen Lally, sat with her mother and sipped herbal tea at Cranks, the new health food restaurant in Carnaby Street. Cranks was the prototype of a million others which were, over the next twenty-five years, to spring up all over the world. Whole food and herbal tea = spiritual and physical health. It was a very new notion at the time and Evelyn sipped her comfrey tea with some suspicion. (Comfrey is now not taken internally, for fear it may be carcinogenic, but only used in external application, so her instinct may have been right.)

'It will comfort you, Mother,' said Helen, hopefully. Evelyn clearly needed comforting. Her eyes were red-rimmed and puffy. She looked plain, desperate and old: not a good combination. On his return from 5 Coffee Place, John Lally had reaffirmed to his wife that her daughter Helen was no longer welcome in Applecore Cottage, that the only possible explanation for the girl's behaviour was that she was no child of his, and had locked himself in the garage. There within, presumably, he now painted furiously. Evelyn set food and drink on the window-sill from time to time: the food would be taken – the window raised quickly then banged shut – but the drink, rather pointedly, left. Home-made wine was stored in the garage so supposedly this was all he required. Black rage seemed to seep out under the garage door. 'It isn't fair,' said Evelyn to her daughter, as if she were the child and not the mother. 'It just isn't fair!'

Nor of course was it. She who had done so much for her husband, dedicated her whole life to him, thus to be treated!

'I try not to let you know how upset I get,' she said, 'but you're a grown girl now, and I suppose this is life.'

'Only if you let it be,' said Helen, secure in the knowledge of her new-found love, and that she for one meant to live happily ever after.

'If only you'd been more tactful about it,' said her mother, as near a reproach as she had ever uttered. 'You have no idea how to manage your father.'

'Well,' said Helen, 'I'm sorry. I suppose it is all my fault. But he keeps shutting himself in. Usually it's the attic: now it's the garage. I don't know why you get so upset about it. It's nothing unusual. If you didn't get so upset, he mightn't do it.'

She was trying to be serious but only managed, to her mother, to sound frivolous. She couldn't help it. She loved Clifford Wexford. So what if her father angered himself to death and her mother grieved herself to an untimely end; she, Helen, loved Clifford Wexford, and youth, energy, future, common sense, and good cheer were on her side, and that was that.

Evelyn presently composed herself and properly admired the unusual stripped pine, country-style of the restaurant, and agreed with her daughter that things had been going on like this for twenty-five years. She expected they'd go on like this for quite a while. Helen was quite right. There was no need to worry and all she had to do was pull herself together. 'Good heavens,' said Evelyn, pulling herself together, 'your hair *is* looking lovely. So curly!'

And Helen, who could afford to be kind, was, and did not instantly try to smooth her hair around her ears, but shook her head so it fluffed out just as her mother liked it. Helen liked to wear her hair straight, flat, silky and smooth long before such a thing was fashionable. Love seemed to be on Evelyn's side in this respect at least, thickening and curling her daughter's hair.

'I'm in love,' Helen said. 'I expect that's it.'

Evelyn looked at her, puzzled. How had life at Applecore Cottage created such naivety?

'Well,' she said presently, 'don't rush into anything just because life at home was so horrible.'

'Oh, Mum, it was never exactly horrible,' protested Helen, though sometimes it truly had been. Applecore Cottage was quaint and charming, but her father's frequent black moods did indeed float like a noxious gas under doors and through cracks, no matter that he shut himself away, both for his family's sake (to protect them from him) and for his (to protect him from their female philistinism and general treachery) and her mother's eyes had been too often red-rimmed, thus somehow dimming the lustre of the copper pans which hung so prettily in the kitchen, throwing back the light from latticed windows; at such times Helen had longed, longed just to get away. Yet at other times they'd been a close family, sharing thought, feeling, aspirations; the two women intensely loyal to John Lally's genius, gladly putting up with hardship and penury on that account, understanding that the painter's temperament was as difficult for him to endure as it was for them. But then Helen had gone – off to Art School, and a mysterious life in London, and Evelyn had to take the full undiluted force, not of her husband's attention, for he gave her little, but of his circling, angry energy, and began to understand that though he would survive, and his paintings too, she, Evelyn, might very well not. She felt far older and more tired than she should. What was more, she understood only too well that if John Lally had to choose between his art and her, he would undoubtedly choose his art. If he loved her, she once told Helen in an uncharacteristic burst of anger, it was as a man with a wooden leg loved that leg. He couldn't do without it, but wished he could.

Now she smiled sweetly at Helen, and patted her daughter's small firm white hand with her large loose one and said, 'It's nice of you to say so.'

'You always did your best,' said Helen, and then, panicky – 'Why are you talking as if we're saying goodbye?'

'Because if you're with Clifford Wexford,' said Evelyn, 'it is, more or less.'

'He shouldn't have burst in on us the way he did. I'm sorry Clifford hit him but he was provoked.'

'It all goes deeper than that,' said Evelyn.

'He'll get over it,' said Helen.

'No,' said her mother. 'You do have to choose.' It occurred to Helen then that with Clifford for a lover, what did she want with a father.

'Why don't you just leave home, Mum,' she said, 'and let Dad get on with his genius on his own? Don't you see it's absurd. Living with a man who locks himself in and has to have his food from a plate left on a garage window-sill.'

'But, darling,' said Evelyn, 'he's *painting*!' And Helen knew it was no use, and, in any case, hardly wanted it to be. It's one thing to suggest to your parents that they part – and many do – quite horrific if they actually act upon that suggestion.

'It's probably best,' said Evelyn to her own daughter, 'if you just stay out of the way for a while,' and Helen was more than ever glad she had Clifford, for a feeling of hurt and terror welled up inside her and had to be subdued. It looked for a moment as if her own mother was abandoning her. But of course that was nonsense. They shared a particularly novel wholewheat and honey biscuit, which Evelyn quite liked, and shared the bill, and once outside, smiled and kissed and went their separate ways, Evelyn no longer with a child, Helen no longer with a mother.

PROTECTIVE CUSTODY

'Good Lord,' said Clifford, when Helen reported the conversation to him that night, 'whatever you do, don't encourage your mother to leave home!'

They were having supper in bed, trying not to get the black sheets sticky with taramasalata, whipped up by Clifford from cod's roe, lemon juice and cream, and cheaper than buying it already made up. Not even love could induce Clifford to abandon his habits of economy – some called it parsimony but why not use the kinder word? Clifford insisted on living well, and also took pleasure in never spending a penny more than he had to in so doing.

'Why not, Clifford?'

Sometimes Clifford confused Helen, just as he confused Angie, but Helen had the quickness and sense to ask for guidance. And unlike Angie, not being stubborn, she was a quick learner. How pretty she looked this evening; enchanting! All thin soft arms and plump naked shoulders, her cream silk slip barely covering a swelling breast – cautiously nibbling, with little, even teeth, the edges of her Bath Oliver, careful not to spill the taramasalata, made by Clifford perhaps just a fraction too liquid.

'Because your mother is your father's inspiration,' said Clifford, 'and though that's hard luck on your mother, sacrifices must be made in the cause of art.

Art is more important than the individual: even than the painter who creates it: your father would be the first to acknowledge that, monster though he is. Moreover, a painter needs his gestalt – the peculiar combination of circumstances which enables him to express his particular vision of the universe. Your father's gestalt, more's the pity, includes Applecore Cottage, your mother, quarrels with neighbours, paranoia about the art world in general and me in particular. It also until now has included you. You've been snatched away. That's shock enough. It's driven him into the garage: with any luck we'll see a change of style when he emerges. Let's just hope that the new is more saleable than the old.'

He carefully removed Helen's Bath Oliver, put it to one side and kissed her salty mouth.

'I suppose,' said Helen, 'you didn't move me in here with you just to make my father's paintings easier to sell?' and he laughed, but there was a little pause before he did, as if he himself almost wondered. Truly successful people often act by an instinct which works to their advantage: they don't have to plot, or scheme. They just follow their noses, and life itself bows down before them. Clifford loved Helen. Of course he did. Nevertheless, John Lally's daughter! Part of a gestalt which needed a shock, a shove, a shaking up –

But they forgot these matters soon enough, and Clifford also forgot to say that Angie Wellbrook's father had called him from Johannesburg during the week.

'I thought I should warn you,' boomed the sad, powerful voice. 'My daughter's on the war-path.'

'What about?' Clifford had been light and cool.

'God knows. She doesn't like the Old Masters. She says the future lies with Moderns. She says Leonardo's is throwing its money away. What did you do? Stand

The Hearts and Lives of Men

her up? No, don't tell me. I don't want to know. Just remember that, though I'm a major shareholder, she acts for me in the UK and there's no controlling her. She's a shrewd girl though a pain in the arse.'

Clifford thanked him and promised to send him the excellent reviews of the Bosch exhibition and press reports of the unprecedented queues outside it, assured him that his investment was well protected, and that the furtherance and support of contemporary art was becoming increasingly part of Leonardo's provenance – in other words that Angie was out on a precarious limb. Then he rang Angie and asked her out to lunch. He forgot to tell Helen about this too. But he left her languid on the bed in such a sensuous swoon he knew well enough she'd be only just recovering when he came back that evening.

Angie and Clifford went to Claridges. Mini-skirts were just coming in. Angie turned up wearing a beige trouser-suit in fine, supple suede, and asked to be shown to Clifford's table. She'd spent the morning in the beauty parlour but the hand of the girl who inserted her false eyelashes had slipped and one of Angie's eyes was red, so she had to wear dark glasses, the wearing of which other than on ski slopes she knew Clifford despised. It made her cross.

'I'm so sorry,' said the Head Waiter, rashly, 'but it is not our policy to allow ladies in trousers into the Grand Restaurant.'

'Really?' enquired Angie, dangerously, made even crosser.

'If you will allow me to take you to the Luncheon Bar –'

'No,' said Angie. 'You just take the trousers.'

And there and then she undid them, stepped out of them, handed them to the Head Waiter, and went on in, mini-skirted, to join Clifford. A pity, Clifford thought, Angie's legs were not better. They quite spoiled the gesture. All the same, he was impressed. So were many of the lunchers. Angie received a round of applause as she sat down.

'I know I'm a bastard,' Clifford said, over quails' eggs, 'I know I let you down, I know I'm a cad and a bounder, but the fact is, I've fallen in love.' And he raised his clear blue eyes to hers, and finding them covered by dark glasses, straightaway removed them.

'One of your eyes is red,' he remarked. 'Quite horrid!' Somehow the gesture, the touch, the remark, made her believe that in love with someone else he might be, but matters between him and her were not finished. She was right.

'So where does that leave us?' she asked, one hand now covering the erring eye, scraping a little fattening mayonnaise from her egg with the knife in the other. He thought that if anything she was too skinny. In his bed she'd kept herself well covered with the black sheet and with good reason. (Thinness, in those days, was not as fashionable as now. A pattern of ribs beneath the skin was seen as unsightly.) Helen, perfectly at ease in her body, could cheerfully expose any part, in any position. Yet Angie's very reticences had their charm.

'Friends,' he said.

'You mean,' she said, 'you don't want my father taking his millions out of Leonardo's.'

'How well you know me,' he said, and laughed, looking directly at her with his bright knowledgeable eyes, and this time he moved her shielding hand, and her heart turned over, but what was the use?

'They'll be my millions eventually,' said Angie. 'And

The Hearts and Lives of Men

leaving you and me right out of it, I don't like seeing them in Leonardo's. Art's a high-risk business.'

'Not any more,' said Clifford Wexford, 'not now I'm in charge.'

'But, Clifford, you're not.'

'I will be,' said Clifford.

She believed him. A crowd of photographers and reporters now clustered at Claridges' door. Word had got round. They wanted a glimpse of Angie's legs or, failing that, of the King of the Waiters discomposed: staff barred their way. The general uproar impressed Clifford. Publicity always did.

Angie was not ungratified, either. Well, she thought, Clifford will wear out Helen soon enough. Helen can't command the press, as I can. Helen, the frame-maker's daughter. Just another pretty face! Penniless, powerless, without place in the world except by courtesy of Clifford. He'd soon get bored. Angie decided to forgive Clifford and be content just to hate Helen. Should she say something scathing, unforgettable, about her rival? No. Clifford was too shrewd. He'd see through it. She'd go the other way instead.

'She's a sweet, pretty girl,' she said, 'and just what you need. Though you'll have to sharpen up her dress sense a little. She really shouldn't go round looking so humble. But I give up. I give in. I'll be yours and Helen's friend. And the crits of the Bosch exhibition were really impressive, Clifford. I may have been wrong. I'll give Dad a call and reassure him.'

Clifford stood, moved round to where Angie sat, lifted her dull-complexioned face with its poor eye, and kissed her firmly on her lips. It was her reward. It was not enough, but something. She would claim what she deserved, what she had been promised, when the time was ripe. There was, she supposed, no hurry. She would wait, decades if she had to.

While Angie lunched with Clifford, Evelyn was on the phone to Helen.

'Oh, Mum,' said Helen, gratefully. 'I thought you'd given up on me!'

'Well, I thought you'd better know just how upset your father is,' her mother said. 'He's left the garage, and now he's up in the attic, cutting up his old canvasses with the garden shears. *Fox Plus Chicken Pieces* is in shreds. He threw a section of *Beached Whale With Vultures* downstairs. He's going to be so upset when he calms down and finds out what he's done. He was on the whale painting for two years, Helen. You remember? All through your "A" levels.'

'I think you should go next door, Mum, and wait till he calms down.'

'They're getting so sick of me next door.'

'Of course they're not, Mum.'

'It is so important for your father not to be upset.'

'Mum, don't you see, I am the excuse for his upset, not the reason for his upset.'

'No, Helen, I'm afraid I can't see it that way.'

At three-fifteen Helen rang, crying, through to Leonardo's and left a message for Clifford to call home urgently. But he did not arrive back in the office until five o'clock. How he had been spending his time between two and five, reader, I am not going to divulge in detail. He had not meant such a thing to happen. Let us just say Angie kept a suite at Claridges for her convenience when shopping in Bond Street – her house in Belgravia seeming to her too far from the heart of things, and her actions too closely observed by the butler and other staff – and that opportunity is, if not all, at least four-fifths of illicit and unexpected sexual congress. And Clifford felt he ought to make amends and, to his credit, was amused and more impressed by the newshounds at her heels than he ever had been by her father's millions. Besides, he was so newly in love with Helen the emotion had not had time to affect a deep-rooted habit of life – that is to say, of taking his pleasures when and as he usefully found them.

Be all that as it may, come five-thirty, Clifford reacted strongly and instantly not so much to Helen's tears as to her account of her father's behaviour. *Fox Plus Chicken Pieces* was a minor and flawed piece but *Beached Whale With Vultures*, though unlikeable on account of its subject matter – rotting flesh, stretched in glistening strands across an almost ethereal canvas – was a fine major work and Clifford was not having it under attack. His lawyers were round at Judge Percibar's within the hour – the eloquent Percibar a lifelong friend of Otto Wexford, Clifford's father – and an injunction taken out restraining John Lally from damaging what turned out to be Leonardo's property, inasmuch as, or so they claimed, the artist benefited by a retainer from that august institution. And by the next morning, after a police car and a Leonardo's van had turned up at the cottage, seven John Lally canvases had been transferred to Leonardo's vaults, plus the shreds, recovered from the garden, of *Fox Plus Chicken Pieces*, and catalogued thus:

1 *Beached Whale With Vultures* – damaged
2 *Massacre of the Turtles* – in fine condition
3 *St Peter and Cripple at Heaven's Gate* – scratched
4 *The Feast of Eyes* – stained (coffee?)
5 *Kitten with Hand* – stained (bird droppings?)
6 *Dead Flowerpiece* (in fine condition)

Fay Weldon

7 *Landscape of Bones* (slashed)
8 *Fox Plus Chicken Pieces* (remnant)

The removal was done while John Lally slept off the effect of shock, overwork, temper and home-made wine. Evelyn tried to wake him as the Leonardo's team tramped up and down the steep narrow stairs to the attic, manoeuvring the wide canvasses with some difficulty, but there was no waking him. She left a note and went to neighbours.

Reader, if you know even an amateur painter, or if you daub or dabble yourself, you will understand how any painter worth his salt hates to be parted from his paintings, in just the same way as a mother hates to be parted from her children. This leaves the painter in a terrible fix. If he doesn't sell not only does he not eat, but he paints himself out of house and home: there is the enormous simple practical matter of *space*: where are the paintings to be kept? Yet if he does sell, and so makes room, it is like having a chunk of living flesh torn away. And it is so agitating. What kind of home is the work going to? Will it be safe? Was it bought because it was truly appreciated, or merely because it matched the wallpaper? Not, of course, that John Lally had many worries on the latter score. There was never any question of a Lally canvas *blending*. He is what is called a gallery painter, fit for display on large bare walls and respectful viewing in public places, where little cries of shock and awe and distaste can be quickly sopped up by the warm, gently circulating, stuffy mausoleum air. (And what kind of fate, raged John Lally, is that for a painting? *Kitten with Hand* – the fingers with claws, the paw with nails – had for a time been hoisted into the air between two pine trees in the garden of

The Hearts and Lives of Men

Applecore Cottage, the better for the birds of the air to admire it, mere earth-swarming humans being so lacking in the capacity for proper appreciation.) And as for the small private galleries, run as they are by undiscriminating rogues who will take as much as fifty per cent commission, these are the shit-holes of the Art World. Go to any opening, and see the phoneys and the poseurs gawping and gaping and very publicly writing out their cheques. On the whole John Lally preferred simply to give paintings away to friends. Then at least he could control who owned them, on whose wall they hung. Friends? What friends? For as quickly as his occasional charm won them, his paranoia and temper would drive them away. There were few enough about qualified to be Lally recipients. This was why, driven to fever pitch by the impossibility of solving the problem, or so John Lally saw it, he had consented to accept a retainer from Leonardo's. And Leonardo's (that is to say, Clifford Wexford) had done him other favours: taken a few canvasses off his hands; had the broken-down garage rebuilt, damp-coursed and air-conditioned so that other paintings could be safely stacked and stored. They had let window lights into the attic roof the better to illuminate his work with good natural north light. If John Lally chose to paint in the garage and store in the attic no great harm would be done. But if John Lally took shears to his canvasses, Leonardo's would step in to claim what turned out, thanks to the Wexford small print, to be Leonardo's property.

And John Lally had, in a way, trusted Clifford, while yet hating and despising him, because in spite of everything Clifford had some sort of proper response to his work and he'd felt sure that whatever else befell, he would at least never do what some collectors did –

put the paintings in a bank vault somewhere for safe keeping. This being to the painter the same as rendering him blind and deaf.

And now Clifford had done exactly this. And not, John Lally was convinced, when he roused himself from his stupor, and found the paintings gone, simply in order to preserve the canvasses – they had survived many such a storm before and even as he shredded *Fox Plus Chicken Pieces* he was working out a new improved version in his head – but to be revenged. John Lally the impoverished artist, breaking down, splintering Clifford Wexford's bedroom door, bursting in upon him – no, it was not forgotten, let alone forgiven! No. This was why eight fine paintings were now immured in Leonardo's vault, while Clifford smiled and said lightly, 'It's for John Lally's own good,' and stretched his white daughter yet again upon the black satanic sheets. It was the artist's punishment.

It was fifteen days before Evelyn dared to creep back into Applecore Cottage and start washing up and sweeping up again, and three months before life returned to anything resembling normal. John Lally then got on with *The Rape by the Sabine Women* in which he depicted the latter as insatiable harpies. A silly idea, but well executed: he painted it on the wall of the hen-house, on the grounds that it could then hardly end up in Leonardo's vaults. Rather, wind and rain would presently obscure the painting altogether.

LITTLE NELL'S INHERITANCE

For six weeks now little Nell snuggled tenderly and safely in Helen's womb. She had inherited at least a

The Hearts and Lives of Men

degree of her maternal grandfather's artistic talent, but not, you will be relieved to hear, his temper or his neuroses: she had all and more of her maternal grandmother's sweetness, but not her tendency to the acute masochism which so often goes with it. She had her father's energy and wit and not his, well, sneakiness. She was all set up to have her mother's looks: but, unlike her mother, to feel it below her dignity to lie. All this, of course, was simply the luck of the draw: and not just Nell's luck but ours as well – all of us who were to encounter her in later life. But our Nell had another quality too – her capacity to attract towards her the most untoward, even dangerous events, and the most disagreeable people. Perhaps it was in her stars: an event proneness inherited from Clifford's father Otto – his early life, too, was lived in hazard – or perhaps it was, as my own mother would have it, that where you have angels, you have demons too. Evil circles good, as if trying to contain it: good being the powerful, moving, active force: evil the nagging, restraining one. Well, you must make up your own mind as you read Nell's story. This is a Christmas tale, and Christmas is a time for believing in good, rather than bad: for seeing the latter, not the former, on the winning side.

As for Helen, she suspected that perhaps Nell, or someone, had come into existence, inasmuch as she suffered from a faint dizziness which affected her whenever she stood too suddenly, and because her breasts were so swollen and sore she could scarcely forget they were there – which most women do, most of the time, unless and until they're pregnant. These symptoms, mind you, or so she told herself, might be due to love, and nothing more. The fact was that Helen didn't want to be pregnant. Not yet. There was far too much to be done, seen, explored, thought about in the world which so suddenly and newly included Clifford.

And how could she, Helen, scarcely yet herself properly in the world, bring someone else along into it? And how could Clifford love her if she was pregnant; that is to say sick, swollen, tearful – as her mother had been during her last disastrous pregnancy, only five years back. That baby had miscarried, horribly and bloodily late in the pregnancy, and Helen had been horribly sorry and bloodily relieved when it happened, and confused by her own conflicting emotions. And John Lally had sat and held her mother's hand, with a tenderness she had never seen before, and she had found herself jealous – and planned there and then to leave home after 'A' levels and go to Art College, and Get Out, Get Out –

Well now, what it added up to was that Helen now just wanted to forget the past and love Clifford and prepare for a glittering future and *not* be pregnant. Because Clifford had asked her to marry him. Or had he asked her? Or just somehow said, some time in the middle of one of their lively, enchanted nights, part sticky, part silky, part velvet black, part glowing lamp-light, 'I must tell my parents about all this. They'll want some kind of marriage ceremony, they're like that,' and so, casually, the matter had been settled. Since the bride's parents were so clearly incapable of arranging anything, it would be left to the bridegroom's. Besides, the latter's income exceeded the former's by a ratio of 100 to 1, or thereabouts.

'Perhaps we should just be married quietly,' Helen said to Otto's wife, Cynthia, when the whens and hows of the wedding were discussed. Clifford had taken her down to the family home in Sussex to introduce her for the first time and say they were to be married all on the one day. Impetuous lad! The house was Georgian and stood in twelve acres. Dannemore Court, reader. Its gardens are opened to the public once a year. Perhaps you know it. The place is famous for its azaleas.

'Why a quiet wedding?' asked Cynthia. 'There is nothing to be ashamed of. Or is there?' Cynthia was sixty, looked forty and acted thirty. She was small, dark, elegant, vivacious and un-English, for all her tweeds.

'Oh no,' said Helen, although she had risen in the night twice to go to the bathroom, and in those days, before the pill was in common use, the symptoms of pregnancy were all too well known to every young woman. And being pregnant, and unmarried, was in most circles still something to be ashamed of.

'So let's make all the fuss we possibly can of such an important occasion,' said Cynthia, 'and as for who pays – poofey! All that etiquette is so stuffy and boring, don't you think?'

That was in the big drawing-room after lunch. Cynthia was arranging spring flowers in a bowl: they were fresh from the garden, and of amazing variety. She seemed to Helen more concerned over their welfare than that of her son.

But later Cynthia did say to Clifford, 'Darling, are you sure you know what you're doing? You've never been married before, and she's so young, and it's all so sudden.'

'I know what I'm doing,' said Clifford, gratified by her concern. It was seldom shown. His mother was always busy, looking after his father's needs, or flowers in vases, or making mysterious phone calls, and dressing up and rushing off. His father would smile fondly after her; what pleased his wife pleased him. There seemed no room for Clifford, either as a child or now he was grown, between them. They made no space for him. They squeezed him out.

'In my experience of men,' said Cynthia (and Clifford thought sadly, yes, that's quite considerable) 'when a man says he knows what he's doing it means he doesn't.'

'She's John Lally's daughter,' said Clifford. 'He's one of the greatest painters this country has. If not the greatest.'

'Well I've never heard of him,' said Cynthia, on whose walls were a minor Manet and a nice collection of Constable sketches. Otto Wexford was a director of The Distillers' Company: the days of the Wexford poverty were a long time ago.

'You will,' said Clifford, 'one day. If I have anything to do with it.'

'Darling,' said Cynthia, 'painters are great because they have a great talent, not because you or Leonardo's make them so. You are not God.'

Clifford just raised his eyebrows and said, 'No? I mean to run Leonardo's, and in the Art World that makes me God.'

'Well,' said Cynthia, 'I can't help feeling someone like Angie Wellbrook, with a couple of goldmines behind her –'

'Six –' said Clifford.

'– would have been a less, shall we say, surprising choice. Not that your Helen isn't very sweet.'

It was agreed they were to be married on Midsummer's Day, in the village church (Norman, plus lych-gate) and have the reception in a big marquee on the lawn, for all the world as if the Wexfords were landed gentry.

Which of course they were not. Otto Wexford, builder, had fled with his Jewish wife Cynthia from Denmark to London in 1941, with their young son. By the end of the war – which Cynthia spent in a munitions factory, wearing a headscarf, and Clifford running wild as an evacuee in Somerset – Otto was a Major in the Intelligence Forces and a man with many influential friends. Whether or not he actually left the Secret Service was never made clear to his family but, be that as it may, he had risen briskly through the world of post-war finance and property development, and was now a man of wealth, power and discernment, and kept a Rolls-Royce as well as horses in the stable block of his Georgian country house, and his wife rode to hounds and had affairs with the neighbouring gentry. All the same, they never quite 'belonged'. Perhaps it was just that their eyes were too bright: they were too lively: they read novels: they said surprising things. Call to tea, and you might find the stable-hand sitting in the drawing-room, chatting, as bold as brass. No one refused the wedding invitation, all the same. The Wexfords were liked, though cautiously: young Clifford Wexford was already a name: too flashy for his own good but entertaining, and the champagne would be plentiful, and the food good, though un-English.

'Mother,' said Clifford to Cynthia, on the Sunday morning, 'what does Father say about my marrying Helen?' For Otto had said very little at all. Clifford waited for approval or disapproval, but none came. Otto was friendly, courteous and concerned, but as if Clifford was the child of close friends, rather than his own and only son.

'Why should he say anything? You're old enough to know your own mind.'

'Does he find her attractive?' It was the wrong question. He was not sure why he asked it. Only with his father was Clifford so much at a loss.

'Darling, I am the wrong person to ask,' was all she replied, and he felt he had offended her as well. Though she was cheerful and flighty and charming enough all day, heaven knows: Otto went hunting: Cynthia stayed home especially to be nice to Helen.

'This house is like a backdrop,' Clifford complained to Helen on the Sunday night. They were not leaving until the Monday morning. They had been put in separate bedrooms, but on the same corridor, so naturally, and as was expected, Clifford had made his way to Helen's room.

'It isn't real. It isn't home. It is a cover. You know my father's a spy?'

'So you've told me,' but Helen found it hard to believe.

'Well, what do you make of him? Do you find him attractive?'

'He's your father. I don't think of him like that. He's old.'

'Very well then. Does he find you attractive?'

'How would I know?'

'Women always know things like that.'

'No they don't.'

They quarrelled about it, and Clifford returned to his own room, without making love to her. He did not, in any case, like his mother's expectation that he would, putting them in separate rooms, but near. He felt insulted by her, and irritated by Helen.

But early in the morning Helen crept into his room: she was laughing and teasing, unimpressed by his bad moods, as she usually was in the first flush of their relationship – and he forgot he was angry. He thought

The Hearts and Lives of Men

Helen would make up for what his parents had never given him – a feeling of ease and closeness, of not talking behind his back, conspiring against him. When he and Helen had children he would make sure of a proper space for them, between the pair of them. Meanwhile, close together in their white-sheeted bed, in the master bedroom, Cynthia and Otto talked.

'You should take more interest in him,' said Cynthia. 'He feels your lack of interest.'

'I wish he'd stop fidgeting: he's always fidgeting,' said Otto, who moved slowly, serenely and powerfully through life.

'He was born like that,' said Cynthia. So he had been, nine months to the day after his parents' meeting, as if protesting at the suddenness and strangeness of it all. His mother barely seventeen, wild cast-off daughter of a wealthy banking family: his father, already at twenty running his own small firm of builders. Otto had been up a ladder, replacing glass in a conservatory, and had looked down at Cynthia, looking up, and that had been that: neither of them had expected the baby, nor the pursuing vengeance of Cynthia's family: snatching contracts from under Otto's nose; condemning them to poverty and a perpetual moving on: nor would it have altered their behaviour had they known. And no one expected the overwhelming vengeance of the German occupation, the deportation and murder of the Jews: Cynthia's family got to America; Cynthia and Otto went underground, joined the Resistance, Clifford handed from household to household the while: until all three were shipped to England, the better for Otto to function. The habit of secrecy was never lost for either of them. Cynthia's love affairs were all to do with it: Otto knew it and put up with it. They were no insult to him: merely the addict's passion for intrigue. He got his fixes with MI5: but where could she get hers?

'I wish he'd find himself a more solid occupation,' said Otto. 'A picture dealer! Art is not for profiteering.'

'He had a hard childhood,' said Cynthia. 'He feels the need to survive, and to survive he has to scheme. It is our example: it is what we did, you and I, and he watched us.'

'But he is the child of peace,' said Otto. 'And we were the children of war. Why is it that the products of peace are always so ignoble?'

'Ignoble!'

'He has no moral concern, no political principle; he is eaten up by self-interest.'

'Oh dear,' said Cynthia, but she did not argue. 'Well,' she said, 'I hope this one makes him happy. Do you find her attractive?'

'I see what he sees in her,' said Otto cautiously. 'But she'll lead him a dance.'

'She's soft and natural, not like me. She'll make a good mother. I look forward to grandchildren. We may do better with the next generation.'

'We've waited long enough,' said Otto.

'I just hope he settles down.'

'He's too fidgety to settle down,' said Otto, serenely, and they both slept.

Helen wept a little when she returned to Clifford's home, Clifford's bed.

'What's the matter?' he asked.

'I just wish my parents were coming to my wedding,' she said, 'that's all.' But in her heart she was glad. Her father would only make some kind of scene: her mother turn up in the old blue ribbed cotton dress, her eyes red-rimmed from the previous night's row. No. Better forget

The Hearts and Lives of Men

them. If only now she weren't beginning to feel sick in the mornings. There still might well be reasons – the change in routine, the nights of wild love-making, the many dinners out – and she so accustomed to frugal student's fare, or the pork, beans and cider-if-you're-lucky routine of the Lally household – but it was beginning to seem unlikely. No quick pregnancy tests in those days: no vacuum abortions on the side. Just, for the former, a toad which got injected with your urine and laid eggs and died forty-eight hours later if you *were* pregnant, and laid eggs and survived if you weren't, and for the latter an illegal operation which you, like the toad, had to be lucky, or very rich, to survive.

But of course the mere fact of worrying could so upset your cycle you never knew where you were. Oh, reader, what days! But at least then the penalty for untoward sex was a new life and not, as it can be now, a disagreeable and disgraceful death.

Another month and Helen could not disguise from herself the fact that she was in fact and in truth pregnant, and that she didn't want to be, and that she didn't want Clifford to know, let alone his parents, and that to go to doctors (two were required) for a legal abortion would require more lies about how more damaging to her health and sanity pregnancy would be than she – so sane and healthy – could sustain, and that she couldn't tell her friends because she couldn't trust them not to gossip, and her father would kill her if he knew and her mother simply commit suicide – round and round the thoughts flew in Helen's head, and there was no one she could turn to for help and advice, until she thought of Angie.

Now, reader, you may think this is no more than Helen deserved, to turn for help to a woman who bore her nothing but malice, however good – and she was *very* good – at disguising it Angie had so far been: giving little dinners for the handsome young couple, chatting away to Helen on the phone, recommending hairdressers and so on – but I do beg you to feel as forgiving as you can about Helen and this initial rejecting of her newly conceived child, our beloved Nell.

Helen was young and this was her first child. She had no idea, as established mothers have, of what she would be throwing away, losing along with the bathwater. It is easier for the childless woman to contemplate the termination of a pregnancy, than for those who already have children. So, please, continue to bear with Helen. Forgive her. She will learn better, with the years, I promise you.

GOING TO ANGIE FOR HELP

Helen rose out of her snowy white bed one morning, holding her pale, smooth stomach, which was in inner turmoil, and telephoned Angie.

'Angie,' she said, 'please come round. I have to talk to someone.'

Angie came round. Angie walked up the stairs and into the bedroom where she had spent four memorable if actually rather unsatisfactory nights with Clifford, in all their eleven months together: well, not exactly together, but in the promise of – eventually – together, or so she had assumed.

'So, what's the matter?' Angie asked, and noticed, for Helen was feeling too ill to so much as fasten her brown silk nightie properly, that Helen's white, full breasts were fuller than ever, almost too full, and felt for once rather proud of the chic discretion of her own, and quite confident that, if she managed this right, Clifford would eventually be hers.

Helen didn't reply. Helen flung herself back upon the fur bedspread and lay crumpled and dishevelled but still beautiful, and wept instead of speaking.

'It can only be one thing,' said Angie. 'You're pregnant. You don't want to be. And you don't dare tell Clifford.'

Helen did not attempt to deny it. Angie was wearing red hot-pants, and Helen did not even have the spirit to marvel at Angie's nerve, considering her legs, in so doing. Presently words formed out of tears.

'I can't have a baby,' wept Helen. 'Not now. I'm too young. I wouldn't know what to do with one.'

'What any sensible person does with babies,' said Angie, 'is hand them over to nannies.'

And this, of course, in the world in which Angie moved, was just what mothers did. But for all that Helen was only twenty-two and (as we have seen) as selfish and irresponsible as any other pretty, wilful girl of her age, she at least knew better than Angie in this respect. She knew that the handing over of a baby would be no easy matter. A baby draws love out of its mother, like a Christmas streamer out of a box, and the necessities occasioned by that love can change the mother's life altogether: make her as desperate, savage and impulsive as any wild animal.

'Please help me, Angie,' said Helen. 'I can't have the baby. Only I don't know where to go and anyway abortions cost money and I don't have any.'

Nor had she, poor girl. Clifford was not the kind of man to put money in a woman's bank account and not ask for proof of where every penny had gone, not even if that woman was his legitimate fiancée. Clifford might eat at the best restaurants, where it was useful to be seen, and might sleep between the finest, most expensive cotton sheets, because he liked to be comfortable, but he kept very careful accounts. So this had to be done without Clifford's knowing. What a fix Helen was in! Just consider the times. Only twenty years ago, and a pregnant girl, unmarried, was very much on her own: no Pregnancy Advice Centres then; no payments from the State, just trouble whichever way she turned. Helen's best friend, Lily, at seventeen, had an apparently successful abortion but after two days had been rushed to hospital with septicaemia. She'd hovered between life and death for some six hours, and Helen sat on one side of the bed and a policeman sat on the other, and he was waiting to charge Lily for procuring an illegal abortion operation. Lily died, and so was spared the punishment. Probably two years inside, the policeman said, and no more than she deserved. 'Think of the poor baby!' he said. Poor little Lily, was all Helen could think. Now how frightened she found herself: frightened to have the baby, frightened not to.

Angie thought fast. She was wearing fashionable hot-pants but did not (as we know) have the best legs in the world. They were podgy around the knees, and gnarled about the ankles; and as for her face, well, the thick make-up the times required was unkind and the hot South African sun had toughened her skin, and somehow greyed it, and she had a thick, fleshy nose. Only her eyes were large, green and beautiful. Helen, curled up on the bed, tearful and unhappy, soft, pale, female, tugging at her brown silk nightie (suddenly too small) in the attempt to make it cover her properly, and altogether too beautiful, inspired in Angie a great desire for revenge. It is really not fair that some women should have the luck of looks, and others not. You must agree.

'Darling Helen,' said Angie. 'Of course I'll help you! I know an address. An excellent clinic. Simply everyone goes there. Very safe, very quiet, very discreet. The de Waldo Clinic. I'll lend you the money. It just has to be done. Clifford wouldn't want you pregnant at his wedding. Everyone would think he'd married you because he had to! And it's going to be a white wedding too, isn't it, and simply everyone looks at waists.'

Simply everyone, simply everyone! Enough to frighten anyone.

Angie booked Helen into the de Waldo Clinic that very afternoon. Helen had the misfortune – rather expected by Angie – of being put into the care of a certain Dr Runcorn, a small, plump, fiftyish doctor with pebble glasses through which he stared at Helen's most private parts, while his stubby fingers moved lingeringly (or so it seemed to Helen) over her defenceless breasts and body. What could the poor girl do about it? Nothing. For in handing herself over to the de Waldo Clinic it seemed that Helen had surrendered dignity, privacy and honour: she felt she had no right to brush Dr Runcorn's hand away. She deserved no better than its tacky assault. Was she not doing away with Clifford's baby without his knowing? Was she not outside the law? Whichever way she looked, there was guilt, and Dr Runcorn's water-glinting eyes.

'We don't want to leave the little intruder in there any longer than we have to,' said Dr Runcorn, in his wheezy, nasal voice. 'At ten tomorrow we'll set about getting you back to normal! A shame for a girl as pretty as you to waste a single day of her youth.'

The little intruder! Well, he wasn't so far out. That's

what Nell felt like, to Helen. But the phrase still made her squirm. She said nothing. She knew well enough that she depended on Dr Runcorn's goodwill as well as on his greed. No matter how much he charged, his clinic was always full. If he 'did you' tomorrow, rather than in four weeks' time, you were, quite simply, in luck. For the first time in her life Helen truly understood necessity, truly suffered, and held her tongue.

'Next time you go to a party,' said Dr Runcorn, 'remember me and don't get up to mischief. You've been a very naughty girl. You'll stay in the clinic tonight, so we can keep an eye on you.'

And a very terrible night it was. Helen was never to forget it. The thick yellowy carpets, the pale green wash-basin, the TV and radio headphones did nothing to disguise the nature of the place she was in. As well train roses up the abattoir wall! And she had to call Clifford, and tell another lie.

It was six o'clock: Clifford was at Leonardo's, negotiating the purchase of an anonymous painting of the Florentine School with a delegation from the Uffizi Gallery. Clifford had a shrewd notion the painting was a Botticelli: he was banking on it, paying over the odds to obtain it, but not too much in case they looked too hard at what they were selling. Just sometimes the Italians, accustomed as they were to a sheer superfluity of cultural richness, did miss something wonderful and extraordinary beneath their very noses. Clifford's blue eyes were bluer than ever: he tossed back the wedge of his thick fair hair so it glinted – he had grown his hair long, as was the fashion then amongst the sophisticated young, and was not thirty-five still young? He wore jeans and a casual shirt. The Italians, portly and in their fifties, displayed their cultural and worldly achievement with formal suits, gold rings and ruby cuff-links. But they were at a disadvantage. They were confused. Clifford meant to confuse them. What was this young man, who belonged so much to the present, doing within these solid elderly marble portals? It unbalanced the Italians' judgement. Why was Clifford Wexford of all people foraging back into the past? What did he mean by it? Did he know more than they, or less? Was he offering too much: were they asking too little? Where were they? Perhaps life was not serious and difficult after all? Perhaps the plums went to the frivolous? The telephone rang. Clifford answered it. The men from the Uffizi clustered together and conferred, recognizing a reprieve when they heard one.

'Darling,' said Helen brightly, 'I know you hate being disturbed in the office, but I won't be at Coffee Place when you get back tonight. My mum rang to say I was allowed home. So I'm going to stay at Applecore Cottage for a couple of nights. She says she might even come to the wedding!'

'Take garlic and a crucifix,' said Clifford. 'And ward your father off!'

Helen laughed lightly and said, 'Don't be such a goose!' and rang off. The men from the Uffizi raised their price a full thousand pounds. Clifford sighed.

The phone rang again. This time it was Angie. Since such considerable millions of her father's money were invested in Leonardo's the switchboard put through her call. This privilege was accorded only to Helen, Angie and Clifford's stockbroker; the last played a chancy game of instant decisions and played it very well, but sometimes needed a quick yes or no.

'Clifford,' said Angie, 'it's me, and I want to have breakfast with you tomorrow.'

'Breakfast, Angie! These days,' he said, trying to keep the Uffizi mesmerized with his smile, and hoping Angie would get off the line quickly, 'I have breakfast with Helen. You know that.'

'Tomorrow morning you won't,' said Angie, 'because she won't be there.'

'How do you know that?' He sensed danger. 'She's gone to visit her mother. Hasn't she?'

'No she hasn't,' said Angie flatly, and would elaborate no further and Clifford agreed to meet the next morning at 8 a.m. for breakfast at Coffee Place. The early hour did not, as he had hoped, discourage her. He'd suggested Claridges but she said he might need to scream and shout a bit so he'd be better off at home. Then she rang off. The men from the Uffizi pushed up the price a further five hundred and would not be deflected and by now Clifford had lost his nerve. He reckoned the two phone calls had cost him fifteen hundred pounds. When the Italians had gone, smiling, Clifford, unsmiling, made a quick phone call to Johnnie, his father's stable-man and chauffeur – a man who'd been with Otto in the war, and still had 00 rating – and asked him to visit the Lally household and investigate. Johnnie reported back at midnight. Helen was not in the house. There was only a middle-aged woman, crying into the washing up, and a man in the garage painting what looked like a gigantic wasp stinging a naked girl.

RESCUE!

Clifford spent as bad a night as did Helen; one that he was never to forget. Into the great bubbling cauldron of distress we call jealousy goes dollop after dollop of every humiliation we have ever endured, every insecurity suffered, every loss we have known and feared; in goes our sense of doubt, futility; in goes the prescience of decay, death, finality. And floating to the top, like scum on jam, the knowledge that all is lost, in particular the hope that some day, somehow, we can properly love and trust and be properly loved and trusted in our turn. Plop! into Clifford's cauldron went the fear that he had only ever been admired and envied, and never truly liked, not even by his parents. Plop! the knowledge that he would never be the man his father was; that his mother saw him as some kind of curiosity. Plop! the memory of a call-girl who'd laughed at him, despising him more than he despised her, and plop! and plop! again, other occasions he had been impotent, and embarrassed; not to mention school, where he'd been fidgety, weedy, skinny, short when others had been tall – he didn't start growing until he was sixteen – and the hundred daily humiliations of childhood. Poor Clifford; both too tough and too sensitive for his own good! How these ingredients stirred and boiled and moiled into a great solid tarry wedge of distress, sealed by the shuddering conviction that Helen was in someone else's arms as he lay unsleeping in their bed: that Helen's lips were pressed beneath the searching mouth of someone younger, fiercer, kinder, yet more virile – no, Clifford was never to forget that night; nor, I'm afraid, was he ever properly to trust Helen again, so potent was the trouble brewed by Angie.

At eight o'clock the doorbell went. Unshaven, distracted, drugged by his own imaginings, affected by a woman as he had never thought possible, Clifford opened the door to Angie. 'What do you know?' he asked. 'Where is she? Where is Helen?'

Still Angie wouldn't tell him. She walked up the

stairs and took her clothes off, and lay down upon the bed, rather quickly covering herself with the sheet, and waited.

'For old times' sake,' she said. 'And for my father's millions. He'll need some consoling about the Botticelli, if it is one. I keep telling you, money is in Modern Art, not in Old Masters.'

'It's in both,' he said.

Now what Angie said was persuasive. And she was, to Clifford, familiar territory, and he was distracted beyond belief and anyway Angie was *there*. (I think we have to forgive him, yet again.) Clifford joined her on the bed, tried to pretend it was Helen there beneath him, and almost succeeded, and then on top of him and totally failed. He knew the moment it was over that he regretted it. Men do seem to regret these things even more easily than do women.

'Where is Helen?' he asked, as soon as he was able.

'She's in the de Waldo Clinic,' said Angie, 'having an abortion. The operation is booked for ten this morning.'

It was by that time 8.45. Clifford dressed, in haste.

'But why didn't she tell me?' he asked. 'The little fool!'

'Clifford,' said Angie, languorously from the bed, 'I can only suppose because it isn't your baby.'

That slowed him down. Angie knew well enough that if you have just deceived your one true love, as Clifford had just done, you are all the more ready to believe you are yourself deceived.

'You're so trusting, Clifford,' added Angie, to Clifford's back, and it was a pity for her that she did, for Clifford caught a glimpse of Angie in the big wall-mirror, gold mounted and mercury based, three hundred years old, in which a thousand women must have stared, and it somehow cast back a strange reflection of Angie. As if indeed she was the wickedest woman who had ever looked into it. Angie's eyes glinted with what Clifford suddenly perceived was malice, and he realized, too late to save his honour, but at least in time to save Nell, what Angie was up to. He finished tying his tie.

Clifford said not another word to Angie: he left her lying on the fur rug on the bed, where she had no right to be – it was after all Helen's place – and was at the de Waldo Clinic by 9.15 and it was fortunate there was at least some time to spare, for the reception staff were obstructive and the operation had been brought forward by half an hour. Dr Runcorn, I have a terrible feeling, could not wait to get his hands on Helen's baby and destroy it from within. Abortion is sometimes necessary, sometimes not, always sad. It is to the woman as war is to the man – a living sacrifice in a cause justified or not justified, as the observer may decide. It is the making of hard decisions – that this one must die that that one can live in honour and decency and comfort. Women have no leaders, of course: a woman's conscience must be her General; there are no stirring songs to make the task of killing easier, no victory marches and medals handed around afterwards, merely a sense of loss. And just as in war there are ghouls, vampires, profiteers and grave robbers as well as brave and noble men, so there are wicked men, as well as good, in abortion clinics and Dr Runcorn was an evil man.

Clifford pushed aside a Jamaican nurse and two Scottish ward orderlies, all three fed up with wages in the public sector and so gone into private health care, or so they told their friends, and since no one would tell him where Helen was, stalked along the shiny, pale corridors of the Clinic, throwing open doors as he went, doing without help. Startled, unhappy women, sitting up neatly in bed in frilly or fluffy bedjackets, looked up at him in sudden hope, as if perhaps here at last was their saviour, their knight in shining armour, he who was to come if all was to be explained, made happy and well. But of course it was not so: he was Helen's, not theirs.

Clifford found Helen on a trolley in the theatre annexe, white-gowned, head turbanned; a nurse bent over her; Helen was unconscious, ready to go into the theatre. Clifford tussled with the nurse for possession of the trolley.

'This woman is to go back to the ward at once,' he said, 'or by God I'll have the police in!' And he pinched her fingers nastily in the trolley's steering mechanism. The nurse yelled. Helen did not stir. Dr Runcorn emerged to see what the matter was.

'Caught red-handed!' said Clifford, bitterly, and indeed Dr Runcorn was. He had just disposed of twins, rather late on in a pregnancy, and a very messy matter it had been. But Dr Runcorn prided himself on his record for twins – not out of his clinic those frequent cases where one twin has been aborted, the other gone on, unobserved by everyone but a bewildered mother, to full term. No, if there was a twin, Dr Runcorn would weed it out.

'This young lady is about to have an exploratory examination of her abdomen,' he said, 'of her own free will. And since you are not married to her, you have no legal rights in the matter.'

At this Clifford simply hit him, and quite right too. Just occasionally violence can be seen to be justified. In his life Clifford was to hit three men. The first was Helen's father, who tried to prize him apart from Helen, the second was Dr Runcorn, who was trying to deprive him of Helen's baby, and the third we have not come to yet, but that was to do with Helen too. This is the effect some women have on some men.

Dr Runcorn fell to the ground and got up with his nose bloodied. I am sorry to say none of his staff assisted him. He was not liked.

'Very well,' he said wearily, 'I will call a private ambulance. On your own head be it.'

And as the ambulance doors closed he remarked to Clifford, 'You're wasting your time on this one. These girls are nothing but sluts. I don't do what I do for money. I do it to spare the babies a hellish future, and to save the human race from genetic pollution.'

Dr Runcorn's puffy face was puffier still from Clifford's blow, and his fingers were like red garden slugs; he seemed, all of a sudden, to want Clifford's approval, as the defeated so often do of the victor, but such was not of course forthcoming. Clifford merely despised Dr Runcorn the more thoroughly for his hypocrisy, and a little of that despising rubbed off, alas, on Helen, as if – quite leaving aside the purpose of her visit to the de Waldo Clinic – the mere stepping inside so awful and vulgar a place had been enough to taint her, and permanently.

The ambulance men carried the still unconscious Helen up the stairs of the Goodge Street house, and laid her on the bed, suggested Clifford called a doctor, and departed. (The de Waldo Clinic was later to send a bill, which Clifford declined to pay.) Clifford sat beside Helen, and watched, and waited and thought. He didn't call a doctor. He reckoned she'd be all right. She breathed easily. Anaesthesia had passed into sleep. Her forehead was damp, and her pretty hair curled and clung in dark tendrils which framed her face. Fine veins in her white temples showed blue: thick eyelashes fringed pale translucent cheeks: her eyebrows made a delicate yet confident arch. Most faces need animation to make them beautiful: Helen's was flawless even in tranquillity; as near the perfection of a painting as Clifford was ever likely to find. His anger, his outrage, failed. This rare creature was the mother of his child. Clifford knew that Angie's insinuations were absurd, by virtue of the sheer intensity of the feelings that welled up in him when he considered how narrow his baby's escape had been. This had been the first act of rescue. He did not doubt but that there would be others. He could see all too clearly that Helen was capable of deceit and folly, and lack of judgement, and worst of all, lack of taste. His child, brushed so near, so early, to the appalling Dr Runcorn! And as Helen grew older these qualities would become more apparent. The baby must be protected. 'I'll look after you,' he said aloud. 'Don't worry.' Absurdly sentimental! But I think he meant Nell, not Helen.

Clifford should have been at Leonardo's that afternoon. The Hieronymus Bosch Exhibition was to be extended a further three months. There was a great deal to be done, if the maximum publicity for the Gallery, the maximum advantage for himself, was to be gained. But still Clifford did not leave Helen's side. He let his fingers stray over her forehead. He had wanted her from the moment he saw her: so that no one else could have her and because she was John Lally's daughter, and because that in the end would open more doors to him than Angie's millions ever would – but he had not known until the torments of the previous night just how much he loved her, and in the loving exposed himself to danger. For what woman was ever faithful? His mother Cynthia had betrayed his father Otto half a dozen times a year, and always had. Why should Helen, why should any woman, be different? But now there was the child – and in that child Clifford focused all emotional aspiration, all trust in human goodness, quite bypassing poor Helen, who had been trying to save Clifford as well as herself.

Helen stirred, and woke, and seeing Clifford, smiled. He smiled back.

'It's all right,' he said. 'You still have the baby. But why didn't you tell me?'

'I was frightened,' she said simply. And then she added, abandoning herself to his care, 'You'll just have to look after everything. I don't think I'm fit.'

Clifford, conscious of simply everyone and thickening waists, rang his parents and said no church wedding, after all. He'd rather make it the Caxton Hall.

'But that's only a trumped up registry office,' complained Cynthia.

'Everyone who's anyone gets married there,' he said. 'And this is a modern marriage. God need not be present.'

'Or only his substitute here on earth,' said Cynthia.

Clifford laughed and did not deny it. And at least he'd said 'everyone' and not 'simply everyone'.

LEAPING INTO THE FUTURE

The wedding between Clifford Wexford and Helen Lally took place on Midsummer's Day, 1965. Helen wore a cream slipper satin dress, trimmed with Belgian lace, and everyone said she should have been a model, she was so exquisite. (In fact Helen was altogether too robust in her early twenties to be anything of the sort. It was only later, when trouble, love and general upset had fined her down that she was able thus to earn a living.)

Clifford and Helen made a spectacular pair; his leonine hair shone, and her brown hair curled, and everyone who was anyone was at the wedding: everyone, that is to say, except the bride's father, John Lally. The bride's mother, Evelyn, sat at the back wearing the same old blue ribbed dress she had worn at the party where Clifford and Helen first met and fell in love. She had defied her husband to attend the ceremony. It would mean a week of not-speaking, possibly more. She did not care.

Simon Harvey, the New York writer, was Clifford's best man. Clifford had known him from way back: had met him in a pub, lent him his first typewriter. Now he had to lend him the fare over, but a friend's a friend, and though Clifford's acquaintances were many, his friends were few. Simon wrote funny novels, on homosexual themes, too early for their popularity. (The word 'gay' was only just finding its feet: to be homosexual a deathly earnest, whispered matter.) Presently he would be a millionaire, of course.

'What do you think of her?' Clifford asked.

'If you have to marry a woman,' Simon said, 'she's the best you could do.' Nor did he lose the ring, and he made an affectionate speech; it was worth the air fare, which Clifford knew he would never get back.

Helen's Uncle Phil, Evelyn's brother, gave her away. He was a car salesman; middle-aged, red-faced and noisy, but all the younger men she knew had at one time or other been her lovers, or nearly been, and that seemed even less suitable – even though they would not have said and Clifford would not have known. She wanted her marriage to start without lies. Clifford didn't seem to mind Uncle Phillip, strangely, just said it was useful to have someone in the car trade in the family,

The Hearts and Lives of Men

and set up a deal at once – a Mercedes for his MG, now he was about to be a married man. And when it came to it Helen was glad her Uncle Phillip was there – the guests being so weighted on the Wexford family and friend side, light on the Lally's. Helen had friends enough, but like many very pretty girls, felt she got on better with men than women, and suffered a little, feeling women didn't like her.

No one (who was anyone) except Clifford knew that Helen was more than three months pregnant on her wedding day – oh, and Angie of course, but she had not been sent an invitation and had returned to Johannesburg to lick her wounds. (Though Angie meant to have Clifford in the end and no amount of 'I will's' and 'I do's' to someone else would daunt her permanently.) It was a wonderful day in any number of ways. Sir Larry Patt came up to Clifford at the reception and said, 'Clifford, I give up. You are the new world. I am the old. I am resigning. You are to be managing director of Leonardo's. The Board decided yesterday. You are much too young, and I told them so, but they didn't agree. So now it's over to you, lad.'

Clifford's happiness was complete. Never would there be such a day as this again! Helen slipped her little white hand in his and squeezed it, and he did not squeeze hers in return, but said, 'How's the baby?' and she said 'Hush!' and had no idea at all that he no longer totally accepted her, but judged her, and thought the squeeze childish and vulgar.

Lady Rowena looked boyish in a grey tunic dress, white frilly blouse and cravat, and fluttered her false eyelashes (everyone was wearing them) at one of Cynthia Wexford's cousins from Minneapolis, and made a rapid assignation with him beneath his wife's nose. Cynthia noticed and sighed. She should never have invited the cousins over: she should have stuck to her principles and kept no contact at all with the family which had so insulted and abused her in her youth. Bad enough that these things ran in the blood. Her father had loved her dearly one day, spurned her totally the next. She had been instrumental in getting the family out of Denmark; had risked torture, life itself, to do it; he had thanked her coldly, but not smiled at her. He would not forgive. She tried not to think of him. Clifford looked like her father: had stared at her with childish eyes as blue as his grandfather's. That was the trouble. She hoped he would be happy, that Helen would do for him what she could not, that is to say, love him. But perhaps he hadn't noticed. She'd always behaved as if she loved him, or thought she had.

Otto and Cynthia went home in their Rolls-Royce. Johnnie drove. He kept a loaded revolver in the glove box, for old times' sake. Cynthia thought Otto was a little subdued.

'What's the matter?' she asked. 'I'm sure if anyone can make Clifford happy, Helen can. Mind you, as a baby he was never exactly content. She'll have her work cut out.'

'All that worries me,' said Otto gloomily, 'is what he'll do for an encore. Head of Leonardo's at his age! It'll go to his head.'

'Too late,' said Cynthia. 'He already thinks he's God.'

Clifford and Helen spent the night in the Ritz, where the double beds are the best and softest and prettiest in London.

'What did your parents give us for a wedding present?' asked Clifford, and Helen wished he hadn't asked. He seemed in an odd mood, both elated and yet somehow restless.

'A toaster,' she said.

'You'd think your father would have given us one of his paintings,' said Clifford. Since Clifford already had a dozen small Lallys on his walls, bought for a song, and eight major paintings in Leonardo's vaults, where no one could see them, Helen didn't think so at all. But she was twenty-two and a nobody, and Clifford was thirty-five, and very much somebody, so she didn't say so. After the episode of the de Waldo clinic, she had become less able to laugh at him, tease him out of his moods, enchant him. She took him, in fact, too seriously for his own good, let alone hers. She had been in the wrong: she was her mother's daughter as well as her father's and it showed.

She had other things to worry about, besides. She lay in bed and worried about them. Clifford had bought a house in Primrose Hill, in the then unfashionable North West London, near the Zoo, to be their marital home. He'd sold Coffee Place for £2,500 and bought the Chalcot Square house for £6,000, judging that presently it would be worth a great deal more. (He was quite right. That very house changed hands recently for half a million pounds.) Clifford hadn't put the property into joint ownership. He didn't see why he should. This, after all, was the sixties, and a man's property was a man's property, and a man's wife serviced it, and was supposed to feel grateful for the privilege. Could she run it properly? She was so young. She knew she was untidy. She had given up her work at Sotheby's, and started going to Cordon Bleu cookery lessons, but even so! Clifford had said, and she could see that he was right, that she would need all her time and energy to run the house, and entertain his friends and colleagues, who, as he himself pointed out, were getting grander and greater all the time. Would there be enough time, enough energy, with a baby on the way? And when would she tell people about the baby? It was embarrassing. Nevertheless, she was full of hope, as befitted a girl on her wedding night. She hoped, for example, Clifford's friends, colleagues and clients would not think her to be an inefficient, stupid child. She hoped that Clifford would not, either. She hoped she would be able to cope with a baby: she hoped she would not yearn for her freedom and her friends, or miss her mother and father too much; she hoped in fact she had done the right thing. Yet what choice had she ever had? You met someone, and that was that.

Clifford kissed her, and his mouth was hot and heavy, and he embraced her, and his arms were lean and strong. It had been a long day; a wedding day; a hundred hands had been shaken; a hundred good wishes received; if she was anxious it was because she was tired. But how strange, that along with the physical reassurances of love, keeping pace, marking step, like some little brother determined to be taken seriously, anxiety came too, and a fear for the future, the sense that life flowed like waves towards the shore, for ever dispersed before they quite arrive; and worse, that the higher the crest, the lower the trough must be, so that even happiness is something to be feared.

In the middle of the night, the pretty gold enamelled telephone on the bedside table rang. Helen answered it. Clifford always slept heavily, never for long, but soundly, his blond head heavy against the pillow, his hand tucked against his cheek, like a child. Helen thought, even as she picked up the receiver, quickly, so he was not disturbed, how wonderful to know so private a thing about so remarkable a man. The call came from Angie in Johannesburg. She was asking how the wedding had been, apologizing for her absence.

'But you weren't even *invited*,' Helen longed to say, but didn't. Could Angie speak to Clifford, Angie asked, and congratulate him on being made managing director of Leonardo's? After all, it was her father who had arranged it.

'It's two in the morning, Angie,' said Helen, as reproachfully as she dared. 'Clifford's asleep.'

'And he sleeps so heavily!' said Angie. 'I know only too well. Try pinching his bum. That usually works. Does he have his hand tucked under his cheek, like a child? Ah, the thought of it. Lucky old you!'

'How do you know?' asked Helen.

'The way so many of us know, darling.'

'When?' asked Helen, bleakly. 'Where?'

'Who, me? Long long in the past, darling, for Clifford. At least a couple of months. Not since your abortive night in the Clinic. That was at Coffee Place. Though before that, of course, many times, many places. But you know all that. Do just wake him. Don't be a jealous little goose. If I'm not jealous, and I'm not, why should you be?'

Helen put the phone down and wept, but quietly and silently, so that Clifford didn't hear, and wake. Then, as a practical gesture, she took the phone off the hook, so Angie couldn't ring back. Outrage and distress would get her nowhere; she knew that. She must calm herself as quickly as she could, and somehow start constructing a new vision of herself, and Clifford, and her marriage.

Fay Weldon

FIRST DAYS

It was remarkable, once the wedding was over, how Helen's waist thickened: two days later and the wedding dress would not fasten; a week, and she could not pull it over her bosom without the seams threatening to give.

'Extraordinary,' said Clifford, who kept asking her to try on the dress, as if to take the measure of her pregnancy by eye. 'I suppose now you feel you can relax. Well, you can't. There's a lot to be done.'

And so indeed there was. The house in Primrose Hill had to be turned from a rooming-house to a dwelling fit for a Wexford, his new burgeoning wife, and to receive the friends he meant to have, and since Clifford was always busy, Helen would have to do it. And so she did. He was solicitous of her pregnancy, but would not allow her to be ill. If she bent retching over the basin in the morning, he would clap his hands briskly and say 'enough!' and by some magic it would be. He required no consultation about paper, paint or furniture, other than the walls should be fit to hang paintings upon, and the furniture be antique, not new, since new had no resale value. He seemed to approve of what she did, or at least he did not say he did not. At weekends he played tennis, and she watched, and admired and clapped. He liked her applause. But then he liked anyone's applause. She understood that.

'You are not very *sportif*,' he complained. She supposed that Angie, perhaps, had been, and others.

On the surface, things went well. Days were sunny and active, the baby kicked; the nights awkward and less wild, but reassuring. Presently acquaintances of Clifford's put in a cautious appearance at the house and, finding his new young wife not as silly as they had feared, stayed around and became friends; her friends came, looked, drifted away, finding her in some way lost to them. How could they, young, poor, mildly bohemian, without ambition, be at ease with Clifford Wexford who required more than mere humanity as a recommendation? How, when it came to it, could she? She saw she must be more Wexford wife, less daughter of Applecore Cottage. She learned to do without the chatter and closeness of her friends, the agreeable warmth of their concern; when they drifted off she did not tug them back. They were nice people: they would have come, Clifford or not. Reader, the truth was, she was weighty, and heavy, and began to lumber – you know how women will in late pregnancy – and the baby pressed upon the sciatic nerve, but she gritted her teeth, and set her smile to fair against weariness and complaint, for Clifford's sake. She would be everything to Clifford. He would never look at another woman again. And at the same time she knew it was no use. She had lost him: though how or why she was not sure.

A TIME OF HAPPINESS

Baby Nell was born on Christmas Day, 1965, in the Middlesex Hospital. Now Christmas is not a good time to have a baby. The nursing staff drink too much sherry and spend their time singing carols; the young doctors kiss them under the mistletoe; senior surgeons dress up as Father Christmas. Helen gave birth to Nell unattended, in a private ward, where she lay alone. Had she been in the ordinary public ward at least one of the other patients would have been there to help; as it was, her red light glowed in Sister's Room hour after hour and no one noticed. It was not yet the fashion for fathers to be present at the birth of their baby, and Clifford, in any case, would have shuddered at the very possibility. As it was, he and Helen had been asked to a Christmas Eve dinner by the eminent painter David Firkin, who was thinking of moving from the Beaux Arts Gallery to Leonardo's, and Clifford did not wish to forgo the invitation. It seemed important. Helen had her first tentative pain in the taxi on the way to the Firkin studio. She did not, of course, want to be a nuisance.

'I don't suppose it's anything,' she said. 'Probably only indigestion. Tell you what, you drop me off at the hospital and they'll have a look at me and send me home and I'll come on to David's in a taxi.'

Clifford took Helen at her word and dropped her off at the hospital, and went on to the dinner alone. Helen did not follow.

'Even if she was in labour,' said David Firkin, 'which I doubt, first babies take for ever so there's no need to worry. It's an entirely natural process. Now don't be a bore and keep calling the hospital.' David Firkin hated children, and was proud of it. Helen was a fine, healthy girl, all the guests said; no need to worry; and no one started counting back on their fingers as to how many months it was since the marriage – or at least, no one that Clifford noticed.

As it was, Helen was indeed a fine, healthy girl, if frightened, and Nell was a fine, healthy baby, and arrived safely, if on her own, at 3.10 a.m. Nell's sun had left Sagittarius and was just into Capricorn, making her both lively and effective; she had the moon in Aquarius rising, which made her kind, charming, generous and good; Venus stood strong in mid-heaven, in its own house, Libra, and that made her full of desires, and

The Hearts and Lives of Men

capable of giving and receiving love. But Mercury was too close to Mars, and Neptune was in opposition to both, and her sun opposed her moon, and so Nell was to be prone to strange events through her life, and to great misfortunes, alternating with great good fortune. Saturn in conjunction with the sun, and powerful, and also opposed in the twelfth house, suggested that prisons and institutions would loom large in her life: there would be times when she would look out at the world from behind bars. Or that's one way of looking at it all. It will do. How better are we to account for the event that fate, and not our natures, cause?

A nurse, shame-faced, came hurrying in on hearing Nell's first cry, and when the baby, washed and wrapped, was finally placed in Helen's arms, Helen fell in love: not as she had fallen in love with Clifford, all erotic excitement and apprehension mixed, but powerfully, steadily, and permanently. When Clifford was wrested from the after-dinner brandy and crackers (Harrods Xmas Best) and came to her bedside at four in the morning, she showed him the baby, almost fearfully, leaning over the crib, pulling back the blanket from the small face. She still never knew quite what Clifford was going to like, or dislike, approve or condemn. She had become shy of him, almost timorous. She did not know what the matter was. She hoped the arrival of Nell would make things better. She did not, you will notice, think of her own pain, or resent Clifford's abandonment of her at such a time; just of how best to please him. In those first few pregnant months of her marriage, she was, as I say, more like her mother than at any other time of her life.

'A girl!' he said, and for a moment Helen thought he meant to disapprove, but he looked at his daughter and smiled, and said, 'Don't frown, sweetheart: everything's going to be okay,' and Helen could have sworn the baby stopped frowning at once and smiled back, although the nurses said that was impossible: babies did not smile for six weeks. (All nurses say this, and all mothers know otherwise.)

He picked the baby up.

'Careful,' said Helen, but there was no need. Clifford was accustomed to handling objects of great value. And there and then he felt, to his surprise, and acutely, both the pain and pleasure of fatherhood – the piercing anxious needle in the heart which is the drive to protect, the warm reassuring glow which is the conviction of immortality, the recognition of privilege, the knowledge that it is more than just a child you hold in your arms, but the whole future of the world, as it works through you. More, he felt absurdly grateful to Helen for having the baby, making the feeling possible. For the first time since he had rescued her from the de Waldo clinic, he kissed her with ungrudging love. He had forgiven her, in fact, and Helen glowed in his forgiveness.

'All be well,' she shut her eyes and said, quoting something she had read, but not quite sure what – and all will be well, and all manner of things will be well,' and Clifford did not even snub her by asking for the source of the quotation. And so it was, very well indeed, for a time.

Until she was nearly a year old, then, Nell lived in the cocoon of happiness created by her parents. Leonardo's flourished under Clifford Wexford's guidance – an interesting Rembrandt was acquired, a few tedious Dutch masters sold, the putative Botticelli labelled and hung as such, to the Uffizi's astonishment, and in the new contemporary section, the price of a David Firkin, now required to paint no more than two paintings a year, lest he spoil his own market, soared to five figures. Helen lost a whole stone and worshipped Clifford and baby Nell in turns. It is even pleasanter – if more difficult – to love, than to be loved. When both happen at once, what higher joy can there be?

A TIDAL WAVE OF TROUBLE

Reader, a marriage that is rapidly put together can rapidly unravel: like a hand-knitted jumper, which if you snip just one strand and pull, and go on pulling, comes to nothing at all. Just a pile of wrinkled junk. Or put it another way: you think you're living in a palace but actually it's just a house of cards. Disturb one card and the whole lot falls and flattens and is nothing. When Nell was ten months old, the Wexford marriage fell in ruins about the poor child's ears: phut, phut, phut – one nasty event falling fast upon another quicker than you can imagine.

This is how it happened.

The Conrans gave a November 5th firework party. Remember? Terence, who started Habitat? And Shirley, later of *Superwoman* and *Lace*? Everyone who was anyone was there, and that included the Wexfords.

Helen left Nell behind with the Nanny: she didn't want the child frightened by bangs and crashes. She went ahead of Clifford, who was coming straight from Leonardo's. She wore an embroidered leather coat and boots with many tassels, and looked slim, vulnerable, very pretty and tender, and somehow amazed, and slightly stunned, as young women recently married to active men do tend to look: that is to say, very attractive to other men, making them behave like stags in the rutting season, all locked mighty antlers and 'I'll have what's yours, by God and nature that I will!' If she'd worn her old blue duffle it mightn't have happened.

Clifford arrived later than Helen expected. She felt sulky. Leonardo's took up too much of his time and attention. Sausages crackled and hot potatoes went splut! in cinders; rockets rippled and fountains of light poured skyward, and cries of amazement and delight drifted on a light wind over Camden Town gardens, along with the bonfire smoke. There was a lot of rum in the hot toddy. If there had been less none of it might have happened.

Helen looked through a veil of smoke and saw Clifford approaching. She forgave him: she began to smile. But who was that by his side? Angie? Helen's smile faded. Surely not. Angie, last heard of, had been in South Africa. But yes, that's who it was. Fur coated, fur hatted, high leather booted, mini-skirted, showing the bare stretch of stockinged thigh fashionable at the time; Angie, smirking at Helen, even while Angie most affectionately squeezed Clifford's hand. Helen blinked and Angie was gone. Worse still. What was she hiding? What collusion was this? Helen had kept Angie's wedding-night phone call to herself: biting pain and insult back, forgetting it, putting it out of her mind. Or that's what she thought she'd done. If only she had, and not just thought she had, none of it might have happened.

Clifford took Helen's arm, comfortingly uxorious. Helen shook it petulantly free – never what a woman should do to a man of high self regard. But she'd had four hot toddies, waiting for Clifford, and was less sober than she knew. If only she'd let him hold her arm. But no!

'That was Angie, you came with Angie, you've been with Angie.'

'It was, I did, I have,' said Clifford coolly.
'I thought she was in South Africa.'
'She's over here helping me set up the Contemporary Section. If you took any interest at all in Leonardo's, you'd know.'
Unfair! Wasn't Helen going to daily courses in the History of Art, in order to catch up? Wasn't she, at twenty-three, running a house and servants, and entertaining, and looking after a small child as well? Wasn't she neglected by her husband for Leonardo's sake? Helen slapped Clifford's face (if only she hadn't) and Angie stepped out of the bonfire smoke, and smiled again at Helen, a little victorious smile, which Clifford didn't see. (No suggesting Angie could have behaved other than how she did. No sirree!)
'You're completely mad,' said Clifford to Helen, 'insanely jealous,' and left the party forthwith with Angie. (Oh, oh, oh!) Well, he was cross. No man likes to be hit in public, or accused of infidelity, without reason. And there certainly was no recent reason. Angie was biding her time: her relationship with Clifford had of late indeed been bounded by Leonardo's new Contemporary Section: Clifford had all but forgotten it had ever been anything else, or would he have brought Angie to the party? (If only he hadn't! It is to Clifford's credit that he, like Helen and unlike Angie, was capable of moral choice.)
Clifford took Angie back to her house in Belgravia and went straight home to Primrose Hill and listened to music and waited for Helen to come home. He decided to forgive her.
He waited until morning, and still she did not come. Then she rang to say she was at Applecore Cottage: her mother was ill. She put the phone down fast. Clifford

had heard that one before – he sent Johnnie to check. Of course Helen was not at Applecore Cottage. How could she be? Her father still barred her from his door. The very folly of the lie compounded her offence.

And where had Helen been last night? Well, I'll tell you. After Clifford had left the party with Angie on his arm, Helen, many hot toddies later, left it on the arm of a certain Laurence Durrance, script writer, and husband of little Anne-Marie Durrance, neighbour and close friend. (After this particular choice of action, there was no going back. No more if onlys. Flop, flop, flop, flop – down came the house of cards.)

Anne-Marie, four foot ten inches and six stone of *jolie-laide* energy, stayed behind to weep and wail and tell *everyone*, very excitedly, that Helen Wexford and her husband had left the party together. Not content with that, she wrung a confession out of Laurence the very next morning. (I took her to my office. On the sofa. Very uncomfortable. You know all those books and papers. I was terribly drunk. Someone had spiked the hot toddy. She seemed so upset. *She* seemed so upset! *Anne-Marie*. Just one of those things. Sorry, sorry, sorry.) And, having heard all that, and before Helen returned from wherever (staying with a girlfriend, actually, trying to compose herself, so great was her guilt), Anne-Marie went round and told Clifford where Helen had been the night before, with many unnecessary and untrue embellishments.

So when Helen did come home, Clifford was unforgiving in the most permanent kind of way. Indeed, Johnnie was just finishing changing the locks. Helen was on the doorstep in the keen November wind: her husband and baby on the other side of a locked door, in the warm.

'Let me in, let me in,' cried Helen, but he didn't. Even

though Nell set up a sympathetic wail, his heart stayed hardened. An unfaithful wife was no wife of his. She was worse than a stranger to him: she was an enemy.

So Helen had to go to a solicitor, didn't she, and Clifford was already seeing his – he wasted no time. Anne-Marie had barely finished her tale than he was on the phone – and a very powerful and expensive solicitor he was and not only that, Anne-Marie thereupon decided to take the opportunity of divorcing Laurence and citing Helen, and by Christmas not only one but two marriages had been destroyed. And the cocoon of warmth and love in which Nell lived had been unwound, faster than the eye could see let alone the mind comprehend it seemed to Helen, and words of hate, despair and spite filled the air around Nell's infant head, and when she smiled no one returned her smile, and Clifford was divorcing Helen, citing Laurence, and claiming custody of their little daughter.

You may not know about the custom of 'citing'. In the old days, when the institution of marriage was a stronger and more permanent thing than it is now, it was seen to need outside intervention to push asunder any married couple. A marriage didn't just 'irretrievably break up' as a result of internal forces. Someone came along and *did* something, usually sexual. That someone was known as 'the third party'. Sheets would be inspected for evidence, photographs taken through keyholes by private detectives, and the third party cited by the aggrieved spouse and get his (her) name in the papers. It was all perfectly horrid; and even if neither spouse was sincerely aggrieved, but simply wanted to part, the motions of sheets and keyholes would have to be gone through. Mind you, every cloud has a silver lining; a whole race of girls grew up who would inhabit seaside hotels and provide required evidence, and who earned a good and frequently easy living, sitting up all night drinking cups of coffee and embracing only when the light through the keyhole suddenly went dark.

The only other mildly glittery lining to this particular cloud was that Helen made a kind of peace with her father – any enemy of Clifford was a friend of his, albeit his own daughter (*alleged* daughter: he would not give Evelyn the comfort of ceasing to disown Helen as his flesh and blood) – and was allowed back into the little back bedroom of Applecore Cottage to weep her shame and anguish away, there where the familiar robin sat on the apple tree branch, just outside her bedroom window, red-breasted, head on one side, clucking and chirruping at her distress, promising her better times to come.

LIES, ALL LIES!

There are some babies whom nobody fights over. If they are plain, or dull, or miserable or mopey, divorced and erring mothers are allowed to keep them and toil for them through the years. But what a charmer Nell was! Everyone wanted her: both parents, both sets of grandparents. Nell had a bright clear skin and a bright clear smile, and hardly ever cried, and if she did was quickly pacified. She was a hard and dedicated worker – and no one has to work harder than babies – when it came to developing her skills: learning to touch, to grasp, to sit, to crawl, to stand, to utter the first few words. She was brave, brilliant and spirited – a prize worth having, rather than a burden just about worth the bother of bearing. And how they fought over her.

'She isn't fit to be a mother,' said Clifford to Van

Erson, his freckled, ferocious solicitor. 'She tried to abort the child. She never wanted it.'

'He only wants her to get back at me,' wept Helen to Edwin Druse, her gentle hippie adviser. 'Please make him stop all this. I love him so much. Just that one stupid time, that silly party, I'd had too much to drink, I was only getting back at him for Angie. I can't bear to lose Nell too. I can't. Please help me!'

Edwin Druse put out a gentle hand to soothe his distraught client. He thought she was too young to cope. He thought Clifford was a very negative kind of person indeed. She needed looking after. He thought perhaps he, Edwin Druse, would be the best person to do the looking after. He could convert her to vegetarianism, and she would no longer be prey to such despair. In fact he thought he and she could get on very well indeed if only Clifford and little Nell were out of the way. Edwin Druse was not perhaps the best legal representative Helen could have chosen, in the circumstances. However, there it was.

Add to that the fact that Clifford wanted Nell, and was in the habit of getting what he wanted, and you will see that in the struggle for her custody he had everything on his side. Money, power, clever barristers, outraged virtue – and his parents Otto and Cynthia behind him, to back him up with extra dollops of the same.

'Sweetness alone is not enough,' said Cynthia of Helen. 'There must be some sense and discretion too.'

'A man can put up with many things from a wife,' said Otto, 'but not being made a fool of in public.'

And Helen had nothing, except loveliness, and helplessness and mother-love, and Edwin Druse's conscience, to put in the scales. And it was not enough.

Clifford divorced Helen for adultery, and there was no

way she could deny the fact: what is more, Anne-Marie actually stood up there on the stand and testified, as she had done in her own divorce, 'and I came home unexpectedly and found my husband Laurence in the bed with Helen. Yes, it was the marital bed. Yes, the pair of them were naked.' Lies all lies! Helen did not even try to counter-claim that Clifford had committed adultery with Angie Wellbrook – she did not want to bring him into public calumny, and Edwin Druse did not attempt to persuade her so to do. Helen was all too ready to believe she had lost Clifford through her own fault. Even while she hated him, she loved him; and the same could be said of him, for her. But his pride was hurt: he would not forgive, and she would not hurt him further. And so he came out of the divorce the innocent, and she the guilty party, and it was in all the papers for the space of a whole week. I am sorry to say that Clifford Wexford was never averse to the publicity. He thought it would be good for business and so it was.

Angie's father rang from Johannesburg and boomed down the line, 'Glad to see you're rid of that no-good wife of yours. It'll cheer Angie up no end!' Which of course it did. That, and the amazing success of David Firkin's paintings, which now hung on the trendiest walls in the land.

'See,' said Angie. 'All that Old Master junk is out, out, out.'

At the custody proceedings, a month later, Helen was to wish she had fought harder. Clifford brought up various matters to prove her unsuitability as a mother; not just her initial attempt to abort Nell, which she had expected, but her father's insanity – a man who cut up his own paintings with the garden shears could hardly be called sane – which she might have inherited, and

Helen's own tendency to gross sexual immorality. Moreover, Helen was practically an alcoholic – had she not attempted to justify her sinning with the co-respondent, Durrance, on the grounds that she'd had too much to drink? No, Nell's mother was vain, feckless, hopeless, criminal. Moreover, Helen had no money: Clifford had. How did she mean to support a child? Had she not given up even her meagre part-time job at the drop of a hat? Work? Helen? You're joking!

Whichever way the poor girl turned, Clifford faced her, accusing, and so convincing she almost believed him herself. And what could she say against him? That he wanted Nell only to punish her? That all he would do would be to hand little Nell over to the care of a nanny; that he was too busy to be a proper father to the child; that her, Helen's, heart would break if her baby was taken away from her? Edwin Druse was not persuasive. And so Helen was branded in the eyes of the world, a second time, as a drunken trollop, and that was that. Clifford won the custody proceedings.

'Custody, Care and Control,' said the Judge. Clifford looked across the courtroom at Helen, and for the first time since the proceedings had begun actually met her eyes.

'Clifford!' she whispered, as a wife might whisper her husband's name on his deathbed, and he heard, in spite of the babel all around, and responded in his heart. Rage and spite subsided, and he wished that somehow he could put the clock back, and he, she and Nell could be together again. He waited for Helen outside the court. He wanted just to talk to her, to touch her. She had been punished enough. But Angie came out before Helen, dressed in the miniest of mini leather skirts, and no one looked at her legs, just at the gold and diamond brooch she wore, worth at least a quarter of a million pounds sterling, and tucked her arm into his, and said, 'Well, that's an excellent outcome! You have the baby and you don't have Helen. Laurence wasn't the only one, you know,' and Clifford's moment of weakness passed.

What happened to Laurence, you ask? Anne-Marie his wife forgave him – though she never forgave Helen – and they remarried a couple of years later. Some people are just unbearably frivolous. But by her one act of indiscretion Helen had lost husband, home and lover – which happens more often than I care to think – not to mention a child, and a friend, and a reputation too. And when Baby Nell took her first steps her mother was not there to see.

Edith Wharton
Pomegranate Seed

I

Charlotte Ashby paused on her doorstep. Dark had ascended on the brilliancy of the March afternoon, and the grinding rasping street life of the city was at its highest. She turned her back on it, standing for a moment in the old-fashioned, marble-flagged vestibule before she inserted her key in the lock. The sash curtains drawn across the panes of the inner door softened the light within to a warm blur through which no details showed. It was the hour when, in the first months of her marriage to Kenneth Ashby, she had most liked to return to that quiet house in a street long since deserted by business and fashion. The contrast between the soulless roar of New York, its devouring blaze of lights, the oppression of its congested traffic, congested houses, lives, minds and this veiled sanctuary she called home, always stirred her profoundly. In the very heart of the hurricane she had found her tiny islet – or thought she had. And now, in the last months, everything was changed, and she always wavered on the doorstep and had to force herself to enter.

While she stood there she called up the scene within: the hall hung with old prints, the ladderlike stairs, and on the left her husband's long shabby library, full of books and pipes and worn armchairs inviting to meditation. How she had loved that room! Then, upstairs, her own drawing-room, in which, since the death of Kenneth's first wife, neither furniture nor hangings had been changed, because there had never been money enough, but which Charlotte had made her own by moving furniture about and adding more books, another lamp, a table for the new reviews. Even on the occasion of her only visit to the first Mrs Ashby – a distant, self-centred woman, whom she had known very slightly – she had looked about her with an innocent envy, feeling it to be exactly the drawing-room she would have liked for herself; and now for more than a year it had been hers to deal with as she chose – the room to which she hastened back at dusk on winter days, where she sat reading by the fire, or answering notes at the pleasant roomy desk, or going over her stepchildren's copy books, till she heard her husband's step.

Sometimes friends dropped in; sometimes – oftener – she was alone; and she liked that best, since it was another way of being with Kenneth, thinking over what he had said when they parted in the morning, imagining what he would say when he sprang up the stairs, found her by herself and caught her to him.

Now, instead of this, she thought of one thing only – the letter she might or might not find on the hall table. Until she had made sure whether or not it was there, her mind had no room for anything else. The letter was always the same – a square greyish envelope with 'Kenneth Ashby, Esquire' written on it in bold but faint characters. From the first it had struck Charlotte as peculiar that anyone who wrote such a firm hand should trace the letters so lightly; the address was always written as though there were not enough ink in the pen, or the writer's wrist were too weak to bear upon it. Another curious thing was that, in spite of its masculine curves, the writing was so visibly feminine. Some hands are sexless, some masculine, at first glance; the writing on the grey envelope, for all its strength and assurance, was without doubt a woman's. The envelope never bore anything but the recipient's name; no stamp, no address. The letter was presumably delivered by hand – but by whose? No doubt it was slipped into the letter-box, whence the parlour maid, when she closed the shutters and lit the lights, probably extracted it. At any rate, it was always in the evening, after dark, that Charlotte saw it lying there. She thought of the letter in the singular, as 'it', because, though there had been several since her marriage – seven, to be exact – they were so alike in appearance that they had become merged in one another in her mind, become one letter, become 'it'.

The first had come the day after their return from their honeymoon – a journey prolonged to the West Indies, from which they had returned to New York after an absence of more than two months. Re-entering the house with her husband, late on that first evening – they had dined at his mother's – she had seen, alone on the hall table, the grey envelope. Her eye fell on it before Kenneth's, and her first thought was: 'Why, I've seen that writing before,' but where she could not recall. The memory was just definite enough for her to identify the script whenever it looked up at her faintly from the same pale envelope; but on that first day she would have thought no more of the letter if, when her husband's glance lit on it, she had not chanced to be looking at him. It all happened in a flash – his seeing the letter, putting out his hand for it, raising it to his short-sighted eyes to decipher the faint writing, and then abruptly withdrawing the arm he had slipped through Charlotte's, and moving away to the hanging light, his back turned to her. She had waited – waited for a sound, an exclamation; waited for him to open the letter; but he had slipped it into his pocket without a word and followed her into the library. And there they had sat down by the fire and lit their cigarettes, and he had remained silent, his head thrown back broodingly against the armchair, his eyes fixed on the hearth, and presently had passed his hand over his forehead and said: 'Wasn't it unusually hot at my mother's tonight? I've got a splitting head. Mind if I take myself off to bed?'

That was the first time. Since then Charlotte had never been present when he had received the letter. It usually came before he got home from his office, and she had to go upstairs and leave it lying there. But even if she had not seen it, she would have known it had come by the change in his face when he joined her – which, on those evenings, he seldom did before they met for dinner. Evidently, whatever the letter contained, he wanted to be by himself to deal with it; and when he reappeared he looked years older, looked emptied of life and courage, and hardly conscious of her presence. Sometimes he was silent for the rest of the evening; and if he spoke, it was usually to hint some criticism of her household arrangements, suggest some change in the domestic administration, to ask, a little nervously, if she didn't think Joyce's nursery governess was rather young and flighty, or if she herself always saw to it that Peter – whose throat was delicate – was properly wrapped up when he went to school. At such times Charlotte would remember the friendly warnings she had received when she became engaged to Kenneth Ashby: 'Marrying a heartbroken widower! Isn't that rather risky? You know Elsie Ashby absolutely dominated him'; and how she had jokingly replied: 'He may be glad of a little liberty for a change.' And in this respect she had been right. She had needed no one to tell her, during the first months, that her husband was perfectly happy with her. When they came back from their protracted honeymoon the same friends said: 'What have you done to Kenneth? He looks twenty years younger'; and this time she answered with careless joy: 'I suppose I've got him out of his groove.'

But what she noticed after the grey letters began to come was not so much his nervous tentative fault-finding – which always seemed to be uttered against his will – as the look in his eyes when he joined her after receiving one of the letters. The look was not unloving, not even indifferent; it was the look of a man who has been so far away from ordinary events that when he returns to familiar things they seem strange. She minded that more than the fault-finding.

Though she had been sure from the first that the handwriting on the grey envelope was a woman's, it was long before she associated the mysterious letters with any sentimental secret. She was too sure of her husband's love, too confident of filling his life, for such an idea to occur to her. It seemed far more likely that the letters – which certainly did not appear to cause him any sentimental pleasure – were addressed to the busy lawyer than to the private person. Probably they were from some tiresome client – women, he had often told her, were nearly always tiresome as clients – who did not want her letters opened by his secretary and therefore had them carried to his house. Yes; but in that case the unknown female must be unusually troublesome, judging from the effect her letters produced. Then again, though his professional discretion was exemplary, it was odd that he had never uttered an impatient comment, never remarked to Charlotte, in a moment of expansion, that there was a nuisance of a woman who kept badgering him about a case that had gone against her. He had made more than one semi-confidence of the kind – of course without giving names or details; but concerning this mysterious correspondent his lips were sealed.

There was another possibility: what is euphemistically called an 'old entanglement'. Charlotte Ashby was a sophisticated woman. She had few illusions about the intricacies of the human heart; she knew that there were often old entanglements. But when she had married Kenneth Ashby, her friends, instead of hinting at such a possibility, had said: 'You've got your work cut out for you. Marrying a Don Juan is a sinecure to it. Kenneth's never looked at another woman since he first saw Elsie Corder. During all the years of their marriage he was more like an unhappy lover than a comfortably contented husband. He'll never let you move an armchair or change the place of a lamp; and whatever you venture to do, he'll mentally compare with what Elsie would have done in your place.'

Except for an occasional nervous mistrust as to her ability to manage the children – a mistrust gradually dispelled by her good humour and the children's obvious fondness for her – none of these forebodings had come true. The desolate widower, of whom his nearest friends said that only his absorbing professional interests had kept him from suicide after his first wife's death, had fallen in love, two years later, with Charlotte Gorse, and after an impetuous wooing had married her and carried her off on a tropical honeymoon. And ever since he had been as tender and loverlike as during those first radiant weeks. Before asking her to marry him he had spoken to her frankly of his great love for his first wife and his despair after her sudden death; but even then he had assumed no stricken attitude, or implied that life offered no possibility of renewal. He had been perfectly simple and natural, and had confessed to Charlotte that from the beginning he had hoped the future held new gifts for him. And when, after their marriage, they returned to the house where his twelve years with his first wife had been spent, he had told Charlotte at once that he was sorry he couldn't afford to do the place over for her, but that he knew every woman had her own views about furniture and all sorts of household arrangements a man would never notice, and had begged her to make any changes she saw fit without bothering to consult him. As a result, she made as few as possible; but this way of beginning their new life in the old setting was so frank and unembarrassed that it put her immediately at her ease, and she was almost sorry to find that the portrait of Elsie Ashby, which used to hang over the desk in his library, had been transferred in their absence to the children's nursery. Knowing herself to be the indirect cause of this banishment, she spoke of it to her husband; but he answered: 'Oh, I thought they ought to grow up with her looking down on them.' The answer moved Charlotte, and satisfied her; and as time went by she had to confess that she felt more at home in her house, more at ease and in confidence with her husband, since that long coldly beautiful face on the library wall no longer followed her with guarded eyes. It was as if Kenneth's love had penetrated to the secret she hardly acknowledged to her own heart – her passionate need to feel herself the sovereign even of his past.

With all this stored-up happiness to sustain her, it was curious that she had lately found herself yielding to a nervous apprehension. But there the apprehension was; and on this particular afternoon – perhaps because she was more tired than usual, or because of the trouble of finding a new cook or, for some other ridiculously trivial reason, moral or physical – she found herself unable to react against the feeling. Latchkey in hand, she looked back down the silent street to the whirl and illumination of the great thoroughfare beyond, and up at the sky already aflare with the city's nocturnal life. 'Outside there,' she thought, 'skyscrapers, advertisements, telephones, wireless, aeroplanes, movies, motors, and all the rest of the twentieth century; and on the other side of the door something I can't explain, can't relate to them. Something as old as the world, as mysterious as life . . . Nonsense! What am I worrying about? There hasn't been a letter for three months now – not since the day we came back from the country after Christmas . . . Queer that they always seem to come after our holidays! . . . Why should I imagine there's going to be one tonight!'

No reason why, but that was the worst of it – one of the worst! – that there were days when she would stand there cold and shivering with the premonition of something inexplicable, intolerable, to be faced on the other side of the curtained panes; and when she opened the door and went in, there would be nothing; and on other days when she felt the same premonitory chill, it was justified by the sight of the grey envelope. So that ever since the last had come she had taken to feeling cold and premonitory every evening, because she never opened the door without thinking the letter might be there.

Well, she'd had enough of it; that was certain. She couldn't go on like that. If her husband turned white and had a headache on the days when the letter came, he seemed to recover afterward; but she couldn't. With her the strain had become chronic, and the reason was not far to seek. Her husband knew from whom the letter came and what was in it; he was prepared beforehand for whatever he had to deal with, and master of the situation, however bad; whereas she was shut out in the dark with her conjectures.

'I can't stand it! I can't stand it another day!' she exclaimed aloud, as she put her key in the lock. She turned the key and went in; and there, on the table, lay the letter.

II

She was almost glad of the sight. It seemed to justify everything, to put a seal of definiteness on the whole blurred business. A letter for her husband; a letter from a woman – no doubt another vulgar case of 'old entanglement'. What a fool she had been ever to doubt it, to rack her brains for less obvious explanations! She took up the envelope with a steady contemptuous hand, looked closely at the faint letters, held it against the light and just discerned the outline of the folded sheet within. She knew that now she would have no peace till she found out what was written on that sheet.

Her husband had not come in; he seldom got back from his office before half-past six or seven, and it was not yet six. She would have time to take the letter up to the drawing-room, hold it over the tea-kettle which at that hour always simmered by the fire in expectation of her return, solve the mystery and replace the letter where she had found it. No one would be the wiser, and her gnawing uncertainty would be over. The alternative, of course, was to question her husband; but to do that seemed even more difficult. She weighed the letter between thumb and finger, looked at it again under the light, started up the stairs with the envelope – and came down again and laid it on the table.

'No, I evidently can't,' she said, disappointed.

What should she do, then? She couldn't go up alone to that warm welcoming room, pour out her tea, look over her correspondence, glance at a book or review – not with that letter lying below and the knowledge that in a little while her husband would come in, open it and turn into the library alone, as he always did on the days when the grey envelope came.

Suddenly she decided. She would wait in the library and see for herself; see what happened between him and the letter when they thought themselves unobserved. She wondered the idea had never occurred to her before. By leaving the door ajar, and sitting in the corner behind it, she could watch him unseen . . . Well, then, she would watch him! She drew a chair into the corner, sat down, her eyes on the crack, and waited.

As far as she could remember, it was the first time she had ever tried to surprise another person's secret, but she was conscious of no compunction. She simply felt as if she were fighting her way through a stifling fog that she must at all costs get out of.

At length she heard Kenneth's latchkey and jumped up. The impulse to rush out and meet him had nearly made her forget why she was there; but she remembered in time and sat down again. From her post she covered the whole range of his movements – saw him enter the hall, draw the key from the door and take off his hat and overcoat. Then he turned to throw his gloves on the hall table, and at that moment he saw the envelope. The light was full on his face, and what Charlotte first noted there was a look of surprise. Evidently he had not expected the letter – had not thought of the possibility of its being there that day. But though he had not expected it, now that he saw it he knew well enough what it contained. He did not open it immediately, but stood motionless, the colour slowly ebbing from his face. Apparently he could not make up his mind to touch it; but at length he put out his hand, opened the envelope, and moved with it to the light. In doing so he turned his back on Charlotte, and she saw only his bent head and slightly stooping shoulders. Apparently all the writing was on one page, for he did not turn the sheet but continued to stare at it for so long that he must have re-read it a dozen times – or so it seemed to the woman breathlessly watching him. At length she saw him move; he raised the letter still closer to his eyes, as though he had not fully deciphered it. Then he lowered his head, and she saw his lips touch the sheet.

'Kenneth!' she exclaimed, and went out into the hall.

The letter clutched in his hand, her husband turned and looked at her. 'Where were you?' he said, in a low bewildered voice, like a man waked out of his sleep.

'In the library, waiting for you.' She tried to steady her voice: 'What's the matter! What's in that letter? You look ghastly.'

Her agitation seemed to calm him, and he instantly put the envelope into his pocket with a slight laugh. 'Ghastly? I'm sorry. I've had a hard day in the office – one or two complicated cases. I look dog-tired, I suppose.'

'You didn't look tired when you came in. It was only when you opened that letter –'

He had followed her into the library, and they stood gazing at each other. Charlotte noticed how quickly he had regained his self-control; his profession had trained him to rapid mastery of face and voice. She saw at once that she would be at a disadvantage in any attempt to surprise his secret, but at the same moment she lost all desire to manoeuvre, to trick him into betraying anything he wanted to conceal. Her wish was still to penetrate the mystery, but only that she might help him to bear the burden it implied. 'Even if it *is* another woman,' she thought.

'Kenneth,' she said, her heart beating excitedly, 'I waited here on purpose to see you come in. I wanted to watch you while you opened that letter.'

His face, which had paled, turned to dark red; then it paled again. 'That letter? Why especially that letter?'

'Because I've noticed that whenever one of those letters comes it seems to have such a strange effect on you.'

A line of anger she had never seen before came out between his eyes, and she said to herself: 'The upper part of his face is too narrow; this is the first time I ever noticed it.'

She heard him continue, in the cool and faintly ironic tone of the prosecuting lawyer making a point: 'Ah; so you're in the habit of watching people open their letters when they don't know you're there?'

'Not in the habit. I never did such a thing before. But I had to find out what she writes to you, at regular intervals, in those grey envelopes.'

He weighed this for a moment; then: 'The intervals have not been regular,' he said.

'Oh, I dare say you've kept a better account of the dates than I have,' she retorted, her magnanimity vanishing at his tone. 'All I know is that every time that woman writes to you –'

'Why do you assume it's a woman?'

'It's a woman's writing. Do you deny it?'

He smiled. 'No, I don't deny it. I asked only because the writing is generally supposed to look more like a man's.'

Charlotte passed this over impatiently. 'And this woman – what does she write to you about?'

Again he seemed to consider a moment. 'About business.'

'Legal business?'

'In a way, yes. Business in general.'

'You look after her affairs for her?'

'Yes.'

'You've looked after them for a long time?'

'Yes. A very long time.'

'Kenneth, dearest, won't you tell me who she is?'

'No. I can't.' He paused, and brought out, as if with a certain hesitation: 'Professional secrecy.'

The blood rushed from Charlotte's heart to her temples. 'Don't say that – don't!'

'Why not?'

'Because I saw you kiss the letter.'

The effect of the words was so disconcerting that she instantly repented having spoken them. Her husband, who had submitted to her cross-questioning with a sort of contemptuous composure, as though he were humouring an unreasonable child, turned on her a face of terror and distress. For a minute he seemed unable to speak; then, collecting himself with an effort, he stammered out; 'The writing is very faint; you must have seen me holding the letter close to my eyes to try to decipher it.'

'No. I saw you kissing it.' He was silent. 'Didn't I see you kissing it?'

He sank back into indifference. 'Perhaps.'

'Kenneth! You stand there and say that – to me?'

'What possible difference can it make to you? The letter is on business, as I told you. Do you suppose I'd lie about it? The writer is a very old friend whom I haven't seen for a long time.'

'Men don't kiss business letters, even from women who are very old friends, unless they have been their lovers, and still regret them.'

He shrugged his shoulders slightly and turned away, as if he considered the discussion at an end and were faintly disgusted at the turn it had taken.

'Kenneth!' Charlotte moved toward him and caught hold of his arm.

He paused with a look of weariness and laid his hand over hers. 'Won't you believe me?' he asked gently.

'How can I? I've watched these letters come to you – for months now they've been coming. Ever since we came back from the West Indies – one of them greeted me the very day we arrived. And after each one of them I see their mysterious effect on you, I see you disturbed, unhappy, as if someone were trying to estrange you from me.'

'No, dear; not that. Never!'

She drew back and looked at him with passionate entreaty. 'Well, then, prove it to me, darling. It's so easy!'

He forced a smile. 'It's not easy to prove anything to a woman who's once taken an idea into her head.'

'You've only got to show me the letter.'

His hand slipped from hers and he drew back and shook his head.

'You won't?'
'I can't.'
'Then the woman who wrote it is your mistress.'
'No, dear. No.'
'Not now, perhaps. I suppose she's trying to get you back, and you're struggling, out of pity for me. My poor Kenneth!'
'I swear to you she never was my mistress.'
Charlotte felt the tears rushing to her eyes. 'Ah, that's worse, then – that's hopeless! The prudent ones are the kind that keep their hold on a man. We all know that.' She lifted her hands and hid her face in them.

Her husband remained silent; he offered neither consolation nor denial, and at length, wiping away her tears, she raised her eyes almost timidly to his.

'Kenneth, think! We've been married such a short time. Imagine what you're making me suffer. You say you can't show me this letter. You refuse even to explain it.'

'I've told you the letter is on business. I will swear to that too.'

'A man will swear to anything to screen a woman. If you want me to believe you, at least tell me her name. If you'll do that, I promise you I won't ask to see the letter.'

There was a long interval of suspense, during which she felt her heart beating against her ribs in quick admonitory knocks, as if warning her of the danger she was incurring.

'I can't,' he said at length.
'Not even her name?'
'No.'
'You can't tell me anything more?'
'No.'

Again a pause; this time they seemed both to have reached the end of their arguments and to be helplessly facing each other across a baffling waste of incomprehension.

Charlotte stood breathing rapidly, her hands against her breast. She felt as if she had run a hard race and missed the goal. She had meant to move her husband and had succeeded only in irritating him; and this error of reckoning seemed to change him into a stranger, a mysterious incomprehensible being whom no argument or entreaty of hers could reach. The curious thing was that she was aware in him of no hostility or even impatience, but only of a remoteness, an inaccessibility, far more difficult to overcome. She felt herself excluded, ignored, blotted out of his life. But after a moment or two, looking at him more calmly, she saw that he was suffering as much as she was. His distant guarded face was drawn with pain; the coming of the grey envelope, though it always cast a shadow, had never marked him as deeply as this discussion with his wife.

Charlotte took heart; perhaps, after all, she had not spent her last shaft. She drew nearer and once more laid her hand on his arm. 'Poor Kenneth! If you knew how sorry I am for you –'

She thought he winced slightly at this expression of sympathy, but he took her hand and pressed it.

'I can think of nothing worse than to be incapable of loving long,' she continued; 'to feel the beauty of a great love and to be too unstable to bear its burden.'

He turned on her a look of wistful reproach. 'Oh, don't say that of me. Unstable!'

She felt herself at last on the right tack, and her voice trembled with excitement as she went on: 'Then what about me and this other woman? Haven't you already forgotten Elsie twice within a year?'

She seldom pronounced his first wife's name; it did not come naturally to her tongue. She flung it out now as if she were flinging some dangerous explosive into the open space between them, and drew back a step, waiting to hear the mine go off.

Her husband did not move; his expression grew sadder, but showed no resentment. 'I have never forgotten Elsie,' he said.

Charlotte could not repress a faint laugh. 'Then, you poor dear, between the three of us —'

'There are not —' he began; and then broke off and put his hand to his forehead.

'Not what?'

'I'm sorry. I don't believe I know what I'm saying. I've got a blinding headache.' He looked wan and furrowed enough for the statement to be true, but she was exasperated by his evasion.

'Ah, yes; the grey-envelope headache!'

She saw the surprise in his eyes. 'I'd forgotten how closely I've been watched,' he said coldly. 'If you'll excuse me, I think I'll go up and try an hour in the dark, to see if I can get rid of this neuralgia.'

She wavered; then she said, with desperate resolution; 'I'm sorry your head aches. But before you go I want to say that sooner or later this question must be settled between us. Someone is trying to separate us, and I don't care what it costs me to find out who it is.' She looked him steadily in the eyes. 'If it costs me your love, I don't care! If I can't have your confidence I don't want anything from you.'

He still looked at her wistfully. 'Give me time.'

'Time for what? It's only a word to say.'

'Time to show you that you haven't lost my love or my confidence.'

'Well, I'm waiting.'

He turned toward the door, and then glanced back hesitatingly. 'Oh, do wait, my love,' he said, and went out of the room.

She heard his tired step on the stairs and the closing of his bedroom door above. Then she dropped into a chair and buried her face in her folded arms. Her first movement was one of compunction; she seemed to herself to have been hard, unhuman, unimaginative. 'Think of telling him that I didn't care if my insistence cost me his love! The lying rubbish!' She started up to follow him and unsay the meaningless words. But she was checked by a reflection. He had had his way, after all; he had eluded all attacks on his secret, and now he was shut up alone in his room, reading that other woman's letter.

III

She was still reflecting on this when the surprised parlour-maid came in and found her. No, Charlotte said, she wasn't going to dress for dinner; Mr Ashby didn't want to dine. He was very tired and had gone up to his room to rest; later she would have something brought on a tray to the drawing-room. She mounted the stairs to her bedroom. Her dinner dress was lying on the bed, and at the sight the quiet routine of her daily life took hold of her and she began to feel as if the strange talk she had just had with her husband must have taken place in another world, between two beings who were not Charlotte Gorse and Kenneth Ashby, but phantoms projected by her fevered imagination. She recalled the

Pomegranate Seed

year since her marriage – her husband's constant devotion; his persistent, almost too insistent tenderness; the feeling he had given her at times of being too eagerly dependent on her, too searchingly close to her, as if there were not air enough between her soul and his. It seemed preposterous, as she recalled all this, that a few moments ago she should have been accusing him of an intrigue with another woman! But, then, what –

Again she was moved by the impulse to go up to him, beg his pardon and try to laugh away the misunderstanding. But she was restrained by the fear of forcing herself upon his privacy. He was troubled and unhappy, oppressed by some grief or fear; and he had shown her that he wanted to fight out his battle alone. It would be wiser, as well as more generous, to respect his wish. Only, how strange, how unbearable, to be there, in the next room to his, and feel herself at the other end of the world! In her nervous agitation she almost regretted not having had the courage to open the letter and put it back on the hall table before he came in. At least she would have known what his secret was, and the bogey might have been laid. For she was beginning now to think of the mystery as something conscious, malevolent: a secret persecution before which he quailed, yet from which he could not free himself. Once or twice in his evasive eyes she thought she had detected a desire for help, an impulse of confession, instantly restrained and suppressed. It was as if he felt she could have helped him if she had known, and yet had been unable to tell her!

There flashed through her mind the idea of going to his mother. She was very fond of old Mrs Ashby, a firm-fleshed clear-eyed old lady, with an astringent bluntness of speech which responded to the forthright and simple in Charlotte's own nature. There had been a tacit bond between them ever since the day when Mrs Ashby senior, coming to lunch for the first time with her new daughter-in-law, had been received by Charlotte downstairs in the library, and glancing up at the empty wall above her son's desk, had remarked laconically: 'Elsie gone, eh?' adding, at Charlotte's murmured explanation, 'Nonsense. Don't have her back. Two's company.' Charlotte, at this reading of her thoughts, could hardly refrain from exchanging a smile of complicity with her mother-in-law; and it seemed to her now that Mrs Ashby's almost uncanny directness might pierce to the core of this new mystery. But here again she hesitated, for the idea almost suggested a betrayal. What right had she to call in any one, even so close a relation, to surprise a secret which her husband was trying to keep from her? 'Perhaps, by and by, he'll talk to his mother of his own accord,' she thought, and then ended, 'but what does it matter? He and I must settle it between us.'

She was still brooding over the problem when there was a knock on the door and her husband came in. He was dressed for dinner and seemed surprised to see her sitting there, with her evening dress lying unheeded on the bed.

'Aren't you coming down?'

'I thought you were not well and had gone to bed,' she faltered.

He forced a smile. 'I'm not particularly well, but we'd better go down.' His face, though still drawn, looked calmer than when he had fled upstairs an hour earlier.

'There it is; he knows what's in the letter and has fought his battle out again, whatever it is,' she reflected, 'while I'm still in darkness.' She rang and gave a hurried order that dinner should be served as soon as possible –

Pomegranate Seed

just a short meal, whatever could be got ready quickly, as both she and Mr Ashby were rather tired and not very hungry.

Dinner was announced, and they sat down to it. At first neither seemed able to find a word to say; then Ashby began to make conversation with an assumption of ease that was more oppressive than his silence. 'How tired he is! How terribly over-tired!' Charlotte said to herself, pursuing her own thoughts while he rambled on about municipal politics, aviation, an exhibition of modern French painting, the health of an old aunt and the installing of the automatic telephone. 'Good heavens, how tired he is!'

When they dined alone they usually went into the library after dinner, and Charlotte curled herself up on the divan with her knitting while he settled down in his armchair under the lamp and lit a pipe. But this evening, by tacit agreement, they avoided the room in which their strange talk had taken place, and went up to Charlotte's drawing-room.

They sat down near the fire, and Charlotte said; 'Your pipe?' after he had put down his hardly tasted coffee.

He shook his head. 'No, not tonight.'

'You must go to bed early; you look terribly tired. I'm sure they overwork you at the office.'

'I suppose we all overwork at times.'

She rose and stood before him with sudden resolution. 'Well, I'm not going to have you use up your strength slaving in that way. It's absurd. I can see you're ill.' She bent over him and laid her hand on his forehead. 'My poor old Kenneth. Prepare to be taken away soon on a long holiday.'

He looked up at her, startled. 'A holiday?'

'Certainly. Didn't you know I was going to carry you

off at Easter? We're going to start in a fortnight on a month's voyage to somewhere or other. On any one of the big cruising steamers.' She paused and bent closer, touching his forehead with her lips. 'I'm tired, too, Kenneth.'

He seemed to pay no heed to her last words, but sat, his hands on his knees, his head drawn back a little from her caress, and looked up at her with a stare of apprehension. 'Again? My dear, we can't; I can't possibly go away.'

'I don't know why you say "again", Kenneth; we haven't taken a real holiday this year.'

'At Christmas we spent a week with the children in the country.'

'Yes, but this time I mean away from the children, from servants, from the house. From everything that's familiar and fatiguing. Your mother will love to have Joyce and Peter with her.'

He frowned and slowly shook his head. 'No, dear; I can't leave them with my mother.'

'Why, Kenneth, how absurd! She adores them. You didn't hesitate to leave them with her for over two months when we went to the West Indies.'

He drew a deep breath and stood up uneasily. 'That was different.'

'Different? Why?'

'I mean, at that time I didn't realize —' He broke off as if to choose his words and then went on, 'My mother adores the children, as you say. But she isn't always very judicious. Grandmothers always spoil children. And she sometimes talks before them without thinking.' He turned to his wife with an almost pitiful gesture of entreaty. 'Don't ask me to, dear.'

Charlotte mused. It was true that the elder Mrs Ashby

had a fearless tongue, but she was the last woman in the world to say or hint anything before her grandchildren at which the most scrupulous parent could take offence. Charlotte looked at her husband in perplexity.

'I don't understand.'

He continued to turn on her the same troubled and entreating gaze. 'Don't try to,' he muttered.

'Not try to?'

'Not now – not yet.' He put up his hands and pressed them against his temples. 'Can't you see that there's no use in insisting? I can't go away, no matter how much I might want to.'

Charlotte still scrutinized him gravely. 'The question is, *do* you want to?'

He returned her gaze for a moment; then his lips began to tremble, and he said, hardly above his breath, 'I want – anything you want.'

'And yet –'

'Don't ask me. I can't leave – I can't!'

'You mean that you can't go away out of reach of those letters!'

Her husband had been standing before her in an uneasy half-hesitating attitude; now he turned abruptly away and walked once or twice up and down the length of the room, his head bent, his eyes fixed on the carpet.

Charlotte felt her resentfulness rising with her fears. 'It's that,' she persisted. 'Why not admit it? You can't live without them.'

He continued his troubled pacing of the room; then he stopped short, dropped into a chair and covered his face with his hands. From the shaking of his shoulders, Charlotte saw that he was weeping. She had never seen a man cry, except her father after her mother's death, when she was a little girl; and she remembered still how the sight had frightened her. She was frightened now; she felt that her husband was being dragged away from her into some mysterious bondage, and that she must use up her last atom of strength in the struggle for his freedom, and for hers.

'Kenneth – Kenneth!' she pleaded, kneeling down beside him. 'Won't you listen to me? Won't you try to see what I'm suffering? I'm not unreasonable, darling; really not. I don't suppose I should ever have noticed the letters if it hadn't been for their effect on you. It's not my way to pry into other people's affairs; and even if the effect had been different – yes, yes; listen to me – if I'd seen that the letters made you happy, that you were watching eagerly for them, counting the days between their coming, that you wanted them, that they gave you something I haven't known how to give – why, Kenneth, I don't say I shouldn't have suffered from that, too; but it would have been in a different way, and I should have had the courage to hide what I felt, and the hope that some day you'd come to feel about me as you did about the writer of the letters. But what I can't bear is to see how you dread them, how they make you suffer, and yet how you can't live without them and won't go away lest you should miss one during your absence. Or perhaps,' she added, her voice breaking into a cry of accusation – 'perhaps it's because she's actually forbidden you to leave. Kenneth, you must answer me! Is that the reason? Is it because she's forbidden you that you won't go away with me?'

She continued to kneel at his side, and raising her hands, she drew his gently down. She was ashamed of her persistence, ashamed of uncovering that baffled disordered face, yet resolved that no such scruples should arrest her. His eyes were lowered, the muscles of his face quivered; she was making him suffer even more than she suffered herself. Yet this no longer restrained her.

'Kenneth, is it that? She won't let us go away together?'

Still he did not speak or turn his eyes to her; and a sense of defeat swept over her. After all, she thought, the struggle was a losing one. 'You needn't answer. I see I'm right,' she said.

Suddenly, as she rose, he turned and drew her down again. His hands caught hers and pressed them so tightly that she felt her rings cutting into her flesh. There was something frightened, convulsive in his hold; it was the clutch of a man who felt himself slipping over a precipice. He was staring up at her now as if salvation lay in the face she bent above him. 'Of course we'll go away together. We'll go wherever you want,' he said in a low confused voice; and putting his arm about her, he drew her close and pressed his lips on hers.

IV

Charlotte had said to herself: 'I shall sleep tonight,' but instead she sat before her fire into the small hours, listening for any sound that came from her husband's room. But he, at any rate, seemed to be resting after the tumult of the evening. Once or twice she stole to the door and in the faint light that came in from the street through his open window she saw him stretched out in heavy sleep – the sleep of weakness and exhaustion. 'He's ill,' she thought – 'he's undoubtedly ill. And it's not overwork; it's this mysterious persecution.'

She drew a breath of relief. She had fought through the weary fight and the victory was hers – at least for the moment. If only they could have started at once – started for anywhere! She knew it would be useless to ask him to leave before the holidays; and meanwhile the secret influence – as to which she was still so completely in the dark – would continue to work against her, and she would have to renew the struggle day after day till they started on their journey. But after that everything would be different. If once she could get her husband away under other skies, and all to herself, she never doubted her power to release him from the evil spell he was under. Lulled to quiet by the thought, she too slept at last.

When she woke, it was long past her usual hour, and she sat up in bed surprised and vexed at having overslept herself. She always liked to be down to share her husband's breakfast by the library fire; but a glance at the clock made it clear that he must have started long since for his office. To make sure, she jumped out of bed and went into his room; but it was empty. No doubt he had looked in on her before leaving, seen that she still slept, and gone downstairs without disturbing her; and their relations were sufficiently loverlike for her to regret having missed their morning hour.

She rang and asked if Mr Ashby had already gone. Yes, nearly an hour ago, the maid said. He had given orders that Mrs Ashby should not be waked and that the children should not come to her till she sent for them ... Yes, he had gone up to the nursery himself to give the order. All this sounded usual enough; and Charlotte hardly knew why she asked, 'And did Mr Ashby leave no other message?'

Yes, the maid said, he did; she was so sorry she'd forgotten. He'd told her, just as he was leaving, to say to Mrs Ashby that he was going to see about their passages, and would she please be ready to sail tomorrow?

Charlotte echoed the woman's 'Tomorrow,' and sat staring at her incredulously. 'Tomorrow – you're sure he said to sail tomorrow?'

'Oh, ever so sure, ma'am. I don't know how I could have forgotten to mention it.'

'Well, it doesn't matter. Draw my bath, please.' Charlotte sprang up, dashed through her dressing, and caught herself singing at her image in the glass as she sat brushing her hair. It made her feel young again to have scored such a victory. The other woman vanished to a speck on the horizon, as this one, who ruled the foreground, smiled back at the reflection of her lips and eyes. He loved her, then – he loved her as passionately as ever. He had divined what she had suffered, had understood that their happiness depended on their getting away at once, and finding each other again after yesterday's desperate groping in the fog. The nature of the influence that had come between them did not much matter to Charlotte now; she had faced the phantom and dispelled it. 'Courage – that's the secret! If only people who are in love weren't always so afraid of risking their happiness by looking it in the eyes.' As she brushed back her light abundant hair it waved electrically above her head, like the palms of victory. Ah, well, some women knew how to manage men, and some didn't – and only the fair – she gaily paraphrased – deserve the brave! Certainly she was looking very pretty.

The morning danced along like a cockleshell on a bright sea – such a sea as they would soon be speeding over. She ordered a particularly good dinner, saw the children off to their classes, had her trunks brought down, consulted with the maid about getting out summer clothes – for of course they would be heading for heat and sunshine – and wondered if she oughtn't to take Kenneth's flannel suits out of camphor. 'But how absurd,' she reflected, 'that I don't yet know where we're going!' She looked at the clock, saw that it was close on noon, and decided to call him up at his office. There was a slight delay; then she heard his secretary's voice saying that Mr Ashby had looked in for a moment early, and left again almost immediately . . . Oh, very well; Charlotte would ring up later. How soon was he likely to be back? The secretary answered that she couldn't tell; all they knew in the office was that when he left he had said he was in a hurry because he had to go out of town.

Out of town! Charlotte hung up the receiver and sat blankly gazing into new darkness. Why had he gone out of town? And where had he gone? And of all days, why should he have chosen the eve of their suddenly planned departure? She felt a faint shiver of apprehension. Of course he had gone to see that woman – no doubt to get her permission to leave. He was as completely in bondage as that; and Charlotte had been fatuous enough to see the palms of victory on her forehead. She burst into a laugh and, walking across the room, sat down again before her mirror. What a different face she saw! The smile on her pale lips seemed to mock the rosy vision of the other Charlotte. But gradually her colour crept back. After all, she had a right to claim the victory, since her husband was doing what she wanted, not what the other woman exacted of him. It was natural enough, in view of his abrupt decision to leave the next day, that he should have arrangements to make, business matters to wind up; it was not even necessary to suppose that his mysterious trip was a visit to the writer of the letters.

Pomegranate Seed

He might simply have gone to see a client who lived out of town. Of course they would not tell Charlotte at the office; the secretary had hesitated before imparting even such meagre information as the fact of Mr Ashby's absence. Meanwhile she would go on with her joyful preparations, content to learn later in the day to what particular island of the blest she was to be carried.

The hours wore on, rather were swept forward on a rush of eager preparations. At last the entrance of the maid who came to draw the curtains roused Charlotte from her labours, and she saw to her surprise that the clock marked five. And she did not yet know where they were going the next day! She rang up her husband's office and was told that Mr Ashby had not been there since the early morning. She asked for his partner, but the partner could add nothing to her information, for he himself, his suburban train having been behind time, had reached the office after Ashby had come and gone. Charlotte stood perplexed; then she decided to telephone to her mother-in-law. Of course Kenneth, on the eve of a month's absence, must have gone to see his mother. The mere fact that the children – in spite of his vague objections – would certainly have to be left with old Mrs Ashby, made it obvious that he would have all sorts of matters to decide with her. At another time Charlotte might have felt a little hurt at being excluded from their conference, but nothing mattered now but that she had won the day, that her husband was still hers and not another woman's. Gaily she called up Mrs Ashby, heard her friendly voice, and began, 'Well, did Kenneth's news surprise you? What do you think of our elopement?'

Almost instantly, before Mrs Ashby could answer, Charlotte knew what her reply would be. Mrs Ashby had not seen her son, she had had no word from him and did not know what her daughter-in-law meant. Charlotte stood silent in the intensity of her surprise. 'But then, where *has* he been?' she thought. Then, recovering herself, she explained their sudden decision to Mrs Ashby, and in doing so, gradually regained her own self-confidence, her conviction that nothing could ever again come between Kenneth and herself. Mrs Ashby took the news calmly and approvingly. She, too, had thought that Kenneth looked worried and overtired, and she agreed with her daughter-in-law that in such cases change was the surest remedy. 'I'm always so glad when he gets away. Elsie hated travelling; she was always finding pretexts to prevent his going anywhere. With you, thank goodness, it's different.' Nor was Mrs Ashby surprised at his not having had time to let her know of his departure. He must have been in a rush from the moment the decision was taken; but no doubt he'd drop in before dinner. Five minutes' talk was really all they needed. 'I hope you'll gradually cure Kenneth of his mania for going over and over a question that could be settled in a dozen words. He never used to be like that, and if he carried the habit into his professional work he'd soon lose all his clients . . . Yes, do come in for a minute, dear, if you have time; no doubt he'll turn up while you're here.' The tonic ring of Mrs Ashby's voice echoed on reassuringly in the silent room while Charlotte continued her preparations.

 Toward seven the telephone rang, and she darted to it. Now she would know! But it was only from the conscientious secretary, to say that Mr Ashby hadn't been back, or sent any word, and before the office closed she thought she ought to let Mrs Ashby know. 'Oh, that's all right. Thanks a lot!' Charlotte called out cheerfully, and hung up the receiver with a trembling hand. But perhaps by this time, she reflected, he was at his mother's. She shut her drawers and cupboards, put on her hat and coat and called up to the nursery that she was going out for a minute to see the children's grandmother.

Mrs Ashby lived nearby, and during her brief walk through the cold spring dusk Charlotte imagined that every advancing figure was her husband's. But she did not meet him on the way, and when she entered the house she found her mother-in-law alone. Kenneth had neither telephoned nor come. Old Mrs Ashby sat by her bright fire, her knitting needles flashing steadily through her active old hands, and her mere bodily presence gave reassurance to Charlotte. Yes, it was certainly odd that Kenneth had gone off for the whole day without letting any of them know; but, after all, it was to be expected. A busy lawyer held so many threads in his hands that any sudden change of plan would oblige him to make all sorts of unforeseen arrangements and adjustments. He might have gone to see some client in the suburbs and been detained there; his mother remembered his telling her that he had charge of the legal business of a queer old recluse somewhere in New Jersey, who was immensely rich but too mean to have a telephone. Very likely Kenneth had been stranded there.

But Charlotte felt her nervousness gaining on her. When Mrs Ashby asked her at what hour they were sailing the next day and she had to say she didn't know – that Kenneth had simply sent her word he was going to take their passages – the uttering of the words again brought home to her the strangeness of the situation. Even Mrs Ashby conceded that it was odd; but she immediately added that it only showed what a rush he was in.

'But, Mother, it's nearly eight o'clock! He must realize that I've got to know when we're starting tomorrow.'

'Oh, the boat probably doesn't sail till evening. Sometimes they have to wait till midnight for the tide. Kenneth's probably counting on that. After all, he has a level head.'

Charlotte stood up. 'It's not that. Something has happened to him.'

Mrs Ashby took off her spectacles and rolled up her knitting. 'If you begin to let yourself imagine things —'

'Aren't you in the least anxious?'

'I never am till I have to be. I wish you'd ring for dinner, my dear. You'll stay and dine? He's sure to drop in here on his way home.'

Charlotte called up her own house. No, the maid said, Mr Ashby hadn't come in and hadn't telephoned. She would tell him as soon as he came that Mrs Ashby was dining at his mother's. Charlotte followed her mother-in-law into the dining-room and sat with parched throat before her empty plate, while Mrs Ashby dealt calmly and efficiently with a short but carefully prepared repast. 'You'd better eat something, child, or you'll be as bad as Kenneth . . . Yes, a little more asparagus, please, Jane.'

She insisted on Charlotte's drinking a glass of sherry and nibbling a bit of toast; then they returned to the drawing-room, where the fire had been made up, and the cushions in Mrs Ashby's armchair shaken out and smoothed. How safe and familiar it all looked; and out there, somewhere in the uncertainty and mystery of the night, lurked the answer to the two women's conjectures, like an indistinguishable figure prowling on the threshold.

Pomegranate Seed

At last Charlotte got up and said, 'I'd better go back. At this hour Kenneth will certainly go straight home.'

Mrs Ashby smiled indulgently. 'It's not very late, my dear. It doesn't take two sparrows long to dine.'

'It's after nine.' Charlotte bent down to kiss her. 'The fact is, I can't keep still.'

Mrs Ashby pushed aside her work and rested her two hands on the arms of her chair. 'I'm going with you,' she said, helping herself up.

Charlotte protested that it was too late, that it was not necessary, that she would call up as soon as Kenneth came in, but Mrs Ashby had already rung for her maid. She was slightly lame, and stood resting on her stick while her wraps were brought. 'If Mr Kenneth turns up, tell him he'll find me at his own house,' she instructed the maid as the two women got into the taxi which had been summoned. During the short drive Charlotte gave thanks that she was not returning home alone. There was something warm and substantial in the mere fact of Mrs Ashby's nearness, something that corresponded with the clearness of her eyes and the texture of her fresh firm complexion. As the taxi drew up she laid her hand encouragingly on Charlotte's. 'You'll see; there'll be a message.'

The door opened at Charlotte's ring and the two entered. Charlotte's heart beat excitedly; the stimulus of her mother-in-law's confidence was beginning to flow through her veins.

'You'll see – you'll see,' Mrs Ashby repeated.

The maid who opened the door said no, Mr Ashby had not come in, and there had been no message from him.

'You're sure the telephone's not out of order?' his mother suggested; and the maid said, well, it certainly wasn't half an hour ago; but she'd just go and ring up to make sure. She disappeared, and Charlotte turned to take off her hat and cloak. As she did so her eyes lit on the hall table, and there lay a grey envelope, her husband's name faintly traced on it. 'Oh!' she cried out, suddenly aware that for the first time in months she had entered her house without wondering if one of the grey letters would be there.

'What is it, my dear?' Mrs Ashby asked with a glance of surprise.

Charlotte did not answer. She took up the envelope and stood staring at it as if she could force her gaze to penetrate to what was within. Then an idea occurred to her. She turned and held out the envelope to her mother-in-law.

'Do you know that writing?' she asked.

Mrs Ashby took the letter. She had to feel with her other hand for her eyeglasses, and when she had adjusted them she lifted the envelope to the light. 'Why!' she exclaimed; and then stopped. Charlotte noticed that the letter shook in her usually firm hand. 'But this is addressed to Kenneth,' Mrs Ashby said at length, in a low voice. Her tone seemed to imply that she felt her daughter-in-law's question to be slightly indiscreet.

'Yes, but no matter,' Charlotte spoke with sudden decision. 'I want to know – do you know the writing?'

Mrs Ashby handed back the letter. 'No,' she said distinctly.

The two women had turned into the library. Charlotte switched on the electric light and shut the door. She still held the envelope in her hand.

'I'm going to open it,' she announced.

She caught her mother-in-law's startled glance. 'But, dearest – a letter not addressed to you? My dear, you can't!'

'As if I cared about that – now!' She continued to look intently at Mrs Ashby. 'This letter may tell me where Kenneth is.'

Mrs Ashby's glossy bloom was effaced by a quick pallor; her firm cheeks seemed to shrink and wither. 'Why should it? What makes you believe – It can't possibly –'

Charlotte held her eyes steadily on that altered face. 'Ah, then you *do* know the writing?' she flashed back.

'Know the writing? How should I? With all my son's correspondents ... What I do know is –' Mrs Ashby broke off and looked at her daughter-in-law entreatingly, almost timidly.

Charlotte caught her by the wrist. 'Mother! What do you know? Tell me! You must!'

'That I don't believe any good ever came of a woman's opening her husband's letters behind his back.'

The words sounded to Charlotte's irritated ears as flat as a phrase culled from a book of moral axioms. She laughed impatiently and dropped her mother-in-law's wrist. 'Is that all? No good can come of this letter, opened or unopened. I know that well enough. But whatever ill comes, I mean to find out what's in it.' Her hands had been trembling as they held the envelope, but now they grew firm, and her voice also. She still gazed intently at Mrs Ashby. 'This is the ninth letter addressed in the same hand that has come for Kenneth since we've been married. Always these same grey envelopes. I've kept count of them because after each one he has been like a man who has had some dreadful shock. It takes him hours to shake off their effect. I've told him so. I've told him I must know from whom they come, because I can see they're killing him. He won't answer my questions; he says he can't tell me anything about the letters; but last night he promised to go away with me – to get away from them.'

Mrs Ashby, with shaking steps, had gone to one of the armchairs and sat down in it, her head drooping forward on her breast. 'Ah,' she murmured.

'So now you understand –'

'Did he tell you it was to get away from them?'

'He said, to get away – to get away. He was sobbing so that he could hardly speak. But I told him I knew that was why.'

'And what did he say?'

'He took me in his arms and said he'd go wherever I wanted.'

'Ah, thank God!' said Mrs Ashby. There was a silence, during which she continued to sit with bowed head, and eyes averted from her daughter-in-law. At last she looked up and spoke. 'Are you sure there have been as many as nine?'

'Perfectly. This is the ninth. I've kept count.'

'And he has absolutely refused to explain?'

'Absolutely.'

Mrs Ashby spoke through pale contracted lips. 'When did they begin to come? Do you remember?'

Charlotte laughed again. 'Remember? The first one came the night we got back from our honeymoon.'

'All that time?' Mrs Ashby lifted her head and spoke with sudden energy. 'Then – Yes, open it.'

The words were so unexpected that Charlotte felt the blood in her temples, and her hands began to tremble again. She tried to slip her finger under the flap of the envelope, but it was so tightly stuck that she had to hunt on her husband's writing table for his ivory letter-opener. As she pushed about the familiar objects his own hands had so lately touched, they sent through her the icy chill emanating from the little personal effects of someone newly dead. In the deep silence of the room the tearing of the paper as she slit the envelope sounded like a human cry. She drew out the sheet and carried it to the lamp.

'Well?' Mrs Ashby asked below her breath.

Charlotte did not move or answer. She was bending over the page with wrinkled brows, holding it nearer and nearer to the light. Her sight must be blurred, or else dazzled by the reflection of the lamplight on the smooth surface of the paper, for, strain her eyes as she would, she could discern only a few faint strokes, so faint and faltering as to be nearly undecipherable.

'I can't make it out,' she said.

'What do you mean, dear?'

'The writing's too indistinct . . . Wait.'

She went back to the table and, sitting down close to Kenneth's reading lamp, slipped the letter under a magnifying glass. All this time she was aware that her mother-in-law was watching her intently.

'Well?' Mrs Ashby breathed.

'Well, it's no clearer. I can't read it.'

'You mean the paper is an absolute blank?'

'No, not quite. There is writing on it. I can make out something like "mine" – oh, and "come". It might be "come".'

Mrs Ashby stood up abruptly. Her face was even paler than before. She advanced to the table and, resting her two hands on it, drew a deep breath. 'Let me see,' she said, as if forcing herself to a hateful effort.

Charlotte felt the contagion of her whiteness. 'She knows,' she thought. She pushed the letter across the table. Her mother-in-law lowered her head over it in silence, but without touching it with her pale wrinkled hands.

Charlotte stood watching her as she herself, when she had tried to read the letter, had been watched by Mrs Ashby. The latter fumbled for her glasses, held them to her eyes, and bent still closer to the outspread page, in order, as it seemed, to avoid touching it. The light of the lamp fell directly on her old face, and Charlotte reflected what depths of the unknown may lurk under the clearest and most candid lineaments. She had never seen her mother-in-law's features express any but simple and sound emotions – cordiality, amusement, a kindly sympathy; now and again a flash of wholesome anger. Now they seemed to wear a look of fear and hatred, of incredulous dismay and almost cringing defiance. It was as if the spirits warring within her had distorted her face to their own likeness. At length she raised her head. 'I can't – I can't,' she said in a voice of childish distress.

'You can't make it out either?'

She shook her head, and Charlotte saw two tears roll down her cheeks.

'Familiar as the writing is to you?' Charlotte insisted with twitching lips.

Mrs Ashby did not take up the challenge. 'I can make out nothing – nothing.'

'But you do know the writing?'

Mrs Ashby lifted her head timidly; her anxious eyes stole with a glance of apprehension around the quiet familiar room. 'How can I tell? I was startled at first . . .'

'Startled by the resemblance?'

'Well. I thought –'

'You'd better say it out, Mother! You knew at once it was *her* writing?'

'Oh, wait, my dear – wait.'

'Wait for what?'

Mrs Ashby looked up; her eyes, travelling slowly past Charlotte, were lifted to the blank wall behind her son's writing table.

Charlotte, following the glance, burst into a shrill laugh of accusation. 'I needn't wait any longer! You've answered me now! You're looking straight at the wall where her picture used to hang!'

Mrs Ashby lifted her hand with a murmur of warning. 'Sh-h.'

'Oh, you needn't imagine that anything can ever frighten me again!' Charlotte cried.

Her mother-in-law still leaned against the table. Her lips moved plaintively. 'But we're going mad – we're both going mad. We both know such things are impossible.'

Her daughter-in-law looked at her with a pitying stare. 'I've known for a long time now that everything was possible.'

'Even this?'

'Yes, exactly this.'

'But this letter – after all, there's nothing in this letter –'

'Perhaps there would be to him. How can I tell? I remember his saying to me once that if you were used to a handwriting the faintest stroke of it became legible. Now I see what he meant. He *was* used to it.'

'But the few strokes that I can make out are so pale. No one could possibly read that letter.'

Charlotte laughed again. 'I suppose everything's pale about a ghost,' she said stridently.

'Oh, my child – my child – don't say it!'

'Why shouldn't I say it, when even the bare walls cry it out? What difference does it make if her letters are illegible to you and me? If even you can see her face on that blank wall, why shouldn't he read her writing on this blank paper? Don't you see that she's everywhere in this house, and the closer to him because to everyone else she's become invisible?' Charlotte dropped into a chair and covered her face with her hands. A turmoil of sobbing shook her from head to foot. At length a touch on her shoulder made her look up, and she saw her mother-in-law bending over her. Mrs Ashby's face seemed to have grown still smaller and more wasted, but it had resumed its usual quiet look. Through all her tossing anguish, Charlotte felt the impact of that resolute spirit.

'Tomorrow – tomorrow. You'll see. There'll be some explanation tomorrow.'

Charlotte cut her short. 'An explanation? Who's going to give it, I wonder?'

Mrs Ashby drew back and straightened herself heroically. 'Kenneth himself will,' she cried out in a strong voice. Charlotte said nothing, and the old woman went on; 'But meanwhile we must act; we must notify the police. Now, without a moment's delay. We must do everything – everything.'

Charlotte stood up slowly and stiffly; her joints felt as cramped as an old woman's. 'Exactly as if we thought it could do any good to do anything?'

Resolutely Mrs Ashby cried: 'Yes!' and Charlotte went up to the telephone and unhooked the receiver.

Jeanette Winterson

extract from

Sexing the Cherry

Jordan, the Dog Woman's foster son, is a voyager, apprentice and companion to the naturalist John Tradescant. On one of his journeys he meets a miller who advises him to hear the story of the Twelve Dancing Princesses, especially since the girls are still living just down the road and willingly tell their own tale.

I banged on the door and heard a voice behind me asking my name.

'My name is Jordan,' I said, though not knowing to whom. 'Down here.'

There was a well by the door with a frayed rope and a rusty bucket.

'Are you looking for me?'

I explained to the head now poking over the edge of the well that I had come to pay my respects to the Twelve Dancing Princesses.

'You can start here then,' said the head. 'I am the eldest.'

Timidly, for I have a fear of confined spaces, I swung over the edge and climbed down a wooden ladder. I found myself in a circular room, well furnished, with a silver jug coming to the boil with fresh coffee.

'I've brought you some herrings,' I said, awkwardly.

At the word 'herring' there was a sound of great delight and a hand came over my shoulder and took the whole parcel.

'Please excuse her,' said the princess. 'She is a mermaid.'

Already the mermaid, who was very beautiful but without fine graces, was gobbling the fish, dropping them back into her throat the way you or I would an oyster.

'It is the penalty of love,' sighed the princess, and began at once to tell me the story of her life.

We all slept in the same room, my sisters and I, and that room was narrower than a new river and longer than the beard of the prophet.

So you see exactly the kind of quarters we had.

We slept in white beds with white sheets and the moon shone through the window and made white shadows on the floor.

From this room, every night, we flew to a silver city where no one ate or drank. The occupation of the people was to dance. We wore out our dresses and slippers dancing, but because we were always sound asleep when our father came to wake us in the morning it was impossible to fathom where we had been or how.

You know that eventually a clever prince caught us flying through the window. We had given him a sleeping draught but he only pretended to drink it. He had eleven brothers and we were all given in marriage, one to each brother, and as it says lived happily ever after. We did, but not with our husbands.

I have always enjoyed swimming, and it was in deep waters one day that I came to a coral cave and saw a mermaid combing her hair. I fell in love with her at once, and after a few months of illicit meetings, my husband complaining all the time that I stank of fish, I ran away and began housekeeping with her in perfect salty bliss.

For some years I did not hear from my sisters, and then, by a strange eventuality, I discovered that we had all, in one way or another, parted from the glorious princes and were living scattered, according to our tastes.

Sexing the Cherry

We bought this house and we share it. You will find my sisters as you walk about. As you can see, I live in the well.

'That's my last husband painted on the wall,' said the second princess, 'looking as though he were alive.'

She took me through her glass house showing me curiosities: the still-born foetus of the infamous Pope Joan who had so successfully posed as a Man of God until giving birth in the Easter parade. She had the tablets of stone on which Moses had received the Ten Commandments. The writing was blurred but it was easy to make out the gouged lines of the finger of God.

'I collect religious items.'

She had not minded her husband much more than any wife does until he had tried to stop her hobby.

'He built a bonfire and burned the body of a saint. The saint was very old and wrapped in cloth. I liked him about the house; he added something.'

After that she had wrapped her own husband in cloth and gone on wrapping the stale bandages round and round until she reached his nose. She had a moment's regret, and continued.

'He walked in beauty,' she said.

'His eyes were brown marshes, his lashes were like willow trees. His eyebrows shot together made a dam between his forehead and his face. His cheeks were steep and sheer, his mouth was a volcano. His breath was like a dragon's and his heart was torn from a bull. The sinews in his neck were white columns leading to the bolts of his collar-bone. I can still trace the cavity of his throat. His chest was a strongbox, his ribs were made of brass, they shone through his skin when the sun was out. His shoulder-blades were mountain ranges, his spine a cobbled road. His belly was filled with jewels and his cock woke at dawn. Fields of wheat still remind me of his hair, and when I see a hand whose fingers are longer than its palm I think it might be him come to touch me again.

'But he never touched me. It was a boy he loved. I pierced them with a single arrow where they lay.

'I still think it was poetic.'

My husband married me so that his liaisons with other women, being forbidden, would be more exciting. Danger was an aphrodisiac to him: he wanted nothing easy or gentle. His way was to cause whirlwinds. I was warned, we always are, by well-wishers or malcontents, but I chose to take no interest in gossip. My husband was handsome and clever. What did it matter if he needed a certain kind of outlet, so long as he loved me? I wanted to love him; I was determined to be happy with him. I had not been happy before.

At first I hardly minded his weeks away. I did not realize that part of his sport was to make me mad. Only then, when he had hurt me, could he fully enjoy the other beds he visited.

I soon discovered that the women he preferred were the inmates of a lunatic asylum. With them he arranged mock marriages in deserted barns. They wore a shroud as their wedding dress and carried a bunch of carrots as a bouquet. He had them straight after on a pig-trough altar. Most were virgins. He like to come home to me smelling of their blood.

Does the body hate itself so much that it seeks release at any cost?

I didn't kill him. I left him to walk the battlements of

his ruined kingdom; his body was raddled with disease. The same winter he was found dead in the snow.

Why could he not turn his life towards me, as trees though troubled by the wind yet continue in the path of the sun?

You may have heard of Rapunzel.

Against the wishes of her family, who can best be described by their passion for collecting miniature dolls, she went to live in a tower with an older woman.

Her family were so incensed by her refusal to marry the prince next door that they vilified the couple, calling one a witch and the other a little girl. Not content with names, they ceaselessly tried to break into the tower, so much so that the happy pair had to seal up any entrance that was not on a level with the sky. The lover got in by climbing up Rapunzel's hair, and Rapunzel got in by nailing a wig to the floor and shinning up the tresses flung out of the window. Both of them could have used a ladder, but they were in love.

One day the prince, who had always liked to borrow his mother's frocks, dressed up as Rapunzel's lover and dragged himself into the tower. Once inside he tied her up and waited for the wicked witch to arrive. The moment she leaped through the window, bringing their dinner for the evening, the prince hit her over the head and threw her out again. Then he carried Rapunzel down the rope he had brought with him and forced her to watch while he blinded her broken lover in a field of thorns.

After that they lived happily ever after, of course.

As for me, my body healed, though my eyes never did, and eventually I was found by my sisters, who had come in their various ways to live on this estate.

My own husband?

Oh well, the first time I kissed him he turned into a frog.

There he is, just by your foot. His name's Anton.

On New Year's Day, walking through the deep lanes slatted with light, I saw my husband on horseback, wearing his pink coat. He held his hunting horn to his lips and stood in the stirrups. The hunt rode off; soon they were only as big as holly berries hidden in the green.

I walked on, away from the path, through bushes and brambles, frightening partridges and threading a route between the patient cattle whose hooves in the mud were braceleted with beads of water. My boots were thick with mud. Every step was harder and harder to take. Soon I was lifting my feet as you would to climb a ladder. I was angry and sweating. I wanted to get home but I couldn't hurry. I had to get home to fetch the punch into the great hall and fire it with bright blue flames.

Coming with much difficulty to the top of a hill I looked across the widening valley and saw where the snow still patched the fields like sheets left out to dry. I love the thorn hedges and the trees bare overnight as though some child had stubbornly collected all the leaves, refusing to leave even one for a rival.

I saw my own house, its chimneys smoking, its windows orange.

Another year.

Then a stag and five deer came out of the wood and across the fields in front of my eyes. The fields were fenced and the stag jumped over, turning his head to bring the others. Just for a second he remained in the air, but in that second of flight I remembered my past, when I had been free to fly, long ago, before this gracious landing and a houseful of things.

He disappeared into the dark and I turned my back on the house. The last thing I heard was the sound of the hunt clattering into the courtyard.

I never wanted anyone but her. I wanted to run my finger from the cleft in her chin down the slope of her breasts and across the level plains of her stomach to where I knew she would be wet. I wanted to turn her over and ski the flats of my hands down the slope of her back. I wanted to pioneer the secret passage of her arse.

When she lay down I massaged her feet with mint oil and cut her toenails with silver scissors. I coiled her hair into living snakes and polished her teeth with my saliva.

I pierced her ears and filled them with diamonds. I dropped belladonna into her eyes.

When she was sick I wiped her fever with my own towels and when she cried I kept her tears in a Ming vase.

There was no separation between us. We rose in the morning and slept at night as twins do. We had four arms and four legs, and in the afternoons, when we read in the cool orchard, we did so sitting back to back.

I liked to feel the snake of her spine.

We kissed often, our mouths filling up with tongue and teeth and spit and blood when I bit her lower lip, and with my hands I held her against my hip bone.

We made love often, especially in the afternoons with the blinds half pulled and the cold flag floor against our bodies.

For eighteen years we lived alone in a windy castle and saw no one but each other. Then someone found us and then it was too late.

The man I had married was a woman. They came to burn her. I killed her with a single blow to the head before they reached the gates, and fled that place, and am come here now.

I still have a coil of her hair.

We had been married a few years when a man came to the door selling brushes. My husband was at work so I let the man into our kitchen and gave him something to eat. I asked him to show me his bag and he spread out, as you would imagine, a layer of polishing clothes, a pile of round soaps, combs for the hair, combs for the beard of a billy goat, ordinary household things. I bought one or two useful pieces, then I asked him what he had in his other bag, the one he hadn't opened.

'What was it you wanted?' he asked.

'Poison . . .'

'Yes, for the rats.'

'No, for my husband.'

He seemed unsurprised by my intention to murder and opened the other bag. I looked inside. It was full of little jars and sealed bags.

'Is your husband a big man?'

'Very. He is very, very fat. He is the fattest man in the village. He has always been fat. He has eleven brothers, all of whom are as slender as spring corn. Every day he eats one cow followed by one pig.'

'You are right to kill him,' said the man. 'Put this in his milk at bedtime.'

Bedtime came and I stirred my husband's vat of milk and put in the powder as directed. My husband came crashing over to the stove and gulped the milk in one draught. As soon as he had finished he began to swell up. He swelled out of the house, cracking the roof, and within a few moments had exploded. Out of his belly came a herd of cattle and a fleet of pigs, all blinking in the light and covered in milk.

He had always complained about his digestion.

I rounded them up and set off to find my sisters. I prefer farming to cookery.

He called me Jess because that is the name of the hood which restrains the falcon.

I was his falcon. I hung on his arm and fed at his hand.

He said my nose was sharp and cruel and that my eyes had madness in them. He said I would tear him to pieces if he dealt softly with me.

At night, if he was away, he had me chained to our bed. It was a long chain, long enough for me to use the chamber pot or to stand at the window and wait for the late owls. I love to hear the owls. I love to see the sudden glide of wings spread out for prey, and then the dip and the noise like a lover in pain.

He used the chain when we went riding together. I had a horse as strong as his, and he'd whip the horse from behind and send it charging through the trees, and he'd follow, half a head behind, pulling on the chain and asking me how I liked my ride.

His game was to have me sit astride him when we made love and hold me tight in the small of my back. He said he had to have me above him, in case I picked his eyes out in the faltering candlelight.

I was none of these things, but I became them.

At night, in June I think, I flew off his wrist and tore

his liver from his body, and bit my chain in pieces and left him on the bed with his eyes open.

He looked surprised, I don't know why. As your lover describes you, so you are.

When my husband had an affair with someone else I watched his eyes glaze over when we ate dinner together and I heard him singing to himself without me, and when he tended the garden it was not for me.

He was courteous and polite; he enjoyed being at home, but in the fantasy of his home I was not the one who sat opposite him and laughed at his jokes. He didn't want to change anything; he liked his life. The only thing he wanted to change was me.

It would have been better if he had hated me, or if he had abused me, or if he had packed his new suitcases and left.

As it was he continued to put his arm round me and talk about building a new wall to replace the rotten fence that divided our garden from his vegetable patch. I knew he would never leave our house. He had worked for it.

Day by day I felt myself disappearing. For my husband I was no longer a reality, I was one of the things around him. I was the fence which needed to be replaced. I watched myself in the mirror and saw that I was no longer vivid and exciting. I was worn and grey like an old sweater you can't throw out but won't put on.

He admitted he was in love with her, but he said he loved me.

Translated, that means, I want everything. Translated, that means, I don't want to hurt you yet. Translated, that means, I don't know what to do, give me time.

Why, why should I give you time? What time are

you giving me? I am in a cell waiting to be called for execution.

I loved him and I was in love with him. I didn't use language to make a war-zone of my heart.

'You're so simple and good,' he said, brushing the hair from my face.

He meant, Your emotions are not complex like mine. My dilemma is poetic.

But there was no dilemma. He no longer wanted me, but he wanted our life.

Eventually, when he had been away with her for a few days and returned restless and conciliatory, I decided not to wait in my cell any longer. I went to where he was sleeping in another room and I asked him to leave. Very patiently he asked me to remember that the house was his home, that he couldn't be expected to make himself homeless because he was in love.

'Medea did,' I said, 'and Romeo and Juliet, and Cressida, and Ruth in the Bible.'

He asked me to shut up. He wasn't a hero.

'Then why should I be a heroine?'

He didn't answer, he plucked at the blanket.

I considered my choices.

I could stay and be unhappy and humiliated.

I could leave and be unhappy and dignified.

I could beg him to touch me again.

I could live in hope and die of bitterness.

I took some things and left. It wasn't easy, it was my home too.

I hear he's replaced the back fence.

As soon as we were married my husband took me to his family home, far from anyone I knew. He promised me a companion and a library but asked me never to interrupt him during the day. I saw him at night for a few hours, over our dinner, though he never ate much. Nor did he seem anxious to decorate my bed with his body.

I asked him what he did during the day and he said he exercised his mind over the problems of Creation. I realized this could take some time and resigned myself to forgetting the rules of normal life.

One night, as we were eating a pigeon I had shot, my husband stood up and said, 'There is a black tower where wild beasts live. The tower has no windows and no doors. No one may enter or leave. At the top of the tower is a cage whose bars are made of bone. From this cage a trapped spirit peeps at the sun. The tower is my body, the cage is my skull, the spirit singing to comfort itself is me. But I am not comforted, I am alone. Kill me.'

I did as he asked. I smashed his skull with a silver candlestick and I heard a hissing noise like damp wood on the fire. I opened the doors and dragged his body into the air, and in the air he flew away.

I still see him sometimes, but only in the distance.

Their stories ended, the twelve dancing princesses invited me to spend the night as their guest.

'Someone is missing,' I said. 'There are only eleven of you and I have only heard eleven stories. Where is your sister?'

They looked at one another, then the eldest said, 'Our youngest sister is not here. She never came to live with us. On her wedding day to the prince who had discovered our secret, she flew from the altar like a bird from a snare and walked a tightrope between the steeple of the church and the mast of a ship weighing anchor in the bay.

'She was, of all of us, the best dancer, the one who

made her body into shapes we could not follow. She did it for pleasure, but there was something more for her; she did it because any other life would have been a lie. She didn't burn in secret with a passion she could not express; she shone.

'We have not seen her for years and years, not since that day when we were dressed in red with our black hair unbraided. She must be old now, she must be stiff. Her body can only be a memory. The body she has will not be the body she had.'

'Do you remember,' said another sister, 'how light she was? She was so light that she could climb down a rope, cut it and tie it again in mid-air without plunging to her death. The winds supported her.'

'What was her name?'

'Fortunata.'

Virginia Woolf

extract from

To The Lighthouse

The first part of Virginia Woolf's major work, To The Lighthouse, *introduces the Ramsay family and their guests holidaying by the sea as they do each summer. In prose as bold as it is sensitive, the characters of husband and wife and their children are clearly established in the reader's mind – so that the sense of loss which comes with the passing of time in the novel, bringing as it does the death of Mrs Ramsay, of her daughter in pregnancy, of her son in the First World War, may come close to being as deeply felt a grief as it undoubtedly must have been for Virginia Woolf herself, looking back to her own childhood and to the deaths of her mother and brother. Lily Briscoe, Mrs Ramsay's loving antagonist in that she is dedicated to her painting rather than to a man in marriage, survives to celebrate the people she has known and to reassert the triumph of art.*

III

The Lighthouse

I

What does it mean then, what can it all mean? Lily Briscoe asked herself, wondering whether, since she had been left alone, it behoved her to go to the kitchen to fetch another cup of coffee or wait here. What does it mean? – a catchword that was, caught up from some book, fitting her thought loosely, for she could not, this first morning with the Ramsays, contract her feelings, could only make a phrase resound to cover the blankness of her mind until these vapours had shrunk. For really, what did she feel, come back after all these years and Mrs Ramsay dead? Nothing, nothing – nothing that she could express at all.

She had come late last night when it was all mysterious, dark. Now she was awake, at her old place at the breakfast table, but alone. It was very early too, not yet eight. There was this expedition – they were going to the Lighthouse, Mr Ramsay, Cam and James. They should have gone already – they had to catch the tide or something. And Cam was not ready and James was not ready and Nancy had forgotten to order the sandwiches and Mr Ramsay had lost his temper and banged out of the room.

'What's the use of going now?' he had stormed.

Nancy had vanished. There he was, marching up and down the terrace in a rage. One seemed to hear doors slamming and voices calling all over the house. Now Nancy burst in, and asked, looking round the room, in a queer half dazed, half desperate way, 'What does one send to the Lighthouse?' as if she were forcing herself to do what she despaired of ever being able to do.

What does one send to the Lighthouse indeed! At any other time Lily could have suggested reasonably tea, tobacco, newspapers. But this morning everything seemed so extraordinarily queer that a question like Nancy's – What does one send to the Lighthouse? – opened doors in one's mind that went banging and swinging to and fro and made one keep asking, in a stupefied gape, What does one send? What does one do? Why is one sitting here after all?

Sitting alone (for Nancy went out again) among the clean cups at the long table she felt cut off from other people, and able only to go on watching, asking, wondering. The house, the place, the morning, all seemed strangers to her. She had no attachment here, she felt, no relations with it, anything might happen, and whatever did happen, a step outside, a voice calling ('It's not in the cupboard; it's on the landing,' someone cried), was a question, as if the link that usually bound things together had been cut, and they floated up here, down there, off, anyhow. How aimless it was, how chaotic, how unreal it was, she thought, looking at her empty coffee cup. Mrs Ramsay dead; Andrew killed; Prue dead too – repeat it as she might, it roused no feeling in her. And we all get together in a house like this on a morning like this, she said, looking out of the window – it was a beautiful still day.

Suddenly Mr Ramsay raised his head as he passed and looked straight at her, with his distraught wild gaze which was yet so penetrating, as if he saw you, for one second, for the first time, for ever; and she pretended to drink out of her empty coffee cup so as to escape him – to escape his demand on her, to put aside a moment longer that imperious need. And he shook his head at her, and strode on ('Alone' she heard him say, 'Perished' she heard him say) and like everything else this strange morning the words became symbols, wrote themselves all over the grey-green walls. If only she could put them together, she felt, write them out in some sentence, then she would have got at the truth of things. Old Mr Carmichael came padding softly in, fetched his coffee, took his cup and made off to sit in the sun. The extraordinary unreality was frightening; but it was also exciting. Going to the Lighthouse. But what does one send to the Lighthouse? Perished. Alone. The grey-green light on the wall opposite. The empty places. Such were some of the parts, but how bring them together? she asked. As if any interruption would break the frail shape she was building on the table she turned her back to the window lest Mr Ramsay should see her. She must escape somehow, be alone somewhere. Suddenly she remembered. When she had sat there last ten years ago there had been a little sprig or leaf pattern on the table-cloth, which she had looked at in a moment of revelation. There had been a problem about a foreground of a picture. Move the tree to the middle, she had said. She had never finished that picture. It had been knocking about in her mind all these years. She would paint that picture now. Where were her paints, she wondered? Her paints, yes. She had left them in the hall last night. She would start at once. She got up quickly, before Mr Ramsay turned.

She fetched herself a chair. She pitched her easel with her precise old maidish movements on the edge of the lawn, not too close to Mr Carmichael, but close enough for his protection. Yes, it must have been precisely here that she had stood ten years ago. There was the wall; the hedge; the tree. The question was of some relation between those masses. She had borne it in her mind all these years. It seemed as if the solution had come to her: she knew now what she wanted to do.

But with Mr Ramsay bearing down on her, she could do nothing. Every time he approached – he was walking up and down the terrace – ruin approached, chaos approached. She could not paint. She stooped, she turned; she took up this rag; she squeezed that tube. But all she did was to ward him off a moment. He made it impossible for her to do anything. For if she gave him the least chance, if he saw her disengaged a moment, looking his way a moment, he would be on her, saying, as he had said last night, 'You find us much changed.' Last night he had got up and stopped before her, and said that. Dumb and staring though they had all sat, the six children whom they used to call after the Kings and Queens of England – the Red, the Fair, the Wicked, the Ruthless – she felt how they raged under it. Kind old Mrs Beckwith said something sensible. But it was a house full of unrelated passions – she had felt that all the evening. And on top of this chaos Mr Ramsay got up, pressed her hand, and said: 'You will find us much changed,' and none of them had moved or had spoken; but had sat there as if they were forced to let him say it. Only James (certainly the Sullen) scowled at the lamp; and Cam screwed her handkerchief round her finger.

Then he reminded them that they were going to the Lighthouse tomorrow. They must be ready, in the hall, on the stroke of half-past seven. Then, with his hand on the door, he stopped; he turned upon them. Did they not want to go? he demanded. Had they dared say No (he had some reason for wanting it) he would have flung himself tragically backwards into the bitter waters of despair. Such a gift he had for gesture. He looked like a king in exile. Doggedly James said yes. Cam stumbled more wretchedly. Yes, oh yes, they'd both be ready, they said. And it struck her, this was tragedy — not palls, dust, and the shroud; but children coerced, their spirits subdued. James was sixteen, Cam seventeen, perhaps. She had looked round for someone who was not there, for Mrs Ramsay, presumably. But there was only kind Mrs Beckwith turning over her sketches under the lamp. Then, being tired, her mind still rising and falling with the sea, the taste and smell that places have after long absence possessing her, the candles wavering in her eyes, she had lost herself and gone under. It was a wonderful night, starlit; the waves sounded as they went upstairs; the moon surprised them, enormous, pale, as they passed the staircase window. She had slept at once.

She set her clean canvas firmly upon the easel, as a barrier, frail, but she hoped sufficiently substantial to ward off Mr Ramsay and his exactingness. She did her best to look, when his back was turned, at her picture; that line there, that mass there. But it was out of the question. Let him be fifty feet away, let him not even speak to you, let him not even see you, he permeated, he prevailed he imposed himself. He changed everything. She could not see the colour; she could not see the lines; even with his back turned to her, she could only think,

But he'll be down on me in a moment, demanding — something she felt she could not give him. She rejected one brush; she chose another. When would those children come? When would they all be off? she fidgeted. That man, she thought, her anger rising in her, never gave; that man took. She, on the other hand, would be forced to give. Mrs Ramsay had given. Giving, giving, giving, she had died — and had left all this. Really, she was angry with Mrs Ramsay. With the brush slightly trembling in her fingers she looked at the hedge, the step, the wall. It was all Mrs Ramsay's doing. She was dead. Here was Lily, at forty-four, wasting her time, unable to do a thing, standing there, playing at painting, playing at the one thing one did not play at, and it was all Mrs Ramsay's fault. She was dead. The step where she used to sit was empty. She was dead.

But why repeat this over and over again? Why be always trying to bring up some feeling she had not got? There was a kind of blasphemy in it. It was all dry: all withered: all spent. They ought not to have asked her; she ought not to have come. One can't waste one's time at forty-four, she thought. She hated playing at painting. A brush, the one dependable thing in a world of strife, ruin, chaos — that one should not play with, knowingly even: she detested it. But he made her. You shan't touch your canvas, he seemed to say, bearing down on her, till you've given me what I want of you. Here he was, close upon her again, greedy, distraught. Well, thought Lily in despair, letting her right hand fall at her side, it would be simpler then to have it over. Surely she could imitate from recollection the glow, the rhapsody, the self-surrender she had seen on so many women's faces (on Mrs Ramsay's, for instance) when on some occasion like this they blazed up — she could remember the look on Mrs Ramsay's face – into a rapture of sympathy, of delight in the reward they had, which, though the reason of it escaped her, evidently conferred on them the most supreme bliss of which human nature was capable. Here he was, stopped by her side. She would give him what she could.

2

She seemed to have shrivelled slightly, he thought. She looked a little skimpy, wispy; but not unattractive. He liked her. There had been some talk of her marrying William Bankes once, but nothing had come of it. His wife had been fond of her. He had been a little out of temper too at breakfast. And then, and then – this was one of those moments when an enormous need urged him, without being conscious what it was, to approach any woman, to force them, he did not care how, his need was so great, to give him what he wanted: sympathy.

Was anybody looking after her? he said. Had she everything she wanted?

'Oh, thanks, everything,' said Lily Briscoe nervously. No; she could not do it. She ought to have floated off instantly upon some wave of sympathetic expansion: the pressure on her was tremendous. But she remained stuck. There was an awful pause. They both looked at the sea. Why, thought Mr Ramsay, should she look at the sea when I am here? She hoped it would be calm enough for them to land at the Lighthouse, she said. The Lighthouse! The Lighthouse! What's that got to do with it? he thought impatiently. Instantly, with the force of some primeval gust (for really he could not restrain himself any longer), there issued from him such a groan that any other woman in the whole world would have done something, said something – all except myself, thought Lily, girding at herself bitterly, who am not a woman, but a peevish, ill-tempered, dried-up old maid presumably.

Mr Ramsay sighed to the full. He waited. Was she not going to say anything? Did she not see what he wanted from her? Then he said he had a particular reason for wanting to go to the Lighthouse. His wife used to send the men things. There was a poor boy with a tuberculous hip, the lightkeeper's son. He sighed profoundly. He sighed significantly. All Lily wished was that this enormous flood of grief, this insatiable hunger for sympathy, this demand that she should surrender herself up to him entirely, and even so he had sorrows enough to keep her supplied for ever, should leave her, should be diverted (she kept looking at the house, hoping for an interruption) before it swept her down in its flow.

'Such expeditions,' said Mr Ramsay, scraping the ground with his toe, 'are very painful.' Still Lily said nothing. (She is a stock, she is a stone, he said to himself.) 'They are very exhausting,' he said, looking, with a sickly look that nauseated her (he was acting, she felt, this great man was dramatizing himself), at his beautiful hands. It was horrible, it was indecent. Would they never come, she asked, for she could not sustain this enormous weight of sorrow, support these heavy draperies of grief (he had assumed a pose of extreme decrepitude; he even tottered a little as he stood there) a moment longer.

Still she could say nothing; the whole horizon seemed swept bare of objects to talk about; could only feel, amazedly, as Mr Ramsay stood there, how his gaze seemed to fall dolefully over the sunny grass and discolour it, and cast over the rubicund, drowsy, entirely contented figure of Mr Carmichael, reading a French novel on a deck-chair, a veil of crape, as if such an existence, flaunting its prosperity in a world of woe, were enough to provoke the most dismal thoughts of all. Look at him, he seemed to be saying, look at me; and indeed, all the time he was feeling, Think of me, think of me. Ah, could that bulk only be wafted alongside of them, Lily wished; had she only pitched her easel a yard or two closer to him; a man, any man, would staunch this effusion, would stop these lamentations. A woman, she had provoked this horror; a woman, she should have known how to deal with it. It was immensely to her discredit, sexually, to stand there dumb. One said – what did one say? – Oh, Mr Ramsay! Dear Mr Ramsay! That was what that kind old lady who sketched, Mrs Beckwith, would have said instantly, and rightly. But no. They stood there, isolated from the rest of the world. His immense self-pity, his demand for sympathy poured and spread itself in pools at her feet, and all she did, miserable sinner that she was, was to draw her skirts a little closer round her ankles, lest she should get wet. In complete silence she stood there, grasping her paint brush.

Heaven could never be sufficiently praised! She heard sounds in the house. James and Cam must be coming. But Mr Ramsay, as if he knew that his time ran short, exerted upon her solitary figure the immense pressure of his concentrated woe; his age; his frailty; his desolation; when suddenly, tossing his head impatiently, in his annoyance – for, after all, what woman could resist him? – he noticed that his boot-laces were untied. Remarkable boots they were too, Lily thought, looking down at them: sculptured; colossal; like everything that Mr Ramsay wore, from his frayed tie to his half-buttoned waistcoat, his own indisputably. She could see them walking to his room of their own accord, expressive in his absence of pathos, surliness, ill-temper, charm.

'What beautiful boots!' she exclaimed. She was ashamed of herself. To praise his boots when he asked her to solace his soul; when he had shown her his bleeding hands, his lacerated heart, and asked her to pity them, then to say, cheerfully, 'Ah, but what beautiful boots you wear!' deserved, she knew, and she looked up expecting to get it, in one of his sudden roars of ill-temper, complete annihilation.

Instead, Mr Ramsay smiled. His pall, his draperies, his infirmities fell from him. Ah yes, he said, holding his foot up for her to look at, they were first-rate boots. There was only one man in England who could make boots like that. Boots are among the chief curses of mankind, he said. 'Bootmakers make it their business,' he exclaimed, 'to cripple and torture the human foot.' They are also the most obstinate and perverse of mankind. It had taken him the best part of his youth to get boots made as they should be made. He would have her observe (he lifted his right foot and then his left) that she had never seen boots made quite that shape before. They were made of the finest leather in the world, also. Most leather was mere brown paper and cardboard. He looked complacently at his foot, still held in the air. They had reached, she felt, a sunny island where peace dwelt, sanity reigned and the sun for ever shone, the blessed island of good boots. Her heart warmed to him. 'Now let me see if you can tie a knot,' he said. He poohpoohed her feeble system. He showed her his own invention. Once you tied it, it never came undone. Three times he knotted her shoe; three times he unknotted it.

Why, at this completely inappropriate moment, when he was stooping over her shoe, should she be so tormented with sympathy for him that, as she stooped too, the blood rushed to her face, and, thinking of her callousness (she had called him a play-actor) she felt her eyes swell and tingle with tears? Thus occupied he seemed to her a figure of infinite pathos. He tied knots. He bought boots. There was no helping Mr Ramsay on the journey he was going. But now just as she wished to say something, could have said something, perhaps, here they were – Cam and James. They appeared on the terrace. They came, lagging, side by side, a serious, melancholy couple.

But why was it like *that* that they came? She could not help feeling annoyed with them; they might have come more cheerfully; they might have given him what, now that they were off, she would not have the chance of giving him. For she felt a sudden emptiness; a frustration. Her feeling had come too late; there it was ready; but he no longer needed it. He had become a very distinguished, elderly man, who had no need of her whatsoever. She felt snubbed. He slung a knapsack round his shoulders. He shared out the parcels – there were a number of them, ill tied, in brown paper. He sent Cam for a cloak. He had all the appearance of a leader making ready for an expedition. Then, wheeling about, he led the way with his firm military tread, in those wonderful boots, carrying brown paper parcels, down the path, his children following him. They looked, she thought, as if fate had devoted them to some stern enterprise, and they went to it, still young enough to be drawn acquiescent in their father's wake, obediently, but with a pallor in their eyes which made her feel that they suffered something beyond their years in silence.

So they passed the edge of the lawn, and it seemed to Lily that she watched a procession go, drawn on by some stress of common feeling which made it, faltering and flagging as it was, a little company bound together and strangely impressive to her. Politely, but very distantly, Mr Ramsay raised his hand and saluted her as they passed.

But what a face, she thought, immediately finding the sympathy which she had not been asked to give troubling her for expression. What had made it like that? Thinking, night after night, she supposed – about the reality of kitchen tables, she added, remembering the symbol which in her vagueness as to what Mr Ramsay did think about Andrew had given her. (He had been killed by the splinter of a shell instantly, she bethought her.) The kitchen table was something visionary, austere; something bare, hard, not ornamental. There was no colour to it; it was all edges and angles; it was uncompromisingly plain. But Mr Ramsay kept always his eyes fixed upon it, never allowed himself to be distracted or deluded, until his face became worn too and ascetic and partook of this unornamented beauty which so deeply impressed her. Then, she recalled (standing where he had left her, holding her brush), worries had fretted it – not so nobly. He must have had his doubts about that table, she supposed; whether the table was a real table; whether it was worth the time he gave to it; whether he was able after all to find it. He had had doubts, she felt, or he would have asked less of people. That was what they talked about late at night sometimes, she suspected; and then next day Mrs Ramsay looked tired, and Lily flew into a rage with him over some absurd little thing. But now he had nobody to talk to about that table, or his boots, or his knots; and he was like a lion seeking whom he could devour, and his face had that touch of desperation, of exaggeration in it which alarmed her, and made her pull her skirts about her. And then, she recalled, there was that sudden revivification, that sudden flare (when she praised his boots), that sudden recovery of vitality and interest in ordinary human things, which too passed and changed (for he was always changing, and hid nothing) into that other final phase which was new to her and had, she owned, made herself ashamed of her own irritability, when it seemed as if he had shed worries and ambitions, and the hope of sympathy and the desire for praise, had entered some other region, was drawn on, as if by curiosity, in dumb colloquy, whether with himself or another, at the head of that little procession out of one's range. An extraordinary face! The gate banged.

3

So they're gone, she thought, sighing with relief and disappointment. Her sympathy seemed to fly back in her face, like a bramble sprung. She felt curiously divided, as if one part of her were drawn out there – it was a still day, hazy; the Lighthouse looked this morning at an immense distance; the other had fixed itself doggedly, solidly, here on the lawn. She saw her canvas as if it had floated up and placed itself white and uncompromising directly before her. It seemed to rebuke her with its cold stare for all his hurry and agitation; this folly and waste of emotion; it drastically recalled her and spread through her mind first a peace, as her disorderly sensations (he had gone and she had been so sorry for him and she had said nothing) trooped off the field;

and then, emptiness. She looked blankly at the canvas, with its uncompromising white stare; from the canvas to the garden. There was something (she stood screwing up her little Chinese eyes in her small puckered face) something she remembered in the relations of those lines cutting across, slicing down, and in the mass of the hedge with its green cave of blues and browns, which had stayed in her mind; which had tied a knot in her mind so that at odds and ends of time, involuntarily, as she walked along the Brompton Road, as she brushed her hair, she found herself painting that picture, passing her eye over it, and untying the knot in imagination. But there was all the difference in the world between this planning airily away from the canvas, and actually taking her brush and making the first mark.

She had taken the wrong brush in her agitation at Mr Ramsay's presence, and her easel, rammed into the earth so nervously, was at the wrong angle. And now that she had put that right, and in so doing had subdued the impertinences and irrelevances that plucked her attention and made her remember how she was such and such a person, had such and such relations to people, she took her hand and raised her brush. For a moment it stayed trembling in a painful but exciting ecstasy in the air. Where to begin? – that was the question; at what point to make the first mark? One line placed on the canvas committed her to innumerable risks, to frequent and irrevocable decisions. All that in idea seemed simple became in practice immediately complex; as the waves shape themselves symmetrically from the cliff top, but to the swimmer among them are divided by steep gulfs, and foaming crests. Still the risk must be run; the mark made.

With a curious physical sensation, as if she were urged

forward and at the same time must hold herself back, she made her first quick decisive stroke. The brush descended. It flickered brown over the white canvas; it left a running mark. A second time she did it – a third time. And so pausing and so flickering, she attained a dancing rhythmical movement, as if the pauses were one part of the rhythm and the strokes another, and all were related; and so, lightly and swiftly pausing, striking, she scored her canvas with brown running nervous lines which had no sooner settled there than they enclosed (she felt it looming out at her) a space. Down in the hollow of one wave she saw the next wave towering higher and higher above her. For what could be more formidable than that space? Here she was again, she thought, stepping back to look at it, drawn out of gossip, out of living, out of community with people into the presence of this formidable ancient enemy of hers – this other thing, this truth, this reality, which suddenly laid hands on her, emerged stark at the back of appearances and commanded her attention. She was half unwilling, half reluctant. Why always be drawn out and haled away? Why not left in peace, to talk to Mr Carmichael on the lawn? It was an exacting form of intercourse anyhow. Other worshipful objects were content with worship; men, women, God, all let one kneel prostrate; but this form, were it only the shape of a white lampshade looming on a wicker table, roused one to perpetual combat, challenged one to a fight in which one was bound to be worsted. Always (it was in her nature, or in her sex, she did not know which) before she exchanged the fluidity of life for the concentration of painting she had a few moments of nakedness when she seemed like an unborn soul, a soul reft of body, hesitating on some windy pinnacle and exposed without protection to all the blasts of doubt. Why then did she do it? She looked at the canvas, lightly scored with running lines. It would be hung in the servants' bedrooms. It would be rolled up and stuffed under a sofa. What was the good of doing it then, and she heard some voice saying she couldn't paint, saying she couldn't create, as if she were caught up in one of those habitual currents which after a certain time forms experience in the mind, so that one repeats words without being aware any longer who originally spoke them.

Can't paint, can't write, she murmured monotonously, anxiously considering what her plan of attack should be. For the mass loomed before her; it protruded; she felt it pressing on her eyeballs. Then, as if some juice necessary for the lubrication of her faculties were spontaneously squirted, she began precariously dipping among the blues and umbers, moving her brush hither and thither, but it was now heavier and went slower, as if it had fallen in with some rhythm which was dictated to her (she kept looking at the hedge, at the canvas) by what she saw, so that while her hand quivered with life, this rhythm was strong enough to bear her along with it on its current. Certainly she was losing consciousness of outer things. And as she lost consciousness of outer things, and her name and her personality and her appearance, and whether Mr Carmichael was there or not, her mind kept throwing up from its depths, scenes, and names, and sayings, and memories and ideas, like a fountain spurting over that glaring, hideously difficult white space, while she modelled it with greens and blues.

Charles Tansley used to say that, she remembered, women can't paint, can't write. Coming up behind her he had stood close beside her, a thing she hated, as she painted here on this very spot. 'Shag tobacco,' he said, 'fivepence an ounce,' parading his poverty, his principles. (But the war had drawn the sting of her femininity. Poor devils, one thought, poor devils of both sexes, getting into such messes.) He was always carrying a book about under his arm – a purple book. He 'worked'. He sat, she remembered, working in a blaze of sun. At dinner he would sit right in the middle of the view. And then, she reflected, there was that scene on the beach. One must remember that. It was a windy morning. They had all gone to the beach. Mrs Ramsay sat and wrote letters by a rock. She wrote and wrote. 'Oh,' she said, looking up at last at something floating in the sea, 'is it a lobster pot? Is it an upturned boat?' She was so shortsighted that she could not see, and then Charles Tansley became as nice as he could possibly be. He began playing ducks and drakes. They chose little flat black stones and sent them skipping over the waves. Every now and then Mrs Ramsay looked up over her spectacles and laughed at them. What they said she could not remember, but only she and Charles throwing stones and getting on very well all of a sudden and Mrs Ramsay watching them. She was highly conscious of that. Mrs Ramsay, she thought, stepping back and screwing up her eyes. (It must have altered the design a good deal when she was sitting on the step with James. There must have been a shadow.) Mrs Ramsay. When she thought of herself and Charles throwing ducks and drakes and of the whole scene on the beach, it seemed to depend somehow upon Mrs Ramsay sitting under the rock, with a pad on her knee, writing letters. (She wrote innumerable letters, and sometimes the wind took them and she and Charles just saved a page from the sea.) But what a power was in the human soul! she thought. That woman sitting there, writing under the rock, resolved everything into simplicity; made these angers, irritations, fall off like old rags; she brought together this and that and then this, and so made out of that miserable silliness and spite (she and Charles squabbling, sparring, had been silly and spiteful) something – this scene on the beach for example, this moment of friendship and liking – which survived, after all these years, complete, so that she dipped into it to refashion her memory of him, and it stayed in the mind almost like a work of art.

'Like a work of art,' she repeated, looking from her canvas to the drawing-room steps and back again. She must rest for a moment. And, resting, looking from one to the other vaguely, the old question which traversed the sky of the soul perpetually, the vast, the general question which was apt to particularize itself at such moments as these, when she released faculties that had been on the strain, stood over her, paused over her, darkened over her. What is the meaning of life? That was all – a simple question; one that tended to close in on one with years. The great revelation had never come. The great revelation perhaps never did come. Instead there were little daily miracles, illuminations, matches struck unexpectedly in the dark; here was one. This, that, and the other; herself and Charles Tansley and the breaking wave; Mrs Ramsay bringing them together; Mrs Ramsay saying 'Life stand still here'; Mrs Ramsay making of the moment something permanent (as in another sphere Lily herself tried to make of the moment something permanent) – this was of the nature of a revelation. In the midst of chaos there was shape; this eternal passing and flowing (she looked at the clouds going and the leaves shaking) was struck into stability. Life stand still here, Mrs Ramsay said.

'Mrs Ramsay! Mrs Ramsay!' she repeated. She owed this revelation to her.

All was silence. Nobody seemed yet to be stirring in the house. She looked at it there sleeping in the early sunlight with its windows green and blue with the reflected leaves. The faint thought she was thinking of Mrs Ramsay seemed in consonance with this quiet house; this smoke; this fine early morning air. Faint and unreal, it was amazingly pure and exciting. She hoped nobody would open the window or come out of the house, but that she might be left alone to go on thinking, to go on painting. She turned to her canvas. But impelled by some curiosity, driven by the discomfort of the sympathy which she held undischarged, she walked a pace or so to the end of the lawn to see whether, down there on the beach, she could see that little company setting sail. Down there among the little boats which floated, some with their sails furled, some slowly, for it was very calm, moving away, there was one rather apart from the others. The sail was even now being hoisted. She decided that there in that very distant and entirely silent little boat Mr Ramsay was sitting with Cam and James. Now they had got the sail up; now after a little flagging and hesitation the sails filled and, shrouded in profound silence, she watched the boat take its way with deliberation past the other boats out to sea.

4

The sails flapped over their heads. The water chuckled and slapped the sides of the boat, which drowsed motionless in the sun. Now and then the sails rippled with a little breeze in them, but the ripple ran over them and ceased. The boat made no motion at all. Mr Ramsay sat in the middle of the boat. He would be impatient in a moment, James thought, and Cam thought, looking at their father, who sat in the middle of the boat between them (James steered; Cam sat alone in the bow) with his legs tightly curled. He hated hanging about. Sure enough, after fidgeting a second or two, he said something sharp to Macalister's boy, who got out his oars and began to row. But their father, they knew, would never be content until they were flying along. He would keep looking for a breeze, fidgeting, saying things under his breath, which Macalister and Macalister's boy would overhear, and they would both be made horribly uncomfortable. He had made them come. He had forced them to come. In their anger they hoped that the breeze would never rise, that he might be thwarted in every possible way, since he had forced them to come against their wills.

All the way down to the beach they had lagged behind together, though he bade them 'Walk up, walk up,' without speaking. Their heads were bent down, their heads were pressed down by some remorseless gale. Speak to him they could not. They must come; they must follow. They must walk behind him carrying brown-paper parcels. But they vowed, in silence, as they walked, to stand by each other and carry out the great compact – to resist tyranny to the death. So there they would sit, one at one end of the boat, one at the other, in silence. They would say nothing, only look at him now and then where he sat with his legs twisted, frowning and fidgeting, and pishing and pshawing and muttering things to himself, and waiting impatiently for a breeze. And they hoped it would be calm. They hoped he would be thwarted. They hoped the whole expedition would

To The Lighthouse

fail, and they would have to put back, with their parcels, to the beach.

But now, when Macalister's boy had rowed a little way out, the sails slowly swung round, the boat quickened itself, flattened itself, and shot off. Instantly, as if some great strain had been relieved, Mr Ramsay uncurled his legs, took out his tobacco pouch, handed it with a little grunt to Macalister, and felt, they knew, for all they suffered, perfectly content. Now they would sail on for hours like this, and Mr Ramsay would ask old Macalister a question – about the great storm last winter probably – and old Macalister would answer it, and they would puff their pipes together, and Macalister would take a tarry rope in his fingers, tying or untying some knot, and the boy would fish, and never say a word to any one. James would be forced to keep his eye all the time on the sail. For if he forgot, then the sail puckered, and shivered, and the boat slackened, and Mr Ramsay would say sharply, 'Look out! Look out!' and old Macalister would turn slowly on his seat. So they heard Mr Ramsay asking some question about the great storm at Christmas. 'She comes driving round the point,' old Macalister said, describing the great storm last Christmas, when ten ships had been driven into the bay for shelter, and he had seen 'one there, one there, one there' (he pointed slowly round the bay. Mr Ramsay followed him, turning his head). He had seen three men clinging to the mast. Then she was gone. 'And at last we shoved her off,' he went on (but in their anger and their silence they only caught a word here and there, sitting at opposite ends of the boat, united by their compact to fight tyranny to the death). At last they had shoved her off, they had launched the lifeboat, and they had got her out past the point – Macalister told the story;

and though they only caught a word here and there, they were conscious all the time of their father – how he leant forward, how he brought his voice into tune with Macalister's voice; how, puffing at his pipe, and looking there and there where Macalister pointed, he relished the thought of the storm and the dark night and the fishermen striving there. He liked that men should labour and sweat on the windy beach at night, pitting muscle and brain against the waves and the wind; he liked men to work like that, and women to keep house, and sit beside sleeping children indoors, while men were drowned, out there in a storm. So James could tell, so Cam could tell (they looked at him, they looked at each other), from his toss and his vigilance and the ring in his voice, and the little tinge of Scottish accent which came into his voice, making him seem like a peasant himself, as he questioned Macalister about the eleven ships that had been driven into the bay in a storm. Three had sunk.

He looked proudly where Macalister pointed; and Cam thought, feeling proud of him without knowing quite why, had he been there he would have launched the lifeboat, he would have reached the wreck, Cam thought. He was so brave, he was so adventurous, Cam thought. But she remembered. There was the compact; to resist tyranny to the death. Their grievance weighed them down. They had been forced; they had been bidden. He had borne them down once more with his gloom and his authority, making them do his bidding, on this fine morning, come, because he wished it, carrying these parcels, to the Lighthouse; take part in those rites he went through for his own pleasure in memory of dead people, which they hated, so that they lagged after him, and all the pleasure of the day was spoilt.

To The Lighthouse

Yes, the breeze was freshening. The boat was leaning, the water was sliced sharply and fell away in green cascades, in bubbles, in cataracts. Cam looked down into the foam, into the sea with all its treasure in it, and its speed hypnotized her, and the tie between her and James sagged a little. It slackened a little. She began to think, How fast it goes. Where are we going? and the movement hypnotized her, while James, with his eye fixed on the sail and on the horizon, steered grimly. But he began to think as he steered that he might escape; he might be quit of it all. They might land somewhere; and be free then. Both of them, looking at each other for a moment, had a sense of escape and exaltation, what with the speed and the change. But the breeze bred in Mr Ramsay too the same excitement, and, as old Macalister turned to fling his line overboard, he cried aloud, 'We perished,' and then again, 'each alone.' And then with his usual spasm of repentance or shyness, pulled himself up, and waved his hand towards the shore.

'See the little house,' he said pointing, wishing Cam to look. She raised herself reluctantly and looked. But which was it? She could no longer make out, there on the hillside, which was their house. All looked distant and peaceful and strange. The shore seemed refined, far away, unreal. Already the little distance they had sailed had put them far from it and given it the changed look, the composed look, of something receding in which one has no longer any part. Which was their house? She could not see it.

'But I beneath a rougher sea,' Mr Ramsay murmured. He had found the house and so seeing it, he had also seen himself there; he had seen himself walking on the terrace, alone. He was walking up and down between the urns; and he seemed to himself very old, and bowed. Sitting in the boat he bowed, he crouched himself, acting instantly his part – the part of a desolate man, widowed, bereft; and so called up before him in hosts people sympathizing with him; staged for himself as he sat in the boat, a little drama; which required of him decrepitude and exhaustion and sorrow (he raised his hands and looked at the thinness of them, to confirm his dream) and then there was given him in abundance women's sympathy, and he imagined how they would soothe him and sympathize with him, and so getting in his dream some reflection of the exquisite pleasure women's sympathy was to him, he sighed and said gently and mournfully,

> But I beneath a rougher sea
> Was whelmed in deeper gulfs than he,

so that the mournful words were heard quite clearly by them all. Cam half started on her seat. It shocked her – it outraged her. The movement roused her father; and he shuddered, and broke off, exclaiming: 'Look! Look!' so urgently that James also turned his head to look over his shoulder at the island. They all looked. They looked at the island.

But Cam could see nothing. She was thinking how all those paths and the lawn, thick and knotted with the lives they had lived there, were gone: were rubbed out; were past; were unreal, and now this was real; the boat and the sail with its patch; Macalister with his ear-rings; the noise of the waves – all this was real. Thinking this, she was murmuring to herself 'We perished, each alone', for her father's words broke and broke again in her mind, when her father, seeing her gazing so vaguely, began to tease her. Didn't she know the points of the

To The Lighthouse

compass? he asked. Didn't she know the North from the South? Did she really think they lived right out there? And he pointed again, and showed her where their house was, there, by those trees. He wished she would try to be more accurate, he said: 'Tell me — which is East, which is West?' he said, half laughing at her, half scolding her, for he could not understand the state of mind of anyone, not absolutely imbecile, who did not know the points of the compass. Yet she did not know. And seeing her gazing, with her vague, now rather frightened, eyes fixed where no house was Mr Ramsay forgot his dream; how he walked up and down between the urns on the terrace; how the arms were stretched out to him. He thought, women are always like that; the vagueness of their minds is hopeless; it was a thing he had never been able to understand; but so it was. It had been so with her — his wife. They could not keep anything clearly fixed in their minds. But he had been wrong to be angry with her; moreover, did he not rather like this vagueness in women? It was part of their extraordinary charm. I will make her smile at me, he thought. She looks frightened. She was so silent. He clutched his fingers, and determined that his voice and his face and all the quick expressive gestures which had been at his command making people pity him and praise him all these years should subdue themselves. He would make her smile at him. He would find some simple easy thing to say to her. But what? For, wrapped up in his work as he was, he forgot the sort of thing one said. There was a puppy. They had a puppy. Who was looking after the puppy today? he asked. Yes, thought James pitilessly, seeing his sister's head against the sail, now she will give way. I shall be left to fight the tyrant alone. The compact would be left to him to carry out. Cam would never resist tyranny to the death, he thought grimly, watching her face, sad, sulky, yielding. And as sometimes happens when a cloud falls on a green hillside and gravity descends and there among all the surrounding hills is gloom and sorrow, and it seems as if the hills themselves must ponder the fate of the clouded, the darkened, either in pity, or maliciously rejoicing in her dismay: so Cam now felt herself overcast, as she sat there among calm, resolute people and wondered how to answer her father about the puppy; how to resist his entreaty – forgive me, care for me; while James the lawgiver, with the tablet of eternal wisdom laid open on his knee (his hand on the tiller had become symbolical to her), said, Resist him. Fight him. He said so rightly; justly. For they must fight tyranny to the death, she thought. Of all human qualities she reverenced justice most. Her brother was most god-like, her father most suppliant. And to which did she yield, she thought, sitting between them, gazing at the shore whose points were all unknown to her, and thinking how the lawn and the terrace and the house were smoothed away now and peace dwelt there.

'Jasper,' she said sullenly. He'd look after the puppy.

And what was she going to call him? her father persisted. He had had a dog when he was a little boy, called Frisk. She'll give way, James thought, as he watched a look come upon her face, a look he remembered. They look down, he thought, at their knitting or something. Then suddenly they look up. There was a flash of blue, he remembered, and then somebody sitting with him laughed, surrendered, and he was very angry. It must have been his mother, he thought, sitting on a low chair, with his father standing over her. He began to search among the infinite series of impressions which time had laid down, leaf upon leaf,

To The Lighthouse

fold upon fold softly, incessantly upon his brain; among scents, sounds; voices, harsh, hollow, sweet; and lights passing, and brooms tapping; and the wash and hush of the sea, how a man had marched up and down and stopped dead, upright, over them. Meanwhile, he noticed, Cam dabbled her fingers in the water, and stared at the shore and said nothing. No, she won't give way, he thought; she's different, he thought. Well, if Cam would not answer him, he would not bother her, Mr Ramsay decided, feeling in his pocket for a book. But she would answer him; she wished, passionately, to move some obstacle that lay upon her tongue and to say, Oh yes, Frisk. I'll call him Frisk. She wanted even to say, Was that the dog that found its way over the moor alone? But try as she might, she could think of nothing to say like that, fierce and loyal to the compact, yet passing on to her father, unsuspected by James, a private token of the love she felt for him. For she thought, dabbling her hand (and now Macalister's boy had caught a mackerel, and it lay kicking on the floor, with blood on its gills) for she thought, looking at James who kept his eyes dispassionately on the sail, or glanced now and then for a second at the horizon, you're not exposed to it, to this pressure and division of feeling, this extraordinary temptation. Her father was feeling in his pockets; in another second, he would have found his book. For no one attracted her more; his hands were beautiful to her and his feet, and his voice, and his words, and his haste, and his temper, and his oddity, and his passion, and his saying straight out before every one, we perish, each alone, and his remoteness. (He had opened his book.) But what remained intolerable, she thought, sitting upright, and watching Macalister's boy tug the hook out of the gills of another fish, was that crass blindness and tyranny of his which had poisoned her childhood and raised bitter storms, so that even now she woke in the night trembling with rage and remembered some command of his; some insolence: 'Do this', 'Do that'; his dominance: his 'Submit to me'.

So she said nothing, but looked doggedly and sadly at the shore, wrapped in its mantle of peace; as if the people there had fallen asleep, she thought; were free like smoke, were free to come and go like ghosts. They have no suffering there, she thought.

5

Yes, that is their boat, Lily Briscoe decided, standing on the edge of the lawn. It was the boat with greyish-brown sails, which she saw now flatten itself upon the water and shoot off across the bay. There he sits, she thought, and the children are quite silent still. And she could not reach him either. The sympathy she had not given him weighed her down. It made it difficult for her to paint.

She had always found him difficult. She had never been able to praise him to his face, she remembered. And that reduced their relationship to something neutral, without that element of sex in it which made his manner to Minta so gallant, almost gay. He would pick a flower for her, lend her his books. But could he believe that Minta read them? She dragged them about the garden, sticking in leaves to mark the place.

'D'you remember, Mr Carmichael?' she was inclined to ask, looking at the old man. But he had pulled his hat half over his forehead; he was asleep, or he was dreaming, or he was lying there catching words, she supposed.

'D'you remember?' she felt inclined to ask him as she passed him, thinking again of Mrs Ramsay on the beach; the cask bobbing up and down; and the pages flying. Why, after all these years, had that survived, ringed round, lit up, visible to the last detail, with all before it blank and all after it blank, for miles and miles?

'Is it a boat? Is it a cork?' she would say, Lily repeated, turning back, reluctantly again, to her canvas. Heaven be praised for it, the problem of space remained, she thought, taking up her brush again. It glared at her. The whole mass of the picture was poised upon that weight. Beautiful and bright it should be on the surface, feathery and evanescent, one colour melting into another like the colours on a butterfly's wing; but beneath the fabric must be clamped together with bolts of iron. It was to be a thing you could ruffle with your breath; and a thing you could not dislodge with a team of horses. And she began to lay on a red, a grey, and she began to model her way into the hollow there. At the same time, she seemed to be sitting beside Mrs Ramsay on the beach.

'Is it a boat? Is it a cask?' Mrs Ramsay said. And she began hunting round for her spectacles. And she sat, having found them, silent, looking out to sea. And Lily, painting steadily, felt as if a door had opened, and one went in and stood gazing silently about in a high cathedral-like place, very dark, very solemn. Shouts came from a world far away. Steamers vanished in stalks of smoke on the horizon. Charles threw stones and sent them skipping.

Mrs Ramsay sat silent. She was glad, Lily thought, to rest in silence, uncommunicative; to rest in the extreme obscurity of human relationships. Who knows what we are, what we feel? Who knows even at the moment of intimacy, This is knowledge? Aren't things spoilt then, Mrs Ramsay may have asked (it seemed to have happened so often, this silence by her side) by saying them? Aren't we more expressive thus? The moment at least seemed extraordinarily fertile. She rammed a little hole in the sand and covered it up, by way of burying in it the perfection of the moment. It was like a drop of silver in which one dipped and illumined the darkness of the past.

Lily stepped back to get her canvas – so – into perspective. It was an odd road to be walking, this of painting. Out and out one went, further and further, until at last one seemed to be on a narrow plank, perfectly alone, over the sea. And as she dipped into the blue paint, she dipped too into the past there. Now Mrs Ramsay got up, she remembered. It was time to go back to the house – time for luncheon. And they all walked up from the beach together, she walking behind with William Bankes, and there was Minta in front of them with a hole in her stocking. How that little round hole of pink heel seemed to flaunt itself before them! How William Bankes deplored it, without, so far as she could remember, saying anything about it! It meant to him the annihilation of womanhood, and dirt and disorder, and servants leaving and beds not made at mid-day – all the things he most abhorred. He had a way of shuddering and spreading his fingers out as if to cover an unsightly object, which he did now – holding his hand in front of him. And Minta walked on ahead, and presumably Paul met her and she went off with Paul in the garden.

The Rayleys, thought Lily Briscoe, squeezing her tube of green paint. She collected her impressions of the Rayleys. Their lives appeared to her in a series of scenes; one, on the staircase at dawn. Paul had come in and gone to bed early; Minta was late. There was Minta, wreathed, tinted, garish on the stairs about three o'clock in the morning. Paul came out in his pyjamas carrying a poker in case of burglars. Minta was eating a sandwich, standing halfway up by a window, in the cadaverous early morning light, and the carpet had a hole in it. But what did they say? Lily asked herself, as if by looking she could hear them. Something violent. Minta went on eating her sandwich, annoyingly, while he spoke. He spoke indignant, jealous words, abusing her, in a mutter so as not to wake the children, the two little boys. He was withered, drawn; she flamboyant, careless. For things had worked loose after the first year or so; the marriage had turned out rather badly.

And this, Lily thought, taking the green paint on her brush, this making up scenes about them, is what we call 'knowing' people, 'thinking' of them, 'being fond' of them! Not a word of it was true; she had made it up; but it was what she knew them by all the same. She went on tunnelling her way into her picture, into the past.

Another time, Paul said he 'played chess in coffee-houses'. She had built up a whole structure of imagination on that saying too. She remembered how, as he said it, she thought how he rang up the servant, and she said 'Mrs Rayley's out, sir', and he decided that he would not come home either. She saw him sitting in the corner of some lugubrious place where the smoke attached itself to the red plush seats, and the waitresses got to know you, playing chess with a little man who was in the tea trade and lived at Surbiton, but that was all Paul knew about him. And then Minta was out when he came home and then there was that scene on the stairs, when he got the poker in case of burglars (no doubt to frighten her too) and spoke so bitterly, saying she had ruined his life. At any rate when she went down to see them at a cottage near Rickmansworth, things were horribly strained. Paul took her down the garden to look at the Belgian hares which he bred, and Minta followed them, singing, and put her bare arm on his shoulder, lest he should tell her anything.

Minta was bored by hares, Lily thought. But Minta never gave herself away. She never said things like that about playing chess in coffee-houses. She was far too conscious, far too wary. But to go on with their story — they had got through the dangerous stage by now. She had been staying with them last summer some time and the car broke down and Minta had to hand him his tools. He sat on the road mending the car, and it was the way she gave him the tools — business-like, straightforward, friendly — that proved it was all right now. They were 'in love' no longer; no, he had taken up with another woman, a serious woman, with her hair in a plait and a case in her hand (Minta had described her gratefully, almost admiringly), who went to meetings and shared Paul's views (they had got more and more pronounced) about the taxation of land values and a capital levy. Far from breaking up the marriage, that alliance had righted it. They were excellent friends, obviously, as he sat on the road and she handed him his tools.

So that was the story of the Rayleys, Lily smiled. She imagined herself telling it to Mrs Ramsay, who would be full of curiosity to know what had become of the Rayleys. She would feel a little triumphant, telling Mrs Ramsay that the marriage had not been a success.

But the dead, thought Lily, encountering some obstacle in her design which made her pause and ponder, stepping back a foot or so, Oh the dead! she murmured, one pitied them, one brushed them aside, one had even a little contempt for them. They are at our mercy.

Mrs Ramsay has faded and gone, she thought. We can override her wishes, improve away her limited, old-fashioned ideas. She recedes further and further from us. Mockingly she seemed to see her there at the end of the corridor of years saying, of all incongruous things, 'Marry, marry!' (sitting very upright early in the morning with the birds beginning to cheep in the garden outside). And one would have to say to her, It has all gone against your wishes. They're happy like that; I'm happy like this. Life has changed completely. At that all her being, even her beauty, became for a moment, dusty and out of date. For a moment Lily, standing there, with the sun hot on her back, summing up the Rayleys, triumphed over Mrs Ramsay, who would never know how Paul went to coffee-houses and had a mistress; how he sat on the ground and Minta handed him his tools; how she stood here painting, had never married, not even William Bankes.

Mrs Ramsay had planned it. Perhaps, had she lived, she would have compelled it. Already that summer he was 'the kindest of men'. He was 'the first scientist of his age, my husband says'. He was also 'poor William – it makes me so unhappy, when I go to see him, to find nothing nice in his house – no one to arrange the flowers'. So they were sent for walks together, and she was told, with that faint touch of irony that made Mrs Ramsay slip through one's fingers, that she had a scientific mind; she liked flowers; she was so exact. What was this mania of hers for marriage? Lily wondered, stepping to and fro from her easel.

(Suddenly, as suddenly as a star slides in the sky, a reddish light seemed to burn in her mind, covering Paul Rayley, issuing from him. It rose like a fire sent up in token of some celebration by savages on a distant beach. She heard the roar and the crackle. The whole sea for miles round ran red and gold. Some winy smell mixed with it and intoxicated her, for she felt again her own headlong desire to throw herself off the cliff and be drowned looking for a pearl brooch on a beach. And the roar and the crackle repelled her with fear and disgust, as if while she saw its splendour and power she saw too how it fed on the treasure of the house, greedily, disgustingly, and she loathed it. But for a sight, for a glory it surpassed everything in her experience, and burnt year after year like a signal fire on a desert island at the edge of the sea, and one had only to say 'in love' and instantly, as happened now, up rose Paul's fire again. And it sank and she said to herself, laughing, 'The Rayleys'; how Paul went to coffee-houses and played chess.)

She had only escaped by the skin of her teeth though, she thought. She had been looking at the table-cloth, and it had flashed upon her that she would move the tree to the middle, and need never marry anybody, and she had felt an enormous exultation. She had felt, now she could stand up to Mrs Ramsay – a tribute to the astonishing power that Mrs Ramsay had over one. Do this, she said, and one did it. Even her shadow at the window with James was full of authority. She remembered how William Bankes had been shocked by her neglect of the significance of mother and son. Did she not admire their beauty? he said. But William, she remembered, had listened to her with his wise child's eyes when she explained how it was not irreverence: how a light there needed a shadow there and so on. She did not intend to disparage a subject which, they agreed, Raphael had treated divinely. She was not cynical. Quite the contrary. Thanks to his scientific mind he

To The Lighthouse

understood – a proof of disinterested intelligence which had pleased her and comforted her enormously. One could talk of painting then seriously to a man. Indeed, his friendship had been one of the pleasures of her life. She loved William Bankes.

They went to Hampton Court and he always left her, like the perfect gentleman he was, plenty of time to wash her hands, while he strolled by the river. That was typical of their relationship. Many things were left unsaid. Then they strolled through the courtyards, and admired, summer after summer, the proportions and the flowers, and he would tell her things, about perspective, about architecture, as they walked, and he would stop to look at a tree, or the view over the lake, and admire a child (it was his great grief – he had no daughter) in the vague aloof way that was natural to a man who spent so much time in laboratories that the world when he came out seemed to dazzle him, so that he walked slowly, lifted his hand to screen his eyes and paused, with his head thrown back, merely to breathe the air. Then he would tell her how his housekeeper was on her holiday; he must buy a new carpet for the staircase. Perhaps she would go with him to buy a new carpet for the staircase. And once something led him to talk about the Ramsays and he had said how when he first saw her she had been wearing a grey hat; she was not more than nineteen or twenty. She was astonishingly beautiful. There he stood looking down the avenue at Hampton Court, as if he could see her there among the fountains.

She looked now at the drawing-room step. She saw, through William's eyes, the shape of a woman, peaceful and silent, with downcast eyes. She sat musing, pondering (she was in grey that day, Lily thought). Her eyes were bent. She would never lift them. Yes, thought

Lily, looking intently, I must have seen her look like that, but not in grey; nor so still, nor so young, nor so peaceful. The figure came readily enough. She was astonishingly beautiful, William said. But beauty was not everything. Beauty had this penalty – it came too readily, came too completely. It stilled life – froze it. One forgot the little agitations; the flush, the pallor, some queer distortion, some light or shadow, which made the face unrecognizable for a moment and yet added a quality one saw for ever after. It was simpler to smooth that all out under the cover of beauty. But what was the look she had, Lily wondered, when she clapped her deer-stalker's hat on her head, or ran across the grass, or scolded Kennedy, the gardener? Who could tell her? Who could help her?

Against her will she had come to the surface, and found herself half out of the picture, looking, a little dazedly, as if at unreal things, at Mr Carmichael. He lay on his chair with his hands clasped above his paunch not reading, or sleeping, but basking like a creature gorged with existence. His book had fallen on to the grass.

She wanted to go straight up to him and say, 'Mr Carmichael!' Then he would look up benevolently as always, from his smoky vague green eyes. But one only woke people if one knew what one wanted to say to them. And she wanted to say not one thing, but everything. Little words that broke up the thought and dismembered it said nothing. 'About life, about death; about Mrs Ramsay' – no, she thought, one could say nothing to nobody. The urgency of the moment always missed its mark. Words fluttered sideways and struck the object inches too low. Then one gave it up; then the idea sunk back again; then one became like most middle-aged people, cautious, furtive, with wrinkles between the eyes and a look of perpetual apprehension. For how could one express in words these emotions of the body? express that emptiness there? (She was looking at the drawing-room steps; they looked extraordinarily empty). It was one's body feeling, not one's mind. The physical sensations that went with the bare look of the steps had become suddenly extremely unpleasant. To want and not to have, sent all up her body a hardness, a hollowness, a strain. And then to want and not to have – to want and want – how that wrung the heart, and wrung it again and again! Oh Mrs Ramsay! she called out silently, to that essence which sat by the boat, that abstract one made of her, that woman in grey, as if to abuse her for having gone, and then having gone, come back again. It had seemed so safe, thinking of her. Ghost, air, nothingness, a thing you could play with easily and safely at any time of day or night, she had been that, and then suddenly she put her hand out and wrung the heart thus. Suddenly, the empty drawing-room steps, the frill of the chair inside, the puppy tumbling on the terrace, the whole wave and whisper of the garden became like curves and arabesques flourishing round a centre of complete emptiness.

'What does it mean? How do you explain it all?' she wanted to say, turning to Mr Carmichael again. For the whole world seemed to have dissolved in this early morning hour into a pool of thought, a deep basin of reality, and one could almost fancy that had Mr Carmichael spoken, a little tear would have rent the surface of the pool. And then? Something would emerge. A hand would be shoved up, a blade would be flashed. It was nonsense of course.

A curious notion came to her that he did after all hear

the things she could not say. He was an inscrutable old man, with the yellow stain on his beard, and his poetry, and his puzzles, sailing serenely through a world which satisfied all his wants, so that she thought he had only to put down his hand where he lay on the lawn to fish up anything he wanted. She looked at her picture. That would have been his answer, presumably – how 'you' and 'I' and 'she' pass and vanish; nothing stays; all changes; but not words, not paint. Yet it would be hung in the attics, she thought; it would be rolled up and flung under a sofa; yet even so, even of a picture like that, it was true. One might say, even of this scrawl, not of that actual picture, perhaps, but of what it attempted, that it 'remained for ever' she was going to say, or, for the words spoken sounded even to herself, too boastful, to hint, wordlessly; when, looking at the picture, she was surprised to find that she could not see it. Her eyes were full of a hot liquid (she did not think of tears at first) which, without disturbing the firmness of her lips, made the air thick, rolled down her cheeks. She had perfect control of herself – Oh yes! – in every other way. Was she crying then for Mrs Ramsay, without being aware of any unhappiness? She addressed old Mr Carmichael again. What was it then? What did it mean? Could things thrust their hands up and grip one; could the blade cut; the fist grasp? Was there no safety? No learning by heart of the ways of the world? No guide, no shelter, but all was miracle, and leaping from the pinnacle of a tower into the air? Could it be, even for elderly people, that this was life? – startling, unexpected, unknown? For one moment she felt that if they both got up, here, now on the lawn, and demanded an explanation, why was it so short, why was it so inexplicable, said it with violence, as two fully equipped human beings from whom nothing should be hid might speak, then, beauty would roll itself up; the space would fill; those empty flourishes would form into shape; if they shouted loud enough Mrs Ramsay would return. 'Mrs Ramsay!' she said aloud, 'Mrs Ramsay!' The tears ran down her face.

6

[Macalister's boy took one of the fish and cut a square out of its side to bait his hook with. The mutilated body (it was alive still) was thrown back into the sea.]

7

'Mrs Ramsay!' Lily cried, 'Mrs Ramsay!' But nothing happened. The pain increased. That anguish could reduce one to such a pitch of imbecility, she thought! Anyhow the old man had not heard her. He remained benignant, calm – if one chose to think it, sublime. Heaven be praised, no one had heard her cry that ignominious cry, stop pain, stop! She had not obviously taken leave of her senses. No one had seen her step off her strip of board into the waters of annihilation. She remained a skimpy old maid, holding a paint-brush on the lawn.

And now slowly the pain of the want, and the bitter anger (to be called back, just as she thought she would never feel sorrow for Mrs Ramsay again. Had she missed her among the coffee cups at breakfast? not in the least) lessened; and of their anguish left, as antidote, a relief that was balm in itself, and also, but more mysteriously, a sense of someone there, of Mrs Ramsay, relieved for a moment of the weight that the world had put on her, staying lightly by her side and then (for this was Mrs Ramsay in all her beauty) raising to her forehead a wreath of white flowers with which she went. Lily squeezed her tubes again. She attacked that problem of the hedge. It was strange how clearly she saw her, stepping with her usual quickness across fields among whose folds, purplish and soft, among whose flowers, hyacinths or lilies, she vanished. It was some trick of the painter's eye. For days after she had heard of her death she had seen her thus, putting her wreath to her forehead and going unquestioningly with her companion, a shadow, across the fields. The sight, the phrase, had its power to console. Wherever she happened to be, painting, here, in the country or in London, the vision would come to her, and her eyes, half closing, sought something to base her vision on. She looked down the railway carriage, the omnibus; took a line from shoulder or cheek; looked at the windows opposite; at Piccadilly, lamp-strung in the evening. All had been part of the fields of death. But always something – it might be a face, a voice, a paper boy crying *Standard, News* – thrust through, snubbed her, waked her, required and got in the end an effort of attention, so that the vision must be perpetually remade. Now again, moved as she was by some instinctive need of distance and blue, she looked at the bay beneath her, making hillocks of the blue bars of the waves, and stony fields of the purpler spaces. Again she was roused as usual by something incongruous. There was a brown spot in the middle of the bay. It was a boat. Yes, she realized that after a second. But whose boat? Mr Ramsay's boat, she replied. Mr Ramsay; the man who had marched past her, with his hand raised, aloof, at the head of a procession, in his beautiful boots, asking her for sympathy, which she had refused. The boat was now halfway across the bay.

So fine was the morning except for a streak of wind here and there that the sea and sky looked all one fabric, as if sails were stuck high up in the sky, or the clouds had dropped down into the sea. A steamer far out at sea had drawn in the air a great scroll of smoke which stayed there curving and circling decoratively, as if the air were a fine gauze which held things and kept them softly in its mesh, only gently swaying them this way and that. And as happens sometimes when the weather is very fine, the cliffs looked as if they were conscious of the ships, and the ships looked as if they were conscious of the cliffs, as if they signalled to each other some secret message of their own. For sometimes quite close to the shore, the Lighthouse looked this morning in the haze an enormous distance away.

'Where are they now?' Lily thought, looking out to sea. Where was he, that very old man who had gone past her silently, holding a brown paper parcel under his arm? The boat was in the middle of the bay.

8

They don't feel a thing there, Cam thought, looking at the shore, which, rising and falling, became steadily more distant and more peaceful. Her hand cut a trail in the sea, as her mind made the green swirls and streaks into patterns and, numbed and shrouded, wandered in imagination in that underworld of waters where the pearls stuck in clusters to white sprays, where in the green light a change came over one's entire mind and one's body shone half transparent enveloped in a green cloak.

Then the eddy slackened round her hand. The rush of the water ceased; the world became full of little creaking and squeaking sounds. One heard the waves breaking and flapping against the side of the boat as if they were anchored in harbour. Everything became very close to one. For the sail, upon which James had his eyes fixed until it had become to him like a person whom he knew, sagged entirely; there they came to a stop, flapping about waiting for a breeze, in the hot sun, miles from shore, miles from the Lighthouse. Everything in the whole world seemed to stand still. The Lighthouse became immovable, and the line of the distant shore became fixed. The sun grew hotter and everybody seemed to come very close together and to feel each other's presence, which they had almost forgotten. Macalister's fishing line went plumb down into the sea. But Mr Ramsay went on reading with his legs curled under him.

He was reading a little shiny book with covers mottled like a plover's egg. Now and again, as they hung about in that horrid calm, he turned a page. And James felt that each page was turned with a peculiar gesture aimed at him: now assertively, now commandingly; now with the intention of making people pity him; and all the time, as his father read and turned one after another of those little pages, James kept dreading the moment when he would look up and speak sharply to him about something or other. Why were they lagging about here? he would demand, or something quite unreasonable like that. And if he does, James thought, then I shall take a knife and strike him to the heart.

To The Lighthouse

He had always kept this old symbol of taking a knife and striking his father to the heart. Only now, as he grew older, and sat staring at his father in an impotent rage, it was not him, that old man reading, whom he wanted to kill, but it was the thing that descended on him – without his knowing it perhaps: that fierce sudden black-winged harpy, with its talons and its beak all cold and hard, that struck and struck at you (he could feel the beak on his bare legs, where it had struck when he was a child) and then made off, and there he was again, an old man, very sad, reading his book. That he would kill, that he would strike to the heart. Whatever he did – (and he might do anything, he felt, looking at the Lighthouse and the distant shore) whether he was in a business, in a bank, a barrister, a man at the head of some enterprise, that he would fight, that he would track down and stamp out – tyranny, despotism, he called it – making people do what they did not want to do, cutting off their right to speak. How could any of them say, But I won't, when he said, Come to the Lighthouse. Do this. Fetch me that. The black wings spread, and the hard beak tore. And then next moment, there he sat reading his book; and he might look up – one never knew – quite reasonably. He might talk to the Macalisters. He might be pressing a sovereign into some frozen old woman's hand in the street, James thought; he might be shouting out at some fisherman's sports; he might be waving his arms in the air with excitement. Or he might sit at the head of the table dead silent from one end of dinner to the other. Yes, thought James, while the boat slapped and dawdled there in the hot sun; there was a waste of snow and rock very lonely and austere; and there he had come to feel, quite often lately, when his father said something which surprised the others, were two pairs of footprints only; his own and his father's. They alone knew each other. What then was this terror, this hatred? Turning back among the many leaves which the past had folded in him, peering into the heart of that forest where light and shade so chequer each other that all shape is distorted, and one blunders, now with the sun in one's eyes, now with a dark shadow, he sought an image to cool and detach and round off his feeling in a concrete shape. Suppose then that as a child sitting helpless in a perambulator, or on someone's knee, he had seen a waggon crush ignorantly and innocently, someone's foot? Suppose he had seen the foot first, in the grass, smooth, and whole; then the wheel; and the same foot, purple, crushed. But the wheel was innocent. So now, when his father came striding down the passage knocking them up early in the morning to go to the Lighthouse down it came over his foot, over Cam's foot, over anybody's foot. One sat and watched it.

But whose foot was he thinking of, and in what garden did all this happen? For one had settings for these scenes; trees that grew there; flowers; a certain light; a few figures. Everything tended to set itself in a garden where there was none of this gloom and none of this throwing of hands about; people spoke in an ordinary tone of voice. They went in and out all day long. There was an old woman gossiping in the kitchen; and the blinds were sucked in and out by the breeze; all was blowing, all was growing; and over all those plates and bowls and tall brandishing red and yellow flowers a very thin yellow veil would be drawn, like a vine leaf, at night. Things became stiller and darker at night. But the leaf-like veil was so fine that lights lifted it, voices crinkled it; he could see through it a figure stooping, hear, coming close, going away, some dress rustling, some chain tinkling.

It was in this world that the wheel went over the person's foot. Something, he remembered, stayed and darkened over him; would not move; something flourished up in the air, something arid and sharp descended even there, like a blade, a scimitar, smiting through the leaves and flowers even of that happy world and making them shrivel and fall.

'It will rain,' he remembered his father saying. 'You won't be able to go to the Lighthouse.'

The Lighthouse was then a silvery, misty-looking tower with a yellow eye that opened suddenly and softly in the evening. Now –

James looked at the Lighthouse. He could see the white-washed rocks; the tower, stark and straight; he could see that it was barred with black and white; he could see windows in it; he could even see washing spread on the rocks to dry. So that was the Lighthouse, was it?

No, the other was also the Lighthouse. For nothing was simply one thing. The other was the Lighthouse too. It was sometimes hardly to be seen across the bay. In the evening one looked up and saw the eye opening and shutting and the light seemed to reach them in that airy sunny garden where they sat.

But he pulled himself up. Whenever he said 'they' or 'a person', and then began hearing the rustle of someone coming, the tinkle of someone going, he became extremely sensitive to the presence of whoever might be in the room. It was his father now. The strain became acute. For in one moment if there was no breeze, his father would slap the covers of his book together, and say: 'What's happening now? What are we dawdling about here for, eh?' as, once before he had brought his blade down among them on the terrace and she had gone stiff all over, and if there had been an axe handy, a knife, or anything with a sharp point he would have seized it and struck his father through the heart. His mother had gone still all over, and then, her arm slackening, so that he felt she listened to him no longer, she had risen somehow and gone away and left him there, impotent, ridiculous, sitting on the floor grasping a pair of scissors.

Not a breath of wind blew. The water chuckled and gurgled in the bottom of the boat where three or four mackerel beat their tails up and down in a pool of water not deep enough to cover them. At any moment Mr Ramsay (James scarcely dared look at him) might rouse himself, shut his book, and say something sharp; but for the moment he was reading, so that James stealthily, as if he were stealing downstairs on bare feet, afraid of waking a watch-dog by a creaking board, went on thinking what was she like, where did she go that day? He began following her from room to room and at last they came to a room where in a blue light, as if the reflection came from many china dishes, she talked to somebody; he listened to her talking. She talked to a servant, saying simply whatever came into her head. 'We shall need a big dish tonight. Where is it – the blue dish?' She alone spoke the truth; to her alone could he speak it. That was the source of her everlasting attraction for him, perhaps; she was a person to whom one could say what came into one's head. But all the time he thought of her, he was conscious of his father following his thought, shadowing it, making it shiver and falter.

At last he ceased to think; there he sat with his hand

on the tiller in the sun, staring at the Lighthouse, powerless to move, powerless to flick off these grains of misery which settled on his mind one after another. A rope seemed to bind him there, and his father had knotted it and he could only escape by taking a knife and plunging it. . . . But at that moment the sail swung slowly round, filled slowly out, the boat seemed to shake herself, and then to move off half conscious in her sleep, and then she woke and shot through the waves. The relief was extraordinary. They all seemed to fall away from each other again and to be at their ease and the fishing-lines slanted taut across the side of the boat. But his father did not rouse himself. He only raised his right hand mysteriously high in the air, and let it fall upon his knee again as if he were conducting some secret symphony.

9

[The sea without a stain on it, thought Lily Briscoe, still standing and looking out over the bay. The sea is stretched like silk across the bay. Distance had an extraordinary power; they had been swallowed up in it, she felt, they were gone for ever, they had become part of the nature of things. It was so calm; it was so quiet. The steamer itself had vanished, but the great scroll of smoke still hung in the air and drooped like a flag mournfully in valediction.]

10

It was like that then, the island, thought Cam, once more drawing her fingers through the waves. She had never seen it from out at sea before. It lay like that on the sea, did it, with a dent in the middle and two sharp crags, and the sea swept in there, and spread away for miles and miles on either side of the island. It was very small; shaped something like a leaf stood on end. So we took a little boat, she thought, beginning to tell herself a story of adventure about escaping from a sinking ship. But with the sea streaming through her fingers, a spray of seaweed vanishing behind them, she did not want to tell herself seriously a story; it was the sense of adventure and escape that she wanted, for she was thinking, as the boat sailed on, how her father's anger about the points of the compass, James's obstinacy about the compact, and her own anguish, all had slipped, all had passed, all had streamed away. What then came next? Where were they going? From her hand, ice cold, held deep in the sea, there spurted up a fountain of joy at the change, at the escape, at the adventure (that she should be alive, that she should be there). And the drops falling from this sudden and unthinking fountain of joy fell here and there on the dark, the slumbrous shapes in her mind; shapes of a world not realized but turning in their darkness, catching here and there, a spark of light; Greece, Rome, Constantinople. Small as it was, and shaped something like a leaf stood on end with the gold sprinkled waters flowing in and about it, it had, she supposed, a place in the universe – even that little island? The old gentlemen in the study she thought could have told her. Sometimes she strayed in from the garden purposely to catch them at it. There they were (it might be Mr Carmichael or Mr Bankes, very old, very stiff) sitting opposite each other in their low armchairs. They were crackling in front of them the pages of *The Times*, when she came in from the garden, all in a muddle, about something someone had said about Christ; a mammoth had been dug up in a London street; what was the great Napoleon like? Then they took all this with their clean hands (they wore grey-coloured clothes; they smelt of heather) and they brushed the scraps together, turning the paper, crossing their knees, and said something now and then very brief. In a kind of trance she would take a book from the shelf and stand there, watching her father write, so equally, so neatly from one side of the page to another, with a little cough now and then, or something said briefly to the other old gentleman opposite. And she thought, standing there with her book open, here one could let whatever one thought expand like a leaf in water; and if it did well here, among the old gentlemen smoking and *The Times* crackling, then it was right. And watching her father as he wrote in his study, she thought (now sitting in the boat) he was most lovable, he was most wise; he was not vain nor a tyrant. Indeed, if he saw she was there, reading a book, he would ask her, as gently as any one could, Was there nothing he could give her?

Lest this should be wrong, she looked at him reading the little book with the shiny cover mottled like a plover's egg. No; it was right. Look at him now, she wanted to say aloud to James. (But James had his eye on the sail.) He is a sarcastic brute, James would say. He brings the talk round to himself and his books, James would say. He is intolerably egotistical. Worst of all, he is a tyrant. But look! she said, looking at him. Look at him now. She looked at him reading the little book with his legs curled; the little book whose yellowish pages she knew, without knowing what was written on them. It was small; it was closely printed;

on the fly-leaf, she knew, he had written that he had spent fifteen francs on dinner; the wine had been so much; he had given so much to the waiter; all was added up neatly at the bottom of the page. But what might be written in the book which had rounded its edges off in his pocket, she did not know. What he thought they none of them knew. But he was absorbed in it, so that when he looked up, as he did now for an instant, it was not to see anything; it was to pin down some thought more exactly. That done, his mind flew back again and he plunged into his reading. He read, she thought, as if he were guiding something, or wheedling a large flock of sheep, or pushing his way up and up a single narrow path; and sometimes he went fast and straight, and broke his way through the thicket, and sometimes it seemed a branch struck at him, a bramble blinded him, but he was not going to let himself be beaten by that; on he went, tossing over page after page. And she went on telling herself a story about escaping from a sinking ship, for she was safe, while he sat there; safe, as she felt herself when she crept in from the garden, and took a book down, and the old gentleman, lowering the paper suddenly, said something very brief over the top of it about the character of Napoleon.

She gazed back over the sea, at the island. But the leaf was losing its sharpness. It was very small; it was very distant. The sea was more important now than the shore. Waves were all round them, tossing and sinking, with a log wallowing down one wave; a gull riding on another. About here, she thought, dabbling her fingers in the water, a ship had sunk, and she murmured, dreamily, half asleep, how we perished, each alone.

11

So much depends then, thought Lily Briscoe, looking at the sea which had scarcely a stain on it, which was so soft that the sails and the clouds seemed set in its blue, so much depends, she thought, upon distance: whether people are near us or far from us; for her feeling for Mr Ramsay changed as he sailed further and further across the bay. It seemed to be elongated, stretched out; he seemed to become more and more remote. He and his children seemed to be swallowed up in that blue, that distance; but here, on the lawn, close at hand, Mr Carmichael suddenly grunted. She laughed. He clawed his book up from the grass. He settled into his chair again puffing and blowing like some sea monster. That was different altogether, because he was so near. And now again all was quiet. They must be out of bed by this time, she supposed, looking at the house, but nothing appeared there. But then, she remembered, they had always made off directly a meal was over, on business of their own. It was all in keeping with this silence, this emptiness, and the unreality of the early morning hour. It was a way things had sometimes, she thought, lingering for a moment and looking at the long glittering windows and the plume of blue smoke: they became unreal. So coming back from a journey, or after an illness, before habits had spun themselves across the surface, one felt that same unreality, which was so startling; felt something emerge. Life was most vivid then. One could be at one's ease. Mercifully one need not say, very briskly, crossing the lawn to greet old Mrs Beckwith, who would be coming out to find a corner to sit in, 'Oh good-morning, Mrs Beckwith! What a lovely day! Are you going to be so bold as to sit in the sun? Jasper's hidden the chairs. Do let me find you one!' and all the rest of the usual chatter. One need not speak at all. One glided, one shook one's sails (there was a good deal of movement in the bay, boats were starting off) between things, beyond things. Empty it was not, but full to the brim. She seemed to be standing up to the lips in some substance, to move and float and sink in it, yes, for these waters were unfathomably deep. Into them had spilled so many lives. The Ramsays'; the children's; and all sorts of waifs and strays of things besides. A washerwoman with her basket; a rook; a red-hot poker; the purples and grey-greens of flowers: some common feeling which held the whole together.

It was some such feeling of completeness perhaps which, ten years ago, standing almost where she stood now, had made her say that she must be in love with the place. Love had a thousand shapes. There might be lovers whose gift it was to choose out the elements of things and place them together and so, giving them a wholeness not theirs in life, make of some scene, or meeting of people (all now gone and separate), one of those globed compacted things over which thought lingers, and love plays.

Her eyes rested on the brown speck of Mr Ramsay's sailing boat. They would be at the Lighthouse by lunch time she supposed. But the wind had freshened, and, as the sky changed slightly and the sea changed slightly and the boats altered their positions, the view, which a moment before had seemed miraculously fixed, was now unsatisfactory. The wind had blown the trail of smoke about; there was something displeasing about the placing of the ships.

The disproportion there seemed to upset some harmony in her own mind. She felt an obscure distress.

It was confirmed when she turned to her picture. She had been wasting her morning. For whatever reason she could not achieve that razor edge of balance between two opposite forces; Mr Ramsay and the picture; which was necessary. There was something perhaps wrong with the design? Was it, she wondered, that the line of the wall wanted breaking, was it that the mass of the trees was too heavy? She smiled ironically; for had she not thought, when she began, that she had solved her problem?

What was the problem then? She must try to get hold of something that evaded her. It evaded her when she thought of Mrs Ramsay; it evaded her now when she thought of her picture. Phrases came. Visions came. Beautiful pictures. Beautiful phrases. But what she wished to get hold of was that very jar on the nerves, the thing itself before it has been made anything. Get that and start afresh; get that and start afresh; she said desperately, pitching herself firmly again before her easel. It was a miserable machine, an inefficient machine, she thought, the human apparatus for painting or for feeling; it always broke down at the critical moment; heroically, one must force it on. She stared, frowning. There was the hedge, sure enough. But one got nothing by soliciting urgently. One got only a glare in the eye from looking at the line of the wall, or from thinking – she wore a grey hat. She was astonishingly beautiful. Let it come, she thought, if it will come. For there are moments when one can neither think nor feel. And if one can neither think nor feel, she thought, where is one?

Here on the grass, on the ground, she thought, sitting down, and examining with her brush a little colony of plantains. For the lawn was very rough. Here sitting on the world, she thought, for she could not shake herself free from the sense that everything this morning was happening for the first time, perhaps for the last time, as a traveller, even though he is half asleep, knows, looking out of the train window, that he must look now, for he will never see that town, or that mule-cart, or that woman at work in the fields, again. The lawn was the world; they were up here together, on this exalted station, she thought, looking at old Mr Carmichael, who seemed (though they had not said a word all this time) to share her thoughts. And she would never see him again perhaps. He was growing old. Also, she remembered, smiling at the slipper that dangled from his foot, he was growing famous. People said that his poetry was 'so beautiful'. They went and published things he had written forty years ago. There was a famous man now called Carmichael, she smiled, thinking how many shapes one person might wear, how he was that in the newspapers, but here the same as he had always been. He looked the same – greyer, rather. Yes, he looked the same, but somebody had said, she recalled, that when he had heard of Andrew Ramsay's death (he was killed in a second by a shell; he should have been a great mathematician) Mr Carmichael had 'lost all interest in life'. What did it mean – that? she wondered. Had he marched through Trafalgar Square grasping a big stick? Had he turned pages over and over, without reading them, sitting in his room in St John's Wood alone? She did not know what he had done, when he heard that Andrew was killed, but she felt it in him all the same. They only mumbled at each other on staircases; they looked up at the sky and said it will be fine or it won't be fine. But this was one way of knowing people, she thought: to know the outline, not the detail, to sit in one's garden and look at the slopes of a hill running purple down into the distant heather. She knew him in that way. She knew that he had changed somehow. She had never read a line of his poetry. She thought that she knew how it went though, slowly and sonorously. It was seasoned and mellow. It was about the desert and the camel. It was about the palm tree and the sunset. It was extremely impersonal; it said something about death; it said very little about love. There was an aloofness about him. He wanted very little of other people. Had he not always lurched rather awkwardly past the drawing-room window with some newspaper under his arm, trying to avoid Mrs Ramsay whom for some reason he did not much like? On that account, of course, she would always try to make him stop. He would bow to her. He would halt unwillingly and bow profoundly. Annoyed that he did not want anything of her, Mrs Ramsay would ask him (Lily could hear her) wouldn't he like a coat, a rug, a newspaper? No, he wanted nothing. (Here he bowed.) There was some quality in her which he did not much like. It was perhaps her masterfulness, her positiveness, something matter-of-fact in her. She was so direct.

(A noise drew her attention to the drawing-room window – the squeak of a hinge. The light breeze was toying with the window.)

There must have been people who disliked her very much, Lily thought (Yes; she realized that the drawing-room step was empty, but it had no effect on her whatever. She did not want Mrs Ramsay now) – People who thought her too sure, too drastic. Also her beauty offended people probably. How monotonous, they would say, and the same always! They preferred another type – the dark, the vivacious. Then she was weak with her husband. She let him make those scenes. Then she was reserved. Nobody knew exactly what had happened to her. And (to go back to Mr Carmichael and his dislike) one could not imagine Mrs Ramsay standing painting, lying reading, a whole morning on the lawn. It was unthinkable. Without saying a word, the only token of her errand a basket on her arm, she went off to the town, to the poor, to sit in some stuffy little bedroom. Often and often Lily had seen her go silently in the midst of some game, some discussion, with her basket on her arm, very upright. She had noted her return. She had thought, half laughing (she was so methodical with the tea cups) half moved (her beauty took one's breath away), eyes that are closing in pain have looked on you. You have been with them there.

And then Mrs Ramsay would be annoyed because somebody was late, or the butter not fresh, or the teapot chipped. And all the time she was saying that the butter was not fresh one would be thinking of Greek temples, and how beauty had been with them there. She never talked of it – she went, punctually, directly. It was her instinct to go, an instinct like the swallows for the south, the artichokes for the sun, turning her infallibly to the human race, making her nest in its heart. And this, like all instincts, was a little distressing to people who did not share it; to Mr Carmichael perhaps, to herself certainly. Some notion was in both of them about the ineffectiveness of action, the supremacy of thought. Her going was a reproach to them, gave a different twist to the world, so that they were led to protest, seeing their own prepossessions disappear, and clutch at them vanishing. Charles Tansley did that too: it was part of the reason why one disliked him. He upset the proportions of one's world. And what had happened to him, she wondered, idly stirring the plantains with her brush. He had got his fellowship. He had married; he lived at Golder's Green.

She had gone one day into a Hall and heard him speaking during the war. He was denouncing something: he was condemning somebody. He was preaching brotherly love. And all she felt was how could he love his kind who did not know one picture from another, who had stood behind her smoking shag ('fivepence an ounce, Miss Briscoe') and making it his business to tell her women can't write, women can't paint, not so much that he believed it, as that for some odd reason he wished it? There he was, lean and red and raucous, preaching love from a platform (there were ants crawling about among the plantains which she disturbed with her brush – red, energetic ants, rather like Charles Tansley). She had looked at him ironically from her seat in the half-empty hall, pumping love into that chilly space, and suddenly, there was the old cask or whatever it was bobbing up and down among the waves and Mrs Ramsay looking for her spectacle case among the pebbles. 'Oh dear! What a nuisance! Lost again. Don't bother, Mr Tansley. I lose thousands every summer,' at which he pressed his chin back against his collar, as if afraid to sanction such exaggeration, but could stand it in her whom he liked, and smiled very charmingly. He must have confided in her on one of those long expeditions when people got separated and walked back alone. He was educating his little sister, Mrs Ramsay had told her. It was immensely to his credit. Her own idea of him was grotesque, Lily knew well, stirring the plantains with her brush. Half one's notions of other people were, after all, grotesque. They served private purposes of one's own. He did for her instead of a whipping-boy. She found herself flagellating his lean flanks when she was out of temper.

If she wanted to be serious about him she had to help herself to Mrs Ramsay's sayings, to look at him through her eyes.

She raised a little mountain for the ants to climb over. She reduced them to a frenzy of indecision by this interference in their cosmogony. Some ran this way, others that.

One wanted fifty pairs of eyes to see with, she reflected. Fifty pairs of eyes were not enough to get round that one woman with, she thought. Among them, must be one that was stone blind to her beauty. One wanted most some secret sense, fine as air, with which to steal through keyholes and surround her where she sat knitting, talking, sitting silent in the window alone; which took to itself and treasured up like the air which held the smoke of the steamer, her thoughts, her imaginations, her desires. What did the hedge mean to her, what did the garden mean to her, what did it mean to her when a wave broke? (Lily looked up, as she had seen Mrs Ramsay look up; she too heard a wave falling on the beach.) And then what stirred and trembled in her mind when the children cried, 'How's that? How's that?' cricketing? She would stop knitting for a second. She would look intent. Then she would lapse again, and suddenly Mr Ramsay stopped dead in his pacing in front of her, and some curious shock passed through her and seemed to rock her in profound agitation on its breast when stopping there he stood over her, and looked down at her. Lily could see him.

He stretched out his hand and raised her from her chair. It seemed somehow as if he had done it before; as if he had once bent in the same way and raised her from a boat which, lying a few inches off some island, had required that the ladies should thus be helped on shore by the gentlemen. An old-fashioned scene that was, which required, very nearly, crinolines and peg-top trousers. Letting herself be helped by him, Mrs Ramsay had thought (Lily supposed) the time has come now; Yes, she would say it now. Yes, she would marry him. And she stepped slowly, quietly on shore. Probably she said one word only, letting her hand rest still in his. I will marry you, she might have said, with her hand in his; but no more. Time after time the same thrill had passed between them – obviously it had, Lily thought, smoothing a way for her ants. She was not inventing; she was only trying to smooth out something she had been given years ago folded up; something she had seen. For in the rough and tumble of daily life, with all those children about, all those visitors, one had constantly a sense of repetition – of one thing falling where another had fallen, and so setting up an echo which chimed in the air and made it full of vibrations.

But it would be a mistake, she thought, thinking how they walked off together, she in her green shawl, he with his tie flying, arm in arm, past the greenhouse, to simplify their relationship. It was no monotony of bliss – she with her impulses and quicknesses; he with his shudders and glooms. Oh no. The bedroom door would slam violently early in the morning. He would start from the table in a temper. He would whizz his plate through the window. Then all through the house there would be a sense of doors slamming and blinds fluttering as if a gusty wind were blowing and people scudded about trying in a hasty way to fasten hatches and make things shipshape. She had met Paul Rayley like that one day on the stairs. They had laughed and laughed, like a couple of children, all because Mr Ramsay, finding an earwig in his milk at breakfast, had sent the whole thing flying through the air on to the terrace outside. 'An earwig,' Prue murmured, awestruck, 'in his milk.' Other people might find centipedes. But he had built round him such a fence of sanctity, and occupied the space with such a demeanour of majesty that an earwig in his milk was a monster.

But it tired Mrs Ramsay, it cowed her a little – the plates whizzing and the doors slamming. And there would fall between them sometimes long rigid silences, when, in a state of mind which annoyed Lily in her, half plaintive, half resentful, she seemed unable to surmount the tempest calmly, or to laugh as they laughed, but in her weariness perhaps concealed something. She brooded and sat silent. After a time he would hang stealthily about the places where she was – roaming under the window where she sat writing letters or talking, for she would take care to be busy when he passed, and evade him, and pretend not to see him. Then he would turn smooth as silk, affable, urbane, and try to win her so. Still she would hold off, and now she would assert for a brief season some of those prides and airs the due of her beauty which she was generally utterly without; would turn her head; would look so, over her shoulder, always with some Minta, Paul, or William Bankes at her side. At length, standing outside the group the very figure of a famished wolfhound (Lily got up off the grass and stood looking at the steps, at the window, where she had seen him), he would say her name, once only, for all the world like a wolf barking in the snow, but still she held back; and he would say it once more, and this time something in the tone would rouse her, and she would go to him, leaving them all of a sudden, and they would walk off together among the pear trees, the cabbages, and the raspberry beds. They would have it out together. But with what attitudes and with what words? Such a dignity was theirs in this relationship that, turning away, she and Paul and Minta would hide their curiosity and their discomfort, and begin picking flowers, throwing balls, chattering, until it was time for dinner, and there they were, he at one end of the table, she at the other, as usual.

'Why don't some of you take up botany? . . . With all those legs and arms why doesn't one of you . . .?' So they would talk as usual, laughing, among the children. All would be as usual, save only for some quiver, as of a blade in the air, which came and went between them as if the usual sight of the children sitting round their soup plates had freshened itself in their eyes after that hour among the pears and the cabbages. Especially, Lily thought, Mrs Ramsay would glance at Prue. She sat in the middle between brothers and sisters, always so occupied, it seemed, seeing that nothing went wrong that she scarcely spoke herself. How Prue must have blamed herself for that earwig in the milk! How white she had gone when Mr Ramsay threw his plate through the window! How she drooped under those long silences between them! Anyhow, her mother now would seem to be making it up to her; assuring her that everything was well; promising her that one of these days that same happiness would be hers. She had enjoyed it for less than a year, however.

She had let the flowers fall from her basket, Lily thought, screwing up her eyes and standing back as if to look at her picture, which she was not touching, however, with all her faculties in a trance, frozen over superficially but moving underneath with extreme speed.

She let her flowers fall from her basket, scattered and tumbled them on to the grass and, reluctantly and hesitatingly, but without question or complaint – had she not the faculty of obedience to perfection? – went too. Down fields, across valleys, white, flower-strewn – that was how she would have painted it. The hills were austere. It was rocky; it was steep. The waves sounded hoarse on the stones beneath. They went, the three of them together, Mrs Ramsay walking rather fast in front, as if she expected to meet some one round the corner.

Suddenly the window at which she was looking was whitened by some light stuff behind it. At last then somebody had come into the drawing-room; somebody was sitting in the chair. For Heaven's sake, she prayed, let them sit still there and not come floundering out to talk to her. Mercifully, whoever it was stayed still inside; had settled by some stroke of luck so as to throw an odd-shaped triangular shadow over the step. It altered the composition of the picture a little. It was interesting. It might be useful. Her mood was coming back to her. One must keep on looking without for a second relaxing the intensity of emotion, the determination not to be put off, not to be bamboozled. One must hold the scene – so – in a vice and let nothing come in and spoil it. One wanted, she thought, dipping her brush deliberately, to be on a level with ordinary experience, to feel simply that's a chair, that's a table, and yet at the same time, it's a miracle, it's an ecstasy. The problem might be solved after all. Ah, but what had happened? Some wave of white went over the window pane. The air must have stirred some flounce in the room. Her heart leapt at her and seized her and tortured her.

'Mrs Ramsay! Mrs Ramsay! she cried, feeling the old horror come back – to want and want and not to have. Could she inflict that still? And then, quietly, as if she refrained, that too became part of ordinary experience, was on a level with the chair, with the table. Mrs Ramsay – it was part of her perfect goodness to Lily – sat there quite simply, in the chair, flicked her needles to and fro, knitted her reddish-brown stocking, cast her shadow on the step. There she sat.

And as if she had something she must share, yet could hardly leave her easel, so full her mind was of what she was thinking, of what she was seeing, Lily went past Mr Carmichael holding her brush to the edge of the lawn. Where was that boat now? Mr Ramsay? She wanted him.

12

Mr Ramsay had almost done reading. One hand hovered over the page as if to be in readiness to turn it the very instant he had finished it. He sat there bareheaded with the wind blowing his hair about, extraordinarily exposed to everything. He looked very old. He looked, James thought, getting his head now against the Lighthouse, now against the waste of waters running away into the open, like some old stone lying on the sand; he looked as if he had become physically what was always at the back of both of their minds – that loneliness which was for both of them the truth about things.

He was reading very quickly, as if he were eager to get to the end. Indeed they were very close to the Lighthouse now. There it loomed up, stark and straight, glaring white and black, and one could see the waves breaking in white splinters like smashed glass upon the rocks. One could see lines and creases in the rocks. One could see the windows clearly; a dab of white on one of them, and a little tuft of green on the rock.

Virginia Woolf

A man had come out and looked at them through a glass and gone in again. So it was like that, James thought, the Lighthouse one had seen across the bay all these years; it was a stark tower on a bare rock. It satisfied him. It confirmed some obscure feeling of his about his own character. The old ladies, he thought, thinking of the garden at home, went dragging their chairs about on the lawn. Old Mrs Beckwith, for example, was always saying how nice it was and how sweet it was and how they ought to be so proud and they ought to be so happy, but as a matter of fact James thought, looking at the Lighthouse stood there on its rock, it's like that. He looked at his father reading fiercely with his legs curled tight. They shared that knowledge. 'We are driving before a gale – we must sink,' he began saying to himself, half aloud exactly as his father said it.

Nobody seemed to have spoken for an age. Cam was tired of looking at the sea. Little bits of black cork had floated past; the fish were dead in the bottom of the boat. Still her father read, and James looked at him and she looked at him, and they vowed that they would fight tyranny to the death, and he went on reading quite unconscious of what they thought. It was thus that he escaped, she thought. Yes, with his great forehead and his great nose, holding his little mottled book firmly in front of him, he escaped. You might try to lay hands on him, but then like a bird, he spread his wings, he floated off to settle out of your reach somewhere far away on some desolate stump. She gazed at the immense expanse of the sea. The island had grown so small that it scarcely looked like a leaf any longer. It looked like the top of a rock which some big wave would cover. Yet in its frailty were all those paths, those terraces, those bedrooms – all those innumerable things. But as, just before sleep, things simplify themselves so that only one of all the myriad details has power to assert itself, so, she felt, looking drowsily at the island, all those paths and terraces and bedrooms were fading and disappearing, and nothing was left but a pale blue censer swinging rhythmically this way and that across her mind. It was a hanging garden; it was a valley, full of birds, and flowers, and antelopes. . . . She was falling asleep.

'Come now,' said Mr Ramsay, suddenly shutting his book.

Come where? To what extraordinary adventure? She woke with a start. To land somewhere, to climb somewhere? Where was he leading them? For after his immense silence the words startled them. But it was absurd. He was hungry, he said. It was time for lunch. Besides, look, he said. There's the Lighthouse. 'We're almost there.'

'He's doing very well,' said Macalister, praising James. 'He's keeping her very steady.'

But his father never praised him, James thought grimly.

Mr Ramsay opened the parcel and shared out the sandwiches among them. Now he was happy, eating bread and cheese with these fishermen. He would have liked to live in a cottage and lounge about in the harbour spitting with the other old men, James thought, watching him slice his cheese into thin yellow sheets with his penknife.

This is right, this is it, Cam kept feeling, as she peeled her hard-boiled egg. Now she felt as she did in the study when the old men were reading *The Times*. Now I can go on thinking whatever I like, and I shan't fall over a precipice or be drowned, for there he is, keeping his eye on me, she thought.

At the same time they were sailing so fast along by the rocks that it was very exciting – it seemed as if they were doing two things at once; they were eating their lunch here in the sun and they were also making for safety in a great storm after a shipwreck. Would the water last? Would the provisions last? she asked herself, telling herself a story but knowing at the same time what was the truth.

They would soon be out of it, Mr Ramsay was saying to old Macalister; but their children would see some strange things. Macalister said he was seventy-five last March; Mr Ramsay was seventy-one. Macalister said he had never seen a doctor; he had never lost a tooth. And that's the way I'd like my children to live – Cam was sure that her father was thinking that, for he stopped her throwing a sandwich into the sea and told her, as if he were thinking of the fishermen and how they live, that if she did not want it she should put it back in the parcel. She should not waste it. He said it so wisely, as if he knew so well all the things that happened in the world, that she put it back at once, and then he gave her, from his own parcel, a gingerbread nut, as if he were a great Spanish gentleman, she thought, handing a flower to a lady at a window (so courteous his manner was). But he was shabby, and simple, eating bread and cheese; and yet he was leading them on a great expedition where, for all she knew, they would be drowned.

'That was where she sunk,' said Macalister's boy suddenly.

'Three men were drowned where we are now,' said the old man. He had seen them clinging to the mast

To The Lighthouse

himself. And Mr Ramsay taking a look at the spot was about, James and Cam were afraid, to burst out:

But I beneath a rougher sea,

and if he did, they could not bear it; they would shriek aloud; they could not endure another explosion of the passion that boiled in him; but to their surprise all he said was 'Ah' as if he thought to himself, But why make a fuss about that? Naturally men are drowned in a storm, but it is a perfectly straightforward affair, and the depths of the sea (he sprinkled the crumbs from his sandwich paper over them) are only water after all. Then having lighted his pipe he took out his watch. He looked at it attentively; he made, perhaps, some mathematical calculation. At last he said, triumphantly: 'Well done!' James had steered them like a born sailor.

There! Cam thought, addressing herself silently to James. You've got it at last. For she knew that this was what James had been wanting, and she knew that now he had got it he was so pleased that he would not look at her or at his father or at any one. There he sat with his hand on the tiller sitting bolt upright, looking rather sulky and frowning slightly. He was so pleased that he was not going to let anybody take away a grain of his pleasure. His father had praised him. They must think that he was perfectly indifferent. But you've got it now, Cam thought.

They had tacked, and they were sailing swiftly, buoyantly on long rocking waves which handed them on from one to another with an extraordinary lilt and exhilaration beside the reef. On the left a row of rocks showed brown through the water which thinned and became greener and on one, a higher rock, a wave incessantly broke and spurted a little column of drops which fell down in a shower. One could hear the slap of the water and the patter of falling drops and a kind of hushing and hissing sound from the waves rolling and gambolling and slapping the rocks as if they were wild creatures who were perfectly free and tossed and tumbled and sported like this for ever.

Now they could see two men on the Lighthouse, watching them and making ready to meet them.

Mr Ramsay buttoned his coat, and turned up his trousers. He took the large, badly packed, brown paper parcel which Nancy had got ready and sat with it on his knee. Thus in complete readiness to land he sat looking back at the island. With his long-sighted eyes perhaps he could see the dwindled leaf-like shape standing on end on a plate of gold quite clearly. What could he see? Cam wondered. It was all a blur to her. What was he thinking now? she wondered. What was it he sought, so fixedly, so intently, so silently? They watched him, both of them, sitting bare-headed with his parcel on his knee staring and staring at the frail blue shape which seemed like the vapour of something that had burnt itself away. What do you want? they both wanted to ask. They both wanted to say, Ask us anything and we will give it you. But he did not ask them anything. He sat and looked at the island and he might be thinking, We perished, each alone, or he might be thinking, I have reached it. I have found it, but he said nothing.

Then he put on his hat.

'Bring those parcels,' he said, nodding his head at the things Nancy had done up for them to take to the Lighthouse. 'The parcels for the Lighthouse men,' he said. He rose and stood in the bow of the boat, very straight and tall, for all the world, James thought, as if he were saying, 'There is no God,' and Cam thought, as if he were leaping into space, and they both rose to follow him as he sprang, lightly like a young man, holding his parcel, on to the rock.

13

'He must have reached it,' said Lily Briscoe aloud, feeling suddenly completely tired out. For the Lighthouse had become almost invisible, had melted away into a blue haze, and the effort of looking at it and the effort of thinking of him landing there, which both seemed to be one and the same effort, had stretched her body and mind to the utmost. Ah, but she was relieved. Whatever she had wanted to give him, when he left her that morning, she had given him at last.

'He has landed,' she said aloud. 'It is finished.' Then, surging up, puffing slightly, old Mr Carmichael stood beside her, looking like an old pagan God, shaggy, with weeds in his hair and the trident (it was only a French novel) in his hand. He stood by her on the edge of the lawn, swaying a little in his bulk, and said, shading his eyes with his hand: 'They will have landed,' and she felt that she had been right. They had not needed to speak. They had been thinking the same things and he had answered her without her asking him anything. He stood there spreading his hands over all the weakness and suffering of mankind; she thought he was surveying, tolerantly, compassionately, their final destiny. Now he has crowned the occasion, she thought, when his hand slowly fell, as if she had seen him let fall from his great height a wreath of violets and asphodels which, fluttering slowly, lay at length upon the earth.

Quickly, as if she were recalled by something over

there, she turned to her canvas. There it was – her picture. Yes, with all its green and blues, its lines running up and across, its attempt at something. It would be hung in the attics, she thought; it would be destroyed. But what did that matter? she asked herself, taking up her brush again. She looked at the steps; they were empty; she looked at her canvas; it was blurred. With a sudden intensity, as if she saw it clear for a second, she drew a line there, in the centre. It was done; it was finished. Yes, she thought, laying down her brush in extreme fatigue, I have had my vision.

Biographical Notes

Mansfield, Katherine 1888–1923
Born in Wellington, New Zealand, she was educated at
Queen's College, London, before returning to New Zealand
to study music. She came back to live in London in 1908
although her search for a cure for tuberculosis took her
frequently to Europe. In the handful of work published
before her early death she established herself as one of the
great practitioners of the modern short story. Short stories
published in her lifetime were *In A German Pension* (1911),
Prelude (1918), *Bliss and Other Stories* (1920) and *The
Garden Party and Other Stories* (1922). *The Dove's Nest
and Other Stories* (1923), as well as letters and journals,
was published posthumously.

Munro, Alice 1931–
Short story writer and novelist. Born in Ontario, she was
educated at the University of Western Ontario. Her first
book of stories, *Dance of the Happy Shades*, was published
in 1968 and was followed by further volumes of short
stories including *Something I've Been Meaning To Tell
You* (1974), *The Moons of Jupiter* (1982) and most recently
Friends of My Youth (1990), as well as the novel *Lives of
Girls and Women* (1971).

Murdoch, Dame Iris 1919–
Novelist and philosopher. Born in Dublin of Anglo-Irish
parents, she was educated at Badminton School and at
Somerville College, Oxford. She worked for some time in
the Civil Service, then lectured in philosophy at Oxford and
at the Royal College of Art in London. Her work includes
studies in philosophy, plays, poetry and fiction. Her first
novel was *Under the Net* (1954) and the most celebrated
books of her prolific career include *A Severed Head* (1961),
dramatized in 1963 by J.B. Priestley, *The Black Prince*

Biographical Notes

(1973), *The Sacred and Profane Love Machine* (1974), *The Sea, The Sea* (1978), which won the Booker Prize, *The Philosopher's Pupil* (1983) and *The Book and The Brotherhood* (1987).

O'Brien, Edna 1932–
Irish novelist and short story writer. Born in County Clare, she was educated at a convent school and studied pharmacy in Dublin. *The Country Girls*, her first novel, was published in 1960, part of a trilogy, which continued with *Girl With Green Eyes* (first published as *The Lonely Girl*, 1962) and *Girls in Their Married Bliss* (1963). Subsequent novels include *August Is a Wicked Month* (1965), and short story collections include *The Love Object* (1968), *A Scandalous Woman and Other Stories* (1974) and *Mrs Reinhardt and Other Stories* (1978).

Page, Kathy 1958–
Novelist and short story writer. She lives in Norwich and divides her time between her own writing and working as a writer in the community. Her novels are *Back in the First Person* (1986), *The Unborn Dream of Clara Riley* (1987) and *Island Paradise* (1989). Her collection of short stories, *As in Music*, was published in 1991.

Plath, Sylvia 1932–63
Poet and novelist. Born in Boston, she was educated at Smith College and won a Fulbright Scholarship to Newnham College, Cambridge. One book of poems, *The Colossus and Other Poems* (1960) was published before her suicide. Posthumous volumes include *Ariel* (1963), her best-known collection, *Crossing the Water* and *Winter Trees* (both 1971). Her novel *The Bell Jar* was published in 1963.

Rhys, Jean 1894–1979
Novelist and short story writer. Born in Dominica, she came to England in 1907, briefly attended the Academy of Dramatic Art, then worked as a chorus girl and film extra. She lived for many years in Paris. Novels include *Voyage in The Dark* (1934), *Good Morning Midnight* (1939) and the book for which she is best known, published late in her career, *Wide Sargasso Sea* (1966). Her collections of short

stories include *Sleep It Off, Lady* (1976); an unfinished autobiography *Smile Please* was published in 1979.

Sagan, Françoise 1935–
French novelist, educated in Paris. She achieved early success with *Bonjour Tristesse* (1954). Other works include *Un Certain Sourire* (1956), *Dans Un Mois Dans Un An* (Eng: *Those Without Shadows*, 1957) and *Les Merveilleux Nuages* (1961).

Shange, Ntozake 1948–
American writer. Best known for her widely celebrated and performed choreopoem *'for colored girls who have considered suicide when the rainbow is enuf'*, she has published two novels, *Sassafrass, Cypress & Indigo* (1982) and *Betsey Brown* (1985) as well as plays and several collections of poetry.

Smart, Elizabeth 1913–86
Poet, journalist and novelist. Born of wealthy Canadian parents, she travelled widely in her teens and worked in New York, Mexico and California before moving to England where she spent much of her adult life. Her long liaison with the poet George Barker inspired her best-known novel, *By Grand Central Station I Sat Down and Wept* (1945). Other published work includes collections of poetry and a second short novel, *The Assumption of the Rogues and Rascals* (1978).

Tan, Amy 1952–
Novelist. Born in Oakland, California, two and a half years after her parents emigrated from China to the USA. Her first novel, *The Joy Luck Club*, was published in 1989.

Walker, Alice 1944–
American novelist, short story writer and poet. Born in Eatonton, Georgia, she was the youngest of eight children of a poor sharecropper family. Her first novel, *The Third Life of Grange Copeland*, was published in 1970 (UK 1985); other novels include *The Color Purple*, which won the 1983 Pulitzer Price for Fiction and was subsequently filmed, and *In the Temple of My Familiar* (1989). Short story

Biographical Notes

collections include *In Love and Trouble* (1984) and *You Can't Keep a Good Woman Down* (1982). Her poetry collections *Revolutionary Petunias* (1973; UK 1988) and *Horses Make a Landscape Look More Beautiful* (1985). She now lives in San Francisco.

Weldon, Fay 1933–
Novelist, dramatist and television screenwriter. Born in Worcester, she grew up in New Zealand and studied at the University of St Andrews. She worked as an advertising copywriter for some time. Her novels include *Praxis* (1978), *Puffball* (1980), *The Life and Loves of a She-Devil* (1983), which was adapted for television and also turned into a feature film, *The President's Child* (1982) and *The Hearts and Lives of Men* (1987).

Winterson, Jeanette 1959–
Novelist. Born in Lancashire, she was educated at the University of Oxford. Her first novel, *Oranges Are Not the Only Fruit*, won the Whitbread First Novel Award in 1985 and was adapted for television. Other novels include *The Passion* (1987) and *Sexing the Cherry* (1989).

Wharton, Edith 1862–1937
American novelist and short story writer. Born into a wealthy New York family, she was educated privately and travelled widely, eventually settling in France. Her novels include *The House of Mirth* (1905), *Ethan Frome* (1911) and the novella *Age of Innocence* (1920) which won the Pulitzer Prize (making her the first woman to receive this honour). She was appointed a Chevalier of the Legion of Honour in 1916 for her wartime relief work. In addition to a prolific career as a novelist, she wrote eleven collections of short stories, travel books and an autobiography *A Backward Glance* (1934).

Woolf, Virginia 1882–1941
Novelist and essayist. She was educated privately, spending much time in the company of her brother and his Cambridge undergraduate friends. After her father's death in 1904 she moved to 46 Garden Square, Bloomsbury – the house which became a meeting place for the writers, philosophers and painters who came to be known as the

Biographical Notes

Bloomsbury Group. In 1912 she married Leonard Woolf and completed her first novel *The Voyage Out*, although her second nervous breakdown delayed its publication until 1915. In 1917 she and her husband founded the Hogarth Press which published Katherine Mansfield, T.S. Eliot, James Joyce and many of the major innovative writers of the day, as well as Woolf's own work. One of the most original novelists of her time, she was also a literary critic, essayist and journalist of distinction. *A Room Of One's Own* (1929) is a classic of feminism. Her best known critical essays were published in *The Common Reader* anthologies (1925 and 1932). She was also a prolific letter-writer and diarist. Her novels include *Jacob's Room* (1922), *Mrs Dalloway* (1925), *To The Lighthouse* (1927) and *The Waves* (1931). *Between the Acts* (1941) is a highly experimental piece of work. It was shortly after finishing it and when oppressed by the fears experienced in the war that she drowned herself near her home at Rodmell, Sussex.